DEBORAH STRIKING

A Novel

Book of Deborah 4

Avraham Azrieli

ISBN: 978-1-953648-09-9

For Carol Wilner,
whose love of books is a constant inspiration.

DEBORAH STRIKING

1

Deborah woke up to find Rogez licking her face. She nudged the horse away and tried to sit up, but found Barac's arms around her. She lay back, inhaled the cool night air, and gazed at the starry sky. The thin crescent moon had reached high, which meant they had slept like this for a while, clinging to each other in the middle of a battlefield strewn with dead men. Her inner thighs were sticky, and a dull ache pulsated in her lower abdomen. Touching the ring on her finger, she relived for a moment the extreme pleasure of their union.

Rogez nuzzled Barac, who groaned and buried his face in her neck. She caressed his curls and kissed his ear. The horse stomped the ground and blew air through his lips, spraying spit on them. They sprung to their feet, protesting and laughing, but quieted down when it became clear why the horse had persisted. The battlefield was no longer still. They heard tapping paws, menacing growls, and crunching noises that, Deborah realized, were produced by powerful jaws on human bones.

She dressed quickly and strapped on her armor and sword. Barac slipped on his blood-crusted tattered robe and picked up his sword. They stood together and stared into the darkness, where long shadows snarled while ripping off chunks of flesh.

The embers left from one of the cooking fires were still red. Deborah felt the ground for dry twigs, threw them on the embers, and blew air until a new fire rose up. The flames threw jittery lights across the battlefield, where jackals, coyotes, and smaller animals were feasting on the bodies. A lone chariot stood near the edge of the cliff, the horse's head hanging low, its back arched, and its tail stiff.

Rogez stepped closer to Deborah.

"Quick," Barac said. "Get in the saddle and ride up the crevice to the ravine."

"What about you?"

"Where you go, I'll go – as soon as I find my horse." He nudged her gently. "Now, before they turn on us."

"Shouldn't we bury these men? It's a sin to let them be eaten like this."

"Worse to get eaten ourselves."

She tossed more twigs into the flames. "The fire will keep them away."

"A bigger fire, maybe," he said, picking up a burning twig.

They stepped over to where the tent had stood. The ground was littered with pieces of cloth, cushions, and empty sacks. They piled everything together, and Barac touched the burning twig to the pile in several spots.

They stepped back while it grew into a great bonfire.

The scavengers retreated into the darkness, growling.

Deborah could tell the bodies apart by the Edomite soldiers' armor and the Hebrews' short robes. There were about fifty Hebrews and twenty Edomite soldiers, as the majority of them had gone over the cliff with their chariots. The corpses were too badly mutilated to recognize individuals, except for General Mazabi, whose missing right arm gave him away even though the animals had left only the skeletal remains of the great warrior.

Averting their eyes from the disfigured faces of the dead, Deborah and Barac dragged the bodies that wore no armor to a spot near the fire, piled them up, and covered them with rocks. Meanwhile, the agitated scavengers lurked just outside the light of the fire.

When the bodies were fully covered, Barac knelt by the mound of stones. "Forgive me, my friends," he said. "You are the heroes of Simeon. Rest in peace. I promise you that I'll go back to Beersheba and defend your mothers, sisters, and young wives." His voice broke. "What I should tell them, I don't know."

"The truth," Deborah said.

He groaned. "What is the truth?"

"God delivered the Edomite army into your hands."

Barac held out his hands, palms up. "My hands?"

"The last man standing after the battle is the victor."

He dropped his hands and clutched the rocks. "That's no victory, with my friends lying dead under these stones. They were the future of Simeon, and they're gone forever while I, the only one among them who's not of Simeon, still walks the earth. How can that be?"

The agony in his voice brought her near tears. "It's not for us to understand God's reasons, or explain His actions."

He didn't respond.

"Perhaps it's because of our forefather Jacob's last words about Simeon."

Looking up at her, Barac waited.

She repeated the quote Goor-Aryeh of Judah had recited when Judge Ohad had condemned him to burn at the stake. "Keep my soul from their company, my honor from dwelling among them, for in malevolence they kill men, on a whim they castrate cattle. Damn their malice, for it's fierce, and their wrath, for it's cruel. I shall cut Simeon off from Jacob and scatter them among Israel."

One of the stones tumbled off the pile, startling them.

Barac picked it up and set it on top. "Harsh words."

"There's only truth in the Holy Scriptures."

"Why did you memorize it?"

"I didn't," she said. "Not specifically. I just remembered it the same way I remember everything."

"Everything people say?"

"And what they do, too."

"You remember everything people say and do." His tone wasn't doubtful, but admiring. "God really loves you, giving you such a gift."

"A gift and a curse. There are many things I'd rather forget, but I can't."

"The Holy Scriptures?"

"No." She smiled. "I don't want to forget the Holy Scriptures. To the contrary, I hope to learn how to read the scrolls by myself."

Watching Barac in the light of the fire, Deborah was relieved he raised no objection to her aspiration, which violated the prohibition against women literacy.

"Jacob's curse came true today," he said. "God snatched a certain victory from Simeon."

"Was it certain?"

He hesitated. "I shouldn't speak ill of the dead."

"How else will you learn from their errors?"

"You're too clever for me."

She felt her face flush. "What was Mamreh's error?"

"There was a weakness in his plan." Barac took a deep breath, shaking his head. "When Sallan broke down and revlealed that the Edomite army was about to attack with many chariots, everyone panicked. Judge Ohad wanted to beat a quick retreat into the desert."

"Let me guess," she said. "Mamreh wanted to fight."

Barac nodded.

"Did Princess Needa say anything?"

"She stood beside Mamreh and held his arm while he spoke. It was an inspiring speech. He explained that the Edomites' deceit and betrayal should be answered with honor and courage, not with flight and cowardice, and that victory was possible. He allowed the men to leave if they wanted to, but no one did. Judge Ohad bemoaned your absence, because you had managed to repel Judah's attack."

"That was different."

"It was also an attack by a superior force on a difficult-to-defend target. Mamreh asked his father to describe in detail what you had done. He asked many follow-up questions. Then, he came up with the idea to imitate your method of forming two lines of men, who would lay in wait for the Edomite army and ignite sudden fires, not to repel the Edomites and send them running, but to drive them to destruction. We only had a few lamps to keep hidden and ready, so he assigned a few men to ignite torches along the line when the Edomite chariots passed through. He predicted that the bursts of fires and the lines closing in like a vice behind the chariots would scare the Edomite horses into a stampede and send them over the cliff."

"Clever," she said. "And brutal, too."

"I suggested we keep some of our men back, hidden in the crevice, with horses ready, and ride in as soon as the Edomite chariots were nearing the cliff."

"Why?"

"In case some of the Edomite soldiers managed to avoid the cliff by jumping off the chariots, or if some were on horses without chariots and swerved away from the cliff. Our men would be on foot, busy with burning sticks and cloth sheets, and armed only with swords, which aren't the most effective weapons against mounted opponents in the best of circumstances."

"And that's exactly what happened. You had predicted it and proposed a good solution. Why did Mamreh reject it?"

"He didn't trust us to control our horses from panicking and going over the cliff like the Edomite beasts."

"Worrying about a few casualties, he ended up losing everyone."

Barac sighed. "He was too confident of his plan's success."

Deborah thought about her own experience. "I planned to ambush Seesya in Ein Gedi, but he got there first and set up a perfect ambush for me, but he still lost the battle."

"What was his error?"

"He made no error. His ambush was as clever as it was ruthless."

"But it failed."

"How could he have predicted that my horse would rise up on his hind legs and take a barrage of spears in his chest to save me? It was a dramatic lesson that even the best planned ambush could fail, turning predator into prey."

"It didn't stop you from setting an ambush in Beersheba for the men of Judah and smiting them."

"We didn't smite them, only scared them away."

"And burned their leader at the stake, which equals smiting, because it'll keep them away for generations."

Deborah hesitated, unsure whether or not to tell him that Goor-Aryeh didn't burn at the stake. She knelt beside Barac, and they recited the Blessing for the Dead together: "Blessed be Yahweh, God of Israel, king of the world, the true judge."

They stayed like this for a long moment, holding hands, giving their final respects to the Hebrew men of Simeon, who would lie forever in a great heap at the cliff's edge overlooking the Ramon Crater.

The bonfire gradually dwindled, and the scavengers crept closer.

With a stick from the fire to serve as a torch, Deborah mounted Rogez. Barac whistled, and his horse galloped in from the darkness. They rode single file up the crevice toward the ravine. Rogez's hooves cluttered on the rocks, and Deborah glanced back over her shoulder at Barac, who smiled at her. Her heart swelled with joy. He was the perfect partner, and she knew without a doubt that, joined together as one, they would win back Palm Homestead and attain the future for which she had suffered a great deal.

Those thoughts made her feel guilty about not telling him the truth about Goor-Aryeh. A true partnership required complete honesty, and she had already failed to be honest.

They tied the horses next to Yael's mare and the princess's horse near the entry to the ravine. Deborah gave Rogez water while Barac did the same for his horse.

"I must tell you something," she said. "The man who burned at the stake in Beersheba was one of the dead soldiers from the battle earlier. The judge of Judah escaped unharmed."

"How do you know?"

"I switched them and let Goor Aryeh go."

"What?" Barac's voice had the edge of anger. "Why?"

"Do not kill," she said.

"But it's war."

"Sibling rivalry is not war. The men of Judah need the water of the wells, that's all."

"And for that water they came at night to spill blood."

"Judge Goor-Aryeh told me he had ordered his men not to hurt anyone in Beersheba, except those who fought back."

"That was a meaningless order. Every man in Beersheba would have fought back."

"That's why he planned to invade at night and capture the city before anyone started fighting."

"And you believed him?"

"I still do. Goor-Aryeh is a man of virtue. I hope you meet him one day."

"On the battlefield, most likely, when he leads his men in another attack, a smarter attack, more determined and deadly." Barac groaned. "Who's going to stop them from taking Beersheba? Not Tsruyah and his band, that's for sure."

"God protects the righteous," she said. "I trust His mercy."

Barac looked toward the battlefield, now shrouded in darkness.

"He was merciful to me and you, but not to my friends."

The flame at the end of the stick fizzled out, and she tossed it away. In the dark, she couldn't tell if he was still angry with her.

Removing her sack from the saddle, she said, "Be careful what you say, because Princess Needa and her maids must continue to believe I'm a young soldier named Borah."

The moonlight reflected in Barac's eyes, and as Deborah stepped toward the ravine, he took her arm, turned her around, and kissed her. She clung to him as happiness filled her chest and softened her knees. Afraid he would break off the kiss before she was ready, Deborah put her arms around him. Her right hand rested at the small of his back, where his robe was coarse with congealed blood that wasn't his. Her left hand's fingers dove into the thicket of curls on the back of his head, and she pressed her lips to his. Barac groaned as his hands slid in under her armor, through her undergarments, onto her bare skin. His touch ignited such heat inside her that she pulled away, terrified of becoming completely overwhelmed and losing the self-control on which her life depended. She shouldered her sack, pecked Barac on the cheek, and hurried into the ravine.

A torch still burned near the spring, all the way at the far end of the ravine. Princess Needa and her two maids were sitting against the sidewall halfway in. Sallan was lying on the ground near the ritual bath, snoring lightly, and Yael stood beside him, holding a sword. She used it to point at the ritual bath, which was covered with rocks. Deborah understood. The women had buried Judge Ohad and Mamreh. She considered reciting a prayer over their grave, but pushed the thought away. How could she pray for men who had forced her to slay them to save herself?

Barac knelt by the mound of stones and recited the prayer over the dead.

Approaching the princess and her maids, Deborah kept her ring hand out of sight. "The battle is over," she said. "Death came to all, Edomites and Hebrews alike."

One of her maids said, "The two of you are still alive."

"We're not your enemy."

Princess Needa sneered, and the maid said, "You murdered our husband."

"Mamreh was nobody's husband. The marriage had not been consummated."

The princess hissed and whispered furiously to her maid, who said, "His brave heart was beating for us until you stopped it."

Deborah recalled the gruesome end of Mamreh and took a deep breath, fighting off a tide of nausea. "I had no choice."

The maid listened to more whispering from the princess and said, "You should have extended your neck under his blade. He was a prince, and you are but a stupid, disloyal, and expendable soldier."

The words triggered a burst of fury in Deborah, who stepped forward, glaring at Princess Needa. "Am I the one who turned her back on her people, on her family, and on her king for a swaggering foreign hothead? Am I the one stranded in the middle of the desert, alone and forsaken, with no kin by her side?"

The princess did not bow her head, her eyes dark inside the slit of her veil

"Who is disloyal, then?" Deborah demanded. "Who is stupid?"

The two maids began to cry.

Barac came up behind Deborah and cleared his throat, but he needn't have worried, because her fury had already dissipated.

"Get some rest," she told them. "At sunrise, we'll start the journey back to Edom."

They looked at Barac, whom they knew as Mamreh's deputy.

"Borah is in charge," he said.

Sallan coughed, and Deborah crouched by his side. Yael gave him water. His face was less swollen, allowing one eye to open. He saw Barac and tried to speak, breaking into a hard cough. He pointed at his sack, and Yael opened it for him. He pulled out a folded travel robe and held it up.

Barac took the robe and felt the cloth with his hand. "Expensive. I've never worn anything like this."

Sallan gestured toward the spring.

Deborah smiled. "He wants you to wash up before putting it on."

Sallan nodded and whispered hoarsely, "Royal color."

Barac looked at Deborah for an explanation.

"You'll see it better in the morning," she said. "It's lined with red threads, which is the color of power and honor in Edom."

"And of blood," Yael said. "You'll feel right at home."

He went to the spring.

Deborah turned to Yael. "Why did you say that?"

"It's the truth. A man covered in the blood of other men is a killer."

"He's a soldier. There's a different."

"What's the difference? That he gets paid for the killing?"

"Isn't that the difference between a wife and a prostitute?"

Yael looked away and didn't answer.

Sallan took Deborah's hand and touched the ring. "Happy?"

She glanced toward the crevice and the battlefield. "All these men are dead. Everyone."

"The boy from Emanuel isn't dead. The princess is alive, too." He coughed. "You won both prizes."

"Not the way I wanted it, not for such a horrendous price, and it's your fault. If not for your deceitful machinations, no one would have died."

"Don't judge me." Sallan's voice was barely audible. "I did what had to be done."

"And you did it all for me, right?" Deborah groaned. "I should thank you for causing the worse bloodshed this desert had seen since the Creation."

"Leave him alone," Yael said. "He got his punishment already."

Looking at Sallan's broken body and swollen face, Deborah had to agree. He had received his due punishment, and there was a tragic truth to what he had said: "You won both prizes." Her journey from Bozra had two goals: taking Princess Needa home and reuniting with Barac. If not for Sallan's conniving maneuvers, the night would have ended with Mamreh keeping both the princess and Barac.

Sallan pressed her hand. "You understand, yes?"

Deborah pulled her hand away. "Where are your boy-servants?"

He sniffled.

Yael answered for him. "They're dead."

"Both of them?"

"Yes."

"Oh, no! How?"

"Mamreh pushed them over the cliff." Yael kept her voice low to prevent the princess from overhearing. "The first boy was killed to pressure Sallan to reveal the Edomites' plans, the second to punish Sallan for what he had done."

Deborah was filled with grief for the two boys, whom she'd known since living in Emanuel, when her sister had been engaged to marry the judge's son and life had held out the prospects of normalcy – marriage, family, and a measure of happiness.

She spoke with difficulty, a lump in her throat. "If they killed the boys, why not Sallan?"

Yael poured water on her hand and patted Sallan's forehead. "Judge Ohad wanted to take him back to Beersheba, hold a public trial, and burn him at the stake. The judge said he would start the fire with the scroll of the fake treaty."

2

Barac tore a piece from his soiled robe, washed it under the spring, and used it to scrub every part of his body, removing the caked mix of sweat, blood, and sand. He stood among the reeds with his back to the women, who were unlikely to see much in the dim light of the fading torch. As he waited to dry up, a chill passed through his body, making him shiver. Sallan's robe slipped on easily, and he smoothed it over his chest, marveling at the softness of the fabric.

He saw Deborah wipe her eyes as she walked away from Yael and Sallan. She began to collect a few twigs and dry reeds. He did the same, and they made a small pile near the mouth of the ravine, a few steps in from the crevice. She untied her sack, took out fire starters, and rubbed them together to produce sparks. As a small flame caught on, she added dry weeds, then twigs and branches, nurturing the fire. Barac watched her face, taking in the small details – the high forehead, drawn with thin creases across, the almond-shaped eyes, almost too large for her delicate face, the splash of freckles on her straight nose, the tear-lined cheeks, and the sheen of moisture on her full lips.

She took off her leather helmet and rubbed her cropped hair, which had started to grow back like new fur on a shorn sheep – soft and pale, almost translucent. He wondered if the pale color would persist as her hair grew, or would it give way to the fiery orange of the glorious, wavy mane of her maiden days in Emanuel.

"Don't stare at me," she said. "They'll notice."

He looked away, embarrassed.

"Was the water cold?"

"Not too bad."

"I'm jealous," she said. "To be clean again – I can't wait."

He glanced toward the princess and her maids, which were but dark shadows by the wall halfway up the narrow ravine. "You can wash. They won't see much."

Deborah chuckled. "Men always underestimate women's ability to know a lot despite seeing little."

They brought the horses into the ravine, tied them near the fire, and gave them water.

From her sack, Deborah took out a blanket, spreading it on the ground. "One day, when we're alone, we'll bathe together."

Barac's heart beat faster, and he could barely breathe, imagining her lanky body, completely naked, slowly immersing in a pond of fresh water, settling into his arms—

"This thing stinks." She pulled a tiger's tail out of her sack and placed it across the foot of the blanket. "But it works."

He was impressed by her forethought: between the lively fire and the odorous tail, no animal would dare creep into the ravine, therefore allowing both of them to sleep, rather than take turns standing guard.

"Do you like Sallan's robe?"

"It's very nice." With his finger, he traced one of the red threads that lined the garment. "Must have cost many coins."

"His mother is wealthy."

"His mother?"

"Women have the right to own property in Edom. Umm-Sallan is wise and decisive, also very kind. She's been a widow for a long time." Stretching out on the blanket, the sack under her head, Deborah took a deep breath and exhaled with a sigh. "I hope we grow old together."

"We will." Barac wished he could lie alongside and take her in his arms, but he remembered her warning about women's perceptiveness. He sat down and spoke softly. "What did Yael say that upset you so much?"

"Sallan's boy-servants. They were sweet and harmless."

He didn't respond.

"I was wrong about Mamreh. He was not a good leader, or a good man."

"It's not that simple."

"A man who murders innocent boys is wholly evil."

Barac didn't want to upset her further, but he felt a duty to defend his fallen commander. "Mamreh's responsibility was to the men of Simeon. Sallan refused to talk, and time was running out. The boys were Sallan's weakness. Hurting them was the only way to make him talk."

"Hurt, maybe, but kill? He's not the first one to use them for that purpose, by the way. Back in Emanuel, Seesya tortured one of them to break Sallan."

"I noticed that one of the boys was missing an ear."

"But not his life," she said. "Even Seesya, whose heart is as dark as the night, didn't kill the boy."

"It's different. Here, Sallan was conspiring to have us all killed."

"That's not true. His plan was only to put everyone to sleep and spirit away the princess."

"He had to realize that putting us to sleep would lead to our slaughter by the Edomite army. Mamreh sensed the mortal danger Sallan represented and used whatever means available to make him talk."

"Do not kill!" Deborah poked the fire. "Yahweh's words mean nothing anymore?"

"Judge Ohad said that the Ten Commandments apply only to Hebrews. Therefore, killing gentiles is not a sin."

"Didn't God create the gentiles, too?"

"Of course, but He chose us to be a nation above all others, gave us His divine laws, and promised us the land of Canaan. Those who conspire to hurt God's Chosen People are conspiring to hurt God, too. His prohibition against killing doesn't apply to them."

"What about compassion? The Holy Scriptures say we shouldn't take eggs from a bird's nest while the mother is nearby, or cook a goat-kid in its mother's milk. If cruelty to animals is forbidden, how could cruelty to people be permitted?"

"Don't we kill goats and birds for our needs?" Barac tried to maintain an even voice, but couldn't hide his impatience. "Forcing Sallan to reveal the Edomites' plans was necessary. How else could we defend ourselves?"

"Threaten, or even hurt one of the boys, but kill?"

"There was no time for slow questioning. Mamreh had to reciprocate Sallan's ruthlessness with equal measures."

"And Sallan talked. He revealed everything. Why did Mamreh kill the second boy?"

"Once Sallan admitted to contaminating our food and drink in preparation for the Edomites' attack, it was clear that his boy-servants had known about it, too. They were as guilty as their master."

"Were they?" Deborah glared at him. "Mamreh was your master. Are you responsible for his sins?"

In the light of the fire, her face mesmerized Barac. Her beautiful features had been with him since Emanuel, but her intensity, her tone, and her confidence were unfamiliar. Gone was the polite, soft spoken, deferential maiden he had known before, replaced by a woman who dressed as a soldier and acted as a general.

"What's wrong? Did you swallow your tongue?"

He leaned closer to her, his voice grave and filled with emotion. "I swore to obey my commander without question, and if that turns me into a sinner, I'll repent by being a better commander when it's my turn. It might take many years but, one day, I will lead a Hebrew army for the glory of God and win freedom for the tribes of Israel."

Now, judging by her expression, she was mesmerized by him.

"I'm sorry Sallan's boys are dead," he said. "My friends are dead, too. That was God's will, but He also willed you and I to live on. We both survived this day against all odds. That was His choice."

Deborah nodded.

"We've both made errors," he said. "Each of us has made many decisions along the way that led to a horrible bloodshed, but we made those decisions while trying to prevent bloodshed. We failed, and the blood of many good boys and men is soaking the ground down by the edge of the crater. Is failure a sin when you try to do the right thing?"

"I don't know," she said.

"I believe God spared us because He had forgiven our errors. We must forgive ourselves and one another." Barac lowered his voice further. "Especially now, that we're husband and wife."

"Not yet." She touched the ring on her finger. "Not until a priest has blessed us and made a sacrifice to God."

"We've done the best part of what's required to seal our

•

marriage."

Her eyes twinkled with reflections of the flames. "Are we sinners?"

"No. Under the circumstances, what we did felt like God's will." Barac's face grew hot. "We'll have the proper ceremony with a blessing and a sacrifice as soon as we find a priest."

"Good." Deborah took a deep breath and exhaled slowly. "You're right. God is the true judge. He ordained what happened to each person tonight, and He will bless our path ahead as He's done for me since I left Emanuel."

"You really believe it?"

"When you pursue your True Calling, God provides the shortcuts."

The words took a moment to sink in, especially as Barac felt dizzy with desire to kiss her lips and press her body against his. "It's true. I've missed the safety of Emanuel and the hills around it, which were like a lush garden compared to the land of Simeon, but in a short time under Mamreh I learned more about becoming a soldier than I would have learned over a lifetime in Emanuel."

"You'll need those skills when we go back to the Samariah Hills."

"Go back?"

"Not immediately. First, we'll bring the princess back home and collect a great reward from the king of Edom. He promised me enough silver to acquire all the supplies and protection needed for the journey to Canaan." Her eyes glistened with excitement. "As soon as we enter the land of Ephraim, we'll have a priest conduct the marriage ceremony and slaughter a goat for God. Then, we'll take possession of Palm Homestead."

Barac didn't want to argue with her, but her plans were unrealistic. "Have you forgotten Seesya? He probably has a hundred soldiers by now, if not more."

"We'll have Yahweh's law on our side, and the people will stand with us, too."

"Why would they?"

Deborah smiled. "We've never actually discussed all of this, which I'm happy about, for it proves that you wanted to be my husband because of your love for me, not because of the prospect of gaining property."

Barac was confused, and her proximity—the glint in her eyes and the scent of her body—made it difficult for him to think clearly. "What property?"

"Palm Homestead has belonged to my family since Joshua parceled out the land of Canaan to the tribes. My father died with no sons, and my sister is also dead now. Under the law, when I marry a man of Ephraim, he will become the rightful owner after my father. If Seesya tries anything, all the other homestead owners will stand with us. I'm sure of it."

The fire illuminated her lovely face, which glowed with happiness, but Barac's own heart sunk as he realized the impending disappointment she was about to suffer.

"You're shocked." She laughed. "Don't worry, I'll help you work the land. Palm Homestead is fertile and abundant."

He nodded, unable to speak.

"Remember the water cistern? It will nourish the fields and orchards. Everything will thrive while I fulfill my father's dream and deliver God's word to our people under the old palm tree."

Barac looked away, unable to meet her eyes, which were filled with hope that would soon collapse into tears.

"What's wrong?"

"I'm sorry," he whispered. "We cannot go back to Palm Homestead."

Deborah pulled the blanket up to her chin. "Why not? You can continue to hone your skills as a soldier in the Samariah Hills. Is that what you're worried about?"

Barac shook his head.

"What, then?"

"To inherit Palm Homestead, I would have to be a man of Ephraim." He sighed. "I am not."

His words seem to confuse her. "What are you talking about? Of course you're of Ephraim."

"I wish, but it's not so. My grandfather came down from Kadesh Naphtali after the Canaanites had taken his homestead. That's why he became a blacksmith – a trade every town needed. Judge Zifron's father welcomed him to Emanuel, and later, my father continued in the trade. That's why he was upset with me. I rejected the trade that had saved our family from a shameful life of nomadic poverty."

"That's impossible," she said. "You lived in Emanuel. Your father and grandfather lived in Emanuel. You're all men of Ephraim – you must be!"

"Naphtali," he said. "We descend from the tribe of Naphtali."

"How could you be of Naphtali? Your father isn't called Abinoam of Naphtali."

"Like all tradesmen living among other tribes, he's named for his trade: Abinoam the Blacksmith."

Her mouth remained open as she gazed at him in disbelief.

"Forgive me." Barac took her hand. "I thought you knew we were strangers in Emanuel."

"How would I know? I was a stranger in Emanuel." She pulled her hand away as fury returned to her face, hotter than before. "Yahweh's mercy! I gave myself to you!"

"Keep your voice down," he whispered. "Everything will be fine. I promise."

She groaned, shaking her head.

"I'll take care of you," he said. "Beersheba is only a few days away, and with Mamreh and his father dead, the people of Simeon need soldiers, especially now, when Judah might attack again. And if you're unhappy in Beersheba, I'll take you to Kadesh Naphtali, where we can join my father. I'll continue to prepare for the great battle against the Canaanites, but I'll also work with my father, harder than my father, and earn enough to support us until we defeat the Canaanites and recover our land. I'll build you a house, bigger than your father's house, with a stove in the center, solid stone walls, and windows overlooking the Sea of Galilee. We'll have many sons and daughters, as God has ordained, and He will watch over us as we grow old together."

Deborah's face softened, giving him hope that the picture he drew of a blessed future comforted her for the loss of Palm Homestead.

"You love me," she said.

"With all my heart."

"I know, but what about my heart?"

"What about it?"

"If you truly loved me, how could you not know what's in my heart."

"I knew your heart belonged to me, as my heart belonged to you."

"Do you really think sweet words could erase bitter facts?"

Barac didn't know how to answer.

"It's my mistake," she said. "A good boy doesn't always become a good man."

The words brought tears to his eyes. "How can you say that?"

"What kind of a man possesses a maiden as his wife without disclosing that he is not of her tribe?"

He wanted to cry that it was she who possessed him, she who had complete and overwhelming power over his mind and body, but he clenched his jaw, holding back such words, which he knew would sound as a lame attempt to deflect responsibly for his actions.

"You're not a man of Ephraim." Her face twisted bitterly as if the words tasted of lemon rind. "Not of Ephraim."

"Please, Deborah." Barac touched her arm. "It didn't occur to me to think of tribes or homesteads when we found each other alive among the dead. All I could think of was God's mercy, allowing us to remain on this earth for each other. We can go somewhere new and build a good life together. My tribal ancestry changes nothing."

"It changes everything." She turned away and pulled the blanket over her head. "Everything!"

Barac pressed her shoulder. "Deborah, we belong together."

A jackal howled in the desert outside the ravine, and the sound echoed from the walls.

She reached out from under the blanket and threw something at him. It sparkled in the dirt, and he looked closely. It was the six-pointed ring he'd given her. He picked it up and held it to his lips while watching Deborah's shoulders tremble with muffled sobs.

3

"Weeping won't solve your problem." The eagle waved her wings to fan the embers in the stove, reviving them into flames. "Chilly tonight, and it's not even New Year yet."

Deborah looked around. "Is this my father's house?"

"Don't you recognize it?"

"It seems smaller than I remember."

The eagle nodded, her head bumping the patchy thatched roof. "It's the same size, but you have grown."

"My body has grown." Deborah leaned back against the wall. "Otherwise, I've remained a foolish girl."

"Beating yourself up is foolish."

"It's all my fault."

"Even a judge knows not to judge himself, or herself."

"I'm not a judge."

"Not yet."

"Women don't become judges."

"Would you like to be the first?"

"I'd like to be with a man of Ephraim." Deborah glanced at her finger, where the six-pointed ring had been. "That's what I'd like."

"Didn't you enjoy your time with the blacksmith's boy?"

Embarrassed, Deborah hoped the eagle didn't know how far their enjoyment had gone. A wave of heat passed through her with the memory of Barac's muscular body clinging to her, rejoicing her until they reached that ultimate moment of complete unity in body and mind at the height of ecstatic pleasure. She fanned her face with her hand and, noticing a goblet on the floor by her hand, grabbed it, gulped a mouthful, and choked, coughing hard. She had expected wine, but the goblet contained lemon water.

"See?" The eagle chuckled. "You expected one thing and got

another."

Deborah pushed the goblet away. "Barac is a lot sweeter than this."

"Which makes your decision that much more bitter." The eagle looked up, where the palm fronds were visible through the long-neglected thatched roof. "Your palm tree seems healthy."

"I know why you brought me here, but this reminder is unnecessary. Have you forgotten how I've risked my life repeatedly, and even killed others, to answer my True Calling?"

The eagle didn't respond.

"Do you think I've lost my resolve to return here to sit under my palm tree and deliver God's message?"

"Your resolve is strong, but not invincible."

"Why not?"

The eagle paused, thinking before she spoke. "Even the strongest resolve is apt to melt in the heat of passion."

Deborah wondered again if the eagle knew how hot her passion for Barac had burned, or how far their love had taken them. "It's a simple choice," she said. "And also impossible."

"It's neither simple, nor impossible." The eagle fanned the embers again, making them glow, but flames no longer appeared. "Look into your heart and answer a single question with honesty. Which one comes first, your duty or your heart?"

Moving her hand, Deborah accidently knocked the goblet over, but instead of lemon water, wine spilled out. "That's an unfair question."

"Unfair?"

She straightened the goblet and repeated what Sallan had once told her. "Young people expect the world to run on wheels of fairness and justice, but that's not how it works."

"Sad, but true."

"Anyway, I don't have a real choice."

"Why?"

"The facts are simple. I love Barac, but my duty is to Yahweh. How could I choose a man over God?"

"Facts reside in the mind, but love burns in the heart, which is why deciding about love based on facts alone will harden your heart into a cold rock where no love will ever burn again."

Deborah noticed the reflection of the flames in the goblet, which was once again full to the brim. She picked it up and inhaled a familiar aroma. It was the wine her father had made from grapes grown on Palm Homestead. She sipped, and it tasted as good as she remembered it.

"Well?"

"Love is a fact, too," Deborah said. "And the heart isn't limited to one love at a time."

The eagle shifted, watching her intently.

Deborah drank the rest of the wine, tilting her head back to empty the goblet, and saw the palm fronds through the thatched roof, swaying in the wind against a clear blue sky. Warmth spread in her chest.

"I love this place," she said. "My heart longs for Palm Homestead. I will return here and deliver God's word to my fellow Hebrews, as my father had envisioned. That's my choice."

The red hue of dawn spilled in through the open doorway, signaling the start of a new day. As Deborah turned toward it, everything disappeared, except for the soft glow of dawn that now illuminated the mouth of the narrow ravine. Beside her, thin smoke wafted from the ashes of last-night's fire. She turned to tell Barac about her discussion with the eagle, to explain her painful choice despite her love for him, but at the spot where Barac had sat, only the ring remained, resting on a flat rock.

4

The path was barely visible in the dark, and the horse was on edge. Was a predator stalking them? Barac realized he had made a grave mistake, leaving the ravine in the middle of the night without a burning torch. He could stop and try to start a fire, but the process of gathering twigs, rubbing stones to produce sparks, and building a big enough fire would take him longer than it would take the predator to catch up and pounce. The only effective defense available to him now was speed, and his survival depended on what kind of an animal was pursuing them. The horse, being able to detect scents and sounds too subtle for men, probably knew the answer, and its jittery nervousness hinted at a dangerous threat.

Barac thrashed the reins and stabbed in with his heals to keep the horse running. Early on, he had hoped it was a bear, or even a lion, neither of which had the stamina for a long chase, but the horse continued to glance back and neigh frightfully, indicating that the predator remained close on their heels. Wolves would have howled, and jackals would have laughed, which left only the most stubborn of the big cats, either a tiger or a mountain lion, both of which were capable of running for a long time while reserving enough energy for the final, deadly sprint.

The sky finally began to acquire a pink tinge as dawn broke over the eastern hilltops. The arrival of a new day was lifesaving, because large cats were known to hunt at night and hide during the day. The path took a steep descent down a sloped bank of a dry streambed, forcing him to slow down. The horse was panting from the long, arduous run. Barac stood up in the stirrups and looked back at the barren desert. Sitting down in the saddle, he pulled a fig from his sack and leaned forward to give it to the horse, a well-earned reward for outlasting whatever beast had stalked them.

Up ahead, the first rays of the sun lit up a mountain with a pointy summit, delighting Barac for having kept true through the darkness to the north for Beersheba.

He wondered whether Deborah was up yet. Had her anger cooled off, or had it transformed into seething hate? He had left the ring by her side last night knowing, without a shred of doubt, that he would never need a ring again. Deborah was the only girl for him, the only wife he would ever have. How could there be another after her?

He imagined Deborah waking up and finding the ring, holding it up, looking at it. There were only two possibilities: Either she would put the ring in her sack for safe keeping until they reunite, or would toss it away as she had done the night before, determined to forget him and seek a man of Ephraim for a husband. Barac's heart longed to hold on to the former possibility, but in his mind he already knew it was the latter. As dedicated as he was to answering his True Calling, Deborah was tenfold more determined to hers, no matter what devastating sacrifices God repeatedly demanded of her.

5

Deborah picked up the ring and gazed at it, her heart pounding. She thought of Barac, sitting beside her the previous night, and imagined how devastated he must have been by her taking off the ring and throwing it at him. She could see that he had brushed off the sand before leaving it for her on the rock, taking his horse, and departing quietly into the night, accepting her rejection despite the fact that only men had the power to cast off their wives, never the other way around. She felt a stab of regret for insulting him over what, in fact, had been her own mistaken assumption about his tribal lineage. Would she be happier if he had ignored her rejection? She imagined waking up to find Barac still by her side, his arms embracing her, his lips kissing her, his firm body possessing her with a perfect balance of lust and kindness, power and gentleness, hunger and sweetness.

She slipped the ring onto the tip of her trembling finger, up to the first joint, but stopped. "Not a man of Ephraim," she said, pulling the ring off and dropping it in her sack. "Not of Ephraim!"

Realizing she had spoken out loud, Deborah glanced back and was relieved to see the princess and her maids asleep under a large blanket. Sallan had remained where he had been lying last night, with Yael curled up on the ground beside him.

Like she did every morning at dawn, Deborah smeared a layer of stubble-paste, but for the first time, it caused a burning sensation on her cheeks. The soreness in her lower belly had subsided to faint discomfort, but when she crouched to relieve herself behind a rock, scorching pain between her legs made her yelp. She expected to see blood on the ground, but there was none.

After packing the blanket and the tiger tail in her sack, Deborah headed down to exit the ravine, but stopped when Rogez became restless. Yael's mare and the princess's horse looked on indifferently while she untiled Rogez and led him along with her out of the ravine. She half-hoped to see Barac's horse, but it wasn't there, which meant that her only true friend was really gone from her life forever.

Her eyes teary and her lips trembling, Deborah stepped to the middle of the crevice, drew her sword, and swung it left, right, up, and down, again and again, slashing, hacking, and stabbing until the muscles in her arms were spent and her eyes were dry.

Panting hard, she sheathed the sword and untied the sling from around her hips. With a stone fitted in the pouch, she rotated the sling and shot the stone down the crevice, where it disappeared long before it hit the ground. A second stone followed, and another, each one going farther than its predecessor and taking with it a sliver of her sadness.

Satisfied with the distance reached by the shots, Deborah focused on improving her aim. She targeted a boulder on the hillside above the crevice. It was a challenging target, both in distance and in elevation. The shot was imperfect, a glancing blow that sent the stone sideways. The next one missed the boulder altogether, and the third fell too short. Selecting a stone more carefully, she fitted it in the pouch and let it dangle by her leg while her eyes focused on the boulder and her mind imagined it to be the head of a person. At first, Barac's smiling face and bushy curls appeared, but she rejected the image and willed her mind to conjure Seesya, with his shoulder-length oily hair and pale face, sliced across by the red scar. Without taking her eyes off the target, she rotated the sling, but just before her thumb let go of the tab, Barac's face reappeared, imposing itself over Seesya's, and the shot went awry.

For some reason, rather than upsetting her, it made her laugh about the way her mind was playing tricks on her, pitting the two young men from Emanuel against each other in a faceoff of extreme opposites – good against evil, handsome against repulsive, loveable against despicable.

It was time, Deborah decided, to stop trying to conjure a hated image, and instead try to hit the boulder without resorting to mind games. She resumed shooting, and her aim gradually improved with minor adjustments to her posture, the speed and angle of rotation, and the looseness of her shoulder, as her thumb lifted off the tab and the sling stretched away in the briefest blink of time before momentum plucked the stone from the pouch. The improved fluidity of the process from rotation to release had a positive impact on the accuracy of her shots until, finally, she achieved a perfect hit, breaking her previous record for distance and elevation.

She chose an even more distant target up the hillside abutting the crevice and continued practicing until the nearby ground was clear of stones and her face was dripping with sweat. Her breasts felt tender, not only the left one, where the knife had nicked the skin, but both of them. She held the chest armor and undergarments off her breasts and blew air down to cool herself, which helped a little.

Rogez whinnied, and she went to him. He lowered his head, pressed his ear to her chest, and didn't move. Was he listening to her heart, making sure it hadn't turned into a cold rock? She ruffled the hair between his ears and combed it down with her fingers. He remained still while her panting slowed down. She pressed her face into his short fur, taking in his familiar smell, and allowed her tears to flow again. For a long time, they stood like this – a great white horse comforting a sad girl in men's armor.

Throat clearing startled Deborah. She turned and saw Yael.

"Sallan is asking for you."

Deborah wiped her eyes and followed Yael, with Rogez following behind.

The morning sun cleared the mountains in the east, casting long shadows into the ravine.

6

Sunrise brought with it a gentle breeze. It came from the north, and Barac took it in, breathing deeply, trying to take the edge off his exhaustion. The path curved around an enormous boulder, twice the size of the horse. He reached out with his right hand and ran the tips of his fingers on the rock. It was smooth, and the night's chill made it feel wet, though it couldn't be, not here, in this parched Negev Desert.

The path passed the great boulder, and he brought his fingers to his lips, which were equally cold. Tapping in with his heels, he signaled the horse to go faster. The response was a sonorous growl, as if his horse had become terribly angry, but he immediately realized the growl was coming from behind.

Barac swiveled in the saddle and looked back.

Atop the boulder, drawn against the early sun, stood a mighty cat with disproportionately large eyes – not two eyes, but four: a yellow pair that straddled the flaring snout, and a larger, white pair with black circles that stuck out over the massive head. As the first pair of eyes blinked, Barac grasped that the second pair on top were actually ears with a pattern that made them look like eyes

All this he absorbed in a brief moment, shorter than the time it took him to inhale sharply. He was still looking back over his shoulder when his horse whinnied frightfully and bucked forward, its hind legs rising for a kick, while the tiger leaped from the boulder, high into the air. The bucking horse jolted Barac up and forward. His headdress flew off, and his loose robe flapped up over his head, turning the world dark. He felt his thighs detach from the saddle, his stomach pressed upward into his throat, and his horse's fur brushing against his lower legs. Something hit the top of his head very hard and stayed pressed to his head as a vice, clasping it on both sides of his scalp, while he flew through the air and came to a hard landing on the rocky earth, followed by a heavy body landing on top of him, clasping him in a powerful grip while claws punctured his chest and abdomen.

The rapid drumming of his horse's hooves faded away while the tiger growled again, which sounded like a roar inside his head. Barac felt a puff of heat on his scalp through the cloth of the robe, followed by foul stench that was similar to the tiger's tail Deborah had lain over her blanket, yet ten times more potent.

The pressure on his head grew worse, and he felt the tiger's teeth poke through the robe and his bushy hair, gradually penetrating through.

7

When Deborah and Yael entered the ravine, Princess Needa and her maids were washing their faces at the spring. Sallan's head was propped up on his black leather pouch, his face less swollen, both his eyes open.

Deborah showed him her hand without the ring. "See? I didn't win."

"What happened?"

She glanced at the princess and her maids, making sure they couldn't hear. "I changed my mind."

"Why?"

"My inheritance depends on marrying a man of Ephraim, and he is not."

"Didn't you know that?"

"Did you?"

Sallan nodded. "I knew his grandfather. He came from the north, one of those troubled Hebrew tribes, I'm not sure which."

"Naphtali."

"It's been many years. I think his tribe lost a battle to the Canaanite king, something like that." Sallan watched her for a moment. "Don't you love the boy?"

"He's wonderful, and he loves me too, but how can I turn my back on—"

A lump formed in her throat, silencing her.

"Keep it together," Yael said. "Soldiers don't cry."

Deborah struggled not to break down.

"There's an Edomite proverb." Sallan paused to cough. "What fails to destroy you makes you harder to destroy."

Deborah regained her composure and said quietly, "Barac didn't try to destroy me."

"Losing someone you love can destroy you." Sallan closed his eyes, taking a deep breath. "That's what happened to me a very long time ago. I was completely destroyed."

"But you recovered," Yael said.

He shook his head. "My cleverness survived, that's all. I'm nothing like I was before losing An."

"In what way?"

"In every way. Do you know what the old king of Edom said about me?"

Yael and Deborah looked at one another and shook their heads.

"It was in the temple, the whole amphitheater crowded with thousands of women, right after I saved Edom from an Egyptian invasion. The high priest refused to permit his daughter – my beloved An – to marry a lowly healer's son. Besides, she was already betrothed to her brother, Qoztobarus, the one you recently slew."

Deborah cringed at the image of high-priest's split head, oozing gray matter.

Pressing her hand, Sallan smiled. "You did the right thing. He deserved it."

"I'm confused," Yael said. "What did the old king say?"

"He announced it from the high balcony." Sallan paused to recall the king's words. "This boy is no longer the mere son of a healer. He is the savior of kings. He is the liberator of nations. He is the great Elixirist. How could any father object to his daughter marrying this young man? In fact, if we had a daughter to give him, we would do so gladly. Surely the high priest doesn't think his daughter is better than a king's daughter, does he?" Despite the cuts and bruises, Sallan's face glowed with joy at the memory. "That's what the old king said about me."

Yael pressed a hand to her heart. "It's beautiful. Did you marry her?"

"Yes, and for a single night, I was the happiest man in Bozra, but in the morning, I lost her, and it destroyed me completely. The people's adoration didn't diminish, but kept growing as my fame spread throughout the region, but I was broken inside, and when the king tired of my popularity, I was too listless to sense the danger."

Deborah felt sorry for him, but only for a moment. "A listless, destroyed man would not be capable of causing a needless battle and a terrible bloodshed."

His face reddened, and he didn't respond.

"Losing Barac hurts, but it won't destroy me." She quoted Kassite's words. "Sometimes good fortune hides behind misfortune."

"Speaking of misfortune," Yael said. "Tell her what you heard from Edom."

"Bad news," Sallan said. "Qozmadorus convinced the king you're a fraud."

"Qozmadorus?"

"The eldest son of Qoztobarus. He's the new high priest."

"Who told you?"

"General Mazabi's grandson."

"The one who returned to camp with the two slaughtered animals for the feast?"

"Yes. Qozmadorus obtained the king's consent to lock up Leola at the temple and prepare for a new ceremony to sacrifice her."

A tremor went through Deborah as she recalled Leola dangling over Qoz's three-pronged thunderbolt, whose sharp spikes were still red from the pig's blood. "When will they do it?"

"At sunset on the day after tomorrow." Sallan coughed, clutching his chest. "Unless you return with Princess Needa beforehand."

"Can we make it back to Bozra in three days?"

"Perhaps, riding day and night, there's a chance."

"Then that's what we'll do."

"Take the princess and ride like the wind." He patted the ground. "I'm staying here."

"No," Deborah said. "I can't do that."

He sighed. "Look at me. I'm nothing but dead weight."

"I agree, and you deserve to die here, but I promised your mother to bring you back home."

Sallan tried to sit up, and his face twisted in pain. "I'm old and badly injured. Leola is young and healthy. Leaving me here is the only rational choice. My mother will understand."

"I'll stay with him," Yael said. "You'll ride with the princess and get there in time to stop the sacrifice. Collect your reward, hire a few soldiers and fresh horses, and come back for us."

"By the time I return, either predators will kill you, or evil men."

"We're wasting time." Yael glanced at the princess and her maids, who were still washing up at the spring. "Even if you wanted to take him, how would you do it? He can't even sit up, let alone ride a horse."

The challenge Yael presented, as insurmountable as it appeared at first, made Deborah think in practical terms. Was there a way to carry an incapacitated man all the way to Bozra?

8

The tiger clutched Barac from behind, wrapping itself around his upper body, using its weight to press him face-down into the ground, and keeping its jaws locked on his head, the fangs boring into his skull. Its front legs encircled Barac's upper arms, the claws hooked into his chest, while the tiger's lower legs were wrapped around his waist, the claws hooked into his lower stomach. Barac tried to push out with his elbows to dislodge the claws from his chest and stomach, but it only caused the animal to tighten its grip on his upper body and clench its jaws on his head. The robe, pulled up over his head and face, caused a disorienting darkness that made it hard to think. He felt a tail slinking between his exposed legs and kicked backward, his heels hammering the tiger's bottom to no effect. Both his arms where locked inside the tight embrace, his left arm pressed against the front of his body, his right arm twisted behind, with his fisted hand pressed to his lower back by the tiger's hairy underbelly. He tried to open his fist, but the tiger growled and tightened its hold even more, leaving him with the ability to take only brief, shallow breaths. Barac finally understood the fate awaiting him: a slow suffocation, an agonizing death, and then, being eaten while his blood was still warm.

In a burst of fear, Barac wriggled and pushed to free himself, which did nothing except leave him out of air.

This was it, he realized.

The end.

A flash of memory came to him of Deborah, naked in his arms, their hot bodies pressed together, the pleasure as extreme and as overwhelming as the pain now being inflicted by the tiger. This was God's punishment, he knew, for possessing a lovely maiden without the blessing of a priest, and for an even worse sin – abandoning her while his seed was still warm inside her. It had been an act of cowardice to leave a girl – and she was a girl despite the soldier's armor, man's weapons, and stubble-paste – to fend for herself in the most inhospitable place in Canaan. Unlike him, she would not abandon those who were dependent on her. How long before she and the pitiful group of four women and an old man perish in that ravine? A day? A week? No wonder God had sent this tiger to devour him.

Barac resigned himself to this just punishment. He only wished that the robe had not flapped up over his eyes, as he would have liked to see the sun one more time and not die like a convict wearing a blindfold at the stake.

The tiger, which must have felt that its human prey had given up the fight, loosened its deathly embrace ever so slightly. The bent fingers of Barac's fisted right hand instinctively sprung open. The movement must have alarmed the tiger and it shifted, clutching him tightly, the claws sinking deeper into his chest and abdomen, the jaws biting harder over the crown of his head with such force that even the bunched-up robe and bushy hair failed to cushion.

The agony unbearable, Barac screamed.

9

Deborah beckoned Yael, ran out of the ravine, mounted Rogez, and rode down the crevice. Yael followed on her mare.

At the bottom, a group of jackals poked at the pile of rocks that covered the dead men. Riding in a wide circle, Deborah recoiled at the sight of coyotes tearing apart three carcasses of horses. The coyotes looked up, but did not retreat.

Several horses crowded together near the sole chariot by the edge of the cliff. Without dismounting, Deborah collected the reins of the chariot horse. Yael pulled along two horses and a camel, which still had some supplies tied up behind its hump.

As they started up the crevice, the horse struggled to pull the chariot over the rocky ground. Finally, they made it up to the mouth of the ravine.

With Yael and the two maids, Deborah carried Sallan out of the ravine and set him down on the floor of the chariot, where a warrior would be standing. They unloaded the camel and secured all the waterskins, dry food, and blankets to the horses. Yael tied her mare behind the chariot, got in the driver's position, and took the reins. The maids helped Princess Needa mount her horse and sit sideways under the canopy. They rode the other two horses.

The small caravan crawled up the crevice, Deborah leading the way on Rogez. Behind them, the abandoned camel uttered a mournful bleat.

10

When his scream died down, Barac tried to refill his lungs, but there was little room for air as the tiger took the opportunity to squeeze in further. The animal's muscles grew tauter in a patient, determined anticipation for its prey's inevitable suffocation and death.

Amidst this terrible anguish, Barac felt oily dampness on the open palm of his right hand, which was pressed between his right buttock and a hairy, hard lump. He realized it was the tiger's male organ. The pain in his head was too great to leave room for disgust, but anger did penetrate through the fog of misery.

With deliberate effort, Barac tilted his right shoulder downward and gradually straightened his arm while reaching as far as down possible with his fingers until his hand came out between the tiger's legs. Bending his fingers around a compact, stubbly sac, Barac felt two small balls inside the sac, which rested snugly in his palm. Drawing on his last bit of consciousness, he clenched his fist, clutched the tiger's testicles, and bent his arm, pulling upward as hard as he possibly could.

The tiger shrieked, jerked its jaws away from Barac's head, and ripped its claws out of his chest and abdomen. The robe tore away with the fleeing tiger, and the rays of the sun stabbed his eyes. He covered his face, curled up on the ground, and took in gulps of air while waiting for the tiger's raging revenge.

11

Once out of the crevice, Deborah took the road north and prodded Rogez into a fast trot. The others followed. Yael managed to drive the Edomite chariot with surprising ease. Deborah recalled the landmarks from the journey south and imagined them in reverse order, starting with the Ramon Crater. Based on her recollection, after the first hillcrest there would be a long, moderate downhill slope leading to a dry stream that Barac had called Aricha Creek. Following the creek upward would bring them to a small oasis, where the convoy had camped for the last night before arriving at the crater. She estimated they would reach that oasis by mid-morning.

The landmarks Deborah remembered appeared as expected while the rising sun baked the desert, the heat slowing down the horses. At the oasis, she allowed everyone a short break to drink and eat. Sallan tried to stand, but he cried in pain and had to lie down. They gave him water, which he drank, and food, which he declined.

Deborah pressed his forearm. "Can we do anything to ease your pain? Perhaps pick up some plants for a potion—"

"In Bozra," he whispered. "My workshop. Everything is there."

She stepped away and found a hidden spot behind a bolder. Crouching to relieve herself, she held her breath, expecting sharp pain, but only felt a mild burning sensation. She jogged back and clapped to get everyone back on the horses.

In the late afternoon, a mountain with a pointed summit appeared up the road as a familiar friend. Deborah remembered Barac calling it Mount Avdat and pointing out, just south of the mountain, a well-trodden east-west road that was a new spice route. She remembered a running spring near Mount Avdat, which would be timely as they were consuming water at an alarming pace. She shook the reins to urge Rogez to go faster. Instead, he stopped.

Everyone behind also stopped.

Deborah kicked in with her heels to urge Rogez forward, but he rocked his head and whinnied. She scanned the surrounding desert to see what had spooked him. There were no animals in sight, only an empty, barren desert. Some distance up a side slope, a dark object caught her eye.

She dismounted and walked off the road to check it out. Halfway there, she could see it was a rag. Up close, she saw dark stains on the bunched-up cloth. She also recognized the smell – same as her tiger's tail, only more pungent. Picking up the cloth, she shook it. A man's robe unfolded. It was sullied with sand and blood. More vigorous shaking cleared some of the sand, revealing a fabric embedded with red threads, resembling the robe Sallan had given Barac. Gazing closely, she saw holes in the cloth, surrounded by bloodstains, and a clutch of fine strands – a lock of dark hair.

12

A sharp poke in his back woke Barac up. He swung his arm around, hitting a black vulture, which crowed angrily, spread its wings, and took off to rejoin its circling kin above. The sun was high, which told Barac he'd been unconscious, or asleep, for a long time. Sitting up caused a jolt of pain in his head. He touched his hair, which was sticky, and when he looked at his hand, it was bloody. His bare chest and abdomen were crusted with congealed blood from four sets of punctures left by the tiger's claws. He wiped his hands on his loincloth. His robe was gone. He imagined the tiger running off with the robe hooked on its fangs.

The vultures crowed, circling above, waiting for him to collapse again. He tried to stand up, but the world began to spin around and he sat on the ground. A brazen vulture dove toward him, changing direction in the last moment when Barac waved his arms and yelled, which caused a new spike of pain in his head. He felt exposed and defenseless. Was this the second part of God's punishment for abandoning Deborah? But how could he have stayed by her side in the ravine after she had pulled off the ring and threw it in his face? And what about his own True Calling? Had he not dedicated himself to becoming a great warrior in order to liberate the Israelite tribes? Was God trying to tell him that his vow of service was unwanted?

His eyes now accustomed to the glare of the sun, Barac noticed something on the road further back. He shaded his eyes and looked harder. It was his belt and sword, which must have fallen off when the tiger had toppled him from the horse. Getting up again, he groaned at the pain and held his arms out to balance against the dizziness, pacing gingerly like a drunken man.

The weight of the sheathed sword strapped against his hip restored a small measure of confidence that God's anger may not be as severe as it had first appeared to be. Was God giving him a chance to redeem himself by going back to save Deborah from perishing in that ravine? Without clothes and water, the heat spelled death within a few hours, even sooner if the tiger returned, or if another predator tracked him. He needed to find shelter, water, and then, somehow, obtain a robe and a headdress, before heading back to the Ramon Crater.

Barac tried to whistle for his horse, producing no sound. Reluctant to inhale deeply for fear of renewed bleeding from the puncture wounds on his chest, he took a shallow breath and whistled again, producing a meek result. He whistled in every direction, but the horse did not return.

The nearby summit of Mount Avdat was like a beacon of hope. He remembered a small oasis by the intersection with the east-west spice route. With the sun scorching his bare skin, he began to walk up the road. The shadows of vultures danced on the pale soil around him. The birds' confidence in his imminent demise seemed well founded, considering how painful each step was and how weak he felt. He kept his eyes on the path and shuffled his legs, placing one foot in front of the other, advancing along at a slow pace, determined to reach water and shelter before the combination of heat and blood loss defeated him. The trek became a blur as his feet continued to move with monotonous stubbornness.

Scents of standing water and animal feces drew him out of his stupor, and he found himself approaching a small pond near a trickling spring. A group of mountain goats looked up at him, their nostrils flaring.

He fell to his knees, cupped water in his hands, and drank. Feeling better, he dunked his head in the pond and splashed water on his chest and abdomen. The wounds hurt, but he kept at it until most of the dry blood washed away.

Crouching in the shade of reeds near the pond, Barac considered what to do next. He felt a powerful urge to turn back and run south, but he had to ask himself a simple question: would he survive the journey? On foot, the Ramon Crater was about two days away. With neither clothes nor water, alone on the road through heat, thirst, and wild animals, he had little chance of making it there alive. Even if he somehow did, his physical condition on arrival would only add to Deborah's burden and hasten her demise.

Resisting the urge to run south, he looked at the field near the pond, where remnants of fires and animal waste told of frequent visitors, and decided to stay until a caravan came by from the east or the west. He had no silver to pay for clothes, a horse, and a waterskin, but he could use stealth to steal, or his sword to rob, because saving Deborah justified all means.

At the nearby base of the mountainside he saw a dark opening of a small cave. He checked it for snakes or scorpions. Finding none, he crawled inside. The rock wall was cool against his back and the sand below was soft. He rested his head on his arm and settled down to wait.

13

Deborah closed her fingers over the lock of Barac's hair and pressed her clenched fist to her mouth to block off a scream. She turned her back to the road so that her companions would not see her face. She struggled to breathe, her chest constricted in terror and grief.

Steps sounded from behind, and Yael appeared beside her.

Deborah showed her the hair and the robe.

Yael's eyes widened and she inhaled sharply.

Unable to speak, Deborah could barely avoid collapsing.

"A large animal," Yael said. "He had no chance."

A groan escaped Deborah's lips. Her rejection had sent Barac into the dark night. It was her fault!

Yael glanced over her shoulder. "The princess is watching. Don't let her see your grief. She'll figure out what you really are."

Shutting her eyes, Deborah brought the lock of hair to her nose. Through the bitter stench of the tiger, she found a trace of Barac's sweet scent.

"At least he didn't suffer," Yael said. "Probably didn't even realize what was happening to him before he was dead."

"No." Deborah shaded her eyes and gazed at the surrounding desert. "He can't be dead."

The doubtful expression on Yael's face spoke louder than words.

"I'm sure of it," Deborah said. "He's alive."

Yael gestured at the bloody robe. "How could anyone survive this?"

It might defy reason, Deborah knew, but she had spent months fearing that Seesya had told the truth about lopping off Barac's head, only to see him alive at Judge Ohad's house in Beersheba, no longer a boy but a strapping young man, bursting with energy and confidence. She would not repeat the same mistake. Just like Seesya, this bloody robe spoke falsely of Barac's violent death. He could not be dead, because he was good and faithful, because dying like this would be wrong and unfair, and because he had not yet answered his True Calling.

"Barac isn't dead," she said. "Yahweh wouldn't allow it."

"Even if he's not dead yet, he will be soon. No one could survive wandering the desert alone, naked, and injured."

"He's not alone. He has his horse."

Again, Yael's face creased in doubt.

"You'll see," Deborah said. "Our God is merciful."

"Where was your God last night?"

"It's not easy to understand His decisions, but I know Barac is alive. Can you whistle?"

Yael put two fingers in her mouth and whistled.

"Keep doing it. The horse will bring Barac back to us, we'll dress his wounds, and all will be well."

As much as Deborah wanted to take the robe and hair with her, she knew that the odor would terrify the horses. She covered them with a few stones and walked back to the road. As she approached Rogez, he turned his head, sniffed her, and whinnied.

"Stop it." She mounted him. "I have enough problems already."

They resumed riding, and Yael whistled repeatedly. For a while, nothing happened, but then, the tapping of hooves sounded, and Barac's horse appeared over a low hill. The saddle was empty, Barac's sack and club still attached to it, his headdress hanging from the saddle horn. They stopped, and the horse came closer, neighing nervously. Deborah dismounted, comforted the horse, and gave him water before tying him behind the chariot next to the mare. Throughout all of this, no one said anything, not even Sallan, who watched her from his perch on the floor of the chariot.

They reached the oasis near Mount Avdat at sunset and stopped to drink water and rest. Soon after, out of the twilight, a small caravan arrived from the east. The man at the head, wearing a rough-brown robe with a hood, steered off the road with his fellow travelers. Princess Needa's elaborate canopy and the mighty chariot must have intimidated them, because they dismounted at the far side of the oasis and began to set up camp.

As twilight darkened, Deborah and Yael carried Sallan off the chariot and set him down with his back against a boulder. They tied the horses together a short distance away and collected weeds and twigs. Deborah started a fire.

Princess Needa sat by the fire while her maids took out bread, dried fruit, and wine. They gave some to Deborah, Yael, and Sallan, who only nibbled on a dry fig, sighing every so often.

When night fell, Deborah stepped away from the group. She knelt in the dark, facing north-east in the general direction of Yahweh's Holy Temple in Shiloh, and pressed her hands to her chest. "I've been faithful to you," she whispered. "Everything I've done, everything I've suffered, everything I've lost, all have been for the glory of your name." She paused to wipe her tears. "You took away my caring parents, Harutz and Raquellah, my lovely sister, Tamar, my righteous friend, Miriam, and my good horse, Soosie. I've accepted each loss, each heartbreak, each stab of deeper loneliness. I've never wavered from my pure devotion to you, or begged you to bring back what you've taken from me, because it's not for me to understand your divine reasons. But Barac?" She was weeping now. "No! Him you may not take! I forbid it!"

14

The sound of voices nearby woke Barac up. Startled, he raised his head to look and banged it on the low ceiling of the cave. Pain shot through his head. He crawled out of the cave and sat up, taking deep breaths while the pain subsided. Had the tiger's jaws cracked his skull? He touched his hair, feeling around for fresh blood, but found only lumps of congealed blood as before. His chest and abdomen hurt, too, but none of the punctures felt wet.

In the darkness at the foot of the hill, two fires burned on opposing ends of the oasis. The sight raised his spirit. Two caravans meant double the chance of successfully stealing a horse, or at least a donkey. If he were lucky, the animal would still be carrying a waterskin and a sack with some food and clothing. If he left soon, mounted on a good horse, he would be back at the Ramon Crater by morning and redeem his sinful error of abandoning Deborah in that desolate ravine. She could hardly remain angry with him, seeing the injuries he had suffered and his determination to come back and save her and her pitiful companions from certain death.

He descended the slope and approached the oasis slowly, pausing every few steps, gazing through the dark. As he came closer, the two groups became distinct. The caravan on the left was noisier, the men talking and drinking, the women caring for children, whose plaintive voices seemed out of place in this desolate land. Their large fire illuminated a cluster of animals – several horses, donkeys, and goats. It would be impossible to steal one of their horses without being noticed. He could wait until they go to sleep, but if one of the men stood guard and raised the alarm, they would give chase and kill him, or take him to sell into slavery.

Getting down on all four, Barac changed course toward the second caravan, whose fire was much smaller, and crouched behind some reeds. The fire was small, and the people sitting near it were mere shadows. There was no tent or smell of cooking. Were they eating bread or fruit, or were they poor travelers with no food or horses? His heart sank as he stared into the dark, searching, but suppressed a sigh of relief when he made out a group of animals tied together further back from the group, where almost no light from the fire reached. Finally, God was smiling on him!

Making a wide detour around the group, Barac crawled on the rocky ground, taking pains to make no noise. His breathing sounded amplified to him, and he stopped to rest. A horse neighed, and Barac realized he must still carry the scent of the tiger on him. He moved ahead anyway, and the horses shifted nervously, stomping the ground. Near the small fire, one of the travelers said something in a soft voice that belonged to a boy or a woman, it was hard to tell.

The smart move would be to retreat into the desert and wait until everyone went to sleep, but while Barac debated what to do, one of the horses jerked its head left and right several times. The others moved about. Barac could see a large box on one of them, and the outline of an open wagon attached to another. Why had the travelers failed to unburden the horses for the night? It was strange.

The agitated horse shook its head again, and the reins must have come loose, because it trotted away from the cluster of shadows. Oddly, it didn't run away from Barac, but came toward him. Was it an aggressive stallion, willing to take on a tiger, or a foolish buck that didn't know better? Only when the horse came through the reeds did Barac realize it was his own horse, with his sack and club still attached to the saddle. The travelers must have found it wondering in the desert.

Back near the fire, they spoke to each other, probably wondering what had spooked the horses. Barac wasted no time. He climbed into the saddle, murmuring thanks to God for giving him an opportunity to redeem himself. Leaning forward, he kicked inward with his heels. The horse bolted, galloping into the night.

Shouts came from behind, and Barac glanced back.

Silhouetted against the small fire was a lanky figure, twirling something.

A sling!

Instinctively, he slapped the horse's neck, causing the beast to veer left.

A stone swished by Barac's right ear, barely missing him. The accuracy was shocking. Was it luck, or was the shooter that good?

He slapped the horse again, swerving to the right as another stone whistled by his left ear. Two lucky shots were unlikely. The shooter was an expert, a trained soldier, not a poor traveler.

The third stone hit the horse's rear. With a terrified neigh, it accelerated even faster, its hooves drumming the hard ground. Barac lowered his upper body all the way down beside the saddle, his head pressed to the horse's neck, and held on. A fourth stone struck his buttock. He cried in pain, but at the same time was relieved, because the hit was not powerful enough to injure him, the great distance having slowed the stone's speed to the point of rendering it harmless. The shooter probably knew it and stopped slinging stones.

Barac glanced back. The fire was now tiny and fading. No one was giving chase, and the lanky figure of the shooter still stood beside the fire, staring after him. It made him think of Deborah, whose skilled slingshots had saved her life several times. He looked back again. The shooter was barely visible. Could it be Deborah? He recalled the shadows of the other horses. The one with the box could have been Princess Needa's royal canopy, and the open wagon could have been a chariot, which would explain how she had extricated Sallan from the ravine. Pulling on the reins, he tried to turn the horse back, but the terrified beast rushed ahead into the dark desert, ignoring him.

Questions swirled in his mind. How had she managed to navigate through the desert so accurately? Where had she found the courage to travel without armed protection with four helpless women and a broken old man? And how had she found his horse?

The answer to all his questions, Barac realized, was that Deborah was no longer the helpless young maiden from Emanuel, whose beauty had haunted him since their separation on the night of Tamar's stoning. Deborah had changed far deeper than the shorn hair and soldier's armor, transforming as much as a caterpillar transformed into a butterfly. She had become a different person altogether, a woman who was like no other woman he had ever known. Deborah didn't need him to protect her, because she was braver than him. She didn't need him to lead her out of the desert, because she was smarter than him. And she didn't need him to marry her, because she was better off without him, free to find a man of Ephraim who would be eligible by law to inherit her father's homestead and ready to stand aside humbly while she stepped up to her mighty palm tree and delivered God's message to His people.

The horse slowed down to a trot. Warm tears trickled down Barac's cheeks as he pulled a blanket out of his sack, draped it over his bare shoulders, and directed the horse toward the northern stars.

15

Deborah tied the sling around her waist. "The damn thief swerved as if he knew a slingshot was coming."

Yael went to calm the remaining horses while the drumming of hooves faded into the night.

The caravan at the other side of the oasis was quiet.

"Our horses are fine," Yael said. "He stole Barac's ride."

Sallan looked up at Deborah, his pale face lit by the fire. She crouched beside him, and he whispered, "It was him."

"Who?"

"The blacksmith's son."

"Are you trying to cheer me up?"

Sallan shook his head.

"Why would Barac steal his own horse?"

"He wasn't stealing."

The statement was technically correct. Barac had the right to take his own horse, which made her all the more certain that the thief could not have been Barac.

Yael rejoined them. "Nothing is missing except for Barac's horse. It went willingly as if the thief was his owner."

Sallan cleared his throat.

"It makes no sense," Deborah said. "Barac wouldn't snatch the horse in the dark and ride away. He would have come over to sit with us by the fire."

"I don't think so," Yael said. "He's ashamed of running off last night and leaving us to our fate."

Princess Needa sneered, and one of her maids said, "Once a coward, always a coward."

Enraged, Deborah was about to defend Barac, but stopped herself. What could she say? That he had left not out of cowardice, but because of her rejection? That she had caused him to ride through the night and get mauled by a predator? No, she couldn't say any of that because it would reveal the truth about her, as well.

"I disagree," she said. "The thief could not have been Barac. A man who survived a tiger's attack, who is bleeding and cold, would have come over to seek our help, dress his wounds, cover his back with another robe, and fill his empty stomach with food."

"You don't know men," Yael said. "A man would rather lose blood than lose face."

"It's true," Sallan said. "It's also possible that he didn't recognize us."

Deborah didn't argue anymore. She hoped they were right. He could have walked from the site of the attack to the oasis, washed and drank water, then hid until dark. A horse would help him endure his injuries and hasten his journey along the desert paths and waterholes. Had God let Barac live because of her prayers, or because of his True Calling? She imagined him reaching Beersheba and defending it from another Judah attack, bolstering his reputation as a great warrior and, one day, liberator of the northern tribes from Canaanite oppression. She could see him as a mature man, his beard full and his face weather-beaten, mounted on a great stallion at the head of a formidable Hebrew army, leading God's Chosen People to victory. Would he still remember their short-lived passion, their youthful love, which felt so true while based on a false assumption? She longed to hold him one more time, but knew it was not to be, because both of them had chosen their divergent True Callings over their love for one another.

Getting up, Deborah went to the horses and pulled two torches from one of the sacks. She came back, lit them in the fire, and kicked sand over the flames to extinguish the fire.

She gave a torch to one of the maids. "Ride in the rear and hold the torch far from your horse, or it'll panic."

Yael supported Sallan as he staggered back to the chariot.

Princess Needa whispered in the maid's ear.

"We're tired," the maid said. "Set up camp for us here. We'll sleep until the morning."

"There's no time." Deborah addressed the princess, whose face was covered by the veil. "We have to reach Bozra before Qozmadorus sacrifices an innocent girl to Qoz."

Princess Needa waved dismissively, and the maid spoke for her. "That's not our concern. We'll sleep here while you stand watch and keep us safe until morning."

Her anger reignited, Deborah struggled to speak calmly. "Get back on your horses now."

The princess murmured to the maid, who said, "We're staying here for the night, soldier. Do as you're told and make sure no one steals our horses, too, or you'll have to carry us on your back all the way to Bozra and up the hill to our palace."

Fuming, Deborah pointed at the princess. "You're an ungrateful—"

Sallan knocked on the wooden bar of the chariot, which Yael started to advance toward them. He gestured to the east.

The maid said, "Obey us, Borah, or our brother will send you to the copper mines to work until you die."

Again, Sallan knocked on the bar and said hoarsely, "The best way to make an obstinate child follow you is to start going."

The princess hissed and murmured to her maid, who said, "Shut up, Sall."

For the first time since before the battle, Sallan smiled. "Calm down, child."

"We're not a child anymore," the maid said. "And don't smile at us."

Deborah mounted Rogez. "Did she call you Sall?"

"It was my name once." The smile faded from his face. "When An died, I added her name to mine. Now, let's go, before another innocent girl dies."

Holding the torch high, Deborah rode off.

Yael hooted, shaking the reins of the chariot horse to make it go faster.

A while later, Deborah glanced back and saw the other torch catching up. Soon, the princess and her maids were close behind the chariot.

16

Barac woke up when the horse suddenly stopped. He sat up quickly, which sent searing pain through his skull. Only the glow of a campfire ahead prevented him from shouting. He took deep breaths while the agony subsided. The air was frosty and, despite the blanket, he was shivering.

Climbing down from the saddle, he tied the reins to a rock, advanced quietly toward the fire, and knelt behind a boulder. The breeze brought over the odor of unwashed bodies. He could see about twenty men in the process of waking up. They had horses and weapons, and he could make out thick beards, white caps, and short robes that ended above their knees. He didn't need to see a yellow banner with a lion to know they were men of Judah. Whatever reason they had to be inside Simeon territory, it wasn't peaceful, and if they caught him, it might be his ending.

As he began to retreat, Barac heard a man speak up.

"Let us pray now."

The men stood in silence.

"Blessed be Yahweh, king of the world, for keeping us safe on the road day and night."

The men chorused, "Amen."

Resisting the urge to retreat, Barac stayed put and listened.

"May He guide us in battle," the man continued, "and give our enemies into our hands as we make true Jacob's deathbed blessing." He paused and recited, "Judah, your brothers will praise you, your hand will be on the neck of your enemies, your father's sons will bow before you. The scepter will not depart from Judah, nor the ruler's staff from between his feet, until he to whom it belongs shall come, and the obedience of the nations shall be his."

"Amen! Amen! Amen!"

The leader clapped to quiet them down. "Dawn is breaking. Fill your stomachs and prepare your horses. I want to attack soon after sunrise while they're praying and eating. We must be swift with our blades, cut down the men of Simeon before they escape into the desert to hide under rocks like rats."

The men laughed and resumed packing up.

Barac returned to his horse and walked it further away from the camp. His head hurt badly, and blood trickled from the puncture wounds on his chest. He glanced at the eastern horizon, where a pale line indicated that dawn was about to break. He must have ridden for a long time in a state of slumber, and if his horse had kept going north, the path would have brought him near Revivim, the small village that had hosted them during the Sabbath on the way south. He felt tired and sad. Why did the men of Judah want to attack Revivim? The answer was likely very simple: greed for land and water.

Taking a wide detour, with dawn as his guide, Barac bypassed the men of Judah and found the road further north. He mounted his horse and rode, first slow and quiet, then breaking into a fast gallop.

Dawn turned into a hazy sunrise when he reached Revivim. At the center of the village, a circular wall protected the small hole in the ground over the water cistern. Several women were drawing water by lowering a bucket through the hole with a rope. A group of men stood under a tree, draped in blue-striped prayer shawls, while a bearded elder recited verses from the Holy Scriptures.

Everyone turned to Barac.

"You must hide," he said. "An attack is coming."

They looked at him, bewildered.

Barac pointed back where he came from. "Men of Judah have spent the night not far from here. I heard them speak of attacking you. There isn't much time. You have to escape and hide in the desert."

The elder stepped forward. "Why would they attack us? We have no silver or gold, not even horses."

"You have fertile land and ample water. Are those not more precious than silver, gold, or horses?"

The words elicited cries from the women.

"You're mistaken," the elder said. "This is Simeon's land. Judah may not settle here."

"They believe Judah is destined to rule over all the land of Canaan, and they're starting with Simeon."

One of the other men asked, "Weren't you here with Judge Ohad on the last Sabbath?"

"I was."

"Where is he now?"

"The Edomite army attacked us at the Ramon Crater. The judge, his son, and our soldiers died. I alone survived."

Everyone stared at him.

"There's no time to waste." Barac dismounted. "How many of you live here?"

The elder thought for a moment. "Eleven men, eighteen women, and thirteen children."

"Fighting would be futile. Escape is the only way. How many donkeys do you have?"

The elder pointed to the corral. "Six."

The situation was getting worse with every answer, and Barac swayed on his feet, feeling dizzy. A girl offered him a jug of water, and he took a drink, which refreshed him.

"God won't allow it," the elder said. "Perhaps you were dreaming."

The girl holding the jug said, "Look at his injuries. They're not from a dream."

Barac was about to explain the true source of his wounds, but thought better of it. "Gather everyone," he said. "We'll run on foot into the desert and find a place to hide."

The men and women hurried to their shacks, calling for their spouses and children.

The elder sat down under a tree. "There's no place to hide."

Barac looked around at the fields and orchards. There were no hills nearby, or deep gorges, only gently rolling desert landscape for a greater distance than what women and children could cover in the short time that remained.

"Do you have weapons?"

"A few knives," the elder said. "And two wooden spears for hunting."

His horse neighed as if urging Barac to get in the saddle and save himself. It was tempting. He had no chance against so many armed men, especially in his current condition. What good would it do to stay here and suffer the same fate as the people of Revivim?

The girl came over and handed him a robe, which he put on. It was made of rough cloth that chafed against his wounds and hanged from his shoulders like a sack. She giggled and tugged on it to make it look better.

"Thank you," he said, noticing for the first time her pretty face. She was about fifteen, with a soft, generous figure that would have looked maternal on an older girl. Her dark hair was chopped unevenly around her shoulders.

Barac felt ashamed for thinking of abandoning her and the others. Deborah wouldn't think of leaving these good people to their fate, as she hadn't abandoned Sallan and the four women at the ravine. Rather, she had managed to extricate the group from that place of death and found the way to the east-west trade route. If Deborah were here, Barac thought, she would have found a clever solution to this situation, too.

He looked around, thinking, what would Deborah do?

The wooden shacks offered no protection. There was no place of high ground to fortify. The only stone structure was the waist-high circular wall above the small opening of the water cistern.

He walked over and glanced down into the cistern. It was dark. Lowering the bucket, he felt it reach the water below. He estimated the length of the rope at about ten steps.

An idea came to him. He ran to a shack that had smoke coming out of its roof. Inside, fire burned in the oven, and a few half-used torches lay beside it. He lit one of the torches and ran back outside. While one of the men held the torch over the opening, Barac climbed over the round wall and used the rope to slide down through the opening, which was barely wide enough to let him through. Inside the cistern, he felt the chill air on his face. He gripped the rope tightly, took a deep breath to overcome his fear – he couldn't swim – and continued sliding down. As the water passed his knees, his feet touched the ground, and he sighed with relief.

"Pull the bucket up," he yelled, "and lower the torch."

When the bucket came down with the torch, Barac held it up to illuminate his surroundings.

The cistern resembled a large cave. Whoever had carved the cistern out of the rock had taken great care to smooth down the floor and the walls, which were plastered with whitewash. There were several holes in the walls, with drip-stains from the inflow of underground streams when it rained in the surrounding desert. Judging by the low level of the water in the cistern, it hadn't rained near Revivim in weeks. He imagined that, when it did rain the way it had rained at the Ramon Crater, this cavernous cistern would fill up higher than his head.

"Young man," the elder called from above. "What should we do?"

Barac yelled, "Lower the children and the women with the rope. Hurry!"

One by one, the small children came down in the bucket. He carried them to the side, where the floor curved up at an angle that made it possible to sit above the water level. The children remained quiet, but when the women were lowered down, each with the rope tied under her arms, the children laughed.

The men slid down the rope quickly, one after another, except for the elder, who remained above. He pulled up the bucket and spoke into the opening.

"They're coming!"

The mothers hushed their children, and everyone sat by the walls all around. Barac dipped the torch in the water, and darkness returned to the cistern, except for the opening above, alight with the morning sun.

The ground above shook under horse hooves. Men were yelling, and the elder cried out in pain. After some time, smoke wafted down through the opening. Barac assumed that the men of Judah were setting the houses on fire. A couple of men stood, their fists clenched, but Barac motioned for them to sit down.

Suddenly, the bucket fell down and hit the water with a splash. A little boy started to say something, and his mother pressed his face to her bosom, silencing him. Everyone held their breath, staring up at the opening.

The rope tightened, and the bucket ascended. A moment later, it dropped down again. Twelve times the men of Judah drew water from the cistern to fill their waterskins, never realizing that the whole village was hiding right below their feet.

There was more commotion above, and the elder cried again. The light from the opening was blocked for a moment, and a body fell in, hitting the water hard. It was the elder, who seemed dead at first, but then his arms and legs twitched, and he sat up, his head above water.

The men got up to help him, but Barac signaled them to stay out of sight from the opening.

A man's voice sounded from above. "Speak up, old man!"

The elder coughed, spitting water, and said, "God will punish you for what you're doing."

"He's punishing you, fool." The man of Judah laughed. "Where are your wretched people?"

Glancing around, the elder smiled wearily. The water around him grew opaque as blood flowed from his wounds.

The bucket appeared through the opening, attached to the rope.

"Speak up," the man of Judah yelled above, "and we'll pull you out."

"I'll speak the words of the Holy Scriptures," the elder said. "And if you disobey Yahweh and fail to keep his laws and prohibitions, curses shall fall upon you."

"You'll die in there," the man said. "Your body will foul the cistern forever, and anyone who drinks from it will die because of you."

"Damned you are in the city," the elder continued quoting, "and damned you are in the field. Damned is your basket, and damned is your dough."

"Damn you," the man yelled. "Tell us where they are!"

"Damned is the fruit of your loins." The elder struggled to his feet, his voice rising. "And damned is the fruit of your land, and of your cattle, and of your sheep!"

The bucket was pulled up though the opening and, a moment later, a stone dropped through, hitting the elder's shoulder. He cried in pain, but continued reciting.

"Damned you are in coming, and damned you are in leaving!"

Another stone came down, bigger this time, and hit him on the head. He collapsed in the water and didn't move. Above, men's voices sounded, then horses neighed, and the earth shook under their hooves as they rode off. Barac waded through the water and pulled the elder to the side. He coughed out water while blood streamed from his head. The men glanced fearfully at the opening above while gathering around the elder.

Coughing, the elder struggled to speak. "You were right, boy. They wish to destroy Simeon and take our land and water."

"Did you hear anything else?" Barac asked. "What's their next target?"

The elder coughed. "Kabetzel."

The facts began to come clear in Barac's mind. "That's where they'll meet up with the rest of Judah's army in order to attack Beersheba."

"My people," the elder said, panting now. "How will they get back up?"

Barac wiped the blood from the elder's face. "Don't worry. We'll find a way."

The elder gripped Barac's hand. "Blessed you are in the city," he whispered, "and in the field."

With a sigh, Barac nodded.

"Blessed is the fruit of your loins—"

In mid-sentence, the elder's jaw slacked, and his eyes froze.

17

The rising sun forced Deborah to shield her eyes, but she didn't mind the inconvenience – a small price to pay for having survived the night. Riding in the dark had been slow, with the road barely visible and obstacle awaiting to trip the horses, though the chilly night had required less stops for rest and water. The surrounding darkness had been alive with jackals' howls, coyotes' laughter, and an occasional screeching of an unfortunate prey, while the burning torches kept predators away from the small convoy.

An oasis appeared ahead. A single caravan was camping there, with a large tent and several horses and donkeys. Two women were already up to rekindle the fire and prepare the morning meal. Deborah stopped at the opposite side of the spring and dismounted. The maids helped the princess, who seemed to be half asleep. Yael, who had spent the whole night on her feet driving the chariot, stepped off and sat on the ground.

With a blanket up to his neck, Sallan was trembling, and his face was pale. He reached under the blanket, took out a cloth pouch, and gave it to Deborah. "For fresh horses," he said weakly. "Make an exchange."

She looked at the caravans, where no men were out yet.

"Go." He touched her sheathed sword. "They'll wake the men up."

"You look deathly. We should find a healer."

He shook his head. "If they have lemons, buy a few."

Seeing Deborah approach, one of the women hurried into the tent. A moment later, a gray-haired man came out, straightening his robe, and said in Moabite, "Good morning, soldier. How can we be of assistance?"

His subservient tone made her want to reassure him she posed no threat, but she held back and spoke in a thickened voice, using the Edomite language. "My horses are tired, but I have no time for resting. Give me four of yours in exchange for four of mine, except for the white one, of course."

He bowed while his eyes darted between the purse in her left hand, the steel-fronted chariot, and the canopy on Princess Needa's horse, before focusing on Rogez. She could see him contemplate the contradictions presented by a single young soldier accompanying four women and a sick man, yet in obvious opulence. He clicked his fingers, and two younger men came out of the tent, each carrying a club.

With a hint of a smile, he said, "It will be an honor to provide you with two fresh horses in exchange for four of yours, including the white stallion, as well as four silver coins."

"The white one stays with me," Deborah said. "The others I need to change."

He sighed with feigned regret. "I must insist."

"That's not a fair exchange." She recalled Abu Zariz telling her a long time ago that a successful trade was based on a fair balance of mutually assured exaggerations and understatements. "My horses are excellent, much better than your horses. Once they're rested, you'll be richer than if you kept your own horses."

He shrugged. "I will lose a day waiting for them to rest. We don't like to wait, do we, boys?"

The two young men shook their heads, grinning as they tapped the clubs against their legs.

"Fair enough," Deborah said. "I'll throw in one silver coin for your time, but we exchange each one of my four excellent horses for one fresh horse of yours. By nighttime, you'll have better horses than before."

"I'll give you three horses for four of yours and eight coins." He smiled. "My next offer will not be to your liking."

Deborah took two silver coins from the purse and held them forth in her open palm. "This, and your four horses, for my four."

He took the two coins and held out his hand. "I'll take the whole purse, and you can forget the horses."

The two younger men shifted positions, one to her left, the other to her right, boxing her in. Glancing left and right, Deborah registered that they were taller than her and much more muscular, but she had speed and agility, as well as a more dangerous weapon, which she knew how to use. Hiding her fear, she laughed.

His forehead creased. "I'm not joking, boy."

"Neither am I." She held his gaze. "My offer is fair. Accept it, and we'll part ways in peace."

"Give me the purse."

"How many more sons do you have, that you're willing to bury these two for a few coins?"

The merchant hesitated, his gaze going back and forth between her purse, her sheathed sword, and her eyes. He reached behind his back and drew a knife. "Time is up, boy."

One of the young men raised his club and came at her.

Without retreating, Deborah simultaneously dropped the purse and drew her sword. The club came at her head, but she was already dodging and, as his body turned with the swinging club, she jabbed the blade into his side between his hip and his ribs, running it through him all the way to the other side. From the corner of her eye she saw the other young man rush at her. She skipped aside, holding on to the hilt. The horizontal pressure on the sword acted as a lever, causing the blade to slice forward through his abdomen and come free, chased by his guts, which spilled out while he was still standing. His brother's club missed Deborah, who grabbed the hilt with both hands and tilted up her sword, where the blade cut into his forearm. He cried, dropped the blub, and bent over, pressing his injured arm to his chest. Deborah stepped around him and held the bloody sword over his neck.

"Don't kill him!" The merchant dropped the knife and fell to his knees. "Take the horses!"

The women screamed and rushed over.

Deborah lowered her sword, picked up her purse, and stepped back.

While the grieving Moabite women wailed, she took the four horses. Yael and the maids switched over the saddles, including the canopy from the princess's horse, the packs of food and waterskins, and the chariot's harness. The three women worked in silence, their eyes avoiding her. She wanted to explain that the Moabite men had left her no choice, that her God had said, "When a person rises to kill you, rise first and kill him." She said nothing, though, hoping that their awkward silence stemmed not from disapproval of her slaying the young man and disabling his brother, but from the primal fear of death that every person experienced when witnessing a life violently taken.

When Deborah said it was time to move on, Princess Needa did not object. Yael gave water to her mare, which was tied behind the chariot, and got back in the driver's position, holding the reins. Deborah mounted Rogez, who showed no signs of fatigue.

They rode on, accompanied by the Moabite women's mournful cries.

Further east, they came upon another merchant caravan and stopped. The leader, a smiling gray-haired Persian, drove a hard bargain, selling her three lemons for a silver coin, but then added a gift of a dozen fresh plums.

He asked, "How does a young man come into possession of such a splendid horse and an Edomite battle chariot?"

Sallan answered for her from the chariot. "We are in the service of King Esau the Twentieth."

"Heading to Bozra?"

"Correct."

"Have you traveled this road before?"

"No," Deborah said. "I haven't."

He pointed east. "It's a rough and arduous road, but well-trodden and easy to navigate. Keep going straight ahead until you reach a busy copper-mining town, which is in Edom."

Searching his face, she saw no ill intentions, and asked, "Who controls this area?"

"The Hebrew tribe of Judah." He glanced around. "A bunch of them rode by yesterday."

"Which direction?"

He pointed west. "Where you came from. Have you not seen them?"

She shook her head.

"Thank your Gods," he said. "Those men were heavily armed and thirsty for blood."

Sallan punctured one of the lemons with his fingernail and squeezed it directly into his mouth, followed by a mouthful of water.

18

The men and women of Revivim waded through the water to congregate around their elder, who had lost his life to defend them. Many wept while one of the men held his hands over the corpse, fingers parted in pairs, and recited, "Blessed is Yahweh, king of the world, the true judge."

For Barac, the sadness was mixed with worry. His clever solution had deceived the attackers, who were gone without achieving their goal, but now, with the bucket and rope out of reach, the men of Judah might in the end unknowingly succeed in destroying the people of Revivim.

They wiped their tears and gazed up at the bright opening above, clearly worried about the same thing.

The girl who had earlier brought him water and a robe said, "Pick me up."

Kneeling, he helped her sit on his shoulders. She was heavier than he expected, but her inner thighs were warm and smooth against his neck, and he felt a stirring in his loins, which embarrassed him.

Several men grabbed his legs and picked him up. The girl reached up, still short of the opening. Below, other men supported the swaying human tower.

"Higher," the girl said.

Barac held her feet while she got up from his shoulders and stood on his hands. To help her stay stable, he pressed his face to the back of her robe, his nose between her upper thighs. When he breathed in, her feminine scent made his heart race. Turning his head sideways, he took a deep breath and slowly raised his hands, lifting her until her robe gave way to her naked calves, which were smooth and moist from the cistern water. He felt her muscles flex and contract against his cheeks while she reached up for the opening, grabbed hold of the stones, and climbed out, her feet leaving his hands.

A moment later, she lowered the bucket with the rope. Barac climbed out through the opening and over the circular wall. He sat on the ground, panting, while the bright sun warmed his face.

The men climbed out of the cistern, one after the other.

The girl knelt beside him and put a water jug to his lips.

He drank some water. "What's your name?"

"Tova. What's yours?"

"Barac, son of Abinoam." He drank more and added, "Of Naphtali."

She smiled, which made her look older. "I've never met a man of Naphtali."

"Neither have I," he said. "Except for my father."

Using a wet cloth, she wiped his face, doing it with gentleness that made it feel like caressing. "I heard stories about Naphtali's land," she said. "Is it really full of rivers and streams that run all the time, even in the summer? Are the forests really so thick that only children can pass between the trunks of the cedars?"

"I don't know about the cedars, but my father said that the Dan River gushes through the forests, its water white with foam, and it fills the Sea of Galilee every spring after the snow melts in the mountains of Lebanon. That's why the Canaanites covet it."

"I'd like to live among streams and forests, instead of this sandy furnace. Wouldn't you?"

He chuckled. Her way of conversing by asking questions reminded him of Deborah, though the similarity ended there. Not only was Tova much shorter and rounder, but also, unlike Deborah's fair complexion and green eyes, she had brown skin and dark eyes. In fact, gazing into Tova's eyes, he could not tell where her pupils ended and her irises started.

Lifting the oversized robe off his chest, she dabbed the puncture wounds and wiped the crusted blood. "Did you fight men with hooked nails?"

"Not men." He chuckled. "A tiger."

She laughed, but looking at him, her laughter faded. "Are you serious? A tiger?"

He nodded.

"Really?"

"It bit me on the head, too."

She touched his thick curls. "There's lots of dry blood. Will you let me wash your hair?"

He sat up. "There's no time."

"Is it hard to be brave?"

"It's harder to be kind." He patted her cheek. "Thank you, girl."

"You're welcome, boy."

He laughed. "I deserved it. Thank you, Tova."

"You're welcome, Barac."

Her self-confidence intrigued him. "Where are your parents?"

"What makes you think I have parents?"

She hurried away before he could respond, which was fine, because he had no answer.

The men of Revivim had climbed out of the cistern, brought up the women and children, and pulled out the elder's body, laying it down in the shade of a tree.

Barac stood up and looked around. The houses were gone, reduced to smoldering ashes. The corral was empty, but he saw a few goats nibble a thorny bush nearby. He whistled several times until he heard the drumming of hooves, and his horse showed up. He gave it water, filled up the waterskin, and got in the saddle.

The men, women, and children of Revivim gathered around him.

He pointed to a low hill nearby. "Build your new houses on high grounds and construct a stone wall around. Make spears and gather rocks inside the wall to throw at attackers. You must be ready to defend yourselves. The men of Judah will come back, and if they don't, others might come—Edomites, Moabites, Philistines, Egyptians, or other gentiles who contrive to take advantage of the fighting among the Hebrew tribes."

"It's not necessary," one of the men said. "God has kept us safe here for many years."

"Look at your village." Barac waved at the smoky ruins. "The Holy Scriptures say that, when the men of Israel violate Yahweh's laws and worship false gods, He turns His face away and allows foreign nations to subjugate Israel. Our northern tribes are already under Canaanite oppression. How long before God's wrath reaches down south?"

They looked up at him with sad eyes. He wanted to turn his horse and sprint away, but felt compelled to give them hope.

"God is still with you," he said. "He always watches over the righteous and gives strength to those who stand up to defend themselves."

They didn't seem comforted.

Gesturing toward the dead elder under the tree, Barac said, "Your wise leader set a good example for his successor."

The men looked at each other, and Barac could tell there was no obvious heir. If he didn't help them choose a new leader, they could end up without one at all.

"Who among you knows the Holy Scriptures?"

The gray-haired man, who had recited the prayer over the corpse earlier, raised his hand.

Barac pointed at him. "Is this man wise and just?"

Most of the men nodded.

"Then he shall be your new elder. I must go now, or the men of Judah will burn down Beersheba, too."

Tova picked up his club from the ground by the cistern and brought it over, holding it up for him.

"Thank you." He pulled on the club.

She didn't let go. "Can I come with you?"

"No." He searched the faces of the men. "Who's in charge of this girl?"

The new elder spoke. "Her father died last week, her mother many months ago. She belongs to no man. You can have her."

Barac shook his head.

Tova asked, "Don't you want a woman?"

He blushed. "I'm a soldier."

"You're also a man, right?"

He tried to shake the club out of her grip.

"Don't you like me?"

Some of the women giggled.

"You're too stubborn," he said.

She held on, and when he pulled harder, she grabbed the tail of his robe with her other hand, pulled herself up, and slipped onto the saddle behind him.

"That's not going to work" He dropped the club into the saddle sheath. "Get off my horse."

Clinging to his back, Tova threw her arms around him.

The new elder said, "May God watch over you," and slapped the horse on the rear.

They galloped away from Revivim, the sun halfway up on the right, the air still chilly from the night. When the horse finally calmed down, Barac heaved on the reins.

"Get off, Tova."

"Why?"

He took a deep breath, controlling his anger. "They'll attack Beersheba in a day or two. I have to get there in time to warn the people and help defend the city."

"Who will tend to your injuries?"

He pulled harder on the reins, bringing the agitated horse down to a trot. "You'll slow me down."

"Am I the one slowing us down now?"

Tova kicked in with her heels, sending the beast forward with renewed energy. Barac cursed, and she began to laugh – a rolling, ringing, beguiling laughter that gradually cooled Barac's anger until he, too, began to laugh.

19

Throughout the day, Deborah allowed only infrequent, brief stops to give the horses water. At midday, they reached another oasis and stopped to eat and fill the waterskins. In the late afternoon, as they came around a bend in the road, she saw a town ahead. A cloud of thick smoke hung over it, and the smell reminded her of a blacksmith shop. Closer yet, she saw the fairgrounds, which had a water well and vendors' stalls offering food and other goods.

Dismounting, she paced back and forth a few times. Having sat in the saddle for hours, her legs were stiff, her crotch throbbed with a dull ache, and her breasts were tender from being chafed by the chest armor. She held the armor off her chest and blew air down to cool her skin.

They gave water to the horses while Yael went to buy food. She came back with bread and figs. The maids took some and served the princess. Yael sat beside the chariot with Deborah. Sallan, who was able to sit up, drink water, and eat a piece of bread.

"We're back to Edom," he said. "You've kept us on the right path."

Deborah took a bite out of a ripe fig. "Do you know this town?"

"It's called Punon."

"The name is familiar."

"Legend says that your ancient Hebrew ancestors stopped here on their exodus from Egypt."

Deborah looked around with renewed interest, but other than the red-tinted rocks, nothing seemed remarkable. "How far from here to Bozra?"

"A day, if we ride fast."

She felt hopeful about reaching Bozra before tomorrow's sunset, in time to save Leola.

"This direction to Bozra." Sallan pointed to the northeast. "It's a good road. I travelled it with my father several times."

Deborah gave Rogez a fig, which he ate noisily, and got in the saddle. Taking the road in the direction Sallan had pointed, she beckoned the others to follow.

At the outskirts of Punon, they passed a fenced area, where guards on horses wielded whips over a column of men in sleeveless shirts and bare feet. The slaves came out of a tunnel in the mountainside, each carrying a straw basket on his bent back. They emptied the baskets onto a large mound of red ore and reentered the mountain through another tunnel. The guards whipped the slaves to hurry them up.

Further down the fenced area, large fires burnt, some in open pits, some inside large stone ovens, spewing dark columns of smoke. Near one of the ovens, a group of guards watched a line of slaves who were kneeling on the ground, their eyes covered with cloth straps. Two of the guards stood beside one of the kneeling slaves and held his arms, and a third guard came behind him and clasped his head. A fourth guard used a bundle of rags to grip the end of a long iron rod and pull it from the oven. The red-hot end of the rod had the shape of a circle, about the size a man could form with a finger and a thumb. Holding the rod horizontally, the guard turned around, careful not to touch one of the other guards, and with the ease of a well-practiced motion pressed the red-hot circle to the slave's left cheek.

The guards dragged the the wailing slave away, dropped him on the ground, and pulled over another slave toward the fire. Riding near the fence, Deborah was close enough to hear the hissing sound of the red-hot circle as it branded the second slave's cheek. The guards moved with quick efficiency, hauling away the screaming slave and pulling over the next one. The sight horrified her. How could they brand living men the way farmers branded goats or cows?

Rogez slowed down, turned his head, and looked at her with a knowing eye.

Dropping the reins, her hand went to the hilt of her sword.

Behind her, Sallan yelled hoarsely, "Keep going, Borah."

She glanced back at the chariot, which Yael struggled to slow down before they collided.

"You can't save them," he said.

Over the chariot, from further back, Princess Needa's eyes bore at Deborah through the slit in the veil while her head tilted slightly in the direction of the guards and the slaves. The implied threat, Deborah knew, wasn't an empty one, coming from the sister of the king, who owned all the copper mines and the branded slaves.

Deborah turned away from the princess and faced forward. Would King Esau break his promise and condemn his sister's rescuer to the copper mines? Or would he deny the promise altogether, now that General Mazabi, who communicated the promise to her, was dead?

She urged Rogez to go faster, and he obeyed, showing no sign of exhaustion despite the arduous journey and lack of sleep. She sensed that he understood what was at stake.

Soon, the branded slaves' screams and the foul odors of Punon were left behind. The road became hilly and, at times, rocky and rough. Near sunset, they stopped by a small village that had a waterhole fed by a spring, where they let the horses drink and topped off their waterskins. Deborah started a small fire, which she used to light two torches, one for her and one for the maid riding behind the princess. They were back on the road while darkness descended on the surrounding hills.

20

"That's Beersheba," Barac said, pointing at the lights in the darkness ahead. He felt Tova lean forward against his back, her chin on his shoulder, her hair caressing his neck. "The lights you see are from the many houses of shop owners and tradesmen with firepits and oil lamps. They're probably finishing their evening meals now."

He had pushed the horse to keep going all day, while the two of them sustained on a few palm dates, which Tova had brought along.

"It's much bigger than Revivim," she said. "Are there no poor people in Beersheba?"

"There are many. They live in the lower part of the city, just inside the walls, near the markets, the workshops, the storage buildings, and the horse stables."

"Is there a temple?"

"A small one, about halfway up the hill."

"With a priest?"

"Yes. Tonight, I will ask him to pray for my friends." Barac thought of all the bodies he and Deborah had piled up near the edge of the Ramon Crater. His grief mixed with dread at the prospect of delivering the terrible news to the people of Beersheba, especially the families of the fallen men. "I hope they don't blame me for the loss of their sons."

"Why would they blame you?"

"I survived. Some might suspect I fled the battle, or betrayed the others. Even I find it hard to believe it's possible that I fought alongside everyone else, and while they fell down, one after the other, I kept fighting, on and on, until there was no one else standing."

Tova was quiet for a moment. "There's always a reason why one person fights harder than others to survive."

"It's true." He hesitated. "There was a girl. I was desperate to stay alive and see her again."

He urged the horse to go faster.

Tova held onto him, gazing ahead over his shoulder, her hair rustling by his ear. "What's her name?"

"Deborah."

"Does she buzz like a bee?"

"No." He laughed. "She wasn't named after a bee. Her name stands for "Word of God," because her father had a dream before she was born in which he saw her deliver God's word to the Hebrew tribes."

"A girl prophet?"

"If any girl can become a prophet, it's Deborah." He shook the reins to prod the horse, whose pace kept slowing down. "She's righteous, wise, and brave as any man I've known, and she has the most incredible green eyes you've ever seen."

"Then why aren't you with her?"

The question hit him hard, and Barac's voice trembled when he answered. "She rejected me."

"Does she love another man?"

"No, she loves me." He took a deep breath. "Still, she pushed me away."

"And you gave up?"

"She had a good reason."

"Girls find reasons to change their minds, sometimes back-and-forth many times."

"Not Deborah. There's no chance she'll change her mind."

"She rejected you and won't change her mind," Tova said in exaggerated astonishment. "The real question is, then, can a foolish girl become a prophet?"

Despite his sadness, Barac laughed again.

Tova hugged him from behind while they approached Beersheba. He could feel her tremble. Several caravans camped in the fairgrounds outside the walls. Near the gate, a single guard sat by a bonfire, drinking wine. Above him, hanging from a wooden pole, was the green flag of Simeon with the drawing of city gates between two masonry guard towers.

The guard got up, swaying on his feet, and raised the jug. "Welcome back."

"You alone guard the city?"

"No, not alone, no." The guard slurred his speech. "We take turns."

Looking in the direction the guard pointed, Barac saw a guard sleeping by the wall some distance away.

Stabbing his heels inward, Barac urged the horse through the gate.

Behind them, the guard yelled, "Where is everyone else?"

Barac didn't answer.

Tova asked, "What's this stench?"

He pointed to the area just inside the walls. "The poor who don't own land are allowed to live here in shacks, huts, or tents, which they share with goats and sheep."

In the houses along the main street, going uphill, cooking fires burned, men and women chatted, children laughed, and babies cried. They rode by the small temple and the priest's house, which was dark. Approaching the top of the hill, a great deal of noise came from the courtyard at Judge Ohad's house, with men singing and women laughing. The gate was open, and Barac directed the horse into the courtyard.

Tall flames danced in the firepit, lighting up the two-story house and the walls around the courtyard. A large group of young men sat at a long table. At one end was the white-robed priest, grim faced, eating grapes from a hefty bunch. At the other end, Tsruyah lounged in the judge's chair. In his lap sat a woman whose lips were painted bright red against her white-powdered face. He pawed her breasts while she sang in the language of the Cainite Clan, flinging her long black hair and crunching her painted face in contrived merriment. A few other Cainite women, in various stages of undress, sprawled over the young men, who groped them and hollered. The table was laden with bowls of food and jugs of wine, and Judge Ohad's servants hurried in and out of the kitchen with fresh servings.

On a pedestal beside Tsruyah stood several wooden effigies. Barac recognized Ra, the Canaanite Sun God that had a man's body and a hawk's head, crowned with a solar disk and a coiled serpent, as well as the two prominent Canaanite deities: Ashtoreth, with her protuberant breasts resting on her forearms while her hands pressed together under her chin as if in prayer to her husband, Baal Amon, God of Fertility, whose elongated head resembled a male organ. A plate of food rested before each effigy.

Shocked by this spectacle of corruption, Barac neglected to pull on his horse's reins until halfway through the courtyard.

Everyone quieted down, gazing at them.

Dismounting, Barac handed the reins to Tova.

Tsruyah shoved the woman off his lap and bolted from his chair, his expression transforming into alarm. "Why has no one told me the judge's coming?"

His assumption, that the rest of Judge Ohad's entourage was right behind Barac, was reasonable, and his men scrambled to their feet, pushing the women away. The priest, however, remained seated, and a grin crept onto his face.

Slapping the table, Tsruyah yelled, "Who's guarding the gates?"

"Two idiots," Barac said. "Drunk sinners, like the rest of you."

The silence that followed Barac's harsh words was interrupted by the priest's soft chuckling as he rose slowly to his feet, pulled a curled ram's horn from under his white robe, and blew into it. The sound echoed from the walls of the courtyard. He inhaled and blew again. The soldiers anxiously strapped on their weapons and formed two lines facing the courtyard gate. The women of the Cainite Clan pulled on their robes and scurried out of the way. The servants retreated to the kitchen, peeking out through the door.

When no other horses appeared at the courtyard gate, Tsruyah rushed out and looked downhill.

The priest kept blowing his horn.

Reentering the courtyard, Tsruyah looked at Barac. "Is the judge coming?"

"No."

The horn blew again. Tsruyah cursed, walked back to the table, and tore the ram's horn away from the priest, whose lips remained circular in mid-blowing. Tsruyah gripped the ram's horn on both ends and broke it in half over his knee.

The priest cried, "No!"

Tossing the remains of the ram's horn toward Barac, Tsruyah

grabbed a wine jug and gulped directly from it. Seeing this, the soldiers' anxiety gave way to relief, the women halted their hasty departure, and the judge's servants hung their heads in disappointment.

Barac picked up the two sections of the ram's horn, kissed each one, and returned them to the priest, who held them with shaking hands, trying to fit together the jagged break-lines. His futile efforts drew hoots from the soldiers, and Tsruyah slumped in the judge's great chair, propped his booted legs on the table, and threw his head back, laughing heartily.

With a shout of frustration, the priest sprang up, ran to the firepit, and threw in the broken ram's horn. This made everyone laugh even harder. Shouting in rage, the priest grabbed the wooden Canaanite effigies and dumped them, too, into the flames.

The act snuffed out the roaring laughter. Tsruyah swung his legs off the table and, with fluid speed, drew his sword while going after the priest, who sprinted toward the courtyard gate. Several men blocked his way, pushing him back toward Tsruyah, who slipped the tip of his sword through the priest's beard under his chin and held it steady, forcing the priest to stand still, his head tilted back, his wide eyes staring down at the blade. Tsruyah moved sideways, compelling the priest to turn in tandem, and made him tiptoe back until his heels bumped against the masonry surrounding the firepit.

The flames licked the back of the priest's robe.

Tsruyah grinned. "What will it be, old man of Levi? Die by the sword, or by the fire?"

Barac gripped the hilt of his sword and approached the firepit.

His face as white as fresh goat's milk, the priest only moaned while the blue fringes at one corner of his robe ignited. The men pointed and cheered, their sweaty faces shining in the red flames.

"In God's name," Barac said. "Stop this."

Tsruyah ignored him and said to the priest, "As your invisible God what to do – impale your stupid head on my blade, or fall back into a purifying fire. Either way, you'll meet Him soon."

Everyone laughed, and the priest moaned, his hands rising toward the blade. The men gathered closer, gulping wine, urging him to choose the sword or the fire. Before Barac could interfere, the priest lost his balance and fell back into the firepit, which gave off a great hiss and an explosion of sparks. Tsruyah stepped back while the flames engulfed the priest, who screamed and flailed his arms and legs.

Leaping forward, Barac pushed through the men. One of the priest's legs stuck out of the fire. Barac clutched it and pulled hard, dragging him out. The priest screamed, his robe in flames. Without stopping, Barac continued to drag the priest across the courtyard to the well and emptied the bucket of water on him. Part of the robe was still on fire, but by now, Tova was at his side, tearing the shards of robe off the priest's back. Barac dropped the bucket into the well, pulled it up by the rope as fast as he could, and emptied it again over the old priest, who curled up on the ground in his wet undergarments, whimpering.

The courtyard became silent.

Tsruyah walked over, wielding his sword. "Ready to fight, boy, or to flee like your cowardly father?"

Barac drew his sword, barely in time to deflect Tsruyah's first jab at his chest, but the larger man immediately rammed him, sending him backward into a group of Cainite women, who screamed and scattered. Barac fell over and dropped his sword. Tsruyah followed him and brought down his blade for a fatal blow, which Barac avoided by rolling sideways. He continued to roll several times, passing under the table while Tsruyah slashed down repeatedly, hitting the dirt ground.

With the massive table separating them, Barac sprung to his feet. His head hurt, his muscles burned, and his eyes misted over. Across the table, Tsruyah was panting, his face red. He rushed to the right, and Barac went left, circling the table until they were again on opposite sides.

The men, meanwhile, had moved out of the way and stood near the courtyard walls, egging their leader on. Tsruyah grinned, jabbed his sword forward above the table and, as Barac leaped back, grabbed a wine jug off the table, gulped from it, and tossed it at Barac, who caught it. The men hooted, and Barac took a sip, which tasted sweet and spread warmth inside his chest. He tossed the jug back to Tsruyah and, while it was still in the air, made a dash toward where his sword was lying in the ground. The wily fighter, however, ignored the flying jug and sprinted around the table in the same direction, forcing Barac to turn and run back in the opposite direction to keep the table between them. This time, however, Tsruyah did not bother to attempt racing around again, but climbed on a chair and up onto the table.

The men cheered.

Grinning, Tsruyah looked down at Barac, unarmed and exposed below him, and swung his sword left and right in a theatrical show of triumph. Behind Tsruyah, Tova pick up Barac's sword, held it horizontally, the blade resting flat on the open palms of her hands, and threw it to Barac, who managed to catch the sword by the hilt. The feat drew applauds from the spectators.

Tsruyah turned to her. "Who are you?"

"My name is Tova, daughter of Matai of Simeon."

"You're too pretty to die, girl, but your father will pay dearly for your rude interference." He waved at his men nearest to the gate. "Go and find that man, Matai, and bring him here."

"My father is already dead," Tova said. "And my mother, too."

"How convenient." Tsruyah stomped his boot on the tabletop. "Where are they buried?"

"In our village, Revivim, and if not for this brave man," she said, pointing at Barac, "all the men, women, and children of Revivim would have died."

"Really? Tell us more." Tsruyah made like he was about to step down from the table to the chair, but turned swiftly and kicked a bowl of fruit at Barac.

Tired and distracted, Barac failed to dodge, and the edge of the clay bowl hit the bridge of his nose. The explosion of pain took over every other sensation. He dropped his sword and pressed both hands to his face while blood burst from his nostrils. Someone pushed him down to the ground, kicked him over onto his back, and pressed down on his chest. Removing his hands from his face, Barac saw through the mist of tears Tsruyah's boot on his chest and the tip of the sword at his throat.

"Time to die, boy," Tsruyah said.

"No!" Tova appeared beside him. "If you kill him, all of you will also die!"

"Nice try," Tsruyah said.

"It's true! A huge army of Judah is coming!"

Barac heard the men around repeat the news to one another.

"They're coming," Tova said. "We rushed here to warn you—"

With his left hand, Tsruyah clutched her hair. "Lying is a sin, girl."

"I'm not lying." Her voice thin with pain, Tova spoke rapidly. "A band of Judah attacked our village, but Barac saved us by taking everyone down into the water cistern. Only our elder remained above and heard them speak of meeting the rest of Judah's army at Kabetzel today in preparation to attack Beersheba. They're coming to kill everyone here!"

"It's about time." The priest bolted up to a sitting position. "Yahweh's punishment is coming for the wicked."

The men's murmuring grew louder.

"She's right." Barac used the side of his forearm to slowly shift aside Tsruyah's blade, slipped from under his boot, and stood up. "An attack is coming."

Still clutching Tova's hair with his left hand, Tsruyah raised the sword in his right and aimed it at Barac's chest. "I'm still going to kill you."

"I'd rather die fighting the men of Judah." Without making any move to defend himself, Barac waved at the anxious men surrounding them. "You don't have enough soldiers, as it is."

The men murmured, and one word repeated loud enough to make out: "Borah."

Tsruyah lowered his sword. "We need Mamreh and his men. How far behind you are they?"

"They're not coming."

"Until when?"

"Never."

A hush fell over the courtyard.

"We were tricked," Barac said. "The Edomite king's treaty was a ruse. He sent an army of steel chariots to liberate his sister. They surprised us by the Ramon Crater. Judge Ohad, Mamreh, and all our men are dead."

A collective cry came from everyone in the courtyard.

"Not everyone's dead," Tsruyah said. "How did you survive?"

"God kept me alive."

"By sneaking away on the eve of battle to frolic with this pretty thing." He tightened his grip on Tova's hair. "Is that what you did?"

For a moment, Barac's mind filled with the memory of lying with Deborah in the middle of the dark battlefield, their bodies melding into one flesh in an explosion of joy. It took all his resolve to drive away the memory and respond.

"This girl wasn't there." He glanced at Tova, whose face was twisted in pain. "She's from Revivim. I stopped there on my way here. Let her go."

"Answer the question," Tsruyah said. "How did you survive? Did you make a deal with the Edomites? Did you sell off the men of Simeon for a benefit to Naphtali?"

The men clustered closer, their faces angry.

"He's injured," Tova said. "Badly."

"Nobody asked you," Tsruyah said, shaking her by the hair.

She squealed, but still, she persisted. "Look at his head. It's soaked with dry blood."

Barac bowed his head to show Tsruyah, and also set aside part of his robe for a quick glimpse of his injured chest. "I fought hard," he said. "And then, I found myself standing alone in the battlefield. That's what happened, I swear to it in God's name."

Having seen him defend the priest at a great risk to his own life, even Tsruyah seemed to believe his oath by the holy name. "Where is Borah?"

"I don't know," Barac said. "Right now, we must prepare for war. A whole army of Judah is gathering in Kabetzel, hundreds of them, maybe thousands."

One of the men said, "We can't fight an army."

"They'll crush us," another said.

"We should escape," said a third one. "Hide in the desert with our families until they leave."

"They won't leave," Barac said. "They want all of Simeon's land and water."

The priest rose from the ground. One of the judge's servants wrapped him in a blanket and brought him a chair. He sat down.

Everyone expected him to speak, but he only mumbled to himself while brushing his silver beard with his fingers.

Tova groaned in pain, and Barac said, "Release her. She's an innocent maiden."

"Just the kind of girl I like." Tsruyah let go of Tova's hair, wrapped his arm around her torso, and picked her up, throwing her over his shoulder, face down. "Let's have us a little party, shall we?"

The priest laughed suddenly, but continued to mumble. The men congregated around him, talking over each other.

"Pray for us!"

"What does God want us to do?"

"Tell Yahweh we repent."

"Yes, tell Him we're sorry."

Tsruyah headed toward the house. "Calm down, men," he yelled. "Nothing to fear."

Barac followed him while Tova struggled in vain.

One of the men said, "We should make a sacrifice."

"For Borah," another one said. "We want him back to save us again."

"A goat," a man yelled toward the kitchen servants. "Bring a live goat, quickly."

Barac glanced over his shoulder and saw the priest shrug, tugging at his beard.

"Please, tell us," a young man cried, falling to his knees before the priest. "What does God want us to do? Should we fight, or run?"

"Neither," Tsruyah shouted as he stopped by the open door at the bottom of the staircase leading up to Judge Ohad's quarters. He turned to face the crowded courtyard. "We're not going to run, or to fight."

The men looked at him, their eyes wide with fear and incomprehension.

"As the new judge of Beersheba, I'll ride to Kabetzel tonight and negotiate peace with the leaders of Judah. There will be no attack, no fighting, and no bloodshed. Get my horse ready."

He turned to enter.

Tova kicked in the air. "Let me go!"

Barac grabbed his robe. "Don't violate her."

Tsruyah paused. "Take your hand off my robe, boy, or I'll kill you for real this time."

Twisting to turn her head in order to see Barac, Tova whispered, "Don't die for me."

Seeing her tears, Barac would not release his hold on Tsruyah's robe.

"Last warning, boy," Tsruyah said. "If I have to put her down and draw my sword, it won't go back in the sheath dry, I swear."

"She's my wife," Barac said, and repeated it louder for everyone to hear. "She's my wife."

21

A scream woke Deborah up. Startled, she sat upright in the saddle and realized that she had dozed off and dropped the torch. Looking back, she saw it on the road behind, where it had spooked the chariot horse, now reared up on its hind legs. Yael screamed again, and the horse came down, left-front hoof landing in the flame. It neighed frightfully and ran off the road and down a slope. The mare, which was tied behind the chariot, was set free when the piece of wood broke off with the reins still attached to it. The chariot's right wheel vaulted over a large rock, catapulting Sallan into the air. He landed on the ground with a cry while the chariot disappeared into the dark night, though the noise of its creaking wheels and Yael's screams continued.

Deborah jumped off the saddle, grabbed her torch from the ground, but it fell apart in her hand, dying off. She ran over to the maid who held the other torch and reached up.

"Give it to me."

The maid raised it out of Deborah's reach and looked at Princess Needa, who shook her head. The maid kicked in to get her horse going, but Deborah caught the tail of her robe and didn't let go as the horse stepped forward and the maid fell. Pulling the torch out of the maid's hand, Deborah ran off the road to where Sallan had fallen. He was unconscious but breathing. A few steps away from him grew a dry thorn bush. Deborah angled the torch to touch the flame to it, and the bush ignited. She went to the other maid's horse, reached into one of the sacks, and took out a few figs.

"Get a new torch," Deborah told her. "Start it before the bush burns out, find another bush to burn, and take care of Sallan."

The sounds of Yael and the chariot died out.

The first maid got up, brushing sand from her robe, and said,

"You must not leave us here unguarded."

"The fires will guard you until I'm back with the chariot. We can't keep going without it."

Princess Needa looked at the maid, who said, "We care nothing for the chariot, the old man, or the whore. Take us to Bozra now."

Heading after the chariot, Deborah yelled over her shoulder, "I care for them more than for you."

The temptation to run was strong, but she forced herself to slow down and held the torch forward to illuminate the tracks left by the chariot's wheels in the sand and rocks. She heard steps behind her and saw Rogez following.

"Good horse," she said. "Watch your steps."

At the bottom of the slope was a dry streambed. She struggled to find the tracks, which appeared only intermittently on patches of sand between the rocks. Occasionally, she stopped and called Yael's name, but heard no answer.

Up another slope and over a hill, she saw the chariot on its side. Coming around the upturned chariot, she saw the horse lying down, its rear legs crushed under the wheel of the chariot. She held a fig in her palm, and the horse took it, chewing while panting.

"Yael?" Deborah looked around. "Where are you?"

"Right here," Yael said in the dark.

Deborah found her sitting on the ground.

"How long was I out?"

"As long as it took me to find you." Deborah crouched beside her. "Are you injured?"

Yael examined herself. "Scratches and bruises, nothing worse."

The horse tried to move and whinnied in pain.

"Let's get you up." Deborah helped Yael to her feet. "Can you walk?"

Yael rotated her arms and stretched her legs, grimacing. "Everything hurts."

The horse whinnied again.

Seeing the horse's condition, Yael turned away with a sigh.

Deborah gave the horse another fig, and while the crippled beast was chewing it, she stepped behind, drew her sword, held it up, and chopped down with all the force she could garner, severing the horse's neck.

Rogez neighed.

"It was necessary," Deborah said, hoping he understood. "A quick death is better than prolonged suffering."

With Yael's help, she removed the harness and the leather breastplate from the dead horse and straightened the chariot. Rogez stood patiently while they attached the harness. Deborah retraced her steps following the same tracks back to the road, which glowed brightly from several burning bushes.

Rogez whinnied happily once he was free from the chariot, which they harnessed to the horse of the maid who had resisted giving her torch to Deborah. They put Sallan, who was still unconscious, on the floor of the chariot and secured him with a rope.

"You can ride the mare," Deborah told the maid.

The maid didn't move. "My mistress says that, because I gave you my torch, I must give you my body."

"You didn't give me the torch. I took it from you by force."

The maid turned around, bent over, and lifted her robe to expose herself. "I'm ready."

Deborah looked away. "Maybe another time."

Yael giggled.

Princess Needa whispered to the other maid, who said, "It wasn't a suggestion, soldier. Do it as the obedient dog that you should be. We will watch."

Without looking, Deborah reached and pulled the maid's robe back down. "Get on the mare. We've wasted enough time."

Princess Needa hissed.

"Please, soldier." The maid again lifted her robe and bent over. "Take me, or my mistress will whip me."

Holding her tongue, Deborah mounted Rogez and urged him into a fast trot. Yael drove the chariot with Sallan tied to the floor. Behind the chariot, the light of the other torch soon followed.

22

"Your wife?" Turning slowly with Tova slung over his shoulder, Tsruyah looked at Barac. "You said she was an innocent maiden, and now you say she's your wife. Which one is the lie?"

"Both things are true."

Tsruyah laughed. "Here's a simple question to answer. Have you possessed her yet?"

His face flushed, Barac said, "Not yet, but she's betrothed to me, and no man may possess her under Yahweh's laws."

"Correct," the priest said, and shut his eyes while quoting the Holy Scriptures. "If there is a betrothed virgin maiden in the town and a man possesses her, you shall take them both to the town's gates and stone them until they die – the maiden for she failed to scream, and the man for he had abused another man's woman, and you shall thus cleanse evil from among you. But if in the field the man finds the maiden and grabs her and possesses her, only the man shall die and the maiden shall not be punished, for it is like a man comes upon another and murders him, so it is here, because in the field she screams and no one is there to save her."

Tova must have been listening, for she screamed at the top of her voice. "Help me! Save me from rape!"

Lowering Tova down, Tsruyah took her small hands and held them for all to see. "Where is the ring?"

Barac didn't know what to say, but Tova answered.

"I lost it," she said, her voice shaking.

"Lost it?" Tsruyah opened his arms in mocked amazement. "Since when does a girl lose her ring of betrothal? Unless, of course, she hates the man who betrothed her."

The men laughed.

"The ring was big," she said. "We rode as fast as the horse could go in order to warn you about the attack. The ring must have fallen off my finger."

Barac reached out and took her arm, pulling her close to him in a demonstration of ownership. The men watched Tsruyah's bearded face, waiting to see what he would do. He stared at the girl hungrily, and Barac wondered what would happen if Tsruyah took Tova in defiance of her alleged betrothal. Would the men challenge him? Not likely, but having just claimed the mantle of a judge, whose main duty in peaceful times was to enforce God's laws, would Tsruyah throw away his credibility at the outset for a brief carnal pleasure?

Tsruyah rested his hand on the hilt of his sword. "Tell me, boy, what inheritance will come to you with this orphan girl? Fields? Orchards? Slaves?"

Barac shook his head.

"Goats, or sheep, perhaps?"

He kept shaking his head.

"Silver?"

"No," Barac said. "There's no inheritance."

"Nothing?" Tsruyah pretended to be shocked. "Am I to believe that a blacksmith's son of Naphtali, an aspiring Hebrew warrior of the Galilee, agreed to betroth a worthless orphan girl?"

The question, put to him with such venomous mockery, threw Barac off.

"I think you didn't," Tsruyah pressed on. "I think you're lying about betrothing her only to deprive me of her company. I think you have no intention of marrying her. Why would you marry a girl who has nothing?"

As Barac looked at Tova, the answer came to him instantly. "She has a good heart," he said. "That's why."

Tsruyah's wily dark eyes measured Tova up and down, and he licked his lips.

A man entered the courtyard with a goat in his arms. "I got one," he yelled. "Let's make a sacrifice to Yahweh so that He brings Borah back to save Beersheba again from the army of Judah!"

"I'll save Beersheba," Tsruyah said. "The goat will be sacrificed to bless a marriage."

The bind he was in, Barac realized, had just become worse.

The smirk on Tsruyah's face grew wider. "Are you ready to marry this poor, worthless orphan for her good heart?"

Barely able to breathe, Barac thought of Deborah, but what could he do now, when his willingness to marry Tova was all that stood between her and Tsruyah's brutality? A girl defiled, willingly or not, was unfit to marry a good man. To survive, she would have to sell her body like the women of the Cainite Clan. His heart belonged to Deborah, but her rejection had been final, as she had made clear on that night in the ravine: "A good boy doesn't always become a good man. What kind of a man takes a maiden as his wife without disclosing that he is not of her tribe?" And then, she pulled off the ring and threw it in his face.

Tsruyah rubbed his hands. "Well, boy?"

"Yes," Barac said. "I am ready."

Beside him, Tova whispered, "Thank you."

"I'm ready, too," Tsruyah said, grinning. "This is my first marriage ceremony to officiate as the new judge of Beersheba, thanks to the Gods."

The reference to multiple gods infuriated Barac, but he said nothing.

A servant bound the goat's front and back legs and placed it on the table. Lying on its side, the goat bleated and writhed, throwing its legs back and forth in a futile struggle to run away. The priest, holding the blanket tightly around his shoulders, joined them.

"We're gathered here," Tsruyah announced, "in this blessed city of Beersheba, to bind in marriage this man, Barac, son of Abinoam of Naphtali, to his betrothed bride, Tova, daughter of Matai of Simeon."

Tova straightened her disheveled hair, tugged at the bottom of her robe, and smiled at Barac. He looked away, lest his eyes betray his feeling of utter anguish at this sudden marriage, which his heart could not embrace. Looking around, he saw that the men were anxious for this to be over with, and a thought came to him that the marriage would actually not take full effect until he possessed Tova's body, which he had no intention of doing. Here was the solution: he would let Tsruyah conduct the ceremony, and when it was over and attention turned to the coming attack, he would release Tova from her betrothal and all would be the same as before.

With the burden of unwanted marriage lifted from his shoulders, Barac was able to return Tova's smile, before one of the women servants draped a veil over her face.

"With this offering," the priest said, "we ask Yahweh to sanctify the marriage, make the bride's womb fertile, and give her many sons to continue her husband's name."

The men mumbled, "Amen."

Someone gave the priest a knife, which he held to the goat's neck while reciting the traditional marriage blessing: "Blessed be Yahweh, our God, king of the world, who created man in His own image and made the woman to lust after her husband and obey him in all matters until death."

The goat bleated desperately as a servant lifted its bound legs so that its neck faced up. With a single slice, the priest cut the goat's neck and silenced its bleating. Blood burst from the severed neck, and the goat's legs jerked rapidly a few times.

Barac expected everyone to turn away and forget about him and Tova.

The priest put down the bloody knife, took Barac's arm, and led him to a door of a room on the ground floor of the house. "When you are done, show us the stained bedsheet to prove that she had not whored with another man before, or she will be stoned to death at the gates as the Holy Scriptures command."

The door slammed behind them, Barac and Tova stood silently by a cot covered with a white sheet.

"It's still me." She pulled off the veil. "No one switched me with an ugly spinster."

Her attempt at humor didn't amuse him. "I can't do this," he said. "I'm sorry."

"I understand." Tova smiled. "You don't have to do anything."

"But—"

"Don't worry." She touched his lips to hush him. "We can at least wash off the dust of the road and lie down to rest. Maybe they'll forget about us."

He noticed a bucket of water by the wall, but was too tired to do anything else but lie down on the cot. "I'm sorry."

"Don't worry," she said. "Close your eyes and rest. No one will bother us for a while. It's the law."

He heard her dip a cloth in the water. She wiped his face, gently cleaning the new wound on his nose and the blood it had oozed. He felt her remove his sandals, and after more sounds of water sloshing, she began to wipe his feet, patiently dabbing each toe, moving on to his ankles and lower legs, slowly and gently, while rolling up his robe. When she reached the top of his thighs, she left his loincloth alone. He raised his midriff to let her roll up the robe and sat up while she pulled it off his shoulders and over his head, all without opening his eyes. She rinsed the cloth again and returned to wipe his chest, careful around the wounds from the tiger, then his neck and underarms. The cool cloth felt pleasant as she worked her way down. When she undid his loincloth, he turned facedown. His breath quickened as she reached between his legs and patiently washed his buttocks and the back of his thighs, and as she wiped his groin, he became aroused.

His face to the wall, Barac listened to the rustle of Tova's robe as she undressed and to the sloshing water while she washed. When she lay down beside him on the cot, her skin was cool against his own, her breath warm on his neck, and the palm of her hand soft on his back, caressing him.

"I can't," he said. "It's not right."

"Hush," Tova whispered in his ear. "Keep your eyes closed and imagine that I am her – the girl you love."

"That's impossible," he said. "She rejected me, and she won't change her mind."

"Imagine she did change her mind. Imagine she's right here with you." Tova resumed caressing his back. "Imagine it's her hand that's touching you, her body beside you."

Barac knew it was wrong, perhaps even a sin, but he could not resist the temptation to imagine that Deborah had actually changed her mind and had come to be with him again, that it was her hand stroking his naked back, her lips kissing his curly hair, her legs wrapping around his hips as he turned to face her, his eyes shut, his nostrils flaring to take in her scent, a mix of desert dust and horse sweat and fresh water – the same scent that had risen from Deborah's skin at the Ramon Crater. He mounted her, as he had done that night, and united with her again, slow at first, forcing his way into her, then faster, and faster, until he was overcome by a frenzy of lust, elation, and joy so intense that nothing else remained of the world but the two of them clinging, panting, joining into one flesh until he reached an explosion of incredible pleasure and shouted her name, "Deborah!"

And then, he opened his eyes and saw Tova's face, red and hot and wet with tears. He rolled off her, covered his face with his hands, and burst out crying with loud sobs and gulps of air like the small boy he had once been, curled up beside his dead mother.

A knock on the door sent them both scrambling to dress up quickly.

"Come in," Tova said, her voice trembling.

The priest entered, wearing a fresh white robe. A woman servant followed him into the room, pulled the sheet off the cot, and held it for the priest to examine. In the center was a moist red stain, about the size of a man's hand. Grunting in approval, the priest tossed a red robe to Tova and left the room, beckoning Barac to follow.

The courtyard was much more crowded than before, with older men gathering at the news of the judge's demise, the fall of Mamreh's small army, and the threat of Judah's second attack. Their faces were tense as they stood in small groups, engaged in hushed conversations.

The woman servant held up the stained sheet, and the priest declared, "The marriage has been lawfully consummated with God's blessings."

The stained sheet landed in the firepit, raising a burst of sparks.

The men returned to their discussions, and the priest left the courtyard without another word. Barac felt his face burning and wished he could go somewhere to be alone. He couldn't look at Tova, ashamed at how he'd used her innocent body to gratify his fantasy of lying with Deborah – yelling her name at the peak of pleasure, no less. Tova was surely brokenhearted by the humiliation, or seething with anger.

She tugged his sleeve, forcing him to turn and face her. She looked even younger in the oversized red robe, which marked her as forbidden to touch due to her feminine blood as a bride. It wasn't unusual, as all girls and women had to wear red every time their periodic bleeding occurred.

He sighed, expecting harsh words, which he deserved.

"Thank you," Tova said softly. "You saved my life."

"You shouldn't thank me." He felt like crying again. "I'm ashamed of what I did."

"You did nothing wrong. I had urged you to think of her."

"But you wept when it was over."

"Tears of joy. I was so happy to share such pleasure with you." She gestured at his chest. "You have a good heart. When you get to know me, you'll see that you also have a good wife."

Tsruyah appeared in the window of the judge's room on the second floor. "Is my horse ready?"

Someone yelled, "Yes."

A moment later, Tsruyah came down the stairs, followed by the face-painted woman of the Cainite Clan, who stood aside and stared at Barac.

Tsruyah mounted his horse, and a few of his men rode into the courtyard to accompany him. The crowd of men made way for them.

"Have no worry," Tsruyah said. "I'll return from Kabetzel with an honorable truce between us and Judah."

Barac stepped forward. "They won't negotiate."

A man nearby asked, "How do you know?"

"I saw them kill the elder of Revivim just for refusing to disclose where his people were hiding."

"I'm not a frail elder." Tsruyah shook the reins, making his horse stomp the ground. "And Beersheba is not Revivim."

"That's why they're gathering to attack," Barac said. "They want the water wells, the fertile land, and the profits from the trade that passes through Beersheba. Our forefather, Jacob, prophesied that Judah will rule over—"

"We need Borah," someone yelled. "We need him to save us again!"

Leaning over the side of his horse toward Barac, Tsruyah spoke to him in a low, menacing voice. "You have a lovely wife now. If you make me angry, there will be unlovely consequences." He snapped his fingers. "Just like that."

Barac's face flushed as he finally understood why Tsruyah had giddily pushed for him to marry Tova. When they had escaped Emanuel, his father had said, "A brave man laughs at danger to himself, but for his wife and children he is always afraid."

More of the men yelled, "Borah! Borah! Borah!"

"Borah is dead," Tsruyah shouted, riding through the courtyard to the gate. "They're all dead."

Barac noticed the Cainite woman who had come down with Tsruyah turn to the wall, bent over in grief.

Tsruyah stopped at the gate and pointed back at Barac. "Borah's friend is here, and he's even more clever than Borah, which is why I'm appointing him to be in charge of defending Beersheba until I'm back with a peaceful truce. Long live the tribe of Simeon!"

With those words, Tsruyah rode out of the courtyard along with his companions. The sound of their horses faded downhill.

Everyone turned to Barac, but he didn't know what to say. It had been his dream to command an army of Hebrew soldiers against an enemy, but in the distant future, after he learned to be a leader, not now, when his only experience in battle had ended in a deadly defeat. What did he know about defending a city?

One of the men asked, "What happened to Borah?"

Barac didn't want to lie. "An Edomite army with steel chariots attacked us at the Ramon Crater. Who can prevail against an army of steel chariots? Not even Borah."

Groans came from the men, but their faith in Deborah made him recall what she had told him about her ingenious ambush that had repelled Judah's previous attack. Repeating it would be futile, but it was a place to start.

"There were three gorges," he said. "In each one there was a group of defenders, and you elected one leader for each of the groups. Are those leaders here?"

Three men made their way to the front.

"You're back in charge," Barac told them. "Summon the groups you supervised ahead of the first attack, together with anyone else available to work – men, women, and children, too, if they can be helpful."

They looked at each other, and the oldest of the three said, "Most of the people have gone to sleep."

"Wake them up," Barac said. "How many people live in Beersheba?"

"About sixteen hundred, but a few hundred more will come in from all the farms and homesteads nearby as soon as they hear about the coming attack."

"Tell everyone that the army of Judah is made of the same cowardly men who ran away last time. But they won't fall for the same trick again. To prevail this time, we have to fight them off. They'll probably be here by sunrise, so we must begin working immediately on plugging the holes in the walls. Also, men should arm themselves with knives, sickles, hammers, clubs, and anything else that can be wielded as a weapon. The women should collect stones and pile them up where they will stand when the attack comes. Divide the city between you, and assign spots to each man and woman, so that the city is defended all around. Post scouts outside the walls in every direction to watch for our enemies and raise the alarm."

"But Tsruyah went to negotiate. Surely he'll be back before an attack.

"He might be too late to stop them, and they might apprehend him before he can turn back to warn us. Or, if God smiles upon us, Tsruyah will succeed in stopping the attack. Either way, it is our duty to prepare for the worst and be ready to defend the city from an attack."

"What chance do we have against them? Beersheba is a city of tradesmen, not of warriors."

Gathering all the confidence he could muster, Barac said, "Defending a city is easier than attacking it, because of the walls and the elevation over the surrounding land. Remember that you're defending your homes and your families against wretched invaders who want to steal, to usurp, and to enslave another tribe of Israel. They're sinners, and Yahweh stands with the righteous."

The men watched him intently.

"Go now," he said. "Prepare the city for the sinners' attack. Don't be afraid."

As the men filed out of the courtyard, the Cainite woman came over, wiping her eyes, and spoke haltingly.

"My daughter went with Borah."

Only now did Barac see the resemblance, which was blurred by the heavy makeup and generous figure. "You speak of Yael?"

"Yes. Do you know her fate?"

Barac leaned closer and spoke in a low voice. "Yael is fine."

She pulled out a small wooden effigy and pressed it to her lips while her dark eyes begged silently for more information.

"Don't worry," he said. "She's on the way to Bozra with the king's sister. I saw them on the road near Mount Avdat."

"Alone? Without men to defend them?"

He lowered his voice further, down to a whisper. "They're with Borah."

Her eyes widened in disbelief.

"Borah is fine, too," he whispered, "Don't tell anyone."

Kissing his hand, she dampened it with her tears.

23

Through the rest of the night, Deborah had passed the burning torch from one tired hand to the other and back, until it burned out completely near dawn. The horses were anxious as jackals' howls and coyotes' laughter echoed nearby. Sallan woke up at sunrise and asked for water. He had fresh bruises over his back, left arm, and the side of his head from hitting the ground after being thrown from the chariot.

They came upon a village in mid-morning. Deborah dismounted. Her legs were stiff and her whole body was achy. Grabbing the rope to raise the bucket from the bottom of the well, she was startled by a scream. It came from the maid, who was pointing at Yael's mare, whose saddle was vacant.

Princess Needa hushed her maid, who lowered her head and went over to the well with the empty waterskins.

Deborah asked, "Where is she?"

"I don't know." Tears flowing, the maid filled a waterskin. "I was sleeping."

Yael tied her mare behind the chariot.

Mounting Rogez again, Deborah rode back the way they came. She stopped at a high point. The road stretched far, and there was no sign of the maid.

Princess Needa, her maid, Yael, and Sallan watched Deborah return.

"Nothing," she said.

"She fell off," Yael said. "We were asleep and kept going."

"I doubt it." Deborah glanced back at the road. "She would have cried in pain, or the mare would have felt her falling and stopped. I think she got off the saddle and prodded the mare to keep going with us."

Princess Needa huffed under the veil to express her displeasure at Deborah's implication that her maid had chosen to stay alone in the desert rather than continue to serve her.

"Let's go." Sallan knuckled the wood on the chariot. "Time is running out."

While giving water to Rogez, Deborah's mind raced with anxious questions. Was the loss of the maid a sign of worse things to come? Had Yahweh taken the maid, who would surely die of thirst or be killed by animals, to show His displeasure? Was it a forewarning that this race back to Bozra was doomed to fail, and that Leola would die?

She got back in the saddle, and Rogez broke into a quick trot without prodding. The others followed.

As they rode on, the road grew wider and less rocky, which indicated that it was frequented by many travelers. Oddly, they didn't cross paths with anyone. In the early afternoon, they turned off the main road to a smaller one, heading west toward a chain of hills. At the top, they saw Bozra at the opposite end of a long verdant valley. The city stood out brightly with its copper roofs and whitewashed walls. It was a magnificent view, and Deborah allowed a brief stop to enjoy the sight, now that they were certain to make it back to Bozra well before sunset.

24

Overnight, Barac visited every part of Beersheba's walls and spoke with countless men and women working to shore up the city defenses. Many asked him about Borah and found comfort in the fact that he had come from the same small town in the Samariah Hills – it lent him a share of Borah's aura of success in fending off the men of Judah. Every time it came up, he felt guilty for sustaining a lie, but knew that telling them the truth – that Borah was a girl who had no knowledge or experience in battle – would throw the whole city into utter confusion and panic. He wondered where Deborah drew her audacity to act with utmost confidence in dangerous, complicated situations that would have confounded grown men. Her daring would be comprehensible if she were insensitive, reckless, or strident, but she was quite the opposite: thoughtful, cautious, and prone to remorse. The contradictions were irreconcilable, unless the answer was positive to the question he had asked Deborah, who wouldn't answer: Did she actually hear God's voice?

At sunrise, he lay down near the gate and slept for a while. Eventually, the rising heat woke him up. Back on his feet, he felt drowsy and weak, but as he climbed the steps onto the wall, a lazy breeze from the west made him feel better. He gazed at the eastern horizon, searching for a dust cloud that a marching army would stir. To his relief, he saw nothing.

Several men followed his example and climbed up to get a good look at the horizon. Everyone was exhausted after a night of hard work, and the fact that the army of Judah had not appeared gave them hope that Tsruyah was successful in his negotiations. Barac listened to their banter, but allowed himself no such hopes. Instead, he urged them to continue fixing the walls and collecting stones.

Exiting the city, Barac rode to the fairgrounds and summoned the leaders of the twenty or so caravans that were camping there. When the foreign merchants gathered, he warned them of the imminent risk of an attack from the east by an army of Judah, and suggested that they go west toward Gaza, or south toward Mount Avdat, where they can take the more remote east-west trade route to their various destinations. To his surprise, none of them seemed alarmed, or gave any indication of leaving. When he inquired why, a Moabite merchant explained that trade is profitable no matter who controls the city, and foreign caravans are always protected in any local skirmish, because each warring party hoped to take over the profitable right of taxation, road tolls, and sale of food and water. With a smile, he added that victorious invaders would ransack the city and enslave its inhabitants, whom they would sell to merchants for transport to the slave market in Gaza, where the Philistines ruled, or in Dibon where, the merchant said, "King Bin-Lot of Moab is fond of Hebrew slaves for their shrewdness and cleanliness."

"Not here," Barac said. "We are descendants of Israel on both sides, and our God forbids selling fellow Hebrews to slavery with other nations."

The Moabite merchant chuckled. "Your God must have made an exception when I bought seven Hebrew men of Benjamin from Hebrew fighters of Dan in Ekron, or when I acquired five lovely women of Manasseh at the market in Gezer from a vintner of Ephraim, or when I bartered five Egyptian crossbows and a goat kid for three healthy boys and two unblemished maidens of Gad from the judge of Reuben who rules the city of Heshbon east of the Jordan River."

Barac was speechless. He could tell that the Moabite merchant spoke the truth, but how could men of Dan, Ephraim, or Reuben sell fellow Hebrews into foreign slavery? Were they not afraid of Yahweh's wrath?

"Don't despair, young man." The merchant patted his shoulder. "What's your name?"

"Barac, son of Abinoam."

"My son Zariz is about your age, and I often have to remind myself of what I learned along the way. Youth is not a chronic illness: you'll eventually grow out of naïve boyish infatuations, sober up from dreamy adolescent enchantments, and see the world for what it really is – a place to embrace every opportunity, do good business, and fill your pockets with silver."

Mounting his horse, Barac rode back to the gates. He looked up at the pole flying the green flag of Simeon. He wished the gates of Beersheba were as mighty as the drawing on the flag, with solid masonry towers to position guards and stocks of stones.

Once inside the city, he turned left along the walls. Only a few men and women were still doing repair work, though much remained to be done. Most of the people had either gone to their homes, or lay down in the shade to rest from a night of worry and labor.

The thought of these men, women, and their children being herded out of Beersheba to be sold as slaves in the markets of Gaza or Moab horrified him. He changed direction and rode up to the judge's house, where the three leaders had returned after managing the work overnight. They were sitting at the table in the courtyard, eating and drinking. He joined them. They were good men with full beards and calloused hands.

Giving them instructions felt presumptuous to Barac, but he did it anyway. "As soon as you're done eating," he said, "go back and set up guards to watch the eastern horizon for the army of Judah. We'll need as much time as possible to summon everyone and get ready to defend the city."

He could see the uncertainty on their weary faces, but they didn't argue and left to do as he said.

Tova brought him a cup of warm milk, which he sipped slowly, enjoying the warmth spreading inside him.

She tilted her head toward the kitchen. "The women are afraid. They're praying that God brings back that young man, Borah, who saved Beersheba from Judah last time."

Barac sipped more milk.

"They say Borah left with you and the judge on the journey south."

He continued to drink.

"It means Borah was with your group, passing through Revivim the first time."

He grunted.

"Was Borah the lanky soldier on the white horse?"

Barac nodded, feigning indifference.

"He looked very young."

"We're all young."

"Are you sure Borah isn't coming back?"

"Yes, I'm positive. Any more questions?" Barac tilted the cup to drink the rest.

"Only one. Is Borah and Deborah the same person?"

He choked on the milk and started to cough.

"That's what I thought." Tova laughed and handed him a rag. "The armor, helmet, and fake stubble couldn't hide her beautiful eyes."

Barac wiped the milk from his chin and put a finger to his lips.

Tova leaned close to him and whispered. "It'll be our secret."

He handed her the cup.

"Would you like some more?"

Shaking his head, he thought of Deborah. Would she serve him warm milk while being agreeable and cheerful? It was hard to imagine, perhaps because Deborah had done everything possible to look and act like a man, whereas Tova seemed to take pleasure in her femininity with her red robe and lush dark hair, which had felt as soft as sheep's wool against his face when their bodies had become one the previous night.

"You're staring at me," Tova said, still smiling. "Do you wish I was Deborah?"

"No, I only wish for your health and safety." He imagined Tova with a baby in her arms, a boy, maybe, with glistening dark eyes and healthy red cheeks, wrapped in a soft blanket. "That's all I wish for, because you're a gift from God, sent to put me back on my true path."

"Thank you, God," Tova said, looking up, her eyelids fluttering in exaggerated piousness that made him laugh.

25

Once they descended the winding road to the valley, Deborah quickened the pace. She noticed that no one was plowing the fields or tending the orchards. The homesteads along the road were quiet, except for a few dogs and the occasional braying from animals in the corrals. Looking ahead, she saw the quiet market at the fairgrounds outside the gates of Bozra. Where had all the people gone?

Drumbeat sounded from the city.

The chariot caught up with Deborah, and Sallan yelled with great effort, "The sacrifice is about to begin!"

Yael whipped the horse, and the chariot sped ahead, with the mare in tow. Rogez followed suit, but the princess and her maid stayed back.

Deborah turned Rogez, sprinted back, and told the princess, "The sacrifice ceremony – they've started it! Hurry!"

The maid said, "That's none of our concern."

"An innocent girl is about to die. Don't you care?"

The princess stopped her horse, and the maid said, "We will wait here. Tell our brother to send servants with appropriate attire and an honor guard."

"You look fine," Deborah said. "Everyone will be happy to see you, and your appearance will stop Qozmadorus from killing the girl."

Princess Needa exhaled audibly.

"Go, boy," the maid said to Deborah. "Tell our brother we are waiting here."

"There's no time – listen to the drums!"

The princess flickered her hand in dismissal.

Burning with fury, Deborah guided Rogez close alongside the princess's horse.

"Obey us," the maid said, "or you will be punished."

Deborah grabbed Princess Needa's robe and pulled her off the canopied saddle. The princess yelped as she fell facedown over Deborah's lap, her veil and hood coming off, releasing her wavy mane of carrot-colored hair.

The maid screamed.

Rogez took off at full speed, Princess Needa lying across the saddle, her legs kicking the air at one side, her long hair flapping down the other. Deborah leaned forward, her left hand clutching the reins, her right hand locked on the saddle horn, both elbows pressing down on the princess's back to keep her from falling off.

Rogez caught up with the chariot near the gates. The guards moved out of the way, and they entered the city. The drumbeat from uphill was loud and heavy. Deborah held on as Rogez raced up the empty switchback street, leaving behind Yael and Sallan in the slower chariot. The princess stopped fighting and slumped inertly across the saddle.

The drumbeat died down, and the silence was even more ominous. Rogez galloped uphill with ease, as if this was the start of a new adventure, not the conclusion of a long voyage through a harsh desert. Up ahead, a cheer sounded, deep and sonorous as only a huge mass of people could produce, throbbing through the air with powerful reverberations.

The guards at the entrance to the amphitheater were looking into the arena, and with all the noise, did not hear Rogez, who came up and stopped behind them with the unconscious royal princess facedown over the saddle.

What Deborah saw was bewildering, as if she had travelled back in time to a scene of horror, which she had hoped never to see again. High above the bloodstained spikes of Qoz's thunderbolt, Leola dangled on a rope, which was threaded through a pulley attached to the horizontal arm of the tall crane. A young priest sat on top, looking down. The rope traveled from the pulley over the sandy arena down to Qozmadorus, who stood under the royal balcony. He was a younger version of the muscular, hairless, copper-painted Qoztobarus, who had fought her in this very arena not long ago while the crowd chanted, "Kill the boy! Kill the boy! Kill the boy!"

Qozmadorus looped the end of the rope around his arm and adjusted his position to bring the sloping rope closer to the balcony railing above. The movements jacked Leola up and down, and she screamed.

On the balcony, King Esau the Twentieth stood at the railing in a red coat and a gold crown. He raised his sword over the railing and brought the blade to the rope, touching it lightly with the edge of the blade.

The crowd became still, their eyes shifting between the king and Leola.

"We give this girl," the king declared in his high-pitched voice, "to you, great Qoz, to have her life in exchange for the life of our sister, Princess Needa, so that you bring her back to us safely from her loathsome Hebrew abductors."

Deborah struggled to breathe, her body rigid with terror and revulsion as she recalled the gray matter inside the high priest's split head, her sword stuck at the top of his chest bone, blood spraying up at her face. With effort, she looked up at Leola and saw the girl's face through the cascade of golden hair.

Their eyes met.

"Save me," Leola cried. "Save me!"

A whisper puffed on Deborah's ear. "Fly. Fly. Fly."

The king swung the sword back over his shoulder, poised to slash the rope.

Deborah kicked in with both heels, and Rogez shot forward through the entrance, past the guards, and into the sandy arena, racing around the huge statue of Qoz with rapid, powerful strides that tossed both Deborah and Princess Needa up and down in the saddle. She gripped the saddle horn and pressed her knees in, hugging the horse's ribs as they closed in on Qozmadorus

The crowd roared as the king swung the sword through the air. Qozmadorus saw the enormous white horse rush at him, released the rope, and ducked sideways, falling on the sand. The king's blade passed over the railing and met the rope, which was no longer taut. The blade cut the rope, but not all the way. The rope flipped aside in the air with the blade's movement, then fluttered upward as the pulley screeched and Leola, with a terrified shriek, descended toward the sharp spikes of the upturned thunderbolt.

Letting go of the saddle horn and the reins, Deborah stood up, her boots pushing down on the stirrups, and leaped up into the air, reaching high with both hands. The rope slithered through her fingers and almost escaped when she clasped hard, the rough threads digging into her palms. She held on, landing hard back in the saddle, her elbows pushing down on Princess Needa's back. Leola's descent halted just as her chest touched the spiked tips of Qoz's thunderbolt. Deborah heard the crowd thunder around the packed arena, but as she pulled on the rope, the partial cut from the king's sword came even with her eyes, and she saw the last remaining threads pop one after another. With a knee jab, she redirected Rogez toward the heavy base of the crane, aiming between the wheels. He sensed what she wanted him to do and, as he reached the box, bumped into it with his chest, pushing it. Deborah gazed up, continuing to urge Rogez forward until Leola cleared the spikes. The young priest sitting on the plank above the pulley lost his balance, rolled to the side and, after hanging briefly by his legs, fell down, missing Deborah, and hit the ground hard with a cracking sound of breaking bones. Meanwhile, the remaining few threads popped quickly and, just as Deborah made Rogez stop, the rope tore apart.

Leola dropped.

Leaning sideways in the saddle, half-turning, Deborah held out her arms and caught Leola. As delicate as the girl was, her downward momentum hit Deborah with a force that ripped her out of the saddle and threw her to the ground, with Princess Needa falling over, as well.

The crowd was on its feet, shouting, or cheering, Deborah couldn't tell. Princess Needa came to and sat up, dazed. Deborah, meanwhile, quickly removed the harness from Leola and helped her and the princess stand up.

The three of them faced the high balcony across the arena.

Rogez stepped up close behind Deborah, protecting her rear.

Up on the balcony, the king raised his hand, and the crowd quieted down.

Below the balcony, Qozmadorus sprang to his feet and pointed. "That's the Hebrew boy who murdered my father! Kill him!"

The guards at the three entrances to the amphitheater moved in, raising their spears.

"Kill the boy!" Qozmadorus jabbed the air with both hands toward Deborah, shouting at the top of his voice. "Kill Him!"

Some voices joined him from the crowded circular amphitheater, "Kill the boy! Kill the boy! Kill the boy!"

Deborah sighed, resigned to do what had to be done in order to avoid a repeat of the long ordeal she had endured in fending off his late father's attack. She untied the sling from her hips.

Qozmadorus pumped his fists in the air to rile up the crowd. "Kill the boy! Kill the boy! Kill the boy!"

She reached into the open-top base of the crane and grabbed a stone.

The guards approached, their faces turned up to the king, awaiting his approval.

"Kill Him!" Qozmadorus kept yelling. "Kill the boy!"

The stone fitted into the pouch, Deborah rotated the sling twice and let go. The stone flew straight and true over the white sand of the arena and hit Qozmadorus at the center of his forehead with a clapping sound. He stopped shouting, remained standing for a moment, his mouth still open, and collapsed.

In the silence that ensued, Deborah spoke up, her voice loud and clear. "King Esau the Twentieth, I've kept my promise and brought Princess Needa home safely."

The crowd jumped up and down with deafening cheers.

Deborah nudged the princess forward.

Despite her exposed hair and dirty robe, Princess Needa proceeded across the arena with a straight back and royal grace that befitted her rank.

On the balcony, the king leaned against the railing, staring down in disbelief.

The crowd quieted down.

"King Esau," Deborah spoke up again. "With my promise fulfilled, will you keep yours – to award me fifteen dozen silver coins and a safe passage to Canaan?"

His eyes still on the princess below, a smile broke on the king's young face, and he yelled, his voice as high-pitched as a girl's voice,

"Yes! Yes! Yes!"

The crowd cheered while the king hurried to the end of the balcony, bounded down the steps, and ran to his sister. In what could only be an unguarded display of sincere affection, they clung to each other for a long time.

The king's public confirmation of his promise gave Deborah a reason to exhale in relief. Until now, she only had the words of General Mazabi, who was no longer alive.

Up on the balcony, Umm-Sallan leaned on the arm of Leola's young husband as they made their way to the stairs. The king and his sister, meanwhile, broke their embrace, yet kept holding hands. The crowd continued to cheer, and the two royals waved at their subjects and smiled at each other. Meanwhile, Deborah and Leola walked to the foot of the stairs, bypassing the fainted Qozmadorus. Leola burst out crying as her husband took her in his arms.

Umm-Sallan's gray eyes were dry, but her thin lips trembled when she asked, "My son?"

Someone shouted, "The Elixirist!" and the crowd roared with renewed intensity.

Turning to look, Deborah saw the chariot enter the arena. Yael held the reins while Sallan sat up, smiling and waving. They went around the arena, circling Qoz's massive throne, and stopped before the king and his sister. Yael helped Sallan off the chariot, and he bowed before the king, who gave him his hand to kiss while the people of Edom cheered with unbridled joy.

26

Whistling sounded, followed by excited voices. Barac hurried to the courtyard gate and out to the street, where he could see all the way downhill. Some people were running down to the main gates, others up to their houses. Many were yelling, but he couldn't make out their words. Tova pulled his horse out to the street and handed him the reins.

"Go back inside," he said. "Hide somewhere until I come back for you."

Tova was pale. "God be with you."

He rode downhill, passing by the temple, where the priest stood outside in his white robe with blue fringes, holding a ram's horn that was longer than the one Tsruyah had broken the previous night. A large crowd had gathered at the main gates, and the poor inhabitants of the huts and tents in the lower city climbed on the wall to see outside the city.

The crowd parted to let Barac ride through. Gazing eastward, shading his eyes with his hand, he saw a column of dust above the road from Kabetzel. He knew it would take many feet and hooves to stir up so much dust, but all he could see ahead of the dust was a clutch of riders advancing at a moderate pace. He turned to face the crowd.

"The army of Judah is coming from the east. They want to steal this land and take the wells that our forefathers Abraham and Isaac dug. God's divine decree gave this land to the tribe of Simeon. He expects you to defend it. Go to your assigned spots inside the walls, stand ready with your weapons and stones, and pray for victory over the sinners of Judah."

The priest, who stood in the back of the crowd, blew the ram's horn until he ran out of air.

Barac took a deep breath, raised his fist, and shouted, "God is with us!"

The gates were shut, and the people ran to their posts around the city. The poor went into their huts and tents.

Barac stationed his horse right inside the gate and stood in the stirrups to watch over the top of the gate.

The army of Judah split up and began to fan out from the road in both directions. They were mostly on foot, with one in a hundred or so mounted on a horse. Barac wondered how long it would take the two columns to meet west of the city to complete a ring around it.

Meanwhile, a group of approximately fifty riders continued advancing on the main road toward Beersheba. One of them carried a rod with the golden flag of Judah. When they were about a thousand steps away, the group stopped, except for two riders. The one on the left was dressed as a man of Judah, but the other rider wore the full beard, long robe, and drooping headdress in the style of a desert dweller. It was Tsruyah. Barac focused on the other man, who must have been the leader of Judah's army, but had a slight build that did not match Deborah's description of Goor-Aryeh's tall stature and wide shoulders.

The two riders slowed down.

"Open the gates," Barac said. "I'll meet them on the road."

Riding out, he noticed the merchant caravans in the fairgrounds a short distance to the right. None of them had left. If anything, there were a few more caravans. The merchants stood at the edge of the fairground and watched the events unfold like a flock of scavengers perched on a tree branch overlooking a pride of predators surround a prey.

Barac rode the short distance up the road to the singed stake, where sinners were burnt after trials, and stopped there to wait. When the two riders reached him, rather than stop, they went past him and continued. Barac turned and followed them to the front of the gates, where they stopped.

"People of Beersheba," Tsruyah shouted. "I bring you peace in our time!"

Many heads popped up over the gates and the walls extending in both directions.

"The Gods have granted me success," he continued. "On behalf of Simeon, I have negotiated a truce with our elder brothers of the mighty tribe of Judah, our powerful neighbor on the north, south, east, and west."

Barac understood the implied threat underlying Tsruyah's words, reminding everyone of the historical prominence of Jacob's fourth son, Judah, among the other sons, as well as its current superiority in numbers and territorial holdings – from Jerusalem, Hebron, and Bethlehem in the north to Kadesh near the Sea of Reeds in the south, and from the fertile Ayalon Valley and rich Lachish in the west to the Sea of Salt in the east – a territory that land-locked Simeon on all sides. Judah's three advantages – ancestral privilege, numerical supremacy, and territorial chokehold – bolstered the implication that resistance was futile. Tsruyah was preempting any opposition to the truce with Judah, no matter what the actual terms of his bargain were. The message was that, even if Beersheba managed to beat back Judah's second invasion, it would make no difference because, in the end, Judah would win by force of history, size, and geography.

"As your new judge," Tsruyah continued, "it is my great honor to introduce Yoaz, son of Lamon, who is the brave commander of Judah's army and the wise judge of the city of Bethlehem."

The leader of Judah's army reclined his head briefly. "I humbly address you, the great men of Simeon. Your judge and I have negotiated as equals under Yahweh's divine blessing."

"As equals," Tsruyah repeated. "We agreed to live in peace and share the abundance of the land and water that our forefathers bequeathed us after they had conquered Canaan on their return from Egyptian slavery. No more wars! No more bloodshed! No more bereavement!"

Barac listened carefully and tried to memorize the words, as Deborah would have done. He had a feeling that this truce wasn't as fair as it sounded.

Inside the walls, hushed murmuring could be heard, but no cheering. Obviously, the people didn't have much faith in Tsruyah as a judge or as a negotiator. They knew him only as Judge Ohad's heavy-handed enforcer.

Barac spoke up. "Where is Goor-Aryeh, the judge of Judah and commander of its army?"

Turning sharply, Tsruyah glared at him with eyes that seemed both furious and nervous. Barac realized that Tsruyah still believed Judge Goor-Aryeh of Judah had burnt at the stake and was terrified of reminding Yoaz what the men of Simeon had done to his predecessor in this place only a short time ago.

Yoaz, however, did not seem angry as he turned his horse and tilted his head in an invitation to follow him. They rode up to the singed stake, where Yoaz stopped and spoke softly.

"What is your name, boy?"

"Barac, son of Abinoam."

"You are not of Simeon, are you?"

Barac shook his head. "Of Naphtali."

"Goor-Aryeh is my friend," Yoaz said. "He told me in private how Borah had saved him from the stake, which made him reluctant to lead this attack. That's why it fell to me to subdue Beersheba and, at Goor-Aryeh's request, plead with Borah to join him in Kabetzel, where he is waiting."

"He's waiting in vain. Borah isn't here. And you shouldn't be here, either. Beersheba can defend itself from ten more attacks by Judah."

Yoaz chuckled, taking no offense. "I'm not alone, as you can see."

Barac noticed that the army of Judah had continued to spread, now stretching all the way south and north of the city in a menacing half-circumference that was sure to cause shock and awe within the walls of Beersheba.

"Impressive, isn't it?" Yoaz rubbed his horse's neck. "I was actually looking forward to matching wits with Borah. What shall I tell Goor-Aryeh?"

The tone of his voice made Barac suspect that Yoaz had learned from Goor-Aryeh that the boy Borah was, in fact, a girl named Deborah, but he couldn't be sure, and therefore, answered simply, "Borah is gone."

"Did you take part in the battle at the Ramon Crater?"

"Yes, from beginning to end."

"How many Hebrew men died?"

"Dozens."

"If we attack Beersheba, whether we win or not, many more will die." Turning his horse slowly in a full circle, Yoaz surveyed the whole area before speaking again. "You're young, but so was Borah, and for the unfortunate people of Beersheba, having lost their judge and his son, you are the closest thing to a leader."

Barac waved toward the gates, where Tsruyah was waiting. "They have a new judge."

"A self-appointed illiterate thug doesn't make an effective leader."

Taken aback by the man's blunt honesty, Barac shaded his eyes with his hand and scanned the expanding line of Judah's army, the flimsy wooden gates of Beersheba, and the patchy sections of the walls that were visible from where they stood.

"The people won't listen to Tsruyah," Yoaz said. "To you, however, they'll listen. You can save many lives today by telling them to accept the truce."

"I have a question." Barac spoke quietly, hoping to hide the tremor in his voice. "Will you swear by Yahweh not to injure, whip, rape, or pillage the city and its people?"

Yoaz pressed his hand to his chest. "I swear to it, and I'll punish any man of Judah who does so."

With an explicit gaze at the fairgrounds, Barac asked, "Will you swear not to sell into slavery any men, women, or child of Simeon?"

"I cannot swear to it."

"Why?"

"Swearing under God to a lie is a sin." Yoaz quoted: "Do not raise Yahweh's name in vain!"

Barac knew the third of the Ten Commandments, but that didn't answer his question. "Why should I tell the people to accept a truce that could turn them into slaves?"

"We have expended many resources to come here. Our men left their farms and shops idle. They deserve compensation. For that, we'll take slaves, but only as many as necessary to cover our losses."

"How many?"

"Much less than the number of people who will die if we attack."

Tsruyah rode over to where they stood. "What's the delay?"

Yoaz raised a finger, hushing him, and spoke to Barac. "It's decision time, boy."

There was no good outcome from this predicament, Barac knew, and the burden of decision was too heavy for him, especially as he wasn't a man of Simeon and would not have to live with the consequences of the truce.

He turned toward the gates and shouted, "Summon the three army leaders and the priest to come outside. Lock the gates behind them."

Tsruyah cursed, but Yoaz chuckled.

After a few moments, the four men came out through the gates and walked up the road.

Barac dismounted, and so did Yoaz. Grunting, Tsruyah jumped off his horse, too.

"You heard the offer earlier," Barac said to the four men. "We need your consent."

"No." Tsruyah stepped in. "I will decide."

"Quiet," Yoaz said. "Let them discuss our offer."

The youngest of the four spoke first. "What does it actually mean?" He quoted from memory. "To live in peace and share the abundance of the land and water that our forefathers bequeathed us after they had conquered Canaan on their return from Egyptian slavery."

"Fairness," Yoaz said. "That's what it means."

"How?"

"By sharing," Barac said. "If the land and water of both tribes is to be shared freely from now on, that's a fair solution, which is preferable to fighting."

Yoaz nodded.

"In addition," Barac said, "Judge Yoaz swore in Yahweh's name that Judah's men will not injure, whip, rape, or pillage the city and its people."

"I swear to it again," Yoaz said. "None of your people will be harmed."

"Not physically," Barac said. "However, the men of Judah want to recover the costs of this military campaign by selling some of the people of Beersheba into slavery."

"It's forbidden," the priest said. "Hebrews may not enslave fellow Hebrews."

"I disagree," Yoaz said.

The priest opened his mouth to argue, but his eyes went to the long spear Yoaz was holding, and he held his tongue.

"Allow me to quote from the Holy Scriptures," Yoaz said. "And if a Hebrew man is enslaved, six years he shall work for his master, and on the seventh, he shall go free. If he is enslaved alone, he shall go free alone. If he has a wife, she shall become a slave too, and on the seventh year, go free with him. But if his master gave him a wife during his slavery, and she bore him sons and daughters, he shall go free alone, and the wife and children shall remain slaves."

While he listened, Barac watched the army of Judah continue to spread around the city like a vice whose two prongs were no longer visible from where he stood. Soon, they would meet somewhere on the other side of the city and create a complete siege.

"That is correct," the priest said. "Slavery is allowed to pay debt between Hebrews, but that's all. Selling to non-Hebrews is forbidden."

The three army leaders glanced at the fairgrounds.

"I agree," Yoaz said. "The slaves will be distributed among the men of Judah. We will not enslave more men, women, and children of Simeon than necessary to recover our expenses and losses in our rightful pursuit of this land and its water, to which we have a claim against Simeon by force of God and ancestry, which is like a debt."

"A debt must be paid." Tsruyah rubbed hands. "I'll make sure you have as many slaves as you need."

The group leaders were too nervous to speak, but the priest asked, "How many?"

"Only as many as necessary," Yoaz said. "I swear to that."

"We need a number." The priest pointed his ram's horn at the city. "The people deserve to know how heavy is the price they must pay to avoid being murdered on their own God-given land by sinful invaders."

"Shut up, fool." Tsruyah pushed him. "How dare you insult our guest."

"Leave him be," Yoaz said. "A man of God may speak his mind freely."

The priest brushed the front of his white robe where Tsruyah's hand left a mark. "How many, then?"

"It depends," Yoaz said. "If they are healthy and strong, I think one in ten is a fair share."

The priest groaned, and the three group leaders looked at each other with wide eyes.

Yoaz asked, "How many people are in the city now?"

"About two thousand," the priest said.

"More than that," Tsruyah said. "At least three thousand."

"It's decided, then," Yoaz said. "We'll take three hundred."

"Three hundred sins." The priest raised the ram's horn to his lips.

"Don't blow," Tsruyah said, "or I'll break this one, too."

Yoaz smiled. "You can blow after we're done here. I'm sure God will forgive us the sin of enslaving others in light of our efforts to prevent bloodshed."

"Who will you take?" The priest waved toward the city. "You should divide the burden fairly among all the families of Beersheba, as Joshua had divided the burden of drafting soldiers among our people when he prepared to conquer Canaan."

Tsruyah laughed. "You compare our ancestors' honorable service in Joshua's army to slavery?"

"Yes."

"I won't break up our prominent families for this."

"Why not? Everyone is equal before God."

"Before God, maybe, but not down here on earth. The tradesmen, merchants, and landowners give work to the peasants, charity to the poor, and taxes to the judge."

One of the three leaders spoke up. "We cannot hand over so many people into slavery. Have you no mercy?"

"Am I not merciful?" Yoaz leveled the spear and stabbed it in the air toward the spreading troops of Judah. "Look at this army. We can crush your defenses and kill every man within these walls, rape every woman, and enslave every child. Instead, we only ask for one in ten to recover our costs."

"Fair enough," Tsruyah said. "It's a price I'm happy to pay."

"Is it fair?" Barac gestured toward the walls. "If you attack, the people of Beersheba will fight hard for their homes with swords, knives, scythes, clubs, and rocks. They'll kill many men of Judah before the battle is decided."

"We don't intend to fight," Yoaz said. "We will hurl burning tumbleweeds over your walls and start a thousand fires that will burn the city down without us stepping a foot inside the walls. What good would your scythes and rocks be then?"

Barac felt his face redden. "We have plenty of water to douse the flames."

"We will win," Yoaz said. "In the end, the preeminence of Judah is preordained. Fighting will bring terrible consequences for the people of Beersheba, not to mention fueling the flames of hatred between our tribes until they burn in perpetuity. This truce is the epitome of wisdom and the embodiment of mercy."

"True," Tsruyah said.

Yoaz pointed his spear at the gates. "Once you hand over the slaves, painful as that might be, our tribes shall live in peace side by side as loving brothers. Agreed?"

The three leaders bowed their heads, consenting through silence. Barac said nothing, cognizant that this truce was the lesser of two evils. Tsruyah rubbed his hands, grinning in satisfaction. And the priest said, "May Yahweh have mercy on your souls."

Mounting his horse, Yoaz said, "Talk to your people and arrange the selection. I don't care how you do it, but those you choose better be healthy and strong, without a single gray hair on their heads, or we'll need more slaves to cover the difference in the value of their labor. You have until tomorrow morning to hand them over, or we'll take by force what we deserve, and more."

Tsruyah got on his horse, too, and looked down at Barac. "Go back and summon the prominent men of the city to the judge's house. I'll speak to them when the sun is halfway down to the west."

"Wait," Barac said. "Who is prominent enough to invite, and who isn't?"

"Isn't it obvious?" Tsruyah snorted. "Men who own houses and land, that's who. And until I meet with them, say nothing about the price we agreed to pay, or there will be riots and attempts to escape."

"And bloodshed," Yoaz said. "My men will kill anyone trying to flee."

No one responded. What was there to say?

Yoaz raised his hand. "God's blessings upon you."

He and Tsruyah rode together, rejoining the group of men of Judah up the road. All of them, including Tsruyah, rode on toward the ring of soldiers surrounding Beersheba.

Barac, the priest, and the three leaders walked down to the gates, with Barac's horse following behind. Once inside, the gates clung shut. Along the walls in both directions, many men and women stood beside piles of stones, some holding sharp tools, farming implements, or plain wooden sticks. On the right, the open area near the mass of shacks, huts, and tents was crowded with hundreds of men, women, and children, who had come out in their tattered clothes and bare feet to watch the unfolding drama.

"Stay alert," Barac said to the three group leaders. "Send some men to prepare jugs of water in case of fires, and keep your people at their posts by the walls around the city to watch the men of Judah for any sign of action. Truce or no truce, we can't trust Yoaz until it's over."

The priest grabbed Barac's forearm. "It's Tsruyah we shouldn't trust."

"There's no choice," one of the three men said. "He is the new judge."

"Judge?" The priest sneered. "He doesn't read the Holy Scripture, he hasn't studied the laws of God, and he can't tell good from evil. How can he be our judge?"

"He's got soldiers."

"Force doesn't make a judge." The priest pointed his ram's horn uphill. "We should summon the prominent men now, before he returns, and elect a real judge for Beersheba."

"The truce he negotiated is better than war. If they attack us, we won't need a judge anymore, because we'll all be dead."

Barac pried the priest's fingers from his forearm. "You heard their decision. Now, blow your horn."

The priest inhaled deeply, put the horn to his lips, and blew a long, sad moan that tapered off without a finite ending.

A crowd congregated around them, and Barac spoke at the top of his voice.

"Today, when the sun is halfway down to the west, every man of Simeon who owns a house or a plot of land must come to the judge's house." He paused, trying to sound confident. "With God's help, we shall have peace again."

27

King Esau the Twentieth and Princess Needa walked hand-in-hand to the doors under the balcony and entered the palace. The crowd cheered and clapped while a string of men with rattles, hand drums, horns, pipes, oboes, flutes, and small harps ran out of the palace, playing their instruments while jogging around the arena. It reminded Deborah of the joyous celebration that had taken place immediately after she had slain Qoztobarus. Now, as then, a group of acrobats rushed into the arena, cartwheeling and hand walking to the crowd's explosive delight. The jugglers came next, tossing multi-colored jars in the air while the acrobats formed a human pyramid that shook precariously, earning yelps and cries from the spellbound crowd when a boy did a handstand at the very top. The people of Edom applauded and sang to the music as clowns on tall stilts traipsed into the arena.

After some time, two guards came out with a chair to carry Sallan. Umm-Sallan told Leola and her husband to go home and followed Sallan with Yael and Deborah. They passed by Qozmadorus, who was coming to, blood oozing from his forehead, while several young priests knelt around him with grim faces. A group of guards marched over, picked him up by his arms, and led him away. The young priests watched in silence.

Entering through the doors, Deborah glanced back and saw the king's horsemen give water to Rogez, the chariot horse, and Yael's mare. Meanwhile, the crowd began to leave the amphitheater.

The guards shut the doors. It was dark inside the palace. As her eyes adjusted, Deborah saw a long hallway, dimly lit with an oil lamp in a wall holder. The floor was tiled with stones. At the end of the hallway, another set of doors led into a cavernous hall, brightly lit with dozens of burning torches attached to the walls at regular intervals all around. The floor was covered with red carpets and the ceiling was painted red. The guards put down Sallan's chair in the middle of the room and lined up along the walls, standing in attention.

The front part of the room was elevated with a platform. At the center was a smaller replica of the giant statue of Qoz in the arena, with the same blank eyes and a round head that sprouted three stubby horns. The throne also had armrests resembling a bull and a cow, but unlike the one in the arena, this throne had a large seat carved into the base between Qoz's legs, creating a throne within a throne. Deborah thought it was a clever idea, bestowing the divine authority of the great deity on the flesh-and-blood monarch.

The rest of the platform was occupied by copper replicas of life-sized animals, standing in staggered positions on both sides of Qoz, as if to protect it. Deborah saw a lion, a tiger, and a bear, as well as a graceful antelope, a lithe gazelle, and a muscular bull. There were also apes, crocodiles, and even a snake as thick as a man's torso. Above each shining copper animal, the stuffed original hung upside down from hooks fixed in the ceiling.

"Don't be alarmed," Sallan said. "The old king styled himself a great hunter, traveling far and wide with a hundred expert trappers and a thousand soldiers."

His mother caressed his gray hair and looked at Deborah. "You kept your promise to bring him home alive."

"It wasn't easy," Deborah said. "That promise was the only thing that kept me from killing him myself."

He chuckled and coughed. "I think Borah loves and hates me in equal measures."

Umm-Sallan shook her head. "The punishment for living too long is to see your son grow into a foolish man."

"He lied to me," Deborah said.

"Don't mind him." Umm-Sallan reached up with her hands and cradled Deborah's face. "You are my hero."

"A heartbreaking hero," Sallan said.

Her brow furrowed, Umm-Sallan ran her hands over Deborah's forehead and temples.

"That poor boy." Sallan coughed some more. "Alone in the

desert. Naked. Thirsty. Hopeless."

Yael scoffed. "He deserves it, leaving us at that cursed ravine."

"A boy?" Umm-Sallan took Deborah's hands, pressing them. "The one who refused to cast a stone at your sister?"

Deborah nodded. "Barac."

"He wasn't dead, then." Umm-Sallan pulled Deborah head down and kissed her on the cheeks beside the nose, where there was no stubble-paste. "That's wonderful."

"It was wonderful for a short time." Deborah was overwhelmed with sadness. "But it's over."

"Over?" The matriarch smiled. "Whatever the two of you shared isn't over at all. In fact, it's only starting."

Deborah looked at her. "What do you mean?"

Umm-Sallan kissed her on the forehead and whispered, "Congratulations. You're pregnant."

"What?"

"Your skin is warm, and its scent is unmistakable. You're pregnant."

"That's impossible."

"Doesn't your body feel differently? More attuned, more tender, more sensitive to every—"

"No!" Deborah couldn't breathe. "No!"

Pregnant!

The room began to spin, the soldiers along the walls merging into a connected chain of vague figures, the torches fusing into a circle of light that spun faster and faster until a mighty gust of dark wind extinguished them and whisked her into complete darkness.

Spiraling through the empty darkness, Deborah felt weightless and, for the first time in days, free of the dull aches and the nagging tenderness in her breasts, as if the chest armor was stripped away and she was released from its constant pressure and chafing. She put out her arms to slow the spinning and began to see countless sparks around. They were stars, she realized, but there was no moon. Two of the stars began to grow and turn yellow, coming closer, until the outline of the eagle's head and her wings became discernable against the stars.

"Not here!" Deborah became alarmed. "You must leave

immediately!"

"Why?" The eagle hovered, her wings moving lazily.

"Don't you know what they do? They'll copy you in a bust of copper, stuff you, and hang you up-side-down from the ceiling!"

"I didn't see any birds hanging, did you?"

Realizing the eagle was correct, Deborah felt embarrassed.

"I appreciate your concern, though," the eagle said. "It's a gruesome display. I've always wondered about this puzzling contradiction."

"What contradiction?"

"The more powerful a man grows, the more insecure he becomes."

"The young king seems very confident to me."

The eagle covered Deborah's face with the soft tip of the wing. "Close your eyes and listen to him speaking in your head, not the words, but the voice."

Closing her eyes, Deborah recalled the king speak from the balcony in his high-pitched voice.

The eagle withdrew her wing. "What did you hear?"

"He sounds a bit like a girl."

The eagle chuckled.

Deborah understood. "He's insecure about his manhood."

"A vulnerability even a king cannot escape."

"Doesn't it make him more dangerous?"

"Not if you know how to take advantage of it."

Cool water on her face pulled Deborah away, even though she wanted to ask the eagle how to take advantage of the king's insecurity, why would she need that advantage, and, most urgently, about Umm-Sallan's frightening news.

Pregnant!

"Can you hear me?" It was Yael's voice.

Deborah opened her eyes.

Yael dabbed her face with a wet cloth.

Umm-Sallan stood over them, her white hair framing her face. "It's natural to panic," she said. "Remember that you're not alone. We're your family now, do you understand?"

Deborah nodded.

A trumpet sounded, amplified indoors, and a man announced, "King Esau the Twentieth!"

Yael helped her stand up.

The king entered through a door in the rear of the platform, followed by his scribe and several royal guards in rooster-comb helmets. He had changed into a waistcoat in a lighter shade of red, but had kept the gold crown on. It made his head seem small. Deborah wondered whether Princess Needa had already asked him to send Borah to the copper mines.

Sallan bowed forward in the chair, and everyone else knelt.

Sitting down, the king's shoulders were at level with the bent knees of Qoz, whereas the king's crowned head seemed to rest in the deity's crotch.

He signaled for them to rise. "Where is General Mazabi?"

"I'm sorry to bring bad news," Sallan said in a frail voice. "The general and his soldiers were lost in battle."

Umm-Sallan groaned, and Yael put her arm around her.

"And our chariots?"

"Other than the one outside, all were destroyed, unfortunately."

The king pounded his knee with a fist. "How could it happen?"

"The general attacked after sunset near the edge of the Ramon Crater, but the clever Hebrews spooked the horses with fires, leading them over the cliff."

"May Qoz smite them." King Esau's face flushed with anger. "All the Hebrews!"

He stared at Deborah, and her hand instinctively went to the hilt of her sword.

"Not everyone went over the cliff," Sallan said. "Some managed to jump off the chariots. The general and his grandsons led a bitter fight and died bravely, decimating almost all the men of Simeon."

"Almost?"

"Their leader and his son fled the battle, but Borah managed to kill them."

King Esau sat back in the throne, looking at her. "Killed your fellow Hebrews, did you?"

She nodded.

"Why?"

Deborah knew that her life depended on how she answered this question.

Everyone watched her, waiting.

"It was necessary," she said. "How else would I be able to keep my promise and bring Princess Needa home?"

For a long moment, the king continued to look at her, but in the end, he beckoned his scribe, who handed him a cloth purse.

Deborah's heart beat faster.

The king weighed the purse in his hands. "That's a heavy load of silver for a Hebrew boy."

Deborah approached the platform and knelt before him.

"You kept your promise," he said. "We keep our promises, too."

She reached forward with both hands to receive her reward.

"Will you take another ten coins for your horse?"

The question caught her by surprise, and she just stared back at him.

Up close, his eyes were large, blue, and cold.

"How about twenty coins?" His pink lips curled, though the rest of his face did not partake in the smile. "That's a generous price for a horse."

Behind her, Sallan spoke up. "If I may, my king, the horse only obeys Borah—"

"Silence!" The king's lips remained curled, belying his sharp tone. "Well?"

"Forgive me," Deborah said.

"Thirty, then. Thirty silver coins for your horse."

She looked down. "I'm unable to oblige."

"Unable or unwilling?"

"God gave me this horse. Selling it would be a sin against Him." She gestured up at Qoz. "The God of Edom would disapprove of sinning against a fellow God."

"You Hebrews are too clever." King Esau craned his head to glance up at Qoz. "So be it."

"Thank you," she said.

The king tossed the purse to the floor before her.

Deborah picked it up and, surprised by its heavy weight, held it to her chest and stepped backward. She kept her head bowed and thought how, in a moment, she would be out in the sun again with Yael, Sallan, and his mother, whose shocking detection of a pregnancy Deborah wished to disbelieve. How could she go back to the Samariah Hills now, even with much silver to spend, when a child is growing inside her without a husband at her side? She would have to find Barac and—

The king clapped, interrupting her thoughts. A side door opened, and guards wheeled in a large cage. It was as tall as a man, about five steps wide, and, as they turned it sideways, she could see it was at least ten steps long. The bars were made of forged iron. Inside the cage were two animals, kept apart by another set of bars that divided the cage in two. In the front part was a white lion, in the rear a black tiger. Both paced in tight circles, panting with open jaws filled with sharp teeth.

Turning to Sallan, Deborah saw his face transform from sickly exhaustion to wide-eyed wonder. He rose slowly from the chair and stepped toward the cage. Deborah handed the purse to Yael and took Sallan's arm to support him as he approached the cage and peered at the animals, one at a time, smiling with fascination.

King Esau came down from his throne and joined them in front of the cage.

The lion leapt forward, colliding with the bars, and the cage tilted over. The guards steadied it.

The king laughed, clapping.

"Magnificent," Sallan said. "My father searched for years, but only once did a trader from the land of black people bring us a white lion cub. It died the next day, and I cried bitterly."

"Your father was a loyal subject," the king said. "He used to send for me and my sister whenever traders brought him interesting animals. That's how we grew to love animals like our grandfather and continued to collect them." He gestured at the platform.

"These will also die?" Sallan pointed at the white lion and black tiger.

"As soon as our blacksmiths complete the copper models."

The joy faded from Sallan's face.

His reaction did not escape the king. "The Elixirist disapproves of our enterprise?"

Sallan's silence surprised Deborah, who expected him to wriggle his way out of this with a smooth and convincing denial.

King Esau stomped his foot. "We could add you to our collection!"

Behind them, Umm-Sallan sucked her breath audibly.

The king laughed, but as before, his merry didn't reach his cold eyes. "We were merely jesting," he said.

Sallan bowed. "My king's love for the animals Qoz has created deserves my deepest respect. If it pleases you, I would be honored to take part in the removal of the skins and purchase the remains which, with your permission, may be dissected, dried, and powdered for their medicinal properties."

"We shall consider it." The king walked back to his throne. "Respect is what a king deserves, and lack of respect is what a king cannot tolerate."

Deborah led Sallan back to his chair, where he sat with a sigh of exhaustion. She hoped they would be allowed to leave now.

The door opened again, and the guards led in the young Qozmadorus. The blood from his forehead had smeared the copper paint on his face and chest, exposing light skin underneath. He fell to his knees and bowed before the king.

"Now you bow to us," King Esau said. "In the arena, however, in front of our subjects, you gave orders to our royal guards as if you wore the crown."

Deborah understood he was speaking of the high priest's attempt to have her killed by the guards.

"Qoz put us on this throne," the king said. "Disrespect to us is disrespect to Qoz."

"No, no," Qozmadorus whimpered. "No disrespect."

"What shall we do?" King Esau tapped his knee. "A lesson must be taught, right?"

"I'm young and inexperienced." Qozmadorus wept openly, banging his forehead on the red carpet. "Please, forgive me."

"I forgive you," the king said.

Qozmadorus raised his head. "Thank you!"

"But Qoz doesn't." King Esau pointed up at the deity above him. "He can't forgive you."

"For a sacrifice," Qozmadorus cried. "He'll forgive me for a big sacrifice! He will!"

"An excellent idea," the king said. "We'll make a sacrifice to Qoz, but which animal?"

The young high priest started saying something, but stopped, hesitating.

"A difficult choice." The king looked at Sallan. "The Elixirist can help us. You understand wild animals, don't you?"

Sallan nodded.

"Tell us, then, which of these two splendid creatures is hungrier?"

"The lion," Sallan said.

The king gestured to the guards. Two of them poked the lion with long rods through the bars to keep it back while the others lifted the front bars, threw Qozmadorus into the cage, and closed the bars. He screamed for only a brief moment before the lion pounced on him, bit down on his neck, and broke it with a powerful headshake.

Turning away, Deborah felt sick, yet relieved that Sallan's choice of the more powerful lion granted Qozmadorus a quicker death than the tiger would have delivered.

"Watch," the king shouted. "Watch!"

They watched the lion tear apart the young man's body while the black tiger paced back and forth, growling. After some time, the lion sat down, his paws on top of his prey, and took a break from eating.

King Esau sat back in the throne. "A fitting punishment for disrespect, don't you agree?"

"Yes," Sallan said.

"What about the respect you steal from us by diverting our subjects' affections?"

Sallan didn't answer.

Umm-Sallan spoke up. "My son told the people he would not make potions until the king permits it."

Leaning forward, the king yelled, "And how is that helping us? If we permit it, they would line up in the front of your house, eager to give you all their love, respect, and silver. And if we don't permit it, they would hate us and line up in front of your house to beg you to violate our divine authority!"

The white lion took another bite, and the black tiger banged against the bars, shaking the cage.

"There." King Esau pointed at the cage. "A hungry animal waiting for a meal."

The threat was at once outlandish – how could the king consider feeding Sallan to a wild animal in front of his mother? – and all too real, considering the high priest was still being eaten. Deborah imagined the tiger pouncing on Sallan and tearing him apart while Umm-Sallan dropped to the red carpet, clutching her broken heart. The image so terrified Deborah that she spoke up without stopping to think.

"There is a third choice," she said.

Everyone turned to her.

"The people should line up before this palace." Deborah patted Sallan's shoulder as her idea began to form more clearly in her mind. "The Elixirist will bring his magnificent collection of animal powders to this palace. Surely there's room here for another loyal servant. He'll set up his workshop and mix all the elixirs and potions here so that the people form a long queue outside and pay their respect and silver to their beloved king."

There was a long silence.

King Esau watched her thoughtfully, his hands clasping the lapels of his coat. "What does the Elixirist say?"

Sallan rose from the chair with difficulty, stepped to the foot of the platform, and knelt down, reaching forward with shaking hands. "May I serve the royal court as its most humble servant in the manner Borah described?"

The king smiled. "The Hebrew boy is even cleverer than his kin's reputation. Perhaps he would stay here as our advisor."

Deborah stepped forward and knelt beside Sallan. "It would have been a great honor," she said. "My God, however, has ordered me to return to Canaan."

"Write this down," the king said to the scribe. "A proclamation to the people of Edom. From this day onward, the Elixirist shall be part of our royal court and serve us with complete fidelity, providing our subjects with potions and elixirs from our palace with the grace of Qoz. So ordered. King Esau the Twentieth."

The quill in the scribe's hand scratched on the scroll for a while longer, with frequent dips in the inkwell, until he completed the writing. He read it back to the king, who nodded his approval.

The guards opened the door and began to push out the cage, while the king stood up and headed to the rear of the platform. Deborah felt Umm-Sallan's hand pressing her arm in reassurance. They had survived.

A trumpet sounded, and a man announced, "Princess Needa of Edom!"

Deborah felt a chill run up her spine.

28

As the sun slowly descended from its peak, Barac inspected the defenses and spoke with the men and women guarding the walls. The army of Judah had settled in a full circle around Beersheba, about three hundred steps away. Some of them were sitting under cloth canopies or open-sided tents, and food was being cooked on fires. Judging by the drifting smells, they were roasting meat from animals – either antelopes or wild goats caught in the desert, or livestock plundered last night from roadside homesteads whose owners had fled.

Barac returned to the judge's house when the sun reached halfway down in the west. He joined the priest at the corner of the courtyard, which was filling up with anxious men, who stood in small groups and exchanged hushed words. The afternoon heat bore down on their heads, making them sweat. The servants passed around jugs of water.

It was some time before the sound of pounding hooves foretold of Tsruyah's arrival. He rode into the courtyard, forcing the men aside, and dismounted directly onto the table at the center.

"I bring you brotherly greetings from Yoaz, son of Lamon, judge of the city of Bethlehem, who commands the army of Judah. As I announced earlier by the gates, the Gods had blessed me with success in my first challenge as the new judge of Beersheba. I have negotiated a truce between our tribes. From this day on, Simeon and Judah shall live in peace and share the abundance of the land and water, which our forefathers conquered after the exodus from Egypt. No more war—"

"What's the cost?" The voice belonged to a stocky man in a black coat.

Other men yelled more questions from all around the courtyard.

"Will they take our silver?"

"What about our daughters?"

"How much land must we give up?"

"Which wells are they getting?"

"Will they avenge their judge, whom we burnt at the stake?"

"How much taxes will they levy on us?"

Smiling broadly, Tsruyah raised his hands to hush them. "No one is taking your silver or daughters. Our brothers of Judah aren't here to extort taxes or take revenge, but to live in peace with us on the Promised Land, which our common forefathers bequeathed to all of us, and share its water and harvest. That's all."

"What does it mean?" The man in the black coat shook a finger. "There's no such thing as sharing. Have you agreed to give them our fields? Our water?"

Tsruyah's face reddened. "As brothers share, so shall we, Simeon and Judah!"

"And who will be the older brother among us, the one who takes the lion's share?" The man was now pointing his finger at Tsruyah. "You know what's on Judah's flag, don't you? A lion!"

"That means nothing," Tsruyah said. "They will share with us fairly."

"They'll take a share of our land and our water, yes, but will they share their land and water with us in Hebron, Bethlehem, and Lachish?"

"Yes," Tsruyah said. "You'll be the first to benefit from it."

Before the man could continue to argue, two of Tsruyah's soldiers pushed through the crowd, grabbed his arms, and hustled him out of the courtyard.

Watching this, Barac assumed that Tsruyah was keen to remove the loudest doubter before breaking the news about Judah's demand for slaves. He wondered what was Tsruyah's plan. Would he order the prominent men of the city to hand over the laborers from their shops, the maids from their homes, and the tenant farmers from their land?

"Trust me," Tsruyah said. "This truce is a thousand times better than what war would bring upon us. Does anyone here disagree?"

No one dared to speak up.

"And there's more good news." He clapped the way Judge Ohad had used to do. "In celebration of our eternal bond as Hebrews brothers, the men of Judah will join us tonight in providing food and wine for the poor and needy, as prescribed in the Holy Scriptures." He looked at the priest. "Isn't it?"

The priest quoted. "And you shall take out one-tenth of your harvest and put it out by the gates of your city for the needy, the stranger, the widow, and the orphan, and they shall eat by your gates and be satiated, and thus your God shall bless you in all the deeds that you pursue."

"You heard it," Tsruyah said. "Go now, collect one tenth of all the food and wine in your houses and stores, and bring it outside the gates of Beersheba. Our brothers of Judah will also give one-tenth of all the supplies that they have brought here with them. At sundown tonight, we shall build a giant bonfire at the stake, not to punish a sinner, but to illuminate our righteousness in providing for the poor and needy of our city."

There was some grumbling, but not much. That would change, Barac knew, when they hear about the number of people Yoaz had demanded for enslavement.

"One last thing," Tsruyah said. "And you better listen very carefully now."

The courtyard quieted down, everyone looking up at him. Barac inhaled deeply, waiting to hear how Tsruyah planned on delivering three-hundreds people into slavery.

"Peace depends on trust," Tsruyah said. "And trust depends on verification. Here's what's going to happen this afternoon. I intend to make unannounced visits to your homes and shops in order to inspect your stores and ensure that you gave what the Holy Scriptures prescribed. If I find that you're cheating on the measures or hiding some of what you have, then one-tenth will no longer be enough. I will confiscate all your stores and give everything to the poor."

No one protested, but a few shifted about and looked down at the ground.

"My soldiers will be waiting outside the gates to receive your contributions in preparation for tonight, when the poor and needy will be invited to eat and drink their full, and the peace among the tribes of Israel will be sealed for generations to come."

As the men were leaving, Barac whispered to the priest, "What about the slaves?"

The priest shrugged, gathered the blue fringes from the four corners of his white robe, and pressed them to his lips.

Soon, the courtyard emptied out, and Tova appeared with a jug of wine for him. As Barac gulped the sweet wine, the weight of the last few days pressed down on him with exhaustion that ached all over. He swayed, feeling dizzy and nauseated. She led him to the room where they had lain after the marriage ceremony, helped him lie on the cot, and removed his sandals.

29

Princess Needa had transformed completely. She wore a long, plum-red gown with matching gloves, leather sandals fixed with sparkling jewels, and a necklace of white pearls. Her clean face was paler than the king's, bringing out her blue eyes. Her hair had been done up in a tower that made her appear much taller. She looked like a queen, Deborah thought.

Taking her brother's hand, the princess walked with him back to his throne, while two servants carried a padded armchair for her, placing it next to Qoz. The princess, however, did not sit down. She scanned the room until her eyes landed on Deborah.

"This Hebrew boy." She pointed. "He tried to rape me."

King Esau, who had just sat in his throne, jumped up. "What?"

The guards pulled the cage back inside and shut the door.

The white lion roared, and the black tiger growled.

"He tried to rape me," the princess said. "And when I fought him off, he raped my poor maid right before me. That's why she remained in the desert to die alone, ashamed and destroyed."

Deborah was stunned by this bold attempt at deadly revenge, but immediately realized she should have expected it, not only because of the harsh journey and its humiliating conclusion, but because she had killed the man Princess Needa had loved.

"Punish this Hebrew boy," the princess said. "He is a rapist and a murderer."

"It's not true," Deborah said.

"See?" Princess Needa turned to her brother. "First he tries to rape me, then he calls me a liar."

A sharp cracking sound came from the cage, where the lion crushed a bone between its jaws.

The king pointed at Deborah. "Arrest him!"

As the guards ran to her, Deborah considered drawing her sword, but thought better of it. Instead, she unbuckled her belt, letting the sword drop to the floor while she knelt and folded her arms on her chest.

The guards surrounded her.

Sallan got up from the chair. "I was with them the whole time. Borah did not touch any of the women. It didn't happen, my king. I swear to you in Qoz's name."

Princess Needa sneered. "Does the great Elixirist also call the king's sister a liar?"

"No one is lying here," Sallan said.

The king's face was red as he yelled, "How is that possible?"

"A dream," Sallan said. "Or, more accurately, a nightmare. The princess had a nightmare, that's all."

Laughing bitterly, Princess Needa said, "Am I delusional?"

"My king," Sallan pleaded, "Princess Needa has suffered greatly in the hands of the wretched Hebrews, and such suffering always causes confusion and nightmares, especially as our escape had started with copious bloodshed and continued with non-stop travel through the harsh desert for three days and nights. The princess had to sleep on her horse through the frosty nights and suffer the scorching heat during the days. I assure you that Borah did nothing wrong, only risked his life to save us and deliver your sister home safely, as promised."

"It wasn't a dream." Princess Needa pointed at Deborah. "He exposed himself to me like a dog in heat, ready to rape me, but when I fought him off, he raped my maid instead, right before me. I saw it as I see you now."

"Enough!" The king's voice came with a high-pitched screech. "Feed him to the black tiger!"

The guards grabbed Deborah and dragged her toward the cage.

"Wait," Sallan cried. "I can prove it!"

Princess Needa laughed. "How can you prove that I didn't see what I saw?"

"In the name of Qoz." Sallan limped toward the platform, stumbled, and fell on the carpet. "If I fail to prove Borah's innocence beyond any doubt, feed me to the tiger, too."

King Esau signaled the guards to stop. "How could you possibly prove it?"

The cage erupted in fighting between the beasts as the black tiger reached with its paw through the dividing bars and tore a limb off the body of Qozmadorus. The lion reached through the bars, as well, and the cats slashed at each other, shaking the cage.

Yael helped Sallan stand up. He was pale, his face twisted in pain, and he coughed.

"The Elixirist is the worst liar," Princess Needa said. "That's what our grandfather said, remember?"

The king nodded.

"Only facts," Sallan said hoarsely. "Facts don't lie."

The princess sneered, an all too familiar sound to Deborah's ears.

"I ask only this," Sallan continued. "If I prove Borah's innocence, will our merciful king let him keep his life and his reward?"

King Esau looked at his sister, who shrugged and gestured dismissively.

"We agree." The king sat back, his expression a mix of anger and curiosity. "Go on."

Taking his time, Sallan limped back to the chair, Yael holding his arm.

The lion chomped down on another bone, startling Deborah, who stood close enough to the cage to smell the sour odor of human blood. Strangely, she felt no fear or foreboding, only curiosity about what Sallan could possibly say to disprove Princess Needa's allegations.

Sallan sat down with a sigh. "Our beloved Princess Needa says that Borah exposed himself to her."

"Like a dog," she said.

"A dog in heat?"

"Exactly."

"How terrible." Sallan sighed again. "He actually exposed his male organ to you?"

"Ready to rape me, yes." She pointed at Deborah. "He was as aroused as a dog about to mount a bitch in heat. I saw it, not in a dream, but as awake and as conscious as I am now. An aroused dog he was!"

The king's face twisted in disgust. "We don't wish to hear such details."

"How terrible it would be," Sallan said, "for the princess to see a man's exposed arousal with her own eyes—"

"It was terrible." Princess Needa pressed a hand to her chest. "The vilest sight."

"Our poor princess." Sallan nodded sadly. "And then he raped the helpless maid?"

"In front of me!"

"It's a shame that our beloved princess has such painful memories," Sallan pressed a hand to his chest, which bordered on mockery, if not for his tone, which rang with sympathy. "My memories are painful, too. Back in Egypt, as I labored in the sun near the Nile River, an Egyptian foreman mocked me for my light skin and reddish hair. He said, "You're a pig, and all men of Edom are pigs, because your king is a pig, and his father was a pig, and all your kings since the beginning of Edom were pigs." That's what the foreman said to me."

He paused, and Deborah wondered where he was going with this fictional insult.

"I'm not easily angered," he continued. "However, hearing such defilement of my king and his forefathers ignited a bonfire of fury in me. I told the foreman that the real pigs were him and his fathers and his Pharaohs."

King Esau nodded.

"The next instant, the foreman swung his sword at me. I managed to dodge the blade almost completely, except for my hand."

He held up his hand, fingers open, to show the missing pinky.

Deborah caught herself being mesmerized by his story despite knowing that he was inventing it on the spot, one lie after another. Coming out of his mouth, it all sounded perfectly convincing.

"The foreman tried again," Sallan said. "He raised his sword, and I knew without a doubt that my time under Egypt's hot sun had come to an end, yet I was comforted knowing that I would die defending my king's honor." He paused, taking a deep breath. "And then, at the last moment, a Hebrew boy working nearby jumped forward, inserted himself between us, and struck the Egyptian foreman right here." Sallan tapped his crotch. "The foremen collapsed in agony, and the brave boy was taken away in chains. His name, as I learned later, was Borah."

Princess Needa clapped once, twice, and a third time. "We are in awe, but how does this fable prove that your fellow slave in Egypt is innocent of his vile deeds in the Negev Desert?"

"I'm not finished," Sallan said. "You see, our Egyptian oppressors never missed an opportunity to terrify their captives into submission. Rather than grant Borah an easy death, which would have been a welcome release from a miserable existence, they maimed him in a public spectacle in order to deliver a lesson for anyone who might think of striking an Egyptian foreman."

Finally, Deborah realized what he was doing, and the sheer audacity of it astounded her.

"Maimed him," the king said. "How?"

"Where he had struck the foreman, that's where they maimed him."

King Esau looked aside and groaned.

"The guards stripped Borah," Sallan continued. "They tied him to a pole with his legs spread wide."

The king's hands instinctively dropped to his groin.

"And then, they sliced off all the parts that made him a man."

A high-pitched yelp escaped the king's lips.

Sallan pointed at Deborah. "This Hebrew boy suffered a horrible punishment in the hands of the Egyptians for defending the honor of Edom and its kings."

"You're lying," Princess Needa said.

"It's the truth," Sallan said. "They castrated Borah."

She waved dismissively. "Lies, all lies."

"Show them," Sallan said to Deborah.

"No." King Esau waved his hands. "We don't wish to see it."

"Make him show us," the princess said. "It's a lie."

The guards moved away from Deborah as if castration were contagious. It reminded her of the eagle's advice to take advantage of the king's vulnerability. The worse his discomfort was, the better her chances of survival were. Approaching the platform, she began to undo the straps holding the leg armor pieces to her thighs.

"Look closely," Sallan said, "Do you see his sparse beard, hairless arms, and smooth chest? That's what happens after a young man suffers a complete and total castration."

"Silence!" The king looked away from Deborah. "He must keep his clothes on!"

Princess Needa stomped her foot. "How are we going to know, then?"

"A castrated boy," Sallan continued, "grows into a young man who not only has no masculine parts, but also has no desire to use what he doesn't have. That's why I'm certain that our beloved princess suffered a terrible nightmare, and that Borah is innocent."

Princess Needa put her lips by her brother's ears and whispered something.

"Good idea." King Esau turned to the scribe. "Check him with your hand and tell us what you feel."

The scribe, an older man of small stature and milky skin, put down his scrolls, ink, and feather. He approached Deborah slowly, his face a mask of revulsion, and crouched before her. She took his hand and led it to the inside of her right thigh, under the armor, and through her undergarments. When his hand reached her crotch, she spread her knees and pressed his palm to her most private place. He whimpered and pulled his hand out.

"Tell us," the king said. "What's there?"

"Nothing." The scribe gagged.

"Nothing?"

"He's completely emasculated." The scribe stumbled aside and puked.

Deborah wanted to do the same, but the danger of being fed to the black tiger had not yet passed. Princess Needa stared down at her with unbridled hate, which Deborah understood. The rape accusation was a mere substitute for a murder accusation, which the princess could not bring up, because she would have to confess her love for Mamreh and her desire to stay with him, rather than return to Edom. Deborah could hardly blame her for making the false accusation of rape. If anyone killed Barac, she would have sought deadly revenge with equal fury. To quell the princess's quest for revenge, Deborah had to communicate to her somehow that she regretted killing Mamreh and lamented depriving the princess of his love.

Going down on her knees, Deborah kept her eyes on the princess. "I am not guilty of what you accused me, but I am guilty of many failures. From the start, I tried to prevent bloodshed, but I failed repeatedly. To defend myself, I have slain worthy men, ending precious lives that were dear to those who loved them. My family is all dead, but at least I managed to bring you home to your loving brother. I pray that your Gods comfort your sorrow, heal your heart, and bless you with peace so that, one day, you may forgive me."

The corners of Princess Needa's lips curled down and her eyes moistened. She turned and, with her back straight and her head high, walked through the display of life-sized copper animals to the rear of the platform and out the door.

Glancing back after his sister, King Esau said, "The Hebrew eunuch may keep his reward, but he must leave Bozra at sunrise tomorrow."

30

When Barac woke up, the room was dark, except for a candle in the corner, where Tova was packing two sacks with blankets and food. He sat up, rubbing his eyes. She saw that he was awake and smiled. He wanted to touch her, but her red robe stood between them as a barrier. She went outside to fetch his sandals, which were clean and oiled. He put them on and stood, stretching his achy arms and legs. She went out again and brought him a plate with meat stew and boiled barley, as well as a cup of wine. He sat cross-legged on the floor and ate.

Tova gestured at the sacks. "The servants gave me supplies for the road. The horse is fed and ready, too."

Barac peeked outside. The courtyard was empty, but the flames were high in the firepit, and the long table was set for a meal with many plates. "Did Tsruyah order us to leave?"

"Not yet," she said.

He chuckled. "Do you always expect the worst?"

"It's not funny. The people look up to you. Tsruyah is envious. I can see it in his eyes. He wants to destroy you."

"He won't dare."

"Not in public, but he'll find an underhanded way to do it. Let's leave now, while he is busy, and everyone else is celebrating the peace." She took his empty plate. "God won't mind. Beersheba is safe now."

Barac got up and strapped on his sword. "Not yet. The leader of Judah expects delivery of slaves – one tenth of all the people of Beersheba."

Inhaling in shock, Tova covered her mouth.

"I must stay," he said. "When people find out their husbands, wives, sons, or daughters are to be sold at the fairgrounds to merchants and taken to the slave markets of Gaza or Bozra, never to be seen again, how will they react?"

"They'll riot," she said.

"And die by the soldiers' swords." He adjusted his robe. "Tsruyah is betraying his own tribe in the service of Judah. I don't know why, but I have to stop him."

Tova stood at the door. "Don't go. Please."

He smiled, waiting until she moved aside. "Don't worry. God had spared me at the battle by the Ramon Crater so that I return here to defend Beersheba. I cannot leave until the people are safe again."

She wiped tears. "I don't want you to die."

Barac paused at the door. "I believe God has many more plans for me."

He walked down the hill through an eerily vacant city. He could hear the noise of a large crowd outside the gates, but no sounds of fighting. When would Tsruyah move to enforce the mass enslavement? How would he do it?

Reaching the gates, Barac ran into a dense river of people heading back into the city. Men and women with anxious faces hurried up the hill through the main street and off to the side streets. None went to the right toward the shacks and tents of the poor, which appeared to be empty. He stood aside to let the crowd pass before stepping out through the gates.

A huge bonfire burned at the stake. In the open area beside it, hundreds of poor men, women, and children stood around large piles of food and many wine jugs, eating and drinking. Tsruyah sat on his horse beside Yoaz and watched as many men of Judah in short robes, white caps, and sandals ambled casually, using their spears as walking sticks, gradually encircling the poor inhabitants of Beersheba, who were too busy eating and drinking to notice anything.

Finally, Barac understood Tsruyah's plan. He wasn't going to force all the men of Beersheba to hand over family members, laborers, and servants for slavery. Rather, under the pretense of a righteous act of charity prescribed by the Holy Scriptures, he collected tithing of food and wine to lure out every hungry man, woman, and child, who were now being rounded up to be taken into slavery by the men of Judah.

The audacity of the unfolding atrocity took Barac's breath away. Yahweh's mercy!

He ran toward the bonfire, waving his hands, yelling, "Escape! They're going to take you!"

A few of the poor looked in his direction while eating and drinking.

"Run away! Now!"

From the corner of his eye, Barac saw something, and a spear hit the ground right before him with a thud. Too late to veer, he bumped into it hard, spun around, and fell flat on his back. Momentarily stunned by the fall, he looked up at the clear sky, dotted with stars and bursts of sparks rising from the bonfire. Tsruyah appeared above him. He leaned over in the saddle and pulled the spear out of the ground.

Barac began to rise.

"Stay down," Tsruyah said. "You're still alive because you're useful, but I'm getting tired of your smug righteousness."

Defying the threat, Barac got up and stood, Tsruyah's spear at his chest.

Yoaz rode over and signaled Tsruyah to move back.

"This is a terrible sin." Barac gestured toward the mass of poor people, who were oblivious to the encircling men of Judah and the danger they represented. "God will punish you."

"It's not a sin," Yoaz said.

"Sins," Barac said. "Every person you enslave is another sin. You have to stop it, or I will."

Tsruyah held his spear ready and looked at the judge of Judah.

Yoaz dismounted, put his arm over Barac's shoulder, and made him turn back to the gates. "Think rationally, young man. Would God want his Chosen People to kill each other by the hundreds tonight, or would He rather allow the enslavement of these poor, wretched, lazy people, whose lives as slaves will probably be an improvement over their current conditions?"

Barac glanced over his shoulder. "Why does God have to choose?"

"It's a necessary choice," Yoaz said, leading him toward the gates. "The march of Hebrew history brought me and my men here to take

Beersheba and its wells, either by the sword, or by the slaves. Which is better?"

Screaming sounded behind them.

Barac didn't look back. "The march of Hebrew history didn't bring you here."

"What, then?"

"Greed."

Yoaz chuckled. "Don't you believe in the Holy Scriptures?"

"I do."

"Then you know what our forefather Jacob said of Simeon." Yoaz quoted. "Keep my soul from their company, my honor from dwelling among them, for in malevolence they kill men, on a whim they castrate cattle. Damn their malice, for it's fierce, and their wrath, for it's cruel. I shall cut Simeon off from Jacob and scatter them among Israel."

Barac glanced at Tsruyah, who shrugged as if the words didn't concern him.

"It's not all," Yoaz said. "Do you know what Jacob said of my tribe?"

"I do," Barac said.

Yoaz quoted it anyway. "Judah, your brothers will praise you, your hand will be on the neck of your enemies, your father's sons will bow before you."

Guessing how Deborah would respond, Barac said, "Your brothers will praise you? For what? Attacking them? Enslaving them? Jacob's prediction will fail because of your actions."

Yoaz laughed, patting Barac's back. "In theory, oppression should incite rebellion, but in reality, the subjugated often idolize their masters, because it's people's nature to shrink before those who make them kneel."

A great wail of many voices rose behind them, accompanied by staccato of whips, and the sporadic high-pitched cries of children.

Tears filled Barac's eyes, and he wiped them with the back of his hand.

"You have a good heart." Yoaz tightened his arm around Barac's shoulders, shaking him affectionately. "An effective leader hardens his heart in order to win a battle, or better yet, to win without a battle."

They reached the gates. No one was in sight. Barac looked toward the dormant shacks and tents on the right. His tears kept flowing, not only for the fate of the poor, but for his own failure to prevent this catastrophe.

"Don't beat yourself up," Yoaz said. "If not for my spies' reports of the strong defenses you put around the city, I would have skipped negotiations and taken it by force. Think of all the men who didn't die, all the women who didn't get raped, and all their daughters who're still virgins. You saved all of them, and we would have taken slaves either way, do you understand?"

Barac nodded.

Behind them, the screaming subsided, while men shouted orders.

"Very good." Yoaz patted his shoulder. "Go back to the house and tell your new wife how lucky she is not to be going into slavery with you tonight."

The implied warning was clear, and Barac knew he had no chance of prevailing in a confrontation, which would end, as Yoaz had just said, in slavery for Tova and himself. There was only one path open for him, and he made the request in a deferential tone.

"I humbly ask that you grant me and my wife a safe passage to the north, so that I can rejoin my tribe of Naphtali."

Yoaz glanced at Tsruyah before answering. "Come back and talk to me in the morning. We'll work something out."

31

It was dark outside when a royal wagon and a company of guards took them back to Umm-Sallan's house, with Rogez and Yael's mare in tow. The servants ran out to help, and two of them carried Sallan, who pointed to his workshop by the side of the house. Deborah followed. Once inside, he sat in a chair while the servants lit several oil lamps and brought a jug of water.

The air in the workshop was a musty mix of sharp scents. Deborah paced down one of the rows of shelves, gazing at the jars and bottles. Wooden cutouts, shaped as various animals, were nailed to the shelves to identify the powders in each of the container. Along the walls, workbenches held measuring scales, clay bowls, wooden barrels, and mixing spoons. Unlike her first visit, when everything had been covered with spider webs and a thick layer of dust, the place was thoroughly clean.

"Tell me what to bring you." She peered at the wooden cutouts. "This shelf has bear parts. And the next is either tiger or lioness, I'm not sure."

"Is it spotted?"

She looked closer. The wooden cutout in the shape of a large cat was dotted with small indentations. "Yes."

"A beautiful animal," he said. "Like golden honey with brown spots like many eyes."

"What do you need?"

He sighed. "It depends."

"What do you mean?" Deborah returned to where he was sitting. "Surely you can mix a potion that would help you heal."

Sallan looked at her, his bruised face puffy and colorful. "Healing is possible only if nothing is ruined." He passed his hand over his chest and abdomen. "When a man receives a severe beating, many things can break or rip inside. The bones, muscles, and organs that keep us going are fragile. No potion can fix a mashed-up liver or a torn stomach."

Deborah felt weak with worry. "Can you tell if something is ruined inside?"

He shrugged, and his face twisted in pain. "A few ribs are broken, I can feel it, but ribs can mend by themselves."

"That's good, right?"

"Unless they puncture an organ." He coughed. "In that case, I'll die before the ribs mend." He pressed on the lower side of his back, sighing. "There's blood inside, hardened, like bruises you can't see."

Inhaling deeply, she fought off a wave of nausea. "We shouldn't worry about what we don't know. What can be done to help you heal?"

"The body can heal itself, unless a high fever attacks it while it's weak."

"Is there a potion for keeping high fever away?"

He nodded.

"Let's make it. What do you need?" She gazed at a wooden cutout. "A lion's heart?"

"Like the one you have?"

She moved down the aisle. "How about a fox's brain? Oh, you already have that."

He laughed, which caused him another coughing attack.

Deborah gave him water, and he calmed down.

"Go there." He pointed. "The last aisle."

She did, and the wooden cutouts there were not shaped as animals, but fruit.

"Pomegranate," he said.

She found the wooden cutout in the shape of a pomegranate and picked up a small jar of powder. "Got it. What else?"

"Lemon."

That was more difficult, as several cutouts looked similar. She removed one of the lamps from the wall holder and used it to look closer, discovering that the cutouts bore the remnants of paint. One was yellow.

"I see a lemon," she said.

"Next to it, similar shape, rounder, and painted orange."

"Got it."

"Now, a few jars over, there's carrot powder."

Her hands full, Deborah carried the jars to the desk near where he sat.

"Go further down," he said. "Green leaves."

She found it. "What's that?"

"It grows in the warm countries near water. My father had a name for it." He paused to think. "Terred."

She used a wooden spoon to scoop powder from each jar in quantities he indicated, added water, and mixed everything in an open bowl until there were no lumps. He tasted the potion, nodded, and held the spoon for her.

"I'm not injured," she said.

"It's good for you. Powder holds the essence of the original fruit. Once spoonful of this potion is like a basket of medicinal fruit."

Deborah relented and tasted the potion. It was bitter and sandy.

"Don't spit it out," he said. "Let your saliva soften it, then swallow."

She did as he said, and it went down easily.

He took a spoonful himself, sloshing it in his mouth, and swallowed. "Thank you for saving me from becoming a tiger's meal."

"It was nothing compared to how you saved my life."

"A crafty lie, wasn't it?"

She laughed. "Did you see how his hands dropped to his crotch?"

Sallan imitated the king. "I knew it would terrify him."

"You were right, but had he insisted on a proper examination of my private parts, you would have lost your life."

"The life you saved only moments earlier, turning me from a threat to his royal popularity into a serving member of his royal palace." He poked her with feigned irritation. "How am I going to weasel my way out of that servitude?"

"I'm sure you'll manage."

He sighed. "It'll be hard without you."

She held his hand, the stump of his severed pinky rough against her palm. "You'll visit me in the Samariah Hills."

He brought her hands to his lips, which were dry and cracked from the journey. "Will you let me live in your palace when you rule over Canaan?"

"Only Canaan?" She kissed his forehead. "Mamreh must have hit your head, judging by the nonsense you speak."

He held her, their faces close. "You know I'm right."

"About what?"

"About your greatness." Sallan's bloodshot eyes bore into her. "Admit it, Deborah. You feel it in your heart. You think it in your mind. And you see it in your dreams. You do, don't you?"

She sat on the ground by his chair and rested her head on his knee. He caressed her short hair.

A while later Umm-Sallan came in. "It's time for you two to wash and rest. We'll discuss the future at dinner."

She snapped her fingers, and the servants appeared to carry Sallan to the house.

A hot bath and a clean bed awaited Deborah in a private room. For the first time in what seemed like a lifetime, she washed thoroughly and slipped into a bed with soft linen, a roof overhead, and four solid walls to protect her. She closed her eyes, took a deep breath, and pushed away all thoughts of what had happened to her in the last few days, what was happening inside her at this very moment, and what would happen at sunrise as she rode away from this home, out the gates of this glorious city, and into the harsh desert, embarking on a journey whose outcome was uncertain.

32

Later that evening, as Barac lay awake, he heard commotion in the courtyard. He opened the door and saw Tsruyah's soldiers bring in a large group of men, women and children, whose tattered clothes and foul smell told him they were part of the enslaved poor.

Tsruyah's voice came from the window of the judge's room above. "Tie them up with ropes. If anyone as much as whines, use the whip.

Stepping out to the courtyard, Barac looked up.

Tsruyah stood in the window. "You again?"

"Who are these people?"

"They're my share." Tsruyah grinned. "One in ten slaves. It's only fair, isn't it?"

His ruthlessness no longer surprised Barac. He quickly counted them. "There are more than fifty here. How many did you give the men of Judah?"

"As many as they could handle. We don't need paupers and beggars in Beersheba."

Barac inhaled, struggling to control his rage. "What will you do with these people?"

"Sell them. Word has gone around the region, drawing more merchants. I'll get top prices for them and collect taxes on everything, lots more than Judge Ohad, the old fool."

Barac knew Tsruyah was goading him to do something rash, providing an excuse to unleash the soldiers on him. Instead, he spoke in a neutral tone of someone trying to be helpful. "If you want to get top prices, you should give them water to wash, clean shirts, and good blankets so that they look healthy and rested when they reach the market."

Tsruyah considered it for a moment. "You are clever, like Borah."

Barac knew he wasn't as clever as Deborah, who would have thought of a way to liberate all these people from the evil net that Tsruyah had sprung on them.

Addressing the soldiers, Tsruyah said, "You heard him. Do it."

With help from the soldiers and several women, including Tova, Barac had the poor men, women, and children wash with water from the well, put on clean shirts, and lay down with blankets to sleep on the ground in the courtyard.

33

The window was dark when Deborah woke up from her nap. The house smelled of roasted meat, which made her realize how hungry she was. A clean robe had been left by the bedside. She slipped it on and went outside.

The family had gathered in the front garden for a late meal. An empty seat waited between Sallan and his mother. Deborah hesitated, wondering if word of her supposed castration had reached some of the members of Sallan's family. It was the oddest of situations, a girl sitting for a meal with a group of people who thought her to be either a man, or a eunuch.

Yael, who sat on Sallan's other side, noticed her and beckoned. Deborah came over and sat down.

Unlike the last meal Deborah had attended, Leola and her husband did not sit at the opposite end of the table, Sallan raised no toasts, and no drumbeat interrupted the continuous arrival of large bowls of roasted meats, boiled barley, warm breads, sliced fruits, and honey cakes. Umm-Sallan's daughters, their husbands, children, and grandchildren ate, chatted, and laughed with a relaxed pleasure that seemed almost otherworldly to Deborah. She wondered about her own future. Could she ever have a large family that dines together with such amiable joy?

Glancing at Umm-Sallan, who ate little while watching over her progeny, Deborah knew it had taken the matriarch a lifetime of hard work, wise choices, and fierce determination – not to mention divine blessings – to raise such a family. Deborah imagined herself at an old age, sitting with her many descendants and watching them with joy.

She placed a hand over her lower belly, pressed lightly against the robe, and wondered whether this child would be the first of many, the beginning of a long journey to an old-age matriarchy, or yet another hopeful promise cut short by heartbreak and disappointment.

After the evening meal, a table was set in the back of the house with warm milk and cakes for Sallan, who had to be carried over, as well as his mother, Deborah, and Yael.

When they sat down, Deborah held Umm-Sallan's hand. "I'm sorry about General Mazabi."

The matriarch nodded. "I'll miss him, especially his wit. Did you notice it? Most people were too busy fearing him to notice his wit."

"Just before the battle," Deborah said, "I pleaded with him not to attack because Yahweh would punish him for killing the Hebrews, and he immediately countered." She recalled the general's exact words. "Perhaps the opposite. The Hebrews have sinned. Their God is angry. I'm their punishment. It's possible, right?"

Umm-Sallan chuckled. "As it turned out, you were both correct."

Deborah thought about the general's violent death in Barac's hands. Yahweh had poured his wrath on both sides that night, decimating all the men, except Barac – a lone survivor, spared by God for a purpose, but what was that purpose? To father her child? To save Simeon from Judah? To grow into a great warrior, fight the Canaanites, and liberate the Hebrew tribes? Perhaps all three, she thought, but certainly the first, for she would not be pregnant had God not spared Barac at the Ramon Crater.

"A new life," Umm-Sallan said. "That's the best comfort after so much death."

"Forgive me, mother," Sallan said. "How will there be a new life if Deborah mounts her horse at sunrise and rides back into the desert with no one to protect her and no family to take her in?"

She didn't answer his question, so he answered it himself, turning to Deborah. "You and Yael should go to Kassite's homestead and hide there until the baby comes."

Yael, who was chewing on a piece of honey cake, spoke with her mouth full. "Who is Kassite?"

"A good man," Sallan said. "And a wonderful friend to me and to Deborah, even if she doubts it."

They looked at Deborah, waiting for her to speak.

"He was my master," she said to Yael. "At the tannery."

"Oh, yes," Yael said. "You told me how he shaved your head and made you walk barefoot in a sleeveless shirt while doing hard labor with stinking cowhides for weeks on end and sleep every night among the savage Philistine slaves, whereas he pretended to be the real Elixirist and strung you along with promises of mixing the Male Elixir until you came up with a plan to float all the slaves down the river to Philistia and leave behind a bloody scene to make the owner think that the Philistines had killed their master before escaping, while you led him and a few lusty Edomite slaves to the town of Emanuel and liberated the real Elixirist—him!" Panting, Yael pointed at Sallan. "Right?"

By the time Yael finished this breathless monologue, the three of them were laughing.

"Mistakes were made," Sallan said, holding his hands up in faux surrender. "It's all in the past. We're in Edom now, and Kassite is no longer an enslaved tannery foreman. While he keeps Deborah safe in the Red Hills, I'll join the king's court, earn his royal affection, and make him richer with the people's silver." Sallan turned back to Deborah. "In nine months, when you're a young mother, with your hair grown back to its bright colors and your skin as light as an Edomite girl, all resemblance to Borah will be gone. We'll bring you back to Bozra and make up a good story about tragedy and widowhood on the distant frontier. You'll live with us here as a relative. In time, there will be a good husband, smitten by your beauty, more children to fill the void in your heart, and a happy future for you and your family, right here in Bozra."

Umm-Sallan patted his forearm. "My son thinks like a man in love."

"Fatherly love," Sallan said.

"A father would not send his pregnant girl to live in a desolate homestead over an abandoned copper mine with a group of lascivious former slaves."

"Kassite will protect her."

"She'll need women to care for her," Umm-Sallan said.

"Yael will be there."

"If you had experienced the agonizing pains, anxieties, and

complications of childbearing, you'd understand that a girl delivering her first baby needs the help of mature women, who know what she's facing and how to help her. That's why she must be right here in this house, where we can care for her until the baby comes."

"But mother, the king's order was clear."

"It was indeed."

"How can we defy the king?"

"We won't. As the king ordered, Borah will ride out of the city tomorrow at sunrise on her white horse. Later, at a discreet spot along the road, we'll arrange a change of attire and horses, and a girl will come back to Bozra to stay with us. The white horse can go to Kassite for the time being, or sold to a caravan heading north."

"Good idea," Sallan said. "That magnificent creature attracts too much attention."

"Here's another idea," Umm-Sallan said. "You could leave it here as a gift to the king and earn his gratitude, as well."

They looked at Deborah.

She took her time forming a response that would not insult them. "I'm grateful for your kindness and generosity. My child, however, deserves both a mother and a father. I must reunite with Barac. It's my duty."

"He left you," Yael said. "A little argument, that's all it took. He waited for you to fall asleep and snuck away, abandoning you at night in a desolate ravine."

"It wasn't like that." Deborah said.

"Yes, it was. I was awake the whole time, and I saw it."

"There you have it," Sallan said. "No use chasing a man who flees after violating you."

Deborah glared at Yael. "Were you spying on me?"

The girl blushed. "I was worried about you. He had just killed so many men, and now he was hissing at you in anger."

"Not good," Umm-Sallan said. "Bad temper is incompatible with a happy marriage."

"He wasn't hissing," Deborah said. "He wasn't angry, and he didn't sneak away, either."

The three of them looked at her with skeptical expressions.

"To inherit my father's land, I needed a Hebrew man of Ephraim, my tribe. I assumed Barac was of Ephraim, but then, I discovered he's from Naphtali and told him to leave." Her face burning, Deborah looked away. "He begged me to change my mind, promised me a good life together, but I refused and threw the ring in his face."

"Ouch." Yael shook her head. "That's cruel."

"I was angry, but it doesn't matter now. With his baby growing inside me, I must find Barac, plead for his forgiveness, and obey his wishes as a good wife."

There was a long silence, broken by Sallan's chuckle. "A good wife? You?"

"God gave me this child," she said. "He wants me to become a mother and a wife. It's his will that I take a different path, but in the end, this path will also lead me to Palm Homestead. I'm sure of it."

"A winding path," Sallan said.

"That's how it looks now – a diversion, a delay, but I still believe in what a wise priest once said." Deborah quoted the words that had fortified her at every setback. "When you pursue your True Calling, God provides the shortcuts."

"Or the detours," Sallan said. "That blacksmith's son could be anywhere, if he's still alive."

"Barac is alive," Deborah said. "Yahweh will not let him die now, after all that's happened."

"How will you find him?"

"He felt it was his duty to defend Beersheba in case of another attack by Judah. They need him, having lost their judge, his son, and many soldiers. Barac will stay there for a while. That's where I'll find him."

"I forbid it." Sallan stood up, but his face twisted in pain. Yael helped him sit down, and he sipped warm milk, recovering. "My body is broken," he said weakly. "And now my heart, too. I fear you'll die in the desert."

"Danger aside," Umm-Sallan said, "she belongs with the child's father."

"Deborah doesn't belong to anyone." Sallan said. "I won't allow you to leave, a pregnant girl, on the road, alone."

"I'm never alone," Deborah said.

"Of course." Sallan groaned. "The invisible, inaudible, intangible

Hebrew God."

"Not Him," Yael said. "She was talking about me."

Umm-Sallan laughed. Sallan and Yael joined her, and then, Deborah, taken by a fit of laughter that fed on itself until they were all hollering so loudly that the servants rushed over.

When they finally calmed down, Sallan sat back, wiping tears. "I needed that."

"We all did," his mother said. "Deborah, is this your final decision?"

"Yes."

"Then we must prepare." Umm-Sallan got up. "I'll have the servants obtain a couple of extra horses and pack up supplies for the road. Do you want to hire soldiers?"

"Not here. Perhaps in Beersheba, with Barac's help. He is a capable leader of soldiers."

"Then you need a caravan to travel with. I'll send a servant down to the fairgrounds to find a caravan that's heading to Beersheba and make the arrangements."

Deborah stood and put her arms around the matriarch. "Thank you."

Sallan slowly rose to his feet. He took Deborah's hands and looked up at her. "You were shorter than me in Emanuel, and now, you're a head taller." He smiled through moist eyes. "May the Gods keep you safe on your travels and help you find what you seek."

She kissed him on both cheeks.

"But if they don't," he said, "come back to Bozra. Promise me that, at least, will you?"

Deborah smiled and kissed him one last time on his forehead. "I promise."

34

Early the next morning, banging noises woke Barac up. He stepped out of the room. The sun wasn't up yet, and in the twilight of dawn, he made his way between the new slaves sleeping in the courtyard and opened the gate.

Across the street, slightly higher on the hillside, a group of men in short robes and white caps set down wooden beams and hammered them together in large squares, each the size of a room. Up front, an armed man, also of Judah, stood guard by a pole fixed in the ground. It flew a large piece of yellow fabric with a drawing of a lion perched on a swell of land, gazing into the distance. Barac was taken aback by the sight of Judah's flag flying at the highest point in Beersheba. He glanced up at the arch over the courtyard gate, where a threadbare piece of green cloth remained of the flag of Simeon.

He crossed the street and asked the guard what was being built.

"A house for the judge," the man said, leaning on his spear.

"For Tsruyah?"

He grinned, shaking his head. "Our judge."

Barac was confused. "Isn't Yoaz the judge in Bethlehem?"

The man shrugged and didn't answer.

The size of the expanding foundations told of a sizable house, possibly the largest in Beersheba.

Crossing the street back, Barac heard sounds of hammering from downhill. Changing directions, he walked down the main street. At every vacant lot of land, abutting the street or behind an existing house, men of Judah were laying foundations for new houses. At every site, an armed guard stood up front beside a yellow flag, some hanging on mere sticks or from a low bush, yet as explicit in the early sun as a torch in the dark. Men and women of Simeon trickled out of their houses to watch, but the presence of armed guards dissuaded anyone who might have considered protesting.

At the temple, Barac was surprised to see several men of Judah sweeping the ground and scrubbing the walls. Another group was building a new altar. The priest paced about in a clean white robe with blue fringes, followed by two Levite boys in matching outfits.

Further down, Barac saw men of Judah knocking on doors and collecting small items, which they gathered in a large basket. He peered into the basket. It was half-full with effigies of foreign gods, made of wood or clay.

Down by the gates, the water wells were guarded by armed men of Judah. On the east side, a swarm of workers were tearing down the shacks, huts, and tents where the poor had lived until the previous day. Poles and beams from the dismantled structures were loaded on wagons and transported to building sites, while everything else was hauled outside the city and burned in a large fire, whose smoke drifted over the desert, fading into the grim sky.

Stepping through the gates, Barac wasn't surprised to see a new pole, twice as tall as the one bearing Simeon's limp green flag, flying a massive yellow flag with the lion of Judah.

Further out, across from the fairgrounds, hundreds of poor men, women, and children, slept on the ground where they had been lured with food and drink the previous night, guarded by men of Judah. To the left, in an area abutting the city walls, he saw a new encampment. In addition to men of Judah, some sleeping, some already up, there were many women and children, as well. He stepped closer and noticed Yoaz with a group of men, engaged in conversation.

Yoaz beckoned him over. "Good morning. An early riser, aren't you?"

"It's noisy in there." Barac gestured at the city. "Your men are busy demolishing the dwellings of those you've enslaved and building new homes on every vacant plot of land, beside guarding the wells as if the water had become your property."

"The guards are there to maintain order, nothing more. Under the terms of the truce, we have the right to share the land and water as long as we live with Simeon like brothers."

"Caine and Abel were brothers."

Yoaz laughed.

Barac looked at the families of Judah, rising for the day. "Your women and children are already here, eager to settle on Simeon's land."

"How can we share if we're not here?"

"That's not sharing. That's taking."

"Taking our share. What's wrong with that? The men of Simeon agreed to it."

"Under threat of bloodshed."

"Compromise happens only when there's a conflict and the two sides agree that the bloody cost of confrontation justifies a peaceful give and take."

"In Revivim, the men of Judah killed the elder and burned the village down. They didn't offer a compromise."

"Is that a rumor, or did you witness it yourself?"

"Saw it with my own eyes and heard it with my own ears. When your fellow men of Judah prepared to attack, their leader said, "We must be swift with our blades, cut down the men of Simeon before they escape into the desert to hide under rocks like rats." The villagers only survived because I managed to reach Revivim and helped them hide in the water cistern, except for their elder, whom your men tortured and murdered."

His face flushed, Yoaz left Barac and went to speak with a group of about a dozen men sitting by a small fire and eating the morning meal. Barac recognized the leader from the camp south of Revivim. At first, voices were low, but the discussion became heated, with Yoaz pointing and shaking his finger. In the end, the men mounted their horses and rode off. Barac watched as they took the road east toward Kabetzel.

Yoaz returned. "You spoke the truth. I banished them back to their village at Be'er Rahma, far to the south, and ordered them to send gifts to Revivim and beg forgiveness."

"What's happening here isn't much better than what happened in Revivim."

"There's no comparison," Yoaz said. "Here, we made a fair bargain. The men of Simeon had time to consider the terms of the truce, and they accepted it."

"These people didn't accept." Barac pointed at the mass of poor people, lying under guard. "And the rest of Beersheba still doesn't know that you bribed Tsruyah with fifty slaves for delivering into your hands the city, the land, and the water without a fight."

Yoaz's face hardened. "Are you trying to offend me?"

"I'm telling the truth, and if you're offended, it's your own actions that give offense."

"Is it wise to offend a man more powerful than yourself?"

The implied threat wasn't empty, with many of Judah's armed men listening to the exchange, but the blatant injustice of it all overwhelmed Barac, making silence impossible.

"Is it wise to bribe another tribe's judge?" Barac raised his voice. "Is it wise to steal another tribe's land and water? Is it wise to burn villages and kill their elders?"

Yoaz appeared ready to strike him.

Barac pointed upward. "Is it wise to offend the true judge with evildoing?"

The men closed in, their faces dark.

Yoaz raised his hand to stop them and spoke through gritted teeth. "Listen carefully, Barac, son of Abinoam. We've been patient with you because it's not in our interest to upset the people of Beersheba, who see you as a substitute for their other savior, Borah."

The words made him think of Deborah, and a lump formed in his throat, making it hard for him to speak. "I'm nothing like Borah," he said. "Borah would have found a way to save Beersheba again."

The pain in Barac's voice defused Yoaz's anger. "Your heart and mouth are equal, which is why we forgive your insults."

"God's forgiveness is what we should all seek."

"Indeed." Yoaz adjusted the white cap over his head. "Let's go and pray together for divine forgiveness, shall we?"

Accompanied by a large group of men, they walked into the city and up the street. In front of the temple, a large pile of effigies was going up in flames while a crowd of locals watched from a safe distance.

The temple courtyard had been swept clean and the walls repainted in white. To Barac's puzzlement, the priest welcomed Yoaz with a brotherly embrace, before inviting the other men of Judah to gather closer around the altar.

The Levite boys carried over a bound goat and placed it on the new altar.

"Yahweh, king of the world," the priest intoned. "Forgive your beloved sons of Judah for the sins of battle and conquest, because Judah is the favorite son of Jacob, who blessed Judah on his deathbed." He pulled a scroll from under his new white robe, unrolled it, and read aloud. "Judah is a lion's cub, who dares rouse him? The scepter shall not depart from Judah, nor the ruler's staff from between his feet, until tribute comes to him, and to him shall be the obedience of the peoples."

Rolling up the scroll, he put it aside and accepted a knife from one of his helpers. Slicing the goat's neck, he said, "May this sacrificial offering please God and be accepted by Him as full and eternal redemption for any and all sins that might have been committed by Jacob's chosen son Judah and his descendants, as well as the sins of all the tribes of Israel."

The men chorused, "Amen!"

The young Levites skinned the goat, cleaned its intestines, and laid it on a fire to cook. As the crowd of men began to disperse, Barac noticed that the altar was different from other altars he had seen. The wooden base and stone top were common, but this one had four corner stones that protruded upward like tapered horns, sharpened to pointy ends.

The priest noticed his interest. "This is how an altar should be built. It's written in the Holy Scriptures, as God told Moses." He paused and quoted. "And you shall make the altar of reeds wood, five feet long and five feet wide, square the altar shall be, three feet its height. And you shall build horns at its four corners, where its horns shall rise up."

"It's a beautiful altar," Barac said.

"Isn't it?" The priest ran his hand on the smooth edge of the stone. "And we've inaugurated it with an unblemished sacrifice and a righteous prayer for forgiveness."

"I was wondering," Barac said. "God may forgive the men of Judah for deceiving Simeon, but will He forgive Simeon's judge and its priest for siding with Judah against their own tribesmen?"

Stumbling back as if he were slapped, the priest grabbed the corner of the altar to steady himself. "I'm not Simeon's priest, or Judah's priest. I'm Yahweh's priest, like all men of Levi. Our tribe was chosen to serve." He pointed at the bonfire, where effigies of false gods were burning. "Judah is faithful to the one God, bar none. That's why He made Jacob's blessing come true: Judah above all others!"

35

At sunrise, on the street outside Sallan's family home, Deborah mounted Rogez. Her leather armor, boots, and helmet were clean and oiled, her sling was tied around her hips, her bejeweled sword was sheathed against her thigh, and General Mazabi's copper spear was secured to the saddle. Yael, dressed in a plain robe with the hood low over her eyes, mounted the mare. They rode downhill, followed by two packhorses.

Near the bottom of the hill, coming around the last switchback onto the lowest section of the main street, they saw a large contingency of soldiers in rooster-comb helmets near the gate. The soldiers stood in several straight rows behind a single rider.

Yael stopped her mare. "Are they waiting for us?"

"Keep going," Deborah said. "The gates are open."

Coming closer at a constant trot, more details emerged. The soldiers held spears in the ready, which ruled out a quick escape. The sole rider up front wore a long red robe and sat with both legs to the right. Her face was veiled, but her identity was obvious.

"We're doomed," Yael said.

Deborah signaled with her hand for Yael to stay back. "It's only me she wants."

Princess Needa edged her horse forward and set aside her veil, revealing a pale, cold face.

Rogez stopped, and the two horses sniffed each other, huffing amiably.

Deborah spoke first. "The king promised me safe passage."

The princess sneered.

"Your constant sneering belies your beauty. Are you here to break the king's promise?"

"My brother made the promise to a Hebrew boy named Borah."

"That's me."

"Is it?" Princess Needa maneuvered her horse to come next to Rogez, reached with her hand to Deborah's cheek, and scratched off some of the stubble-paste. "And still, she persists."

Her heart pounding, Deborah grabbed the hilt of her sword, intending to take the princess hostage and make a run for it, but a ray of sun shone on Princess Needa's face, which was free of hate.

Dropping her hand off the hilt, Deborah asked, "How did you figure it out?"

"Once my anger at the Elixirist cooled down, I pondered the whole castration charade and tried to find an explanation. I reflected on the way you had looked at the handsome Hebrew soldier that night in the raving, and how upset you seemed in the morning after he'd left. There could only be one explanation."

"The poor scribe," Deborah said. "He'll never recover."

The princess smiled, which brightened her face. "Once I realized you were a girl, like me, I understood why the words you had said to me in the palace reached into my heart."

"I meant every word," Deborah said. "Before the marriage ceremony by the edge of the crater, Judge Ohad had told me that you actually loved Mamreh and wanted to marry him. I tried to stop Sallan's plans, but he refused, fearing your brother. I rode out to find General Mazabi and begged him to abort the attack and talk to the Hebrews about a truce that would let you stay with Mamreh. He wouldn't listen to me."

"Sall has always been too crafty for his own good, and General Mazabi was too traumatized by a broken truce that cost him an army and an arm, so he barreled ahead with his chariots into the clever ambush that you had inspired."

"Me?"

"The stones and burning tumbleweeds that had welcomed the men of Judah when they approached Beersheba at night – your success gave Mamreh the idea to use fire to drive the chariots over the cliff."

"It's my curse," Deborah said. "The more I try to prevent bloodshed, the worse it gets. I especially regret having to—"

"You had to defend yourself," the princess said. "It doesn't diminish my grief, but we must put our anger in the past to allow for a better future. When you become Queen of the Hebrews and bring peace to Canaan, please come back to visit us, and our respective nations will sign a real treaty of friendship."

Deborah smiled. "May the Gods keep both of us safe until that glorious day arrives."

Princess Needa dropped the veil back over her face and returned her horse to stand in front of the rows of soldiers, who raised their spears up into the air, not in a hurtling posture, but in an honorable salute. Deborah beckoned Yael, and they rode out of Bozra.

36

When Barac reached the top of the hill, the workers across from Judge Ohad's house were already framing the walls of the new house. The guard was sitting on a rock, his back against the flagpole under the yellow banner of Judah.

Inside the courtyard, Barac was relieved to see the new slaves sitting together on the ground and eating bread, cheese, and apples, while a large jar of milk was being passed around.

Tsruyah appeared in the judge's window on the second floor, saw Barac, and leaned with both hands on the windowsill, shaking his head. "What's wrong now, boy?"

"Nothing is wrong," Barac said. "I walked around the city and was very impressed."

"Impressed? Why?"

The courtyard quieted down, everyone listening to the exchange.

"The men of Judah have come prepared to share the city, with hammers to build new houses and many families to live in them."

"That's impossible. How could they have families here already?"

"They planned it," Barac said. "Their families travelled right behind the army, confident in their victory."

The smirk faded from Tsruyah's face. "Based on what?"

"Because Yahweh is with them, not with those who worship false gods. In fact, I think the people of Beersheba seem content to live under the rule of Judah."

"That's a lie," Tsruyah shouted. "I rule Beersheba!"

Barac pointed to the gate. "Have you permitted the building of a bigger house on higher grounds for a new judge of Judah?"

Tsruyah craned his neck to see over the front wall of the courtyard, rising on his toes, but in vein. He groaned in frustration, disappeared from the window, and emerged from the bottom of the stairs, still without headdress or sandals. He ran across the courtyard and out the gate.

The soldiers in the courtyard looked at each other.

A moment later, he was back, his face red. "Bring my horse!"

While Tsruyah ran back upstairs to his room, presumably to get dressed, the Cainite woman came down and approached Barac.

"He says you must leave," she said. "He says you should go quickly, before he changes his mind and whips you for your insults." She held forth a folded robe of fine fabric. "That's from me, for your kindness. My name is Na'ama."

"Thank you." Barac took the robe. "If I see Yael again, I'll tell her that you're well."

Na'ama pressed his hand. "Where will she go with Borah after Edom? Do you know?"

"I expect they'll travel north to Borah's family homestead in the land of Ephraim."

His answer seemed to exacerbate her worries. "We're of the Cainite Clan. Everyone hates us. How will I find my daughter in that vast land?"

"Their homestead is in the Samariah Hills, near Emanuel."

"I heard of Emanuel. What is Borah's father's name, which I should ask for?"

He leaned closer and whispered in her ear. "Don't tell anyone, but Borah's real name is Deborah, daughter of Harutz of Ephraim."

The shock on Na'ama's face quickly turned to joy. She laughed out loud, hugged Barac, and planted a kiss on his cheek, before running back to the stairs leading up to the judge's room.

Tova had already packed food and water for the road. She changed the red robe for a plain travel robe and got in the saddle behind him. They rode downhill. Near the gates, the area formerly taken by the decrepit dwellings of the poor was nearly cleared up, and men of Judah were laying down wooden beams for a new building.

Outside the gates, the enslaved men, women, and children sat on the ground, dust coating their tattered clothes, faces, and hair. Some of the children were crying. None of the men tried to challenge the guards.

He heard Tova sniffle behind him and glanced back at her.

She wiped her eyes. "There was nothing you could have done."

Across the way, the fairgrounds had filled up with more merchant caravans. He saw the old Moabite merchant, who smiled and waved them over.

"Didn't I tell you?" He surveyed the busy fairgrounds as if it were his doing. "Everyone knows there's good bargains to make after a skirmish."

Barac glanced at the captured poor. "Some bargains may be profitable, but still sinful."

"May the Gods forgive us all." The merchant patted Barac's horse. "And may they watch over you on the road."

A young man joined them, bearing a plate of hot breads. He was about Barac's age, though slimmer, with straight black hair, sparse stubble on his chin, and intelligent eyes that narrowed to a slit when he smiled. Barac and Tova dismounted and thanked him, accepting a piece of bread each.

"This is my eldest son," the merchant said. "His name is Zariz, which makes me Abu Zariz."

"I am Barac, son of Abinoam. And this is my wife, Tova."

They stood in a circle, chewing on the bread.

When they were done, the merchant sent his son to bring a jar of wine, which he handed to Barac. "For your journey," he said.

"Thank you, but we cannot drink your wine."

"Why?"

"It's forbidden to us."

Puzzled, the young man looked at his father.

"Take no offense," the old merchant said. "Their God forbids drinking any wine touched by those who don't believe in him."

The puzzlement didn't leave his son's face.

Abu Zariz chuckled. "Most of the Hebrews we meet on our travels aren't keen on this particular prohibition, or on their God's laws in general."

Barac bowed his head. "We're grateful for your kindness."

"Will you have milk?"

"Yes, thank you."

The young man brought a jug of milk, which Tova put in the saddle pocket.

Abu Zariz fed a piece of bread to the horse. "Where are you heading?"

"My family is of Naphtali," Barac said.

"All the way to the north? That's a long journey."

"I wouldn't know. My grandfather came south to the Samariah Hills, and I grew up there and never travelled north, but now I must return to my tribe."

Zariz perked up. "We travelled in the Samariah Hills last spring. Do you know Emanuel?"

His father gave him a stern look.

"Emanuel?" Barac smiled. "That's where I grew up."

Zariz's eyes widened. "Do you know a girl named Deborah? Her parents were killed—"

"Son," Abu Zariz said. "That's enough."

Barac could hardly breathe. "How do you know Deborah?"

Abu Zariz answered for him. "Some months ago, we found her alone on the road north of Emanuel and took her to Shiloh. That's the last we saw of her."

"Now, I remember. You're the Moabite boy who taught her to ride a horse, shoot arrows, and draw a map. She told me about you."

His eyes glistening, Zariz smiled. "She taught me how to throw stones while blindfolded. Is she well?"

"She was when I saw her a few days ago."

Zariz exhaled in relief. "Where?"

"Near Mount Avdat, south of here. She was on her way to Bozra. The king of Edom had promised her a reward for rescuing his sister. It's a long story, but if all goes well, she plans to travel back to Emanuel, marry a man of Ephraim, and claim her father's inheritance."

"No," Zariz cried. "She shouldn't!"

His father placed a calming hand on his forearm. "My son is concerned because we know the trouble awaiting her in Emanuel. She had humiliated the judge's son in a public trial. Everyone speaks of it in the Samariah Hills. We also avoid the place these days, which is unfortunate. Judge Zifron is a reasonable man, but his son is dangerous."

"True," Barac said. "Seesya ambushed Deborah in Ein Gedi, but she managed to defeat his soldiers and injure him badly. He might have drowned in the Sea of Salt, or died in the desert."

Abu Zariz shook his head. "That's the fate he deserved, but it didn't come to him. We heard that he was saved by a Canaanite caravan, treated by the personal healer of the king of Hazor, and returned to Emanuel, nastier than before."

"Father," Zariz said. "We should go to Bozra and warn Deborah."

"Taking sides in local skirmishes is not the way of the travelling merchant. Besides, the Hebrew tribes have been fighting each other since their namesakes were boys in their father Jacob's house. It's their way, and we must keep out of it."

"Then you go," Zariz said to Barac. "Tell her not to return to the Samariah Hills."

Barac chuckled sadly. "I might as well tell the sun not to rise. The only thing Deborah cares about is going back to Palm Homestead. It's what she lives for, and it's what she would die for, if she must. She may already be on her way from Edom to Canaan."

Behind them, men were shouting orders. Barac turned to watch as the men of Judah pushed the newly enslaved poor to line up in rows.

Tova tugged at his sleeve. "We should leave now, before Tsruyah arrives."

"Wait," Zariz said. "What about Deborah?"

"She'll prevail," Barac said. "In the end, Seesya will lay dead at her feet."

"How do you know?"

"God will stand with her."

"Your God hasn't been very kind to Debora, so far. I fear what will happen if Seesya gets another chance to kill her."

Barac felt a wave of kinship with the Moabite boy, who obviously loved Deborah as deeply as he did and would have travelled far and wide to help her, if his father allowed it. Glancing back at Tova, he was relieved when she nodded.

"You're right," Barac said. "She is in danger. Can you tell me the best way to travel to the Samariah Hills from here?"

"Look here." Abu Zariz used a stick to draw a map in the sand. "You have two options. One is to go east to Kabetzel and Arad, then north to Hebron, Bethlehem, Jerusalem, and Bethel, where you'll ride into the Samariah Hills toward Emanuel. The second option is to ride west, but not as far as Gerar, where the Philistines roam in search of easy prey, and take the road north to Lachish and Yarmut, and then east to Gibeon in the land of Benjamin. From there, it's a straight road up to Bethel and Emanuel."

"Which way is better?"

Abu Zariz peered at the map. "Either way, you'll spend most of the time in the land of Judah. In the east, you'll face the risk of outlaws from Arabia, who wander in from beyond Edom and Moab to rob lone travelers. You'll be safer with a larger group, but if it's only you two, then spend the nights in villages or towns, and never camp alone. In the west, the Philistines are wise not to bother merchants like us for fear of disturbing the trade in and out of Gaza, but they're known to enslave any Hebrews they can catch, as the Hebrews do to them."

"I know," Barac said. "Deborah told me about the tannery in Aphek, where the hard labor was done by Philistine slaves. One of those slaves figured out she was a girl and attacked her at night."

"No!" Zariz clenched his fists. "Did he—"

"He failed to actually rape her, thanks to the intervention of a group leader, a Philistine named Petro, who went on to drown the attacker in the river. Later, she repaid him by devising a plan of escape for all the Philistine slaves."

"I knew it was her!" Zariz beamed. "All over the lands of Manasseh and Ephraim men are talking about the great escape from largest tannery in all of Canaan, which was found empty one morning, the guards gagged and blindfolded, and not a single slave left behind to tell the owner how it was done."

"She turned the roofs of the pavilions into rafts, and the Philistine slaves floated down the Yarkon River to the coast of the Great Sea, where they reunited with their people."

"Roofs made into rafts – only Deborah could come up with something like that."

"It won't happen again," his father said. "Now every master brands his slaves on the cheek with hot iron to make sure they'll be never pass for free men or women."

Gazing at the drawn map, Barac memorized it. "We'll take the east route," he said. "It's closer to where Deborah will travel up from Bozra, and if God wills it, our paths will intersect."

The men of Judah, meanwhile, began to inspect the lines of new slaves. They pulled out the elderly and invalid, and sent them back into the city, while their families cried, and whips lashed anyone who objected.

Barely resisting the urge to interfere, Barac mounted his horse, waited for Tova to settle in behind him, and nudged his horse forward while Tova waved back at Abu Zariz and his son.

They rode toward the rising sun, leaving Beersheba and its foul sounds and smells behind. It was some time before he could speak calmly.

"I hope you understand," Barac said. "I cannot sit idle while Deborah falls into the bloody hands of Seesya."

"I expect no less, husband." Tova said from behind. "It's a curious thing how her name pops up everywhere we go."

"And now it will be us who pop up where she's going."

37

After a long day of riding in the heat and a quiet night in Kabetzel, Barac was up early. He watched the sun rising over the horizon and imagined Arad, nestled among the distant peaks where the trade routes split – right to Edom and left to Canaan. He would ride left, heading north into the Judean Mountains, and pass through the great cities of Judah – Hebron, Bethlehem, and Jerusalem.

Before the sun cleared the jagged horizon, they were already back on the road, heading north-east toward Arad. Not much later, Tova tapped his shoulder, and he looked back. Behind them, a band of riders was catching up. Soon, they were upon them.

One of them asked, "Are you Barac, son of Abinoam?"

There was no point in denying. "Yes."

"Judge Yoaz orders you back to Beersheba."

Barac kept his hands on the reins. A sword fight would be futile, and running for it was equally hopeless. "I was told to leave Beersheba by Tsruyah, the judge of Simeon."

"Simeon has no judge. Turn around, or we'll make you."

They rode back with the group of men, who didn't speak and only paused to drink from waterskins that hung from their saddles. By midday, the heat was unbearable, and Tova almost fell off the saddle a few times. In the afternoon, riding into the glaring sun was sheer torture, but the men of Judah kept going.

From a distance, Beersheba glowed in the twilight with countless fires and torches. Closer yet, Barac could see a large number of people between the fairgrounds and the gates of the city. An elevated platform had been erected and, one by one, the newly enslaved climbed up onto the platform to be offered for sale by an auctioneer, whose booming voice travelled far.

"This boy of ten will be like wet clay in its owner's hands," he declared. "Look at his strong arms and legs. Lean and supple as a youthful deer!"

Several hands rose among the pack of foreign merchants, and after a brief auction, the boy was sold and taken away, his arms and legs bound by ropes that allowed him to walk, but not to run. Meanwhile, a man was led up with his wife and a child of about five.

"Three slaves for the price of one-and-a-half," the slave master announced. "And soon, this fertile woman and her healthy husband will give their master more young slaves every year while working in his kitchen, tending his sheep, and harvesting his fields."

The small family was sold quickly.

The men stopped at a large, open-sided tent. In its shade, Tsruyah lounged on cushions, drawing smoke from a wooden pipe. Yoaz sat in an armchair, which Barac recognized as Judge Ohad's chair. He beckoned Barac, who dismounted while Tova stayed in the saddle.

Yoaz offered him a pipe.

Barac declined.

"You left without my blessing."

"Yahweh's blessing is all I seek," Barac said. "I left because Tsruyah told me to go."

"I did not," Tsruyah said, smoke petering from his mouth.

"Your woman delivered the message."

"What woman?"

"Na'ama"

Tsruyah cleared his throat and spat a fat glob of sputum. "A whore of the Cainite Clan doesn't speak for me."

"It doesn't matter," Yoaz said. "You should have sought my permission."

Barac shrugged. "I served as a soldier for Simeon, and the order of dismissal came from the judge of Simeon."

"Simeon no longer has a judge."

Tsruyah looked away, puffing on his pipe.

"It's for the better," Yoaz said. "A judge needs the people's confidence in his wisdom, righteousness, and knowledge of God's laws. Tsruyah agreed that his skills fit better with the important role of leading soldiers, and his first assignment requires your participation."

"I'm not interested," Barac said.

"You're interested in freedom, yes?"

Barac nodded.

"Freedom comes with a price."

"Will I be free to leave with my wife afterward?"

Yoaz smiled. "Yes."

"What's the assignment?"

"It's simple." Yoaz glanced at Tsruyah. "This time of year, Simeon's herds of sheep and goats go to graze in the green pastures near Gerar. We worry that the shepherds might hear the news from Beersheba and seek refuge in the hills, sell the herds to another tribe, or to the Philistines. We must secure the herds as soon as possible. The shepherds know you as Mamreh's deputy. They'll trust your assurances, and Tsruyah will keep them safe on the way back to Beersheba."

Barac understood what was being asked of him, but wasn't sure what God would think of it. "There are two problems," he said. "One, I will not commit the sin of lying."

"Tell them the truth," Yoaz said. "Tell them everything that happened here. Tell them that their families are safe and that no harm shall come to them, either. Tell them that life has returned to normal in Beersheba, with every man living in peace under his vines and fig trees."

"There's a second problem," Barac said. "As soon as the herds are secured, Tsruyah will murder me and my wife."

Tsruyah grinned.

"Wipe the grin off your face," Yoaz said. "Take an oath right now, in the name of Yahweh and all the false Gods you worship, that no harm will come to this young man and his wife."

"Accidents happen," Tsruyah said. "Am I this boy's keeper?"

"Swear to it!"

"I swear in the name of Yahweh and all the other Gods that I and my men will not touch Barac, son of Abinoam, and his wife."

"If you do," Yoaz said, "I'll find out and have you whipped."

Tsruyah shrugged.

"It's settled, then," Yoaz said. "At sunrise, you'll head west and find those herds."

38

Deborah and Yael traveled from Bozra with an Edomite caravan of several merchants and their families. The journey through the hot, barren land was slow, but uneventful. They stopped for the night at a small oasis, nestled in the foothills of the Seir Mountains, where she had stopped with Sallan on the way to Beersheba. They gave the four horses water and food before sitting down to eat.

The leader of the caravan, a gray-haired man with small hands and a large belly, beckoned Yael from the entrance to his tent.

She looked at Deborah.

"Take the tent peg, just in case."

Yael giggled, patted the pocket of her robe, and went over to him.

That night, Deborah slept alone in their tent, waking up several times to the sound of laughter.

They continued the next day, passing over the ridges of the Seir Mountains, followed by a long trudge across the arid desert flats, arriving at Tamar near sunset. In the few remaining moments of light, Deborah visited the grave of the old healer with Yael, who was fascinated with the story. After sunset, Yael left their camp for a long time, returning late at night, coins jingling in her pocket.

"Welcome back," Deborah said.

Yael slipped under the blanket. "Why are you still awake?"

"Not for the same reason as you."

Yael laughed. "I hope not."

"Aren't you afraid of those men?"

"They're merchants and craftsmen, not outlaws. I sell them my pretty goods for a fair price, leaving no one disappointed."

"Some men don't need a reason to hurt a girl."

"They can try." Yael pulled a copper tent peg from her pocket. "I wonder if Judge Ohad realized I was using his gift to finish him off."

The memory made Deborah shudder. "Why did God make men this way?"

"What way?"

"Slaves to their worst depravities – pride, envy, power, greed, lust, hate – I don't understand them."

"Yet you're chasing one across the desert."

Deborah rose on one elbow. "I'm not chasing Barac. I know where he is."

"In the middle of war between the tribes."

"Yes, he's there to defend the people of Simeon, because he's righteous, honorable, and brave, unlike the merchants and craftsmen you cavort with."

"He's no different, I assure you." Yael pulled the blanket up to her chin. "All men are slaves to lust. I bet you there's a girl in his bed tonight."

"You're wrong. Barac is thinking about me with fondness and longing every moment he's awake. We captured each other's heart, which is very different from what you're selling."

"At least I'm honest about what I sell." Yael turned away. "Your problem is that you pretend to be a man, but you have no idea what men are really like."

39

In the morning, Tsruyah left Beersheba with twenty mounted men in long robes and drooping headdresses, heading west along the trade route. Barac, with Tova in saddle behind him, rode some distance behind to stay out of the dusty cloud raised by the riders. Once they left the ring of homesteads in the vicinity of Beersheba, the desert became vast, barren, and empty, except for a couple of merchant caravans coming in the opposite direction from Gaza.

Tsruyah kept a fast pace until midday, when he stopped for water at a spring by the Patish Stream. The men rested in the shade of a droopy jujube tree, while the horses nibbled at a few shrubs by the spring. Resuming the journey, they rode fast at first, but the horses soon slowed down, tired and hot. Tsruyah stopped for one more rest in the afternoon and continued riding through the twilight and into the night. They camped on the side of the road for a few hours of sleep. The next day took them from the flat desert land into low hills. In the evening, they arrived at a hill covered in ruins. Only one house was standing, light glowing in its windows. A farmer came out with a long spear in one hand and a torch in the other. He was a large man who seemed capable of knocking down several men with his bare hands.

"Blessings of Simeon upon you," Tsruyah said. "We come from Beersheba to seek our shepherds. May we camp here for the night?"

Barac noticed that Tsruyah didn't introduce himself by name.

"Welcome to Gerar." The farmer had a strong voice that fit his barrel chest. "You may camp here for the night and, if you have a few coins, you'll receive some food, too."

Tsruyah paid the farmer, who started a fire and brought out dry meat, old bread, and hard cheese. While they ate, the farmer stepped a short distance away with the torch and held it high to illuminate the neighboring ruins.

"These are the remains of Gerar," he said. "It was ruled by a great dynasty of kings called Avimelekh."

The word meant "Father of a king," and Barac chuckled at this literal use of the name.

"Each of them deserved the name, except the last one." The farmer held the torch over a pile of rocks. "This is where our forefather Abraham stood on his arrival from Ur and lied to King Avimelekh, as the Holy Scriptures tell us." He quoted from memory. "And Abraham said of Sarah his wife: "She is my sister." And Avimelekh, king of Gerar, took Sarah for himself, for she was more beautiful than all his wives. That night, God came to him in a dream and said, "The woman whom you took, she is a man's wife." And when King Avimelekh confronted Abraham, he admitted it, saying, "Because I thought: Surely the fear of God is not in this place; and they will slay me for my wife's sake. Moreover, she is indeed my sister, the daughter of my father, but not the daughter of my mother, and so she became my wife." And King Avimelekh gave Abraham many sheep, oxen, and servants, and also, restored Sarah to him as his wife. He said to Abraham, "Behold, my land is before you, dwell where it pleases you." And Abraham settled right here, in Gerar, but God punished King Avimelekh and sealed up all the wombs in the house of Avimelekh, because he had taken Sarah, Abraham's wife."

Tova cleared up the empty bowls and took them inside. She came out with a jug of wine, pour it in the men's cups, and said to Barac, "I'll sleep inside with the women. Good night, brother."

They laughed, and the farmer clapped his big hands.

The men stayed by the fire, drinking wine, while the farmer entertained them with stories about the glorious past of Gerar and its decline from a city to a village, and then, a place of ruins where only one man of Simeon resided with his family in the same spot where Abraham had built a home to share with his beautiful sister-wife Sarah.

40

Before they left Tamar, Yael went to the market and bought bread, goat milk, palm dates, and several colorful dresses, which she packed away. With the sun rising over the ridges of the Seir Mountains, they took the north-west trade route toward Arad. The road was rugged and monotonous, but Deborah recognized occasional landmarks from the recent trip with Sallan. This time, however, no caravans crossed their path.

Two days later, they reached Arad, where a single man of Judah collected a coin from each group for a spot at the empty fairgrounds. Deborah asked him about the absence of caravans heading the other way. He shrugged and said nothing. When darkness came, she noticed that there were only few fires in the town. Had the men of Goor-Aryeh not returned yet, or had they come and gone again for a second attack on Beersheba?

After a modest evening meal by the fire she had started, Deborah watched Yael put on one of her colorful new dresses and go into Arad. Deborah went to sleep. Through the cloth side of the tent, she listened to Rogez breathing, shuffling his hooves, and slapping his tail to ward off flies. Reassured that he would warn her of danger, she was able to fall asleep.

The night was quiet, and she didn't wake up when Yael returned, either because the girl had kept her coins from jingling, or because she had earned none. Deborah did wake up, however, when a baby cried nearby. It seemed like a dream at first, but the sound persisted, and she tossed aside the blanket and got up to look.

A group of women were huddled by the embers left from the fire. She counted six, in addition to their children and the crying baby. With Yael's help, Deborah added twigs and rekindled the fire. She saw that the baby was trying to feed, but kept turning away from the breast, which was likely dry. She gave the mother a waterskin. The mother drank until it was empty. When she brought the baby to her breast, he latched on.

Yael handed out pieces of bread and dry fruit, which they ate quickly.

Deborah asked the mother, "Is this your first baby?"

"Third, all boys, but he's the only one to survive the circumcision fever."

"Circumcision fever? I've never heard of it.

"Who would tell you? The priests?"

"I'm sorry for your loss. What's his name?"

"Zerakh, son of Hamuel of Simeon. I am Leah."

After a while, the baby fell asleep. Leah wiped his lips gently and covered herself. In the light of the fire, his face was peaceful. Deborah could not take her eyes off his tiny features, which were delicate to the point of perfection.

Leah cradled Zerakh in one arm, reached for a piece of bread, and took a bite.

"May I hold him?" As soon as the words left her lips, Deborah realized how strange her request must seem, coming from a soldier. "For a moment," she added, "while you eat."

Leah turned slightly as if to shelter the baby. "It's your fault Zerakh will have no father to raise him."

"My fault?"

"You didn't return to save Beersheba again."

Deborah was stunned. Not only had the woman recognized her as Borah, but she implied that Judah had mounted a second attack on Beersheba. She thought of Goor-Aryeh's words: "We didn't come here to kill the people of Simeon. I ordered my men to subdue the guards and any soldiers they confront and hurt no one who didn't raise a weapon." She feared asking how many had been killed.

Leah rocked the baby. "Why didn't you return, Borah?"

What could she say? That she had gone to Edom instead? "I went with Judge Ohad to bring Mamreh and his soldiers back to Beersheba for reinforcement, but I failed."

"We heard they died at the Ramon Crater." The mother put her ear to the baby's nose to verify he was breathing. "We thought the

Edomites killed you, too, but here you are, alive and well."

"How did you hear about the Ramon Crater?"

"From the blacksmith's son. He alone came back and tried to defend us from Judah, but our new judge negotiated an unfair truce."

"New judge?"

"The cursed Tsruyah. He sold us into slavery. Our husbands went to other masters, we don't even know where they'll be sent."

"How could he do that? The Holy Scriptures forbid enslaving fellow Hebrew as plunder in war."

"God has abandoned us." The mother's voice was flat, devoid of emotions.

"Why did Tsruyah give in to Judah? He likes to fight."

"For fifty slaves, that's what I heard."

Deborah pressed her hands together. "What about the blacksmith's son?"

"When Tsruyah went to negotiate with Judah, the blacksmith's son called up everyone to defend the walls. The people came, because he was Borah's friend." Leah shrugged. "If not for his fortifications, Tsruyah would have let Judah enslaved all the people of Beersheba, not only us – the poor and helpless."

"What happened to him?"

"I told you." Leah looked at her, eyes red with reflections of the flames. "Judah gave him fifty slaves, and he lives in Judge Ohad's house, sleeps with the judge's Cainite whore, and drinks the judge's wine with his soldiers."

Deborah glanced at Yael, who looked away. "I meant, what happened to the blacksmith's son?"

"Oh, him. He left Beersheba with his wife."

"Wife? What wife?"

"The girl he had brought with him."

"Brought from where?"

"A village in the south."

"Are you sure we speak of the same person? Barac, son of Abinoam, the new blacksmith from Emanuel?"

"I'm poor, not stupid," Leah said. "He was Mamreh's deputy. A handsome boy with black curls and a warm smile."

"You must be mistaken. There couldn't be a girl with Barac. He went to Beersheba alone."

"He didn't arrive alone. I heard he got her as a gift from the people of Revivim after he saved them from a band of Judah. She's a nice girl, too, very pretty, with wide hips for childbearing and ample breasts to feed them." Leah's sad face broke into a smile. "His eyes were shining when he looked at her. I could tell he lusted fervently for that girl."

Yael cleared her throat and made a face that said, "I told you."

Deborah became short of breath, as if someone pressed on her chest. "It's impossible. You're confusing him with someone else."

"It was him," Leah said. "I was working at the judge's house when the priest blessed their marriage over a slaughtered goat, and the blacksmith's son possessed the girl in a room off the courtyard. With my own eyes I saw the bloodstain on the bedcloth."

Scrambling to her feet, Deborah ran to the edge of the fairgrounds and into the dark desert, where she stopped and hugged herself, struggling to breathe.

Shining eyes!

Lusted fervently!

A bloody bedcloth!

Her baby was fatherless, like Zerakh!

She fell to the ground and wept.

41

At sunrise, the men got back on the horses. Tova stayed with the farmer's wives and daughters while Barac joined the search for the herds. As they rode west, the desert hills turned to green pasture. They spent the night under a tree by a spring. The next day, they saw a herd of sheep grazing on a distant hill.

Leaving the men behind, Tsruyah and Barac rode over to speak with the shepherd. He seemed wary of Tsruyah, but remembered Barac fondly from before Mamreh had departed Beersheba. Barac told him everything that had happened in the city recently and explained the truce with Judah. The shepherd, whose family was back in Beersheba, agreed to return with the herd, as well as to assist them in finding the other herds.

They spent the rest of the afternoon and the following day gathering the other herds. The shepherds listened to Barac, who assured them that Beersheba is at peace and, although the men of Judah have the upper hand in controlling the city, they seem dedicated to making Beersheba flourish under Yahweh's laws. The shepherds agreed to return home with their flocks.

They travelled slowly, heading south-east, and reached the ruins of Gerar late into the night, when the air was cool and fresh. Barac was happy to reunite with Tova, and she confessed to spending much of the time praying for his safe return.

After a short meal provided by the farmer, the shepherds resumed the journey to Beersheba in the dark, planning to rest during the hot days. Tsruyah's men lit up torches and spread in a wide circle to protect the moving herds from any predators.

Tsruyah mounted his horse and looked down to Barac. "That's it, blacksmith's son. Stay away from the land of Simeon."

"You mean, the land of Judah."

"Cleverness won't help you where you're going." Tsruyah laughed as he turned his horse and rode off.

"Imagine what God is saying," Tova said. "Why did I create Tsruyah? What was I thinking?"

The farmer laughed.

"Don't worry," Barac said. "He can't harm us anymore."

The farmer stayed by the fire with Barac, drinking wine, while Tova went to sleep.

"It's good land," Barac said. "There's pasture and trees a short distance from here."

"It's the moisture in the air," the farmer said. "We're only a couple of days' ride from the coast of the Great Sea."

Indeed, Barac had noticed that the air smelled differently than in Beersheba, or even in Emanuel. "Are there other Hebrew villages nearby?"

"Not anymore. The Philistines have killed or enslaved everyone."

A baby inside cried, and jackals howled in the night. Barac gazed into the dark, imagining a band of Philistines lurking nearby. "Why do you stay here?"

"My oldest wife is a Philistine from Gaza. Her brothers sold her to me. I give them gifts whenever they visit, and they guarantee our safety."

"How often do they come?"

The farmer emptied his cup. "Actually, they were here earlier."

42

The women and children were still asleep when Deborah got up at dawn. She found a crevice a few hundred steps away to practice with her sword. At first, her arms were heavy, her mind numb, and her blade wayward. An all-consuming sadness weighed down on her, almost as heavy as on that terrible day in Emanuel, when she had sat in a circle among the maidens and watched her beautiful, kind, loving sister being stoned to death for a sin she hadn't committed.

With each stab and slash of the blade, Deborah's mind progressed on a staircase of memories. Some stairs went down with painful setbacks that had tested her resolve and fueled her despair, whereas other stairs went up with breakthroughs, such as the day she had finally found Kassite and convinced him to help her, lifting her closer to her True Calling. It was a long staircase, and when she took a step down with the memory of the dreary tunnel at the bottom of Kassite's abandoned copper mine – the lowest point in her journey – she recalled the eagle's visit and the flight they had taken together over the Samariah Hills, allowing her to witness a future that was possible if she persisted. The eagle had said, "Defeatism is self-fulfilling, but so is the determination to win."

When Deborah returned to camp, Yael walked out to meet her, far enough that their voices would not reach the others.

"Last night," Yael said, "I asked Leah if she knew where Barac had gone. Apparently, he left Beersheba with his young wife. Perhaps they went back to Revivim."

Deborah shook her head.

"Where else? The land of Naphtali?"

"It doesn't matter. Barac is dead to me."

"What? You are angry with him?"

"I can't be angry with someone who no longer exists."

"He should be angry at you," Yael said. "Whose fault was it that he left? Who drove him into another girl's arms?"

"A man who hops from one girl to another is like a breeding bull – all loins, no heart."

"All men are." Yael lowered her voice. "Don't you understand? A pretty smile, a shock of luscious hair, a whiff of feminine scent, and they're enthralled in overwhelming lust. It's their nature. Barac can't help being a man."

"My father wasn't like that," Deborah said.

"No girl wants to believe her father can lose his head to lust, but a man is a man."

"Sallan isn't like that, either. He loved one girl, and when she died, he was forever broken."

Yael was quiet for a moment. "Yes, he told me."

"Really?"

"Why are you surprised? Men like to talk, especially to pretty girls who show interest."

Deborah shook her head. "You're too much. I'm lucky not to be a real man."

"You're more a man than many of them. Sallan told me that, as well."

"What else did he tell you?"

"His whole life story. It's very sad. That girl, An, was everything to him, and then, he caused her death."

"How?"

"Apparently, he saved Bozra from an Egyptian army by making a Male Elixir for thousands of women, who became a new army to replace their dead fathers, brothers, husbands, and sons. The girl, An, insisted on drinking it, too."

"And it killed her?"

"In a way." Yael took a deep breath, recalling the story. "After the victory, the king forced An's father, the high priest, to give her to Sallan as a wife. They married before all the people in the temple and spent their first night – the happiest night of his life, Sallan said – in his family home. He stayed in bed, while she went to prepare a meal for him. He was very tired after days of nonstop preparations for the battle – not to mention a night of lovemaking – and fell back asleep.

When he woke up at midday, she was gone."

"Dead?"

"Gone from the house. He later found out that the king had gathered two dozen pretty girls during the night and sent them with guards on a journey to Egypt as a reconciliation gift to the Pharaoh. An heard about it, put on the armor and weapons she still had from serving in the imitation army, got a horse from the stable, and left Bozra to save the girls."

"By herself?"

"Sallan blames his Male Elixir. He thinks it must have infused An with excessive masculine aggression and overconfidence, transforming her into a reckless teenage boy who thinks he's invincible."

"What happened to her?"

"She caught up with them, wielding a sword. The guards mistook her for an outlaw, killed her, and kept going. They later reported that scavengers started tearing up the corpse within moments. Sallan spent weeks scouring the desert for her remains, but only found one of her boots."

They sat in silence for a while, thinking of the brave girl who broke Sallan's heart.

"There's a lesson here," Yael said. "Barac isn't dead. He can still be your husband and a father to your child."

"I'd rather raise the child alone than be a second wife to a man who used me for his carnal pleasure and forgot me the next day."

"No man can forget you."

"He must be an exception." Deborah raised her hand. "Enough. Don't mention his name to me ever again."

"Back to Bozra, then?"

"No."

"You're with a child. Sallan and his mother can protect you."

"Going back won't bring me closer to my destination."

"Your destination is a dangerous place."

Deborah lowered her hand on the hilt of her sword. "I can fight."

"You're brave, but you're also an orphan girl wearing a soldier's costume."

"My strength comes from God, not from weapons."

"Are you trying to get us killed?"

"Of course not." Deborah sighed. "You're turning into an argumentative Hebrew."

"I descend from Cain – the first man to bicker with God."

"My father told us the story of Cain and Abel. Tamar and I laughed when he imitated Cain's feigned innocence." Deborah smiled at the memory. "Am I my brother's keeper?"

Yael looked at her for a long moment. "How can you smile after everything that's happened to you?"

"I think of happy times."

"What about the terrible times, the disasters, the suffering you've gone through?"

"Remember Sallan's proverb?" Deborah imitated his hoarse voice and Edomite accent. "What fails to destroy you makes you harder to destroy."

Yael smiled, nodding slowly. "It's true."

"Besides, I'm not completely without friends in Canaan. We can stay with them until we figure out what to do next."

"Who?"

"A group of lepers in Ein Gedi."

The look of incredulity on Yael's face made Deborah laugh.

A man advanced toward them from the gate across the road. As he came closer, Deborah recognized him by the scar on his left cheek.

"Borah," he said. "Welcome back."

She nodded.

He glanced at Rogez. "No one has killed you for your horse yet?"

"Whoever tries, dies." She kept eye contact with him. "Where is Judge Goor-Aryeh?"

"He's in Ziklag, shamed by leading us into a trap in the first attack on Beersheba."

"It wasn't his fault."

"It was yours." He laughed. "First, you saved the city of Simeon by humiliating the men of Judah, and then, you helped the leader of Judah escape Simeon's fire. Whose side are you on?"

"Yahweh's side."

His laughter died.

"God sent me to Simeon," she said. "He wanted me to find an

Edomite princess and bring her back to her people, who would have otherwise become sworn enemies of all the Hebrews. She's home safely now."

He picked at his scar. "Then why are you here again?"

"Yahweh hasn't told me yet." Deborah pointed at the women and children. "Are these your slaves?"

"Why do you care?"

"I gave them food and water last night. Their owner owes me for it." She held out her hand. "A silver coin would do."

He showed her empty hands. "I have no silver. Only these women to sell."

"In violation of God's laws?"

"They need new husbands, or masters, and I need to feed my hungry children."

"They wouldn't need new husbands if you hadn't sold theirs."

"At least we didn't kill them."

Disgusted, Deborah looked away, her eyes resting on the Edomite caravan, where the women were out preparing the morning meal. "I may be able to talk my Edomite friends into buying the women."

"Really?" He became excited. "Eighteen silver coins for all of them, children included."

Deborah calculated in her head. He was asking three coins per woman. She could afford it, but failing to negotiate would make him suspicious. How did traders negotiate? She recalled Abu-Zariz's advice: "A successful trade is always based on a fair balance of mutually assured exaggerations and understatements."

"The leader is a shrewd merchant," she said. "He might buy the women, but he's not going to waste silver on children who eat and do no work. Will you keep them?"

"I have enough of my own." He sighed. "I'll accept seventeen coins for the whole lot."

"If you throw in three jars of water and three donkeys, I think he would agree to ten coins."

"Sixteen," he said.

"Eleven."

"Fifteen."

"Thirteen, and that's too much already."

"I accept."

"And don't mention my presence here to anyone. If there's any trouble, you'll get nothing."

While he went back into Arad, Deborah told Yael to pack up the tent and prepare the women and children for the road. She put her blanket in the sack and took thirteen silver coins out of the purse. Lying to him about the involvement of the Edomite merchants in the deal was a sin, but otherwise he might have tried to rob her, which would force her to injure, or even kill him. She remembered what the eagle had said: "To do a lot of good, you often have to do a little bit of bad along the way." Here, to save six Hebrew women and their children from a life of slavery, she had to do a little bit of lying.

He returned with the jars of water and three scrawny donkeys. She handed him the coins, and he counted them while Yael filled the waterskins from the jars. Satisfied with the payment, his gaze lingered on Yael.

"Forget it," Deborah said. "Today is a Cainite holiday."

Yael giggled.

He looked at them suspiciously. "What holiday?"

"It's the anniversary of Abel's death."

As Yael burst out laughing, he grabbed the empty jars and hurried back across the road.

The Edomite caravan was getting ready to leave. Deborah told the women about the payment to their master and explained that they were free to stay, return to Beersheba, or join her and Yael on the road north. They immediately decided to join her and helped redistribute the loads between the two packhorses, the three donkeys, and the mare. Each animal carried a woman and two children. Yael joined Deborah on Rogez. As the Edomite caravan turned left out the fairgrounds, heading west toward Kabetzel and Beersheba, Deborah led her convoy to the right, back on the road eastward. It was early in the day, and no guard had been posted yet to collect fees from caravans wishing to stay overnight.

The climb uphill among the ruins was slow, but they reached the top without incident, and soon, Arad was out of sight. They proceeded at a slow pace toward the rising sun.

43

Barac and Tova slept near the animal corral behind the farmer's house. At first light, a kick to his ribs made Barac sit up and reach for his sword, which he'd placed beside him before lying down. The sword was gone, and several men stood over him and Tova, who remained asleep. They wore only loincloths and sandals, and their dark complexion resembled ripe olives. They had rust-colored hair, cropped close to the scalp. One held Barac's sword while the others bound his arms behind his back. They did the same to Tova, who woke up with a yelp.

The Philistines prodded them around the house to the front, where Barac's horse was waiting.

The farmer stood at the doorway.

"Do something," Barac said.

He shook his head. "I told you they'd come back."

"Selling Hebrews to foreign slavery is a sin."

"Tsruyah ordered me to betray you. The sin is on him."

Speaking a strange, harsh language, one of the Philistines snapped at the farmer, who bowed deeply, went inside, and returned with food and a jug of wine.

They used hand motions to direct Tova and Barac to mount his horse and tied them to the saddle horn.

Tova whispered, "Who are they? What will they do to us?"

"Philistines," Barac said. "They've taken us as slaves. With God's help, I'll find a way out."

The farmer heard him and said, "Give up hope. You're as good as livestock now."

The way he was looking at Tova while speaking made Barac's blood cold. "Tell them my wife comes from a sacred bloodline, and if they violate her, our mighty God will make their genitals rot with leprosy."

Hesitating for a moment, the farmer shrugged and spoke to the Philistines, gesturing at Tova and then at his own crotch. They laughed, but Barac could tell they were wary.

One of them led Barac's horse by the reins, and the group began walking on the road west. Barac felt Tova press her face into his back and wondered if she was crying. The situation threatened to drive him to despair, too.

The path soon curved right in a north-west direction. The sun kept rising and, with it, the heat of the day. Once in a while, one of the Philistines held a waterskin to Barac's lips, and then to Tova's. They took a long rest in the shade of a tree and resumed going in the late afternoon.

At night, they camped on the side of the road, tying Barac and Tova's hands in the front so they could eat and relieve themselves. In the morning, they continued riding and, as before, took a long rest in the shade during the hottest hours.

Near sundown, with the waterskins empty, the Philistines engaged in an intense discussion. When it was over, one of them led the way off the road into the hills. They arrived at a homestead, which sustained a Philistine family and a few animals on a dozen palm trees and a well whose water tasted salty. Barac and Tova were placed in a corral with a donkey, an ox, and two goats, again with their hands tied in front. They slept in the corner of the corral. Tova scooted close to him and, after a while, her breathing slowed down as she fell asleep. For Barac, however, the guilt for bringing this disaster upon her head was too great, and he stayed awake while the moon made its way across the sky.

The following morning, the Philistine men put Barac and Tova back on the horse, and the journey resumed. Despite the clear sky and rising sun, the day did not grow hot. In the afternoon, the road softened up into loose sand until it disappeared in the smooth swells of yellow dunes. A fresh breeze picked up, cooling their faces. The air acquired an unfamiliar scent, which grew stronger as they proceeded west.

The horse struggled to keep moving, its hooves sinking deep into the sand. The Philistine men seemed to know their way despite the absence of any landmark. Barac looked ahead, expecting to see a village emerge over the dunes, but all he saw were more dunes, like mounds left by an army of moles.

Tova said, "Look!"

They were coming over a heap of sand and, up ahead, a vast blue surface opened up, stretching to the horizon. They cleared the last dune, and he could see that the golden sand turned dark in a wet strip, where a succession of foamy waves rolled in and crashed, one after the other, with roaring rumbles.

Filled with awe, Barac yelled, "The Great Sea!"

The Philistine men turned sharply, alarmed.

"I've never seen it," Barac said. "My father taught me that our God created it, but even he had not lain eyes on it."

They looked at each other and shrugged. None of them seemed to understand the Hebrew words. The one who held the horse's reins stayed put while the others ran into the water, waded through the waves, and splashed with their hands.

"They're floating," Tova said in awe. "How are they not drowning?"

"If you know how to swim, you don't drown."

"It's like magic," she said. "I want to learn how to swim."

"Me too." Barac glanced back at her. "Let's ask them for a lesson."

For the first time since Gerar, they laughed together.

One of the Philistines came out to switch with the one holding the reins, who ran in to join the others. A while later, they all came out and resumed the trek, heading north along the wet strip of sand, which was firmer than the dunes and easier to ride on. Barac's horse shook his head anxiously and skipped aside every time a wave crashed in. Their captors found it amusing, especially when Barac and Tova almost fell off.

"Next time," Barac said, "we'll actually fall. As soon as we hit the ground, scream and cry as if you're badly injured. They'll untie us, and while they're distracted, I'll grab a weapon and attack them."

"One against six?"

"It will be one against sixty, or six hundred, when we reach their city."

"God help us." Tova was quiet for a moment. "Tell me when."

He looked at the sea, gauging the incoming waves. "The fourth wave out is the largest. As soon as the horse jumps, we drop."

The first wave crashed. Then the second, and the third. When the fourth came in with a loud thunder, the horse skipped aside, and the two of them fell off the saddle. The wet sand was hard, and they hit it together. Tova shrieked. Barac rolled over, his hands still tied, and faced her. She cried, and he realized she might not be pretending, but was truly hurt.

The Philistines surrounded them. The one who had Barac's sheathed sword drew it and, rather than use it to cut the rope binding Tova's wrists, put the tip of the blade against her chest. She screamed again, and Barac realized that the man was about to kill her, assuming her injuries rendered her unfit to be sold as a slave.

"No!" Barac scrambled to his feet, barely able to keep his balance with his hands tied, and placed himself between Tova and the blade. "Don't hurt her!"

Tova stopped screaming.

Barac forced a smile to his face. "She was scared, that's all."

They looked at him blankly.

"I'm speaking Hebrew." He kept smiling. "You don't understand a word I'm saying, do you?"

Rising to her feet, Tova smiled, too. "I'm not hurt. Everything is fine."

The Philistines put the two of them back on the horse and resumed the journey. On the left, the setting sun reflected on the water. Eventually, it touched down on the horizon, where the Great Sea met the sky. The wind picked up, bringing in the scents of salt and spray. A gray bird glided over the water, dove in to snatch a fish, and gobbled it while taking off again.

"Such freedom," Barac said. "Why didn't God give us wings?"

"If only," Tova said. "As long as He didn't give any to the Philistines."

Barac chuckled. "Wings for the Chosen People only."

"Are we still His Chosen People when we're owned by those who worship false gods?"

He wasn't sure whether she wanted an answer or not, but he knew that their only hope was a miracle from God. Young and healthy slaves fetched high prices, and the owners expected a good return, extracted with the whip, if necessary. The thought of Tova being whipped in a field or at a kitchen made his blood boil. He didn't even want to think about what else might happen to her. How stupid he had been, trusting Tsruyah and the conniving farmer! Now Tova would be sold away to spend a short and painful life in a strange land, all because of him. But she wasn't the only victim of his failure: Deborah was heading to Emanuel for a fatal confrontation with Seesya. What chance did a lone girl, brave and daring as she might be, have against dozens of soldiers led by her sworn enemy? The thought sent a frozen hand into his chest, clutching his heart and squeezing.

He groaned.

"What's wrong?" Tova asked.

"It's all my fault," he said. "I failed."

"You'll find a way to save us. I'm sure of it."

Her unbridled confidence made him cringe. "What makes you so sure?"

There was a long silence before she answered. "Because you won't let Deborah down."

Stunned by her insight, Barac felt he should deny it, but he paused, noting that Tova's tone wasn't resentful, or accusatory.

She pressed herself to his back. "I'm not jealous of her, if that's what you're thinking."

He looked back at her over his shoulder, even though he knew she could see admission in his eyes and, worse yet, guilt.

"Why should I be jealous? You betrothed me as your wife, married me by God's altar with a sacrifice to Him and a blessing by His priest, and possessed me as your wife." She kissed his cheek. "What else could I ask for?"

"Your husband's complete devotion."

"Deborah desires God, not you. She wants to become a prophet, not a wife. And you want to help her, not because you hope to change her mind about rejecting you, but because you believe in the truth of her calling."

"I do."

"As your wife, I also believe it." Tova smiled. "And if God

believes it, too, He will save us from the Philistines so that we can go to Emanuel and help Deborah."

"I just realized," Barac said. "Your faith is as strong as hers."

She kissed his cheek again. "And now, you're as impure as I am."

He laughed.

At sunset, the Philistines set up camp on the sand not far from the water. The sound of the crashing waves was constant, and sleep came easily.

44

For two days, Deborah led the caravan back to Tamar, where the major trade routes intersected. On the morning of the third day, instead of heading south-east back to Bozra, Deborah led the way north to the Sea of Salt. The scorching heat was as oppressive as she remembered from the trip south after Seesya's ambush, but Deborah took comfort in knowing that, this time, she would not have to suffer the constant gawking of Kassite's Edomite slaves. That night, they camped by the Zered Creek, which was completely dry.

Travelling north from the Zered Creek, Deborah led her convoy to the southern tip of the Sea of Salt, where they stopped briefly to look out at the enormous expanse of water. The soil under their feet was crusted with salt, and the air was hot and odorous.

Turning left, the road skirted the coastline as it curved from west to north again, where they camped for the night. Deborah stepped away from the camp to relieve herself. Afterward, she dipped her hands in the warm sea water, which brought back mixed memories. When she returned to the camp, the women and children had already gone to sleep, but Yael waited for her by the fire with food and a little wine.

"Tell me," Yael said. "How come you have leper friends in Ein Gedi?"

Deborah sipped some wine to fortify herself before recounting the traumatic events. "On the night of my forced wedding to Seesya, he failed to consummate our marriage. He planned to lie, as he had done with my sister when her bedcloth remained stainless after they lay together, accusing her of having whored with another man beforehand. I saved my life by staining the bedcloth with goat blood. Later that night, he tried to kill me. I knocked him unconscious and ran out of Shiloh. A group of lepers hid me while Seesya and his men searched the fairgrounds. The lepers' leader, Miriam, masqueraded me as a leper, and her nephew, Ramrod, navigated our way through the hills to Aphek. Before we parted ways, I had a dream about them, which I understood to mean that they would heal from the curse of leprosy if they went to the Sea of Salt and rubbed themselves with garlic and olive oil. I told Miriam about my dream and the cure I thought it promised. Many weeks later, after my slavery at the tannery, the escape with Kassite, and standing trial in Emanuel, I ran into Ramrod on the road south, where he had been looking for me."

"Wasn't he with the other lepers?"

"He had gone with them to Ein Gedi initially, but later, he left his aunt and the others there, because he hated the heat and shortage of food, and went to stay with elderly relatives near Bethel."

"Wasn't he a leper too?"

"Only his finger, and it had healed in Ein Gedi."

"So your dream was true."

"I don't know," Deborah said. "Perhaps God decided to lift the curse from him as a test. At any event, he professed his love for me and proposed I settle with him as his wife, which was ridiculous."

"Why?"

"All the reasons in the world."

"Such as?"

"Ramrod abandoned the aunt, who had cared for him from infancy, and the pitiful group of friends, who had been his surrogate family. They needed him in Ein Gedi, and he deserted them for his own selfish motives. Besides, Ramrod is a scrawny little youth, weak, and anxious. He would never become a complete man."

"What happened to him after you refused his proposal?"

"He was caught by Seesya, who scared him into revealing that I was on the way to Ein Gedi with Sallan, Kassite, and a few Edomite slaves. Seesya raced to Ein Gedi with his men via Jerusalem, while we took the slow road down the Jordan River Valley and Jericho. He set a perfect ambush, which failed only because Miriam shouted a warning, paying with her life, and my beloved horse rose up on its rear legs to take a barrage of spears in his chest. There was a battle, I shattered Seesya's jaw with a slingshot, and we killed all his men except one, whom I spared and sent back to Emanuel to tell the people what Seesya had done."

"What happened to Seesya?"

"He escaped by swimming away in the Sea of Salt. Now, do you understand why I despise Ramrod?"

"Because he's a disloyal, ungrateful quitter."

"That's right," Deborah said. "I could forgive him breaking under Seesya's violent pressure, even though it led to Miriam's death, but not for abandoning the other lepers in Ein Gedi with a few equally helpless locals."

"In all fairness, you are the one who sent them to Ein Ged in the first place."

"That's why I also can't forgive myself. I keep wondering how many of them have already died because of my foolish dream."

During the night, Rogez again served as her watchman, but had no reason to wake her. Zerakh cried a few times, but Leah nursed him back to sleep.

At dawn, like every previous day on the road, Deborah woke up and forced herself to rise for her daily practice with the sword, the sling, and the dead general's copper spear. Despite her efforts to forget Barac, he dominated her thoughts. Her feelings alternated between crushing sorrow and fuming rage. Only the necessary concentration demanded by the increasing challenges she set for herself with the weapons gave her momentary reprieves from the storm of conflicting emotions. Fighting skills required endless drills, and she used failures to force herself to try harder, while the occasional perfect strike boosted her mood. The result was that every day, by the time the others woke up, her muscles were aching, but her spirits were up.

This morning, however, Deborah was worried about what was awaiting her in Ein Gedi. When everyone was ready, she led the way north along the narrow strip of land between the water and the craggy cliffs of the Judean Mountains. By the afternoon, as their waterskins were running low, Ein Gedi appeared in the distance.

Deborah glanced back. The mare, donkeys, and horses followed at a slow pace, the women and their children were slumped, their heads covered. She patted Yael's knee, waking her.

"That's Ein Gedi?" Yael leaned forward. "Not much to see."

She was right. From a distance, Ein Gedi looked like a solitary patch of pale greenery on the narrow shore.

The sun descended behind the tall cliffs to their left, casting jagged shadows over the Sea of Salt. They drew near Ein Gedi in the dim twilight. Deborah saw the familiar cluster of fruit trees, the handful of date palms, and the bushes that lined the stream from the mouth of the canyon, across the strip of level ground, to the water's edge, where the flat surface of the Sea of Salt began. Her heartbeat quickened at seeing the site of Seesya's ambush, and she recalled the spears flying from the dark cave, her beloved horse rearing up to shield her, Seesya and his men charging with swords held high, the slingshots knocking them down, the young soldier in the stream, staring up at her as she stabbed him with the sword, and her futile chase after Seesya, who swam away, his broken jaw bleeding into the lifeless sea.

Deborah's hand went to the hilt of Seesya's bejeweled sword, which she had found on the ground just ahead, where his blood stained the salt-crusted soil.

Coming closer, Deborah wondered whether any lepers still lived in the cave, which was coming up on the left about two-stories high in the face of the cliff. There was no stepladder leading up to the cave, answering her question. She hoped some of them had survived and returned to the Samariah Hills.

"This looks new." Yael pointed at fresh cultivation along the narrow shore, with brown soil that must have been brought down from the streambed somewhere up the canyon.

Surprised, Deborah also noticed a channel bringing water from the stream ahead into a modest pond, about three steps across. Smaller channels ran along tidy rows of barley, as well as two lines of very young date palms, not much taller than a man's knee, and other trees that were too young to identify. There were no birds or dogs, the silence broken only by the crunching dry salt under the horses' hooves.

Yael asked, "Where is everybody?"

A horn blew, the sound echoing from the canyon walls ahead and spreading over the Sea of Salt. The sound continued while Deborah arrived at the mouth of the canyon and saw a large assembly of people between the steep slopes.

The horn went silent.

The people were divided in two. On the left, wrapped in black rags from head to toe, stood about a hundred lepers – many more than the twenty or so who had come here with Miriam. On the right was a small group of local men, women, and children. Deborah recognized the few men who had butchered her dead horse for meat, with her heartbroken permission.

Above the assembly, on a ledge halfway up the right side of the canyon, were the locals' wooden shacks, clotheslines, and a corral for their few goats and sheep. On the opposite slope she saw new lean-to structures and clotheslines on which black rags hung to dry.

The man who blew the horn was standing on a rock with his back to her, a white cap on his head. The small horn, she noticed, had only a single twist, not the multiple coils of a proper ram's horn that priests blew on holidays and at trials. The man had Ramrod's thin stature and narrow shoulders, but as he put the horn back to his lips and blasted it with force, skill, and confidence, she knew it couldn't be him.

Rogez whinnied.

The man stopped blowing the horn and turned.

It was Ramrod, and his initial alarm immediately gave way to a bright smile.

"Deborah!" He jumped down from the rock. "Just in time!"

She dismounted. "In time for what?"

"The New Year." He was almost a head shorter than her and had to look up. "It's the first day of the seventh month. Did you forget?"

Deborah's face flushed. It was autumn, and she should have known it was coming – New Year and the start of the ten Days of Awe, which would end with the Day of Atonement. Back in Ephraim, men had spoken of the coming Days of Awe for weeks in advance, but during her time in the Negev Desert, the men of Simeon had not mentioned it.

The mothers and children dismounted and clustered together.

"I made this today." Ramrod held up the short horn. "From a cow. Can you tell? There are no rams here. Better than nothing, right? One of the locals helped me prepare it for blowing. Do you smell the stench? It's foul, but it works. Nice, isn't it?"

His rapid talking hadn't changed. Deborah sniffed the horn and twisted her face.

"You've grown taller." Ramrod kept smiling, showing no resentment as he gazed up at her. "Yahweh is benevolent to bring you here in time for the holy day. Don't you think?"

Deborah nodded. "He apparently brought more lepers, too."

"More are coming every day from all over Canaan, seeking the cure you recommended."

"How do they know to come here?"

"Word got around. It started with the soldier whose life you spared, Mishneh of Ephraim."

Deborah recalled the fear on the young soldier's face as she instructed him what to do. "Tell the people that Seesya ambushed me and my companions, that he attacked us from a cave without provocation, and that he killed an innocent leper woman, Miriam, who was more righteous than the highest priest. Tell the people that we defeated Seesya and his soldiers and spilled their blood because we had no choice. Tell them that I spared your life in order to spread the word, because I believe in justice and I trust that the tribes of Israel will recover their faith in Yahweh and be blessed by Him."

"He kept his word," Ramrod said. "Stopped at every city, town, and village, told them about you – how you sent the lepers here to be cured, how you stood trial in Emanuel for offenses punishable by stoning, how you exonerated yourself while exposing Seesya as a murderer, how the people cheered you when you left Emanuel while Seesya was being whipped, how you were ambushed by Seesya and his soldiers in Ein Gedi and defeated them against all odds, and how you were merciful to an enemy soldier and spared his life."

Deborah looked at the large group of lepers. "They know all this about me?"

"And more," Ramrod said. "Your fame has spread all over Canaan – the girl Deborah, who became the boy Borah to fight evil men. Some say you're famous even in Gaza for liberating many Philistine slaves from a tannery near Aphek."

Embarrassed, Deborah changed the subject. "How many lepers are here?"

"One hundred and twelve, so far. I've struggled to provide them with food and shelter."

"And garlic."

Ramrod laughed. "They bring it with them. I buy everything else in Jericho."

"Buy with what?"

"I trade salt for food. We collect water from the sea, further in, where it's clean, and let it dry in bowls. Pure salt is precious, even in Jericho, where travelling merchants buy it for transport to distant markets. And we're growing food here. Did you see our barley?"

"I did."

"And the date palms? I went up and down every creek in the area to find seedlings. They look good, don't they? They're hardy. And I bought other seedlings in Jericho, too. Did you see the lemon trees? And the pomegranates?"

"We saw all the plants, yes."

"And we built these, also." Ramrod pointed at the lean-to dwellings on the slope "It wasn't simple, you know? Everything has to be built higher up, because of the flash floods. They're deadly here. Have you seen one yet?"

She shook her head.

"So?" He waved his hands around. "Do you like what you see?"

"I'm very impressed," she said. "And a bit surprised, too."

"It's all because of you."

"Me?"

"Don't you remember what you told me?" He quoted her while pointing at the lepers. "They need you to stay here and take care of them, as Miriam had done until she died."

"I didn't expect you to listen."

"How could I not?"

"Miriam would have been very proud of you." Deborah gestured at the assembly. "They're waiting."

"We've all been waiting. For you." He turned to the assembled lepers and locals. "Yahweh answered our prayers and brought back the girl who stood up to evil men and lived – the blessed Deborah!"

They cheered and started chanting her name, "Deborah! Deborah! Deborah!"

Pulling off her helmet, she gave it to Yael, who already had a waterskin ready. Deborah washed off the stubble-paste off her cheeks and chin. Yael put away the waterskin, pulled General Mazabi's copper spear out of the saddle sheath and handed it to her.

Leah led the women and children of Simeon around Deborah, staring at her in bewilderment, and joined the locals on the right.

Deborah mounted the rock and faced the assembly, holding the copper spear as a staff.

A local man at the front of the group knelt and bowed his head. Others did the same, locals and lepers alike.

"Don't bow to me." Deborah pounded the bulging butt of the spear on the rock. "We're Hebrews, the children of Abraham, Isaac, and Jacob. We bow only to our God."

They stood.

Twilight was fading quickly. She nodded at Ramrod, and he blew the horn again, going on at length, keeping the sound steady yet tremulous in a way that touched the heart. He ended on a high note that bounced off the canyon walls.

Everyone looked at Deborah, waiting for her to speak.

Closing her eyes, she was back home at Palm Homestead on the New Year with her parents and Tamar. Their father blew a coiled ram's horn and explained what it meant, which Deborah now conveyed to the people before her.

"On the first day of the seventh month," she said, "as Yahweh had ordained, we blast the ram's horn to celebrate the anniversary of the day He created Adam and Eve. Tonight we begin to count a new year in our existence as men and women, a new year in the life of the animals and the trees, a new year in our freedom from slavery in Egypt and the deliverance to the Promised Land, a new year in the counting of Sabbatical Years, when the land is left alone to rejuvenate, and the Jubilee, when all land goes back to the heirs of the original recipients of every homestead from the time of Joshua."

Some of the local men nodded and murmured to their neighbors.

"We're all strangers here," Deborah said. "We've been driven from our stolen homesteads to live in a place where life itself struggles to survive. Ein Gedi is within the territory of Judah, but no man of Judah wanted it as his family's homestead because it's desolate and hot, a narrow ledge by a sea that sustains no living creatures in it."

They nodded.

"But a desolate place makes for a safe refuge, and now, it's blooming because of your hard work."

"Because of Ramrod," one of the lepers said behind his veil.

Many of the others agreed loudly, including the locals.

Deborah glanced at Ramrod, who shrugged and smiled.

"It warms my heart," Deborah said. "Especially after my long journey from the land of Ephraim to Manasseh, Dan, Benjamin, Judah and Simeon – the bickering tribes of Israel, fighting each other, killing, robbing, and enslaving other Hebrews."

Leah sniffled, pressing her cheek to her baby.

"It's no wonder that our God has allowed the Canaanites to subjugate the Hebrew tribes of Naphtali, Asher, Zebulon, and Issachar, that He permitted the Edomites to conquer towns of Judah and Simeon, and that He empowered the Philistines to carve out the Coastal Plain from Dan and Manasseh. That's why, today, I want to think not of Adam and Eve, but of their sons, Cain and Abel, the progenitors of brotherly enmity. Let us start this new year with a prayer for peace."

"Shalom," one of the men yelled. "Shalom!"

"Yes," Deborah said. "Shalom among the Hebrews. Who among you is of Judah?"

A few locals and lepers raised their hands.

"Of Simeon?"

Others raised their hands, as well as the women from Beersheba.

"Of Manasseh, Dan, Benjamin, or Levi?"

Others raised their hands.

"Of Ephraim?" Deborah raised her hand, as did Ramrod and many of the lepers.

"Let us wish each other a good year," she said. "A year of peace among the sons of Israel."

The men and women turned to each other with greetings and smiles, first separately – men to men, women to women, and lepers to lepers – but then, the dividing gaps narrowed as men greeted women, locals greeted lepers, and even the children imitated the adults and greeted each other with pretended formality, before collapsing in giggles.

"I wish you a good year," Ramrod said to Deborah. "May it continue as wonderfully as it has just started."

"And to you." Deborah turned to Yael. "And to you, too."

Yael stepped forward and hugged her.

Leah came over. "I want to become a man, too. Will you teach me?"

Deborah kissed the baby's head. "You're not only Zerakh's mother, but a mother to all of Simeon. It's a calling you cannot answer as a man."

"Then teach me how to use these." Leah touched the spear and the sword.

"Even better, I'll teach you how to use this." She untied the sling from around her hips and handed it to Leah. "It's the perfect weapon for a woman, because you can keep it hidden until you need it, and when you do, its highly effective."

Leah took the sling and looked at it doubtfully.

"It saved my life several times," Deborah said. "Make a copy of it. You can use leather, rope, cloth, whatever you can find."

Ramrod blew the horn one last time, and everyone dispersed. The locals invited the women and children of Simeon to stay with them. In the absence of fire, which was forbidden until the following night, Ramrod set up a watch rotation between the men. He helped Deborah and Yael feed the horses and donkeys, then showed them to his own lean-to and took his cot outside.

That night, Deborah dreamt of lying with Barac in the battlefield by the Ramon Crater, his lips locked to hers, his bare chest pressed to hers, his body one with hers. The joy she felt was as real as it had been then, but at the moment of her greatest delight, she woke up, realized it was only a dream, and remembered that Barac was now with another girl, a pretty girl, a girl with wide hips and ample breasts for his future children. The collapse from peak elation to deep grief was so jarring that she broke down. With her face buried in her sack, Deborah wept while remembering Barac's face, smiling happily the way he she remembered him from the streets of Emanuel and, later, in Beersheba, with his beard fuller, his jaw firmer, his shoulders wider, but his smile as bright as before. She wept for his smile, which would never sparkle for her again, and for her baby, who would never have a loving father.

45

In the morning, the Philistines continued north on the hard-packed sand by the water's edge. The crushing waves no longer bothered the horse, even when the foamy runoff sloshed at its hooves. In the afternoon, up ahead, Barac saw white triangles rising from the water near the coast. Closer yet, he realized they were sails, attached to masts of wooden ships. He had never seen ships with his own eyes, but remembered his father's stories about the Hebrew tribe of Asher, which lived north-east of Naphtali, and whose territory included the mountains of Lebanon and the northern shores of the Great Sea, where the men of Asher sailed ships out of the cities of Tyre and Sidon to catch big fish and trade with the inhabitants of exotic islands and distant shores.

Tova asked, "What are those things?"

"Sailing ships," he said. "The Philistines are seafaring people. I heard they had come from an island in the north that's so small they call it Button. Every grown child, except the firstborn, must leave the island because there's no room for more people."

"Why do they come here?"

"My father said that they had tried landing all along the coast of Canaan, but the men of Asher, Manasseh, and Dan fought them back to sea. This area was part of Judah's territory, but the men of Judah preferred to settle inland, where there is fresh water and good land to farm. That gave the Philistines a foothold in Canaan, and they grew so numerous that Judah, Dan, and Manasseh could no longer push them back to sea. That's what my father said."

On the rolling sand dunes across from where the ships bobbed on the water, Barac saw a city of many one-story houses with flat roofs. At the center of the city stood a huge building painted blue, featuring a series of columns facing the Great Sea.

By the size of the city he figured it must be Gaza, the Philistines' main city. It was built on flat land, unlike Hebrew settlements, which always sat on a hill or a knoll that offered natural defenses against attacks. Another oddity, which could not be explained by the lack of hills or knolls near the coast, was the lack of protective walls. Were the Philistines too lazy to carry the needed stones from inland, or too arrogant to fear any attackers? He reckoned it was the latter, assuming that the other Philistine men in the city shared the fervent intensity of their captors who, even after the long journey, appeared tireless, alert, and ready for violence.

Near the city, he saw floating wooden ramps, secured to stakes fixed in the sandy shore. The ramps stretched out over the water, lurching and plunging with the waves. The ships were anchored further out to sea, about four or five hundred steps away, if one could walk on the water. Sailors unloaded dripping nets full of fish from several of the ships into small boats, rowed over to the floating wooden ramps, and carried the bursting nets to shore. He was amazed at how they kept their balance on the pitching ramps.

Once on land, other men hauled the nets up the shore and into the city, whose first line of houses was built about two hundred steps inland. Barac wondered whether the waves ever grew large enough during storms to sweep away houses built near the shore.

"Look," Tova said, pointing.

Nearby, little boys with olive-skin were digging in the sand with sticks and carrying water from the sea in clay bowls to fill the holes.

"They're cute," she said.

The boys started to splash on each other, squealing in delight.

"Not so cute when they grow up," Barac said.

The sun was almost gone, and mothers came for their kids. Unlike the scantily dressed men, the women wore brightly colored dresses in red, blue, yellow, and orange, which reached down below their knees and had sleeves down to their elbows. They did not cover their hair, which they wore in long braids down their backs.

Gaza smelled of fish, human waste, and rotting garbage. The fairgrounds occupied a vast area in front of the building with the giant blue columns. Between the columns stood tall statues of various gods. At the center was a deity he had never seen. From the waist up, it was a man whose complexion and bare chest resembled a Philistine man, but there ended the resemblance. The deity had a black beard that came halfway down his chest, long black hair, which curled backward at the nape, and a red crown painted green and black with a gray-bird ornament on top. The deity's hands seemed human, the left reaching out solicitously to the people in the busy fairgrounds, the right hand held up in a greeting. But the most striking part was below the waist, where the lower half of the body was a fish with multi-colored scales and a green tail divided into two fins.

The vast fairgrounds accommodated more than thirty merchant caravans along the south side. The center was filled with numerous stalls of fish and other goods. The north side was fenced off and divided between animal corrals and cages for slaves.

Their captors pulled Barac and Tova down from the horse and presented them to an old slave master. He squeezed Barac's thighs and arms to feel his muscles and poked a finger in his mouth to check his teeth.

"We're Hebrews," Barac told him, speaking loudly to be heard over the noise of the bustling fairgrounds. "We're free Hebrews from the land of Judah."

The slave master ignored him and tugged on his blood-encrusted hair, searching for open wounds, and grunting in displeasure.

"We're not slaves," Barac said. "They kidnapped us."

The slave master turned to check Tova. He prodded her belly, pawed her breasts, and pinched her cheeks.

"Hebrew," Barac said. "Do you understand?"

The slave master engaged in an intense discussion with the man who carried Barac's sword. Tova looked at the slave cages, one for men and one for women and children, each crowded with many slaves, some sitting, some standing at the wooden bars, watching. She wiped her eyes.

Barac turn to face the busy fairgrounds, where torches now lit up the myriad vendors and shoppers, and yelled, "Hebrew, anyone? Do you understand Hebrew?"

The man carrying his sword stopped talking with the slave master, turned to Barac, and punched him in the chest, sending him to the sandy ground.

Tova yelled, "We're Hebrews! We're free Hebrews! Help us!"

The slave master produced a short whip and slashed her across the back, making her scream in pain. He did it again, and she fell to the ground beside Barac, crying.

A purse of coins changed hands, and their captors left, taking Barac's horse with them. The slave master summoned two burly guards, who pushed Barac into the men's cage and Tova into the women's.

A man with a silver beard beckoned Barac to a spot near the bars.

Barac came over and sat down on the ground.

"Shalom," the man said. "Do you have any food?"

Barac patted his robe to show he has nothing on him.

"I'm Mefati of Reuben. And you?"

"Barac of Naphtali."

"You're a long way from home. How did you end up here?"

"We were travelling from Beersheba through Gerar."

"No one is safe west of Beersheba except for merchant caravans and those who pay the Philistine regular tribute for access to pasture. Didn't anyone tell you?"

Barac shook his head. "How did they catch you?"

"They didn't catch me. I was sold."

"By whom?"

"It's a long story."

"We have time.

Mefati sighed. "My father died when I was a boy. My uncle took my mother as a wife, but he already had two wives and many children, so he bartered me to an Ammonite merchant for some goods." He paused, taking a deep breath. "I served my master well for many years, travelling along the trade routes, and when he died, his son inherited me, and I served him for more years than I could count. I've known the boy since he was born, saw him grow up, and helped him became a successful merchant like his father. My own abilities, however, aren't what they used to be. Yesterday morning, I tripped on a tent peg and dropped a clay jug of wine. When my master didn't hit me, I knew it was the end, and I was right. As soon as I collected the slivers of clay and threw them away, he sold me to the slave master for a new clay jug – an empty one." Mefati chuckled sadly.

"That's all I'm worth, and even at that price, no one bought me at the auction this morning."

"What will happen to you?"

"Someone will buy me for pittance to dig holes or clean fish in the market until I drop dead – the sooner the better, please God."

Barac looked away, pained by the man's story. "Your master should have taken you back to the land of Reuben and released you there to die in peace among your own people."

Mefati sighed. "I've given up on this dream a long time ago. And you should stop dreaming, too. Tomorrow morning, someone will pay a good price for you and expect to earn it back with hard work and obedience. The girl, too."

"She's my wife."

"Better you forget her. A pretty thing like her will fetch the best price from the enterprising owner of prostitutes. The sailors pay good silver for a few minutes—"

"No!" The brief image of Tova lying under the crushing weight of a dark-skinned Philistine made Barac dizzy. "Never!"

Inside the women's cage, Tova sat at the bars facing the men's cage, her face cradled in her hands. Barac burned with determination to find a way to regain their freedom before they were sold off. But how? He needed to know more about this place.

"Will there be an auction tonight?"

"In the morning," Mefati said.

"How does it work?"

"The slave master goes up on the platform there." Mefati pointed through the bars. "Everybody lines up, and he tries to get the best price."

"One at a time?"

"Ship owners buy groups sometimes."

"Why?"

Mefati thought for a moment. "Probably to take them to some island or foreign city and sell them for profit. But most slaves go to local buyers and traveling merchants from other nations. I've been to many of those countries – Bashan, Ammon, Arabia, Persia, Moab, Edom, even an Amalekite town once, and here in Gaza, of course, many times."

"Have you gone across the sea?"

"Wouldn't that be exciting, to see those faraway islands? The Philistines are the best seamen in the world."

Barac looked down toward the water, where the ships sat at anchor.

"It's too late for me," Mefati said. "If I were young like you, I'd pray to be sold to a ship owner and leave this cursed place."

"Gaza?"

"Canaan."

"It's our Promised Land."

"It's our damn punishment." Mefati spat on the ground. "Even the Holy Scriptures say of Canaan, "A land that consumes its inhabitants." Perhaps you'll get lucky and a ship owner will take you away."

Barac had no interest in seafaring slavery, but Mefati's words gave him an idea. "Do you speak the Philistines' language?"

"Enough to get by."

"Why don't you ask the slave master for food?"

"He doesn't feed us. It would cut into his profits."

"What about your master? Surely he cares about you after so many years."

"A slave is like a goat. Would an owner visit his old goat after selling her to slaughter, or bring her something to eat?"

The attempt at humor fell flat for Barac. Reality was growing bleaker with every passing moment.

"Look at the bright side, boy," Mefati said. "It's a fitting start for our Days of Awe."

It took a moment for Barac to realize that the old man was right. It was the eve of New Year, and he had completely forgotten!

"You can pray in your heart," Mefati said. "Our God is everywhere, always listening to those who believe in Him. That's what I've done every day for many years. No one can take that from us, unlike false effigies and ugly figurines that can be crushed underfoot like rodents."

Barac was awed by this expression of faith, maintained over a lifetime of slavery among strangers. "Were you the only Hebrew travelling with the caravan?"

"Rabbath, my master's wife's maid, has some Hebrew blood on her mother's side. She's kind, always keeps some food for me when I'm busy setting up camp or taking it down. I saw her this morning in the crowd, watching the auction." Mefati craned his head to look through the wooden bars at the fairgrounds, now quieting down. "Perhaps she'll come again."

They sat in silence while a man crouched beside them and relieved himself on the ground. Barac wanted to move, but the cage was too crowded to find another spot to sit. The stench made him gag. Mefati stood up, lifted the bottom of his robe, and urinated on the fresh pile of feces.

"It dulls the bad odor," he said, sitting back down. "Talking also helps. Tell me, where were you heading when they captured you?"

"North, to Ephraim."

"Ah, Ephraim." He chuckled. "Always in the shadow of big brother Manasseh. Which town?"

Barac didn't feel like talking, his heart heavy with failure and regret. "Emanuel."

"Judge Zifron's domain." Mefati perked up. "We've stopped there many times to trade for their baskets, which are the best in Canaan, but not for long. Last time we were there, his foreman was very sick."

"Sallan?"

"You know him?"

Barac nodded. "His sickness was a trick to get his freedom and return to Edom. Do you know the son of Judge Zifron?"

Mefati's smile faded. "A nasty young man. Even my old master, who was the most gifted charmer since Joseph of Israel, couldn't find a way into that cold heart."

"Because Seesya has no heart."

"But he does have a good head. My master says that Seesya will surpass his father tenfold in wealth and power, unless his violent nature gets in the way."

They sat quietly for a while, before Mefati spoke again.

"And why does a boy of Naphtali want to reach Ephraim?"

"To help a friend, whose parents Seesya murdered for their family homestead."

"You were going to fight the son of Zifron?" Mefati chuckled.

"The Philistines probably saved your life by enslaving you."

On the other side of the cage, a fight erupted between two men, who shouted in the Philistines' language, went on to pushing, punching, and kicking. They fought with murderous rage while everyone scrambled to get out of the way. One of them managed to knee the other in the groin, which disabled his opponent long enough to put on a chokehold from behind. Barac had never seen a man suffocate to death, but the sounds he made while writhing desperately for air were reminiscent of the sounds made by the wounded men on the battlefield at the Ramon Crater as they choked on their blood. Barac got up, intent on breaking the fight, but Mefati grabbed his arm and held on while turning to the bars and yelling something in the Philistines' language. A moment later, two guards rushed into the cage. They tried to dislodge the chokehold by hands and with a whip, but couldn't, and the man died. Only then did the other one let go and dropped to the ground, shielding his head with his arms while the guards continued to whip him until they were tired. They dragged the dead man out of the cage and secured the door.

Distracted by all the commotion, Barac hadn't noticed that Mefati was standing at the bars with a veiled woman, who passed him a small package through the bars. He took it and kissed the tips of her fingers. Barac guessed the woman was the maid Mefati had mentioned, and as she turned to leave, he spoke up in Hebrew.

"Rabbath?"

She paused.

"Mefati told me about your kindness. I wish you a good New Year."

She nodded and glanced around nervously.

"My young wife, Tova, is locked there." He pointed toward the other cage. "We were betrayed and captured, but there are Philistines in Gaza who would help us."

Mefati made a doubtful sound, and the woman turned to leave.

"Have mercy," Barac said. "Ask around the city for any slaves who fled from the tannery in Aphek. My friend Borah led their escape."

"I heard about that," Mefati said. "No one could figure out how they escaped without being seen on the roads in any direction."

"Borah mentioned a Philistine group leader named Petro." Barac pressed his face between the bars. "I beg you, Rabbath. The Day of Atonement is upon us, and Yahweh will judge you favorably if you help fellow Hebrews. Spread the word around Gaza that a friend of Borah is locked up here."

One of the guards noticed them, shouted a warning, and Rabbath ran off.

"Borah liberated them," Barac yelled after her. "The tannery in Aphek! Group leader Petro! Ask around!"

46

For the first time in many days, Deborah slept through dawn. It was daylight outside, and she could hear people talking. Out of habit, she reached into her sack for the jar of stubble-paste, but put it back. It was an odd feeling to be free of the necessity to hide who she really was.

When Deborah came outside, the view startled her. From where she stood, halfway up the side of the canyon, she could see the whole width of the Sea of Salt, all the way to the distant Moab Mountains rising up from the opposite shore. The sun had cleared their jagged peaks and reflected off the water, forcing Deborah to shield her eyes.

Ramrod and Yael were sitting on a rock nearby, eating dates from a bowl, chatting in low voices, their heads close together.

Noticing her, they stopped talking.

"Good morning," she said. "Were you discussing the weather?"

"No, no." Ramrod stood up. "The weather is the same here every day. Very hot. And also the same every night. Very cold. Then hot again in the day. Nothing changes, same weather here, nothing to discuss."

"Relax," Yael said. "She was joking."

"Oh. Right." He shrugged, embarrassed. "Yael was telling me all you have been through in Beersheba and the Negev Desert."

Deborah looked at Yael. "All of it?"

"All the fights you've won – how you saved me from the judge of Simeon, defended Beersheba from the army of Judah, rescued Princess Needa from the Negev Desert, and released the mothers of Simeon from slavery."

"Did I really win anything?" Deborah took a date from the bowl and nibbled at it. "The women of Simeon still lament their husbands, the princess of Edom still grieves for her lover, and the people of

Beersheba still fell into its enemies' hands."

"I've remained free," Yael said.

Deborah put the rest of the date in her mouth and spoke while chewing. "Have you told Ramrod what you do with your freedom?"

"Why not? He's a potential customer."

The horror on Ramrod's face made Deborah burst out laughing, while Yael flipped her dark locks seductively.

"I'm not," he said. "Not a customer, I mean, which is not to say that there's anything wrong, or that you're not beautiful, yes, you are a beautiful girl, but it's not something I would engage in, not ever."

"It's fine if you do." Deborah took another date. "Men are eager to pay her. She must be very good at it."

"I pleasure men," Yael said. "Deborah slays them."

"She had no choice," Ramrod said. "Killing is better than being killed, or seeing someone you love getting killed. I was here when she had to kill the men who ambushed her. If only I could have killed them myself, because it wouldn't be a sin, but a good deed, you know? Seesya hurt people, including me, and he killed my aunt, Miriam, who was like a mother to all of us. He stabbed her in the back like it was nothing, and if Deborah didn't strike him down and kill his men, they would have murdered her and everyone else, the way he killed Miriam!"

Ramrod was shaking, and Deborah pressed his shoulder. "You're right. Miriam was like a mother to me, too. She is with God now, walking peacefully in the Garden of Eden, safe and happy forever."

Standing up, Ramrod put the horn to his lips and blew it, surprising her again with his skill at producing a sound both powerful and delicate.

Across the canyon, the locals came out of their shacks and went down the slope to the open area at the mouth of the canyon near the shore. The lepers also emerged from their dwellings and headed downhill.

"Go ahead," Yael said to Ramrod. "We'll be down in a moment."

As soon as he was out of earshot, she said, "I didn't tell him anything about Barac. Not a word."

"Why not?"

"Isn't it obvious? He's completely enamored with you."

"He'll be cured once he learned the truth about me."

"Nothing will sway him, I can tell." Yael smirked. "And he's got a lot of potential."

"What potential? Look at him, a skinny boy—"

"A young man, at least a year older than you."

"Pouting, with those little eyes and mousy face—"

"He's peculiar, yes, but in an endearing way."

"Rambling on and on with such nervousness—"

"He's intense, restless even, which makes him industrious."

"So eager to please, like he's desperate—"

"And you're desperate to find flaws," Yael said. "Think about the positives, starting with his most important quality: he's a man of Ephraim."

Deborah sighed. "I don't like him."

"You need him."

"I don't want him."

"He wants you, and you want Palm Homestead."

"Not Ramrod," Deborah said. "Not him. It'll never happen."

Yet, even as she said it, Deborah remembered Sallan's words: "Never say never. Even a feeling of absolute certainty is only temporary, subject to a change of mind."

At the bottom of the canyon, Ramrod reached the two groups, mounted the rock, and blew the horn again.

"Watch carefully," Yael said. "To these people, he's not a nervous boy. To them, he's a good man with a warm heart, deep faith, and sincere dedication to others, who are less fortunate than him."

A memory came to Deborah from the balcony facing the great copper statue of Qoz, a moment before Qoztobarus had strung up Leola, "Under all this," Umm-Sallan had gestured at Deborah's leather armor, "there's a girl ready to emerge as a beautiful woman. Let her out and attract a husband – even if you don't like him at first, it doesn't matter. A smart girl uses her head to decide whom her heart should fall for. And when you capture a good man's heart, he'll fight for your inheritance and indulge your desire to serve your God."

"It's not going to happen," Deborah said. "Even if I wanted to, it's not possible, not in my condition."

"In your condition you need a husband even more."

"What man would marry a girl who's pregnant with another man's baby?"

"What girl would tell a smitten man she's already pregnant with another man's baby?"

"An honest girl."

"There's nothing to tell." Yael put her hand over Deborah's mouth. "You're not showing. For all we know, there's no pregnancy."

"But there is."

"Couldn't Umm-Sallan be wrong? In the first week of pregnancy, the signs are very subtle. You can't be sure."

"I'm sure." Deborah pressed her hands to her tender breasts. "I can feel my body changing every day."

"My body also changed after my first time with a man, and I'm not pregnant, that's for sure."

"How do you know?"

"My mother taught me how to prevent it. Didn't your mother—"

"No." Deborah blushed. "And Umm-Sallan wouldn't make such a mistake. I'm pregnant."

"So what? It'll be months before you show. Push it out of your mind and start again, right now. Give yourself to Ramrod as your husband, and when the baby comes, he'll rejoice with his blessings."

"He'll rejoice with a falsehood, which I'll have to sustain morning, noon, and night."

Yael groaned in frustration. "Have you forgotten your True Calling? Every day you'll be doing good for the Hebrews, speaking the word of Yahweh to them, and preventing their nasty sins, which would compensate for your little lie a thousand times over."

"I once heard a similar argument from a higher authority." Deborah quoted the eagle. "To do a lot of good, you must do some bad along the way."

"Exactly."

Below, one of the locals joined Ramrod on the rock and recited verses from the Holy Scriptures. Everyone repeated each verse. Ramrod blew the horn again, and the recital of verses continued. Some of the men wandered aside, praying out loud, raising their hands to the sky. Others stood around the rock and continued reciting the verses with Ramrod and the other men.

"It's too much." Deborah said. "Every moment would require a new lie. How will I be able to serve God while continuing to commit the sin of lying to my husband and my child."

"It's a bigger sin to bring your child into the world without a father."

Deborah looked at the mothers of Simeon, sitting by the side of the canyon with their fatherless children. "It's not my fault that my child's father cares nothing for his mother after possessing her with slick words and feigned affection."

"I'm sure his affection was sincere at the time, and fault is a matter for your God to decide. If I were pregnant and could choose between Ramrod and having no father at all for my child, what would you tell me to do?"

"Every child is better off with a father," Deborah said. "My situation is different, though. God separated me and from Barac for a reason. What if He doesn't want my child to have another father?"

"What if your God's reason was that He agreed with your decision to reject Barac?"

"Why?"

"You told me that Barac wanted to become a great warrior and fight the Canaanites. What if your God wants you to find a man who will have nothing else on his mind but to help you answer your True Calling?"

Deborah thought of the High Priest's words. "When you pursue your True Calling, God provides the shortcuts." She watched Ramrod and wondered, was he a new shortcut from Yahweh?

"Look at him," Yael said. "He's a good man."

"I admit," Deborah said. "He has improved."

"I think he'll be a good father, too."

"Probably, but not for another man's child."

"Here we go again." Yael sighed. "What he doesn't know won't hurt him."

Deborah smiled, calmer now that her dilemma was resolved, and quoted Umm-Sallan. "A secret in a marriage is like a rotten core in an apple."

Ramrod finished another lengthy horn blow, and more men took to praying loudly, walking in circles, arms up, pleading with God to forgive their sins, to cure and feed them, to keep their loved ones safe and healthy. Looking uphill, Ramrod beckoned Deborah and Yael to come down.

"Let's join them," Deborah said.

Yael followed her. "Do you want me to tell him?"

"I'll tell him, and then, you can comfort him."

"That won't be necessary. I bet you a silver coin that he'll still want to marry you."

"It's a bet."

The rest of the morning passed in prayers, horn blasting, and a modest meal at midday, followed by rest and quiet. When darkness came, Ramrod had a fire started, a goat roasted, and a late meal marking the second of the Days of Awe, which started at sunset. While everyone ate, Ramrod helped a group of newly arrived lepers find where to stay until additional lean-to shacks were built.

Late at night, after everyone had gone to sleep and the air grew colder, Deborah started a small fire in front of Ramrod's shack, warmed up a jug of goat milk, and sat on the rock. He joined her, and she poured milk into wooden cups, giving him one. Yael wished them good night and went inside. Deborah assumed she would be eavesdropping.

Ramrod sipped from the milk. "This is good. I prefer goat milk to all other drinks. Wine is good, too, but it clouds the mind, which milk does not, except that it makes me sleepy sometimes. What do you like?"

"Milk is good." A tremor went through her.

"Are you cold?" He put down the cup, hurried inside, and came back with a sheepskin, which he draped over her shoulders. "Here, that's better."

"Thank you," Deborah said. "It's not only the cold. I'm nervous."

"Why?" He moved away from her. "Was I sitting too close? I didn't mean to. Forgive me. I don't pay attention sometimes."

"I need to tell you about a part of my life that's difficult to talk about."

"You don't have to," he said. "Don't tell me anything you don't want to. It won't matter to me. You know how I feel. It's not going to change, no matter what you tell me."

Deborah recalled him standing by his donkey on the road between Bethel and Emanuel, pleading with her not to continue with the Edomites to Bozra, but to come with him. "We have a small homestead, far into the hills, and a small spring. You'll be safe with us, and you won't starve." Her response then was still timely now: "One day I'll tell you why I can never be a good wife." He had reached up and touched her forearm. "I can be good for both of us."

"Hear me out," she said. "No interruptions."

Ramrod nodded, picked up the cup, and took a sip.

Deborah started with the early friendship she and Barac had struck up in Emanuel, his refusal to cast a stone at Tamar, and his story about the mythical Elixirist, which launched her quest to find that Edomite and seek his help in turning into a man. She told Ramrod about her longing for Barac all those months without knowing if he was still alive, of their reunion in Beersheba, their survival at the Ramon Crater, and the ring he put on her finger.

"And there," she said, "in the middle of a battlefield strewn with dead men, we lay with each other as husband and wife, even though we weren't yet blessed by a priest before God."

Ramrod looked away from her, his eyes on the fire, but said nothing.

"And then, I lost him – not once, but twice. First, by my own decision, when I found out he was not of Ephraim, but of Naphtali, which meant he could not inherit my father and bring me back to Palm Homestead. And I lost him again within days as he married another girl whom, according to Leah, Barac loves as much as he had appeared to love me."

Deborah wiped tears on her sleeve, while Ramrod filled up her cup with milk from the jug and handed it to her.

"Barac is gone from my life, but not from my body." She drank a bit of the milk, which warmed her inside. "You see, I am pregnant with his child."

Ramrod, who was in the process of picking up his cup from the ground, dropped it, and turned to her with horrified eyes.

"It's true." She touched her lower belly. "I'm sorry."

Burying his face in his hands, Ramrod began to weep.

Deborah went inside the shack. Yael was lying under her blanket, facing away. Deborah did the same. The night was quiet, except for the crackling of the twigs in the fire and Ramrod's muffled sobs.

47

Barac woke up shortly after dawn. The air was chilly, and torches still burned from the night. The old slave master mounted the auction platform and shouted orders, pointing here and there. Guards entered the women's cage with whips and clubs and prodded them to line up into a queue. Barac caught Tova's eyes, which were wide and fearful.

"Don't look," Mefati said. "All you can do is shut your eyes, your ears, and your heart."

"There's still time. I'm counting on Rabbath."

"Forget her, too."

"But she may have found one of the—"

"Nonsense. You really believe a slave maid would walk around Gaza summoning escaped slaves, or that any of those Philistines would care to help a captured Hebrew man? You can't be that foolish."

Realizing the futility of his hopes, Barac looked down at the ground, his eyes misted.

"Accept it, boy," Mefati said. "You're a slave now. That's your new life."

"No," Barac said. "I'm not a slave. I'm a free Hebrew soldier, and that girl over there is my wife."

On the platform, a man joined the slave master. He was muscular, with bowlegs and a multicolored loincloth, similar to the scales on the half-fish deity at the center of the blue Philistine pantheon. He held a blue plank of wood that was rounded at one end like a handle and honed at the other end into a flat beam.

"A ship owner," Mefati said. "You can tell by the oar he's carrying from rowing a small boat from his ship to the shore."

The slave master shouted an order, and the guards herded the women out of their cage in a long line, one behind the other. Tova was about two-thirds of the way down the line. She looked at Barac, who could tell, even from a distance, that she was terrified.

The man with the multicolor loincloth peered down at each of the women as they approached the platform and used the blue oar to point left or right. It was a process of quick selection, and Barac soon realized the man was sending only young and healthy women to the right. One of the young women tried to pull a little girl with her, but the guards snatched the girl and took her to the left, where an old woman held her while she shrieked for her mother, who collapsed among the women on the right, sobbing bitterly.

When Tova's turn came at the platform, the oar pointed right, and she joined the group of young women, who pressed together in a tight cluster, surrounded by guards brandishing whips and blubs. She kept her head down and no longer looked toward the men's cage. Barac peered through the bars at the fairgrounds, which was starting to fill up, searching for Rabbath. He grabbed the bars, shaking them, groaning with frustration, until a whip whistled and cut across his fingers. He let go of the bars and fell back, pressing his hands to his mouth.

With the selection completed, the ship owner paid the slave master, pointed the oar toward the beach, and jumped down to lead the way as the guards herded the women through the fairgrounds. Barac knew what it meant. Tova was going to sea where, if she didn't drown in a storm or die of disease, abject slavery awaited her under the heavy hands of strange people in a foreign land.

Leaping back to the bars, he shouted, "Tova!"

From among the tight cluster of terrified women, her face lit by the flames of the torches, she gave him a final glance that communicated enough sorrow for an eternity. Then, she was gone.

Barac sat on the ground and buried his face in his hands.

After some time, he felt an arm over his shoulder.

"Come," Mefati said. "It's our turn now."

As the slaves lined up to exit the cage, the crowd of buyers built up in front of the platform. The first slave in line, a young man whose back was lined with red welts from lashing, was pushed onto the platform by a guard and stood there while the slave master lifted his arms and pointed at his muscles, before untying his loincloth, exposing his genitals and making him turn around to show his firm buttocks. Buyers began shouting offers.

Barac stood on his tiptoes, looking toward the beach, trying to see where the women were being taken, but his line of sight was blocked by the tents of merchant caravans. A puff of air brought smoke from a nearby torch into his eyes, and he rubbed them.

"The eastern wind," Mefati said behind him. "It starts just before sunrise. That's why the ships sail off at daybreak. Pray for her. It'll make you feel better, and maybe help her, too."

"I've prayed enough," Barac said.

A merchant bought the young slave, pulled him down from the platform, and led him away. The next slave, a mere boy, was lifted onto the platform, and burst into tears, which made the buyers laugh.

Barac grabbed Mefati's arm. "I'm going to make a break for it."

"How?"

"I'll hit this guard." He gestured at one of them, standing nearby. "I'll take his club and run to the beach."

"You're too young to die," Mefati said. "I'd like to die, but I'm too weak to fight the guards. They'll just push me over and laugh."

He was right, but Barac could no longer stand still, even facing the certainty of death.

The boy was sold quickly, and the buyer, gray-haired and stocky, threw the crying boy over his shoulder and ambled away, grinning with yellow teeth.

The guards prodded the next man onto the platform.

"Accept it," Mefati said. "No use to resist."

"It doesn't matter," Barac said. "I'm a soldier, and soldiers don't surrender. We fight."

"Then fight with your head."

The words made Barac pause. He was a good fighter, as proven at the Ramon Crater. There, however, he had a sword and a club, as well as dozens of comrades fighting by his side against confused opponents who lost their leader and chariots. Here, on the other hand, the guards outnumbered him fifteen to one, bore effective weapons, and had plenty of light between the burning torches and the start of sunrise. What could he do to reverse their advantage?

No, he realized, the correct question was different.

What would Deborah do?

The answer rested with what she had done to succeed in liberating hundreds of slaves from the tannery in Aphek and setting a nighttime ambush for the men of Judah in Beersheba. The common thread wasn't the use of force, but using what was available to gain an advantage. Could he achieve the same here?

Looking around, Barac could see no weapons lying around in wait for his hand, no rocks, or sticks. Fire, however, was all around him, because many torches were still burning.

What could he do with a torch?

The line edged forward.

He glanced back over his shoulder. There were about fifty slaves in line behind Mefati, and another thirty or so ahead of himself. Most of the slaves seemed healthy, yet their faces showed defeat. They were beaten and dispirited. It would take weeks to turn them into a group of fighting comrades, but could they still serve a purpose?

An idea came to him, as simple as one of Deborah's solutions.

He pointed at the columns at the temple and asked Mefati, "What's this half-fish statue in the middle?"

"Their greatest God. His name is Dagon."

"Dagon," Barac repeated. "He will be my savior."

"You chose a strange time to turn away from Yahweh."

"Were you serious about wanting to die?"

Mefati nodded.

"Then help me escape. The worst that can happen is that you'll die, but if you don't, and I succeed, I'll come back for you. Agreed?"

"Tell me what to do."

"I'm going to push the man ahead of me, and you'll turn around and push the man behind you as hard as you can. They'll fall on the next man, he'll fall on the next, and so on. It will create a diversion."

"And then?"

"Start yelling "Dagon" repeatedly. Don't stop yelling, no matter what happens."

Mefati shut his eyes and recited, "Blessed be Yahweh, king of the world, the true God."

Hearing him recite the blessing on the dead, Barac felt a tremor run up his spine. The old man was braver than he'd realized. "Amen," he said. "Ready?"

"I am," Mefati said.

Facing forward, Barac placed his hands on the upper back of the slave ahead of him and shoved him as hard as he could, propelling the man forward, where he bumped into the one ahead of him, who in turn knocked into the next one, each one of them yelping as they collided in a chain of collapses. Barac didn't have to turn to know that Mefati did the same, because a similar commotion sounded from behind.

Mefati shouted, "Dagon! Dagon! Dagon!"

Sprinting to the side of the platform, Barac pulled a burning torch from a bracket and hurled it over the heads of the crowd at the statue of Dagon. It hit the deity's bare chest with an explosion of sparks and landed by the green fins. Barac grabbed another torch and hurled it, as well, while the flames from the first torch began to lick the fins and a few sparks glistened in the black beard.

Mefati's hoarse voice kept shouting, "Dagon! Dagon! Dagon!"

The guards' attention was drawn to the dozens of fallen slaves, who were getting up and attacking each other. The guards descended on the slaves in a frenzy of whipping and clubbing. The slave master, however, saw from his high perch what Barac was doing and pointed at him, shouting orders. Barac grabbed the side of the platform and toppled it, sending the slave master to the ground.

At the center of the pantheon, Dagon's fins were on fire while his beard turned gray with smoke. At the same time, Mefati's yelling made people look in the direction of their chief deity and, seeing it on fire, they too began shouting, "Dagon! Dagon! Dagon!"

Barac grabbed a third torch and ran through the fairgrounds toward the beach, pushing through people and knocking down vendor stalls with heaps of goods. Once he reached the open stretch of sand, he sped up while his eyes searched for Tova and her fellow slaves. They were no longer on the beach or on the floating wooden ramps, but in three boats that headed out toward the anchored ships.

"Tova!" He kept running with the torch held up. "Tova!"

They were too far to hear him over the crashing waves.

Several empty boats bobbed at the far end of the floating ramps.

He ran faster, aiming for the spot where one of the ramps was secured to stakes in the wet sand at the water's edge. Leaping onto the ramp, he ran along it. A wave lifted the ramp, and it tilted sharply. He slipped on the wet wood, fell hard on his chest, and his legs splashed into the water. He lost grip of the torch, which rolled away on the ramp, almost dropping into the water, before resting in the groove between two beams.

The ramp heaved again, and Barac fought to hold on as the water reached his hips and up to his chest. Through the fog of terror, he imagined water filling his mouth and nose, suffocating him. His nails left lines in the soggy wood planks while he continued to slip off until a new wave jolted the ramp and tossed him off. His head went under water, his arms beat around, and his legs kicked about. He could hear Mefati's voice. "You're too young to die." With his lungs burning for air, Barac was about to open his mouth and take in the water, when the soles of his sandals touched bottom. He straightened his legs, shooting upward, and his head bobbed above water just as the ramp sank into a trough between waves. With desperate kicking and pulling, he scrambled back onto the ramp and stayed down flat, his arms and legs spread wide, while the ramp swayed and pitched, trying to toss him back into the water.

Lifting his head, Barac looked ahead and saw the boats gather around one of the ships, whose sails were a third of the way up and its bow pointed west toward the endless sea.

Staying on all fours, Barac clutched the still-burning torch with one hand, angling it up to keep the flame from the water, and advanced along the ramp. Every time it heaved, he lay flat and held on, waiting for calm before continuing forward. At the end of the ramp, a rope secured a boat, which dipped and lurched with the waves. He pulled on the rope to bring the boat alongside the ramp and rolled into it.

Propping the torch inside the boat, he untied the rope, picked up an oar that rested in the bottom and dipped it in the water, moving it backward along the side of the boat the way he saw the Philistine sailors do the previous day. The boat turned, but he quickly switched sides, rowed, and back again, rowing on each side quickly, back and forth. It took a few attempts before he got the hang of it, and the boat began to advance in the right direction.

Up ahead, the boats reached the ship.

Barac rowed faster, which was made easier by the calmer water further out from shore. Birds dove over him, crowing loudly.

The first boat began to unload as the new slaves climbed into the ship.

"Tova!" His screeching voice sounded odd to him. "Tova!"

In one of the boats, her face appeared.

He shoved the oar in the water, pushed it hard, switched to the other side of the boat, and repeated the motion, on and on. His boat moved painfully slow through the water, while the boat Tova was in lined up with the ship. He could see bare-chested sailors pulling the women on board, where they disappeared a moment later under the deck. Other sailors handled ropes, which changed the position of the sails. He realized they were preparing to sail away as soon as the women were on board.

The ship owner climbed out of Tova's boat, holding the blue oar he'd used to make his selections of slaves. Two sailors bent over the side of the ship and pulled the women one by one into the ship.

"Tova!" Barac rowed faster, getting closer. "I'm coming!"

The sailors took notice of him and alerted the ship owner, who pointed his blue oar in Barac's direction. In the boat, the woman ahead of Tova was pulled up into the ship. It was Tova's turn now.

"Don't go in," Barak yelled.

She looked from him to the sailors while retreating to the back of the small boat. One of them jumped from the ship into the boat, which pitched from side to side. Tova sat down as he stepped to her and bent down to get her. She must have resisted, for he raised a hand and slapped her, the sound of the clap travelling over the water to Barac.

"Leave her alone!" He rowed quickly, changing sides to keep the boat straight.

The sailor grabbed Tova, lifted her, and threw her over the railing into the ship. Meanwhile, several sailors gathered in the rear of the ship, shielding their eyes, gazing at Barac, or so he thought before realizing that they were not looking at him, but gazing toward the shore. He glanced over his shoulder and was blinded by the morning sun that just cleared the eastern horizon. Shielding his eyes, as well, he was stunned to see a ball of fire in the middle of the city, almost as bright as the rising sun. People were running up and down the sandy beach with buckets. He almost turned back to the front when something caught his eye.

Almost invisible in the reflections of the sun and the fire over the surface of the water, halfway between him and the shore, there was another boat. Squeezing his eyes to see better, Barac made out two men with oars, one on each side of the boat, rowing rapidly. At the front of the boat was a third Philistine man, leaning forward like a hunter stalking a prey.

Barac turned forward and resumed rowing. The ship was about thirty steps away. Some of its crew still gazed at the city while others were heaving ropes that made the main sail edge up, flapping in the wind. The ship owner was dragging Tova to the back.

"Tova!" Barac stood in the boat and beckoned her. "Jump off!"

She wriggled free of the ship owner and took a few steps away, but he threw the blue oar, hitting her in the back, and she fell down.

Shouting in rage, Barac grabbed the burning torch from where it was perched against the side of the boat and hurled it toward the ship, aiming for the sail. The torch flew in a long arc over the water, hit the upper part of the half-raised sail, and slid down to the bunched-up lower part of the sail, where it stayed.

Sitting down to row again, Barac yelled, "Tova, jump off!"

The ship owner pulled her up, but paused at the sight of smoke coming from the sail. Tova took advantage of this distraction, tore her arm free, and ran forward on the deck.

Twenty steps away, Barac rowed as fast as he could. On the ship, men yelled and ran about. Tova climbed up on the railing and stood there in perfect balance, hesitating, while the ship owner ran toward her.

Tova jumped.

She hit the water legs first and disappeared below.

Shifting the oar from side to side, Barac focused his gaze on the circle of foam where Tova had gone down. As he got closer, she reappeared, her mouth open, her eyes wide, her hands beating the water, before she sank again. On the ship, flames surrounded the main sail while the crew started to empty barrels of barley and fruit over the side and filled them with water to douse the fire.

His boat approached the widening circle of foam, and Barac bent over the side, staring into the water. All he could see was reflections of fire and ripples caused by his still moving boat.

"Tova!" He bent lower, and a ripple splashed his face. "Where are you?"

Wiping the salty water from his eyes, he rushed to the other side, gazing down into the dark water.

Nothing!

The boat was still moving, and he leaped to the rear, staring into the water. "Tova!"

A fleeting movement under water came and went before he could tell what it was. He grabbed the oar and dipped the paddle end into the water, holding the end with both hands, reaching deeper until the whole oar was underwater, as were his forearms. He moved around the boat like this, the edge of the sidewall boring in his armpits while he swayed the oar underwater from side to side.

The oar touched something hard. Barac shifted back, reaching deeper.

A brief tug, perhaps a fish, then nothing.

He slipped over the side of the boat and, grasping the edge with his left hand, stabbed the oar deeper into the water with his right hand, his upper body and head sinking in, too. Blindly, he made circles in the water with the oar while in his mind's eye he saw Tova as she had looked in Revivim, a girl with big, dark eyes, kneeling beside him, holding a jug of water to his lips, wiping his face with a wet cloth. "I heard stories about Naphtali's land," she had said. "Is it really full of rivers and streams that run all the time, even in the summer?" Now, she would never live to see the rivers and forests, because he failed to keep her safe.

Another tug.

He poked the oar around the same area.

Something grabbed hold of the other end of the oar.

Gently, Barac pulled the oar up while raising himself until his head came out of the water beside the boat. Holding on with his left hand, he continued to lift the oar until he saw a hand grasping it, and Tova's head emerged. She coughed, and a jet of water came out of her mouth. Barac pushed her up while tilting the boat over. Tova rolled in, together with a good amount of water. The oar was floating away, but he managed to catch it before climbing into the boat.

Tova was lying on her side at the bottom of the boat, half-submerged in water, coughing hard. Barac wiped his face and looked up.

The ship's main sail was ablaze, and the fire spread to the mast and to a smaller sail behind it. The Philistine crew fought the fire with barrels of water, except for two men, who climbed down into a boat and started rowing in his direction. Meanwhile, the boat that had chased him from shore was closing in fast. He grabbed the oar and started rowing, but with Tova and the water in the boat, it moved much slower than before. As the boat from the ship caught up with him, one of the men put down his oar and placed one foot on the side, ready to leap into Barac's boat, but as soon as they came into range, Barac pulled his oar out of the water and whacked the man, who yelled and stumbled back, causing their boat to rock. Barac resumed rowing, but barely got away when the man he had hit recovered and rejoined the rowing.

Tova stopped coughing. She sat up and pointed. Barac turned to see the other boat coming fast from the left, lined up to intercept him. He rowed hard, hoping to avoid getting caught in a vice between the two boats with a total of five angry Philistines. His single oar, however, barely managed to move the heavy boat, and the two Philistine boats were coming in at high speed from opposite directions.

"Stay down," Barac yelled to Tova. "And pray!"

He stood up, wielding the oar.

The two Philistine boats rammed his boat from both sides simultaneously, their bows mounting the sidewalls and shattering the wood. Barac fell into the water and would have gone down if not for his hand grabbing the side of the boat that came from the ship. Looking up, he saw the Philistine sailor whom he had whacked with the oar standing above him in the boat, a grin spreading on his dark face. The sailor raised his foot and stepped on Barac's hand, forcing him to let go of the sidewall. Barac grabbed it again, but the sailor stepped on his hand and laughed. As Barac kicked hard, trying to stay afloat, the sailor lifted his oar with both hands high above Barac's head.

It was the end, Barac realized, Mefati had been right.

Instinctively, he shut his eyes before the oar landed on his head.

A loud bang sounded, but he felt no pain, and when he opened his eyes, he saw the Philistine sailor still standing above him with his oar held high and his eyes rolled back in his head. Another oar appeared, hitting the sailor's head again. This time, he collapsed and fell over the side on top of Barac, pushing him down into the water.

The sudden dunking caught Barac unprepared, and he swallowed a mouthful of seawater. He struggled to surface, but the heavy body pushed him deeper. A piece of wood touched his hand. He grabbed it and held on as it pulled him up, out of the water, where strong hands rolled him into the boat. A fit of coughing brought a gush of water out of him, accompanied by scorching pain in his chest and throat.

Someone was pounding his back to help him cough out the water. He wiped his burning eyes and looked. It was Tova. Beside her was another Philistine man – the one who had looked like a hunter in the bow of the boat coming from shore. Up close, he appeared short and stocky, with rust-colored hair and missing teeth, exactly as Deborah had described him.

"Husband," Tova whispered. "Say something."

Barac rose shakily to his feet. "Group leader Petro, I presume?"

The Philistine man nodded and said in Hebrew, "They say you're a friend of Borah."

"I am."

"If you lie, you go back there." Petro pointed at the water, where the two sailors from the ship floated facedown beside the wreckage of Barac's boat. "Borah sent you?"

"No," Barac said. "Philistine men captured me and my wife and brought us to Gaza."

"That's no business of mine."

Barac glanced at Tova, who was pale with fear. "Borah told me about freeing you and your friends from the tannery in Aphek. Now you can help Borah's friends regain freedom, too."

"Many people know Borah. Few are Borah's friends."

"I was on my way to help Borah in the Samariah Hills when we were captured."

"Many people say many things, many not true."

On the ship, the flames had caught onto the deck and bow, but the sailors continued to fight the fire.

"I know how you escaped," Barac said. "Borah turned the roofs of the pavilions into rafts, and you floated at night down the Yarkon River to the Great Sea."

"Many people know that, too."

"In Philistia, maybe, but not among the Hebrews."

"This is Philistia," Petro said. "Maybe another slave told you."

"There's one thing no Hebrews or Philistines know, except Borah's friends." Barac took a deep breath. "Borah is a girl."

Petro gave him a long, searching look, before stepping over the side into the other boat, where his two companions waited. They listened while Petro spoke in the Philistines' language, asked him a few questions, and nodded in agreement. Petro beckoned Barac and Tova, and when they were seated safely in the boat, the two men began to row. Petro held on to the empty boat, and as they passed by the ship, he shoved it in its direction. There were two other boats, now filling up with the slave women, evacuating the burning ship.

The fire in the city had subsided, though people were still running up and down the sandy area with buckets. Petro stood at the bow while his companions rowed, and when the boat reached a floating ramp, he jumped over and tied the rope. Barac helped Tova out, and they walked slowly, feet spread wide, down the heaving ramp until their feet finally touched the wet sand of the shore.

Using her fingers, Tova brushed back her wet hair. "That was refreshing."

Petro smiled. "You're brave," he said. "Like Borah."

She turned to Barac, and he laughed, nodding in agreement.

Additional men joined them, forming a protective ring, and they walked quickly down the shore and inland around the outskirts of Gaza. At a large compound of crudely built houses with many connected rooms, Petro was treated with reverence by a large group of men, as well as women and children. Barac asked Petro to free

Mefati, if he had survived, and to find the stolen horse and few belongings that their captors had stolen.

One of the women took Barac and Tova to an airy room with a view of the sea. They washed with rags dipped in fresh water, put on clean robes, and lay down to rest on a straw cot covered with clean linen.

The sun was halfway down over the sea when they woke up. Smells of cooking drew them outside, where a whole sheep was roasting over red embers. Tova joined the women, who greeted her with smiles. Petro was sitting by the firepit. He got up to greet Barac and told him that Mefati had died in the mayhem at the fairgrounds during the fire. Saddened, Barac hoped the old man had not suffered before dying.

The men lined up, holding empty bowls, and Petro sliced chunks of meat off the sheep and served them. Each man bowed and thanked him. The men sat in concentric circles and waited until Petro and Barac joined them before starting to eat.

During the meal, three men showed up with Barac's sack, sword, and club, as well as a purse of coins. They spoke with Petro, who translated what they said for Barac.

"Your horse was sold to an Egyptian merchant. It's gone. The silver is for you. Compensation."

Barac weighed the purse in his hand thinking that he would rather have his good horse back than any amount of silver.

"Don't worry," Petro said. "Egyptians treat their horses as well as they treat their children."

When the meal was over, the men chanted melancholy songs until the sun went down and torches were lit to keep out the darkness. Most of the men left, but a few stayed.

Petro put down the bowl. "When will Borah need your help?"

"She's travelling from Edom to the Samariah Hills to fight her enemy, the judge's son."

"The one with the scar and long black hair?"

"Seesya. You know him?"

"He came looking for her at the tannery. She deserves a better husband."

"I agree."

"Will you take her as your second wife?"

Barac chuckled at the idea. "She'll never share a husband with another woman."

"We cannot go to fight for Borah in Canaan, but we will help you get there. How did you plan to go before you were captured?"

Barac recalled the map Abu Zariz drew for him. "We were going to take the road north to Lachish and Yarmut, and then east to Gibeon in the land of Benjamin. From there, it's a straight road north to Bethel and Emanuel."

"Too dangerous." Petro smoothed down the sand between them and drew with his finger. "If you go north from here, we can keep you safe for two or three days, but when you leave Philistia, it will become dangerous for you and the girl."

"Why?"

"The Hebrew men of Dan conduct raids into the lands of Judah, Benjamin, and even Ephraim. They burn homesteads and villages, steal animals and food, and take young men and women to sell as slaves." Petro drew in the sand. "We can take you east to the pasture lands of Simeon, where you were captured. From there, you can go to Beersheba, continue to the land of Judah, and head north to the Samariah Hills. Much safer that way."

"The new rulers of Beersheba aren't good men. They might arrest me, and Borah would die."

Petro spoke with the other Philistine men for a few minutes, pointing at the map, tracing routes. They argued until he spoke sharply, and they bowed, saying no more. He gave them orders and sent them away.

Barac gazed at the map in the sand. "What's the plan?"

"We'll get a ship and take you by sea." Bending down, Petro traced the way with his finger on the map. "We'll sail north to Jaffa and use the darkness to row into the Yarkon River, about halfway up the river. You'll get off the ship, walk to Aphek, and buy a horse for the ride to the Samariah Hills."

"You're taking a big risk. If you get caught, it's back to slavery."

"Borah gave us freedom," Petro said. "Now, we risk our freedom for Borah."

48

When Deborah stepped out of the shack in the morning, Ramrod was gone, but Leah and the other women of Simeon were sitting by the rekindled fire. Leah got up and handed her the old sling back while holding up a new one she had made. The other five women also held new slings.

"Let's practice," Deborah said.

They walked down the steep slope and out of the canyon, turning right along the narrow shore, past the cultivated squares and young trees, and lined up at the foot of the cliffs, facing the still water. The women watched Deborah demonstrate and began to try their new slings. There were plenty of stones to use, but most of them did not make it far. Many stones fell out of the pouches before a single rotation occurred, others were ejected prematurely in unintended directions, and some clang to the pouches, becoming entangled in knots of straps and fingers. There were laughs, yelps, and cries of pain, but Deborah worked with each woman until they all mastered the basic technique and managed to shoot toward the water without hurting themselves or others.

While the women continued practicing, Deborah walked back north, crossed the stream at the mouth of the canyon, and picked a few plums from the tree that had welcomed her to Ein Gedi the first time. At the corral, Rogez was happy to see her, and even happier with the plums. Yael's mare enjoyed a couple of plums, as well, and she had to go back to pick more for the two other horses and the three donkeys.

Back with the women of Simeon, Deborah continued to correct their techniques, improve their postures, and challenge them to shoot further away.

As the sun rose higher, several local women appeared with slings they had made of various materials and joined the practice. With each new trainee, Deborah became better at teaching the intricacies of sling shooting and the pitfalls that must be avoided to prevent needless injuries. Some of the slings broke, and the women helped each other fix them. Later, local men began to show up, some holding a crying child that needed his mother, others to join in, taking spots at the far end. Finally, lepers began to trickle in, one by one, with slings they had made, too. Missing thumbs and fingers required the lepers to compensate by tying the tab end to their wrist while curling a last remaining finger to hold on to the hook end of the sling while rotating it.

One of the men brought a sack of dry animal bones, which he tossed one by one far into the water to serve as floating targets. Deborah slung several stones, hitting distant bones, which left everyone in awe.

"Here's a trick that works for me," she told them. "To hit a target, imagine it's the face of someone who deserves to be hit."

The shooting resumed, and she could see a slow, but constant improvement. Occasionally, a stone flew sideways, making people dodge and instigating bursts of laughter. She was pleased to see these long-suffering women and men take such pleasure in learning to use the slings and persevering until they hit the targets. It seemed that every man and woman in Ein Gedi – except Ramrod and Yael – had become enamored with slinging, which made the stones scarce even in a place that was literally carpeted with stones.

After a midday break to eat and drink, Deborah taught them how to use the sling as a weapon of whipping, knotting and, if all else failed, blinding an opponent by slapping the tab-end of the sling at his eye. They were amazed at her ability to hit plum pits, sending them flying far away. She explained that her proficiency with the sling was the result of daily practice. She led them into the canyon and spread them out along the stream, where they lashed at leaves on bushes and hooked the slings on branches. Deborah stopped by each person, demonstrating, adjusting, and encouraging.

When sunset approached, there was still no sign of Ramrod. Deborah hiked to the spring at the head of the canyon and tried to sort out her mixed feelings. She had to acknowledge the virtue of his earnest competence in transforming Ein Gedi into a habitable refuge for a rising number of lepers. On the other hand, if he had done all that to impress her, it manifested an obsessive infatuation that repulsed her. While she recognized Yael's logic in accepting Ramrod as a husband who was eligible to inherit Palm Homestead for her, the thought of becoming his wife made her stomach churn. For that reason, she was relieved by his reaction last night and his subsequent disappearance, which could only mean that her pregnancy with Barac's child was too much for Ramrod to accept.

Yael joined her with a fistful of raisins, which they shared.

"He's gone," Deborah said. "Where's my silver coin?"

"It's not over yet."

"Didn't you hear him cry last night?"

Yael nodded. "He's in pain. You're also in pain. It's a good match. You'll heal together, build a family, serve your God, and so on."

"It's not going to happen. What did you tell me about men's pride?" Deborah quoted Yael. "A man would rather lose blood than lose face."

From the bottom of the canyon, a wail came, at first sounding human, then crystallizing into a horn blow that grew stronger and reverberated from the rocky walls.

"Do you hear?" Yael splashed water at her. "He's summoning you!"

Deborah splashed her back. "It's a call for prayers, that's all."

"You'll see." Yael ran her wet fingers through her long hair. "On this matter, I'm the prophet."

"And your prophesy is that I'll sell my body for an inheritance?"

Yael laughed. "Only to a man of Ephraim!"

When they reached the mouth of the canyon, the sun was gone, and a goat was roasting over a fire. The locals and the lepers sat separately on opposite sides of the narrow canyon. Ramrod mounted the rock, blew the horn again, and gestured for Deborah to come up, while he stepped down. She did as he asked.

"Blessed be Yahweh," she said, "king of the world, for creating this food, which we are fortunate to eat here together as we begin the third of the ten Days of Awe, contemplating our sins and making amends before the coming Day of Atonement."

The evening feast was rowdy, everyone talking about their slingshots, target hits, and riotous mishaps. They compared their blisters and bruises, praised their different slings, and suggested improvements. Men and women surrounded Deborah, asking advice and seeking instructions. Ramrod sat with a group of local men, listened to their banter, but did not participate.

After the meal, Ramrod mounted the rock and blew the horn at great length, while everyone gazed up at him. A breeze came up from the east, carrying a tangy odor from the Sea of Salt and breathing new life into the fire. Flames rose up and illuminated Ramrod on the rock, blowing the horn for a long time. When the sound finally died off, he bent over, resting his hands on his knees, panting hard.

Everyone clapped.

Ramrod straightened up and cleared his throat.

"Forgive my absence," he said. "I had to be alone today, walk in the desert, reflect on what has happened in the recent past, and consider what should happen next."

They watched him in silence, the locals on one side, the lepers on the other.

He addressed the lepers first. "We came here following Deborah's dream and, as she had predicted, the curse stopped advancing. For me, it meant a cure for my affliction, which was slight, but for most of you, it only means living a longer life of suffering and hopelessness."

Many of the lepers murmured in agreement.

He turned to the locals. "God saw your kindness and compassion toward those who receive no empathy elsewhere. The Days of Awe, in my opinion, should be called the Days of Praise when it comes to the people of Ein Gedi. May His judgment of you on the Day of Atonement be equally kind and compassionate."

"Amen," everyone chorused.

Now, Ramrod addressed both the locals and the lepers. "We live in a harsh place, but the rest of the land is harsh in worse ways. There's strife among the tribes of Israel, sins against God, and Canaanite subjugation. Has God abandoned His Chosen People?"

Raising his horn, Ramrod blew it again, and when he was done, he took a few deep breaths before continuing to speak.

"I believe God still loves us and wants us back under His wings. I believe He anointed Deborah to deliver His word. And I believe He expects us to protect her from the evil men in Ephraim who plan to kill her. It is a dangerous duty, but an honorable death is better than a wretched life. Each one of you should think about it tonight. At sunrise, I will blow the horn from this rock to summon the righteous for a holy march." Ramrod held the horn up in the air, as one would raise a flag. "He who is for God, join me!"

Later, Deborah started a small fire outside Ramrod's lean-to and warmed up goat milk. Yael and Ramrod sat by the fire, holding their cups as she poured the milk. The three of them drank slowly and listened to the whispers coming from up and down the steep slopes of the canyon.

"I liked your speech," Yael said. "I wish I could join your cause. Unfortunately, I'm not a Hebrew leper."

"Too bad," Deborah said. "There are ways to become one, if you really want."

"No, thanks," Yael said. "Maybe another time."

They laughed, then quieted down and drank more warm milk while the fire crackled and the shacks were alive with murmured conversations.

Ramrod put down his cup. "I have another speech. May I deliver it now?"

Deborah and Yael nodded.

"Last night," he said, "I was in agony and confusion, but walking alone in the desert today, I realized what God has been trying to show me repeatedly. First, He brought you to the gates of Shiloh, where I heard your desperate prayers, saw you faint, and carried you to Miriam's tent. Second, after knocking down Seesya, you hid among us on the journey to Aphek. Third, after winning your trial in Emanuel, you came upon me on the road from Bethel. Fourth, when you survived Seesya's ambush here, I stayed behind with the lepers while you continued on your journey to Edom. But now, the fifth time God has brought us together, I finally understand. Staying by your side is my True Calling."

Deborah felt the urge to get up and run, but she stayed put.

"Deborah," Ramrod said. "Will you accept me as your husband?"

Yael clapped. "I knew it!"

The first thing that came to Deborah's mind were God's words in the Garden of Eden: "And to the woman God said: I shall multiply your pain and agony; in anguish you shall bear children; always you shall lust after your husband, and he shall reign over you." The first part – pain, agony, and anguish – she had plenty of, but there was no chance she would ever lust after Ramrod or let him reign over her. And then, she remembered what Obadiah of Levi, the priest in Emanuel, had said: "Without a husband, you're nothing. The law says that only a man may possess land. If a man dies with no son but a daughter, the local judge will hold the land in trust until the daughter marries and her husband becomes owner of the land, provided that he is from the same tribe." Closing her eyes, Deborah prayed for an answer: Was Ramrod a gift from God, a shortcut on her path to answering her True Calling, or was he the tormenting husband God had promised every woman since Eve?

Reaching over, Ramrod gripped her forearm. "I swear to you, Deborah, that as your husband I'll do everything in my power to help you recover Palm Homestead and deliver God's word to our people."

Somewhere above, Deborah heard wings flapping, but when she looked up, the sky was too dark to reveal anything. Was it the eagle? Had it come to warn her, or to bless this union?

"Also," Ramrod said, "when the time comes, I'll treat the baby as my own."

Her chest constricted with the pressure to give an answer. She searched the sky again, remembering what the eagle had said, back in Judge Ohad's house, about the possibility of marrying Barac: "The prospect of marriage presents a whole new set of fears, duties, and opportunities, which you must weigh very carefully to make sure you are acting based on virtuous reasons and correct assumptions, or your brief moment of happiness will turn into lifelong misery." Those foreboding words had been prescient, as her brief moment of happiness with Barac had in face turned into what could become lifelong misery of an unwed mother to a fatherless child.

"Say yes," Yael said. "Or no. Make a choice."

A choice.

The word reminded her of something else the eagle had said:

"When facing a tough dilemma in life, we tend to fixate on an obvious choice and fail to see other, less obvious choices."

"Yes or no," Deborah said. "That's not my only choice."

They remained quiet, waiting for her to continue.

"Let me tell you my choice. My choice is never to be owned by a man, never to be told by a man what I may or may not do, and never to be silenced by a man when I wish to speak. My choice is not to be treated by a man the way Hebrew wives are treated by their husbands. And if I do agree to marry, my choice is to only accept a husband who will take pride in me when I wield weapons, learn to read and write, and study the Holy Scriptures – a husband who will show me the same honesty, loyalty, and respect that he expects me to show him. That's my choice!"

Her voice had risen as she spoke, travelling up and down the canyon, and when the echoes of her last word faded away, the lepers' murmurs was gone as if they, too, were bewildered by her audacity.

Ramrod stood up, shook his robe to straighten it, and went down on his knees. "I swear to you by Yahweh's name that, as your husband, all my actions and omissions will match perfectly with the desired husband you've just described." He took a deep breath. "Now, will you become my wife?"

Deborah knew he was sincere, but would he manage to keep his vow when, as Umm-Sallan had predicted, the men in Canaan sought her downfall for fear that their wives and daughters might demand the same rights as her?

"I know you're sincere," she said. "The future, however, is impossible to know. Reality might test your resolve in unexpected ways."

"There's only one test I dread," he said. "That the baby's father decides to come back into your life."

"Don't worry," Yael said. "He's not coming back."

Deborah wasn't so sure. Barac had left because of her rejection, not due to any change of heart on his part, and not before he begged her to change her mind. What if he did show up one day, a year or five from now, to plead with her again, saying that his heart still belonged to her, whereas the pretty girl with the wide hips and ample breasts had only served to dull his heartbreak over losing Deborah.

How sweet it would be to hear Barac say those things, but would it change anything? In the end, he was not a man of Ephraim, and his quick departure and marrying another girl proved that his love was shallow and his loyalty feeble.

"Fear not," Deborah told Ramrod. "As long as you keep your vows, I shall keep mine."

He smiled and exhaled in relief.

Deborah turned to Yael. "Bring me my sack."

Yael went into the shack and returned with the sack. Deborah searched inside, found the six-starred ring, and handed it to Ramrod.

His eyes glistening, he slipped it on Deborah's finger. "With this ring," he said, his voice quivering, "I betroth you to be my wife."

Again, Yael startled them by clapping. "We need a priest and a goat."

"Yes," Deborah said, "and a lifetime of keeping vows."

They raised the milk cups in a toast, emptied them, and retired for the night – Ramrod on his cot outside and the two girls in the lean-to shack. Deborah felt sick as if she has eaten spoiled meat. She pulled a coin out of the purse and gave it to Yael, who hugged her tightly.

49

Sunrise over the Great Sea was unlike any of the countless sunrises Barac had seen in his life. He stood with Tova on the deck of the ship, held on to the railing, and watched the sun emerge over the horizon, its reflection sparkling on the choppy blue water.

The previous night, Petro's men had somehow taken possession of this ship and three of its crewmen. Petro brought along five of his men, carrying food and water for a week, as well as clubs, spears, and swords. Taking advantage of the pre-dawn breeze, the three crewmen had raised the sails, weighed anchor, and headed into the sea.

One crewman stood in the rear, holding on to a long wooden rod connected to a wide plank, which was half-submerged behind the ship and controlled the direction it was moving. He kept the ship heading north on a path parallel to the distant shoreline. With the sails under a steady blow from the east, the ship leaned gently to the left, and water occasionally splashed onto the deck through holes at the bottom of the side railing.

As the day grew brighter, Barac realized how tiny the ship was in the vast expanse of water around them. He walked the length of the ship, measuring it to be thirty-three steps. The width was ten steps, and the main mast was about as tall as the length of the ship. There were different ropes to control the sails and to secure goods on the deck.

When night fell, Petro navigated by watching the lights of fires at the Philistines' coastal cities, villages, and homesteads. The wind shifted, coming from the west, and the ship plowed ahead, rising and falling with the waves. Barac and Tova stayed on deck, often retching over the side, which amused Petro and the others, who seemed as comfortable on water as on land.

On the morning of the second day, they felt better. Barac stood at the bow of the ship, the breeze in his face, the water swelling and dropping in an endless cycle.

Tova beckoned him back to the side railing.

In the water, several large fish with fins on their backs swam alongside the ship at the same pace, rising and diving in graceful coordination. At the same time, the pale birds they had seen on the beach at Gaza were flying over the ship, occasionally taking a rest on the railing or the mast, crowing to each other as if in heated arguments.

At midday, the wind died down. It did not come back all night, and through the following day and night. They spent the two nights sleeping fitfully on deck, hot and sweaty, and during the day sat in the shade of the sails while the sea birds crowed above. The delay tested Barac's patience as he imagined Deborah arriving at Emanuel to face Seesya alone.

On the morning of the fourth day, the wind finally picked up again, and the sails filled. They traveled north all day. In the early evening, Petro pointed at the coast. "That's the north end of Philistia. From here on, the land belongs to the Hebrew tribe of Dan. They have fast rowboats to raid ships passing too close to shore."

Under darkness, the helmsman kept the ship in its northward progress. It was a cold night, and Barac and Tova went below deck. With only one narrow entryway, the ship's hold smelled of raw fish and bitter wine. Most of the floor was taken by heaped fishnets, stacked barrels, a bunch of oars, and a pile of weapons. The center, which was the lowest part of the ship, was filled with stones to keep the ship straight. Dirty water sloshed around the stones. They cleared a corner to lie down and rest. Soon, the gentle swaying of the ship put them to sleep.

The fifth day on the ship was tense. Petro and his men stood at the railing, watching for any threat. A few times, a sail appeared in the distance, but none came close. Barac and Tova went below deck to rest.

A crewman woke them up during the night. They went up on deck. Petro stood at the railing, his gaze fixed on the distant shore, where the glow of numerous fires told of a large city.

"That's Jaffa," he said. "Main city of the Hebrew tribe of Dan.

They're cunning and warlike. Their territory extends to the mouth of the Yarkon River – if they spot us, we'll have to turn and sail west into deep waters as fast as the wind can take us."

The helmsman kept the ship on a northerly path beyond the lights. The sea grew calmer as the wind weakened. The moon edged up over the horizon, casting a bleak glow on the surface of the water.

At a signal from Petro, the helmsman began to execute a moderate turn to the right until the bow pointed at the coast. Gradually, the outline of land grew clearer in the moonlight. The crewmen lowered the sails and brought oars from below for everyone except the helmsman, who remained at his position, Tova, who stood in the back of the boat, and Petro, who relocated to front, where he leaned forward over the pointed bow and stared ahead.

The oars, which were much longer than the ones used on the small boats, fitted in holes along the bottom of the railing on both sides. The men knelt on the deck and began to row. Barac was third on the right. He watched the others and did his best to imitate the circular motions and the rhythm of their rowing. At the bow, Petro raised his right or left hand to communicate with the helmsman, who made course corrections accordingly.

While kneeling, Barac's head was just above the railing, giving him a view of Jaffa's lights, far to the south by now, and the lights of a village, coming up on the right.

The ship approached a narrow gap in the coastline. It was the mouth of the Yarkon River. As they came closer, the ship began to shake, its bottom scraping the ground in the shallow water. Plowing through, they rowed hard and got over the invisible underwater hump. Petro whispered an order, and everyone lowered their heads and slowed down the pace of rowing, careful not to make splashing noises with the oars while the ship slipped into the wide mouth of the river. The current flowed in the opposite direction, but it was mild, enabling them to progress against it.

The village was built slightly up from the south bank of the river, which was lined with trees and bushes. A few dogs barked, but none came down to the water. Fires still burned from the evening meals, and voices could be heard of women chatting and children chirping, though Barac could not make out what they were saying. As the ship passed the village, a man yelled in Hebrew, "Bring me wine, woman, or I'll whip you this moment!" She must have obeyed, because the man began to sing.

Slowly, the lights of the village faded behind, the man's singing quieted down, and the ship went into the dark, unnoticed and unmolested. The river narrowed to approximately forty steps wide, with tree branches hanging low over the water. Petro signaled to speed up the rowing.

Despite the growing distance from the village, Barac remained anxious. If the men of Dan deserved their reputation, would they not keep a night watchman? Would they miss a foreign ship coming in from the sea into the river steps away from their village? Reflecting back, he realized that, in his efforts to discern the words, he failed to question why only one man's voice could be heard, while there were numerous women and children.

Barac pulled his oar out of the water, told Tova to go below deck, and went forward to speak with Petro.

"It's not safe yet," he whispered.

Petro waved his hand at the dark river around them as if challenging him to point out any danger.

"Our forefather, Jacob, said of Dan that they are like a snake on the road that bites a horse's heel to topple the rider."

"I know the snake on their flag," Petro said. "But they didn't see us."

"What if they did notice us, but pretended not to? I heard only one man's voice in the village, but many women." Barac pointed to the back of the ship. "They could sneak up on us in boats from behind and climb aboard before we can mount a defense."

Considering this for a moment, Petro made a decision. He left four rowers, and had the others collect weapons from below and crouch behind the railing in the rear of the deck. Each man clutched a sword in one hand and a spear in the other. Intermittently, Petro peeked over the railing.

After a while, Petro stood up. "Nothing," he said. "Any attack would have happened already."

As the men returned to their posts, the ship stopped abruptly, the bow rising up and the rear dropping. In the moonlight, Barac noticed a heavy rope across the front, tied between the riverbanks. The boat began to slide backward, the bow dropping back down and the rear rising. Everyone lost their balance and fell. He heard a soft whistle, and an arrow hit the man beside him in the neck. More whistles followed, while Barac pushed Petro and the other men closer to the railings. The arrows made knocking sounds as they hit the ship. Of the four rowers, one was slumped with an arrow stuck through his ear, while the others hid behind the railing.

The arrows stopped flying, and Barac knew what was coming next.

"Get ready," he yelled, grabbing the sword and club he'd dropped while falling down. "They're coming!"

His prediction of a stealth approach from the rear came true as a man climbed in using the helm as a steppingstone. Petro stabbed him in the chest, and the man fell back into the water with a loud splash. The noise triggered a cacophony of battle cries in Hebrew as more men appeared over the railings around the ship. The Philistine men jumped up and rushed at the attackers, screaming curses in their language. For a brief moment, Barac froze in confusion, his arms refusing to act against Hebrew men, but as one of them jumped over the railing toward him with a raised sword, Barac dodged while angling his sword to run it through the man's underbelly. The man cried, and Barac sliced his throat, silencing him, and pushed him over the railing.

Next to Barac, Petro clubbed an attacker on the head, stabbed him between the ribs, and with the sword still inside, flung him sideways to knock down another attacker, whose arm was then chopped off at the elbow by another Philistine. One of the rowers, meantime, pulled his oar out of the hole and used it to knock several attackers off the railing back into their small rowboats. More attackers climbed over the bow. Barac ran forward, stabbing one of them with his sword while clubbing the other across the face. At the same time, a third one scrambled over, hopped onto Barac, and knocked him down on his back. Drawing a knife from his belt, the man raised his hand high and stabbed down. Barac grabbed the man's wrist, the point of the blade within a hair of Barac's eye. The man pressed down.

"Yahweh curses you," Barac said in Hebrew. "Yahweh will punish you!"

The words distracted the man for a moment, allowing Barac to push his arm up, but then he grinned and pressed down again. The blade touched Barac's eyelid and began to penetrate.

A stone hit the man's head, and he cried, turning to see where had the stone come from. Barac took advantage of this and rolled aside with the man, ending up on top of him, with the knife clutched by both of them. Looking up, Barac saw Tova run along the ship between the fighting men, a second stone in her other hand. She dropped to the deck and pounded the stone on the man's forehead, again, and again until he no longer moved. Barac got up, pulled his sword from the man he had killed before and picked up his club, just in time to confront three more men of Dan, who climbed over the railing near the bow. A crewman joined him, and together they killed two and maimed the third, who fell into the water.

The battle ended as abruptly as it had started. A few attackers rowed downstream furiously in a single boat. Four other boats drifted among the bobbing corpses. On the ship, two Philistine men were dead and two wounded. Barac shuddered at the thought of what the result would have been had the men of Dan managed to surprise them while they were exposed and unarmed.

Tova helped Petro bandage the wounded while Barac and the remaining men rolled the corpses into the water and resumed rowing. The current had carried them a short distance downstream, and when they returned to where the rope was tied across the river, Barac leaned over the bow and hacked the thick rope with his sword until it was cut through. They continued to row upriver. Occasionally, dogs barked from isolated homesteads on either side of the river, but they saw no lights of fires or torches.

When the moon reached its apex in the night sky, Petro signaled the helmsman to veer aside, and the ship came to a stop in the shallows near the south riverbank.

Climbing over the railing, Barac went into the water, which reached up to his chest. He carried his sack and weapons over his head to dry land while Petro carried Tova, as well as a waterskin and some bread.

"Go uphill." Petro pointed. "You'll find a good road. It's called the Sea Highway, because it comes all the way from Egypt. Go left toward the east. By morning, you'll reach Aphek, where the river starts. You can buy a horse there and continue your journey."

Barac bowed. "Thank you."

Wading back into the water, Petro said, "Tell Borah I paid my debt of freedom."

"I'll pass the message." Barac shouldered his sack. "May your Gods bring you back to Gaza safely.

50

When Ramrod blew the horn at sunrise, the lepers packed up their dwellings with great haste, harnessed their carts to donkeys, and loaded their belongings. The locals, meanwhile, prepared bread, cheese, and fruit for the lepers, filled up waterskins at the spring, and brought black-dyed robes and headdresses for Deborah, Yael, and Ramrod to wrap themselves up as lepers. Two of the locals carried a bucket of black dye to the corral and, while feeding Rogez plums, painted him over until he bore no resemblance to his former white self. Deborah wrapped her armor and sword, covered up the copper spear, and secured her sack to the saddle. She went to say goodbye to Leah and the other women of Simeon, who decided to stay with the locals in Ein Gedi for the time being.

Deborah took Leah aside and gave her two-dozen silver coins. "Use it to buy anything you need from passing caravans, or to pay one to take you if you decide to leave Ein Gedi and join us in the Samariah Hills."

"Thank you." Leah hugged her. "May you find happiness where you're going."

Deborah hugged her back. "There was something I wanted to ask you about Beersheba. You said that Tsruyah now lives in Judge Ohad's house. Is he the new judge of Simeon?"

"I heard him declare himself to be the judge, but then, the men of Judah started building a larger house across the street for their judge, who sent armed men to collect all the false gods and burn them at the temple."

"That's good," Deborah said. "Judge Ohad had allowed too many of those in Beersheba, even in his own room."

"A lot of new houses are now being built by men of Judah for their families."

"Inside Beersheba?"

Leah nodded.

"Simeon kneels before Judah," Deborah said. "Exactly as our forefather Jacob predicted countless generations ago."

The sun was barely above the Moab Mountains in the east when the long caravan left Ein Gedi on the coastal road north. The pace was slow, with about half of the lepers on foot while their carts carried those who had difficulty walking. Deborah rode on Rogez with Yael behind her, both of them clad in black. She thought about Barac and Ramrod, who was her choice now, evidenced by the ring on her finger, but not in her heart, where Barac still reigned,

Along the way, they ran into more lepers heading to Ein Gedi. Many of them reversed direction and joined the caravan. At every stop, the lepers picked the desert floor clean of stones and practiced shooting with their slings. It took a while for Deborah to grow accustomed to hearing them laugh behind their black veils, or to see some of them use both hands to compensate for missing fingers.

They stopped for the night at an oasis near a steep mountain, whose cliffside was riddled with out-of-reach caves. After sunset, Ramrod blew the horn to start the fourth of the Days of Awe. After a light meal, they went to sleep. Deborah, Ramrod, and Yael took turns standing watch.

The march resumed at dawn, while the air was still cool, and kept going all day, stopping occasionally for water and rest. They reached Jericho late that night and made camp near the fairgrounds. Ramrod blew the horn to mark the fifth of the Days of Awe.

The next morning, local merchants accepted jars of pure salt, which Ramrod had brought along, in exchange for palm dates and honey cakes, as well as milk and cheese. The caravan started on the road up the Judean Mountains. Dressed in black, Deborah and Yael kept a sheer veil over their faces like the lepers. The journey was slow, but the road was well marked and free of obstacles. They spent two nights by small villages, where vendors sold food and water to replenish travelers' stocks. By the afternoon on the third day, the climbing was over, and Ramrod pointed to a hilltop town in the distance.

"That's Jerusalem," he said. "The men of Judah fought hard to capture it."

Deborah shielded her eyes and gazed.

"It's the highest point along the trade route from the Negev Desert through Hebron and Bethlehem and on to the north. Jerusalem sits on a hilltop, easy to defend on all sides, and there's a vibrant spring right under the city."

They arrived at Bethel long after sunset. The convoy had swelled to well over two hundred lepers. As Ramrod blew the horn to mark the eve of the eighth of the Days of Awe, a dozen other horns blew nearby. The vendors did brisk business with travelers heading to the Holy Temple in Shiloh to make sacrifices before the Day of Atonement.

Late that night, when everyone was asleep, Deborah, Ramrod, and Yael went to the town's ritual bath. While Ramrod and Yael stood watch, Deborah stripped naked and dipped three times in the chilly water.

51

Despite her shorter stature, Tova had kept a fast pace, earning Barac's admiration. They followed the road along the river, which meandered like a giant snake under the moon. Isolated homesteads along the right side of the road were guarded by dogs, which barked incessantly, but didn't attack. Only one time they saw lights, but on the left side of the road, down by the riverbank. It was a large compound that emitted a foul stench. A wooden wall surrounded it, and torches burned at regular intervals all around. Looking down from the road, Barac saw rows of small pools in the middle.

"It's the tannery," he said to Tova. "This is where Deborah worked until the great escape."

They continued walking through the rest of the night and the morning, when they heard the sound of rushing water ahead. Another curve in the road, and the view stopped them in their tracks.

Aphek was even larger than Beersheba. It covered a hillside above the north bank of the river. A narrow gorge roared with several gushing springs – the source of the Yarkon River. Massive walls defended the city from attacks where it wasn't protected by the river, the gorge, or the cliffs, which Barac guessed were the western ridges of the Samariah Hills. The road passed behind the springs in the deep end of the gorge, providing the only passage from south to north or back, between the Great Sea and the Samariah Hills. Now he understood why the Sea Highway had to turn inland along the riverbank until it could cross over here and continue north.

"God almighty," Tova said. "What a beautiful city!"

"It's very old," Barac said. "My father said that, prior to Joshua's war of conquer, an Egyptian governor had ruled here for centuries, sending olive oil, palm dates, wine, and taxes to the Pharaohs."

"Maybe that's his palace."

Tova pointed at a large ornate building with its own fortification walls and guard towers in the center of Aphek. Some of the roof was missing, and the left wing was blackened by fire.

"Probably," Barac said. "Imagine how Egyptian merchants feel when they travel through here and see this – a lesson to anyone doubting our divine claim to the Promised Land."

Two guards stood at the narrow part of the road by the gorge, where anyone wishing to enter the city or continue to travel east or north had to pass through. Near the checkpoint, a makeshift pole flew a black flag. Barac expected to see the white ox of Ephraim on the flag, but it carried Manasseh's white antelope. The two guards were dressed almost like men of Judah, with short robes and sandals, but their heads weren't covered, and their beards were short. One drew his sword, staying slightly back, while the other stepped to the center of the road, facing them.

"Shalom, brothers." Barac kept his right hand away from the hilt of his sheathed sword. "A fine day, isn't it?"

The guard at the center of the road measured Tova up and down.

Barac cleared his throat. "May we pass?"

Looking back at him, the guard asked, "What's in your sack?"

"Food, blanket, and a water skin."

"Open it."

The other guard tapped his sword against his leg, smirking.

Barac put down his sack, untied the neck, and held it open.

The guard put his hand in, felt around, and took out the purse Petro had brought back from their captors in Gaza. "What's this?"

"A few coins for the journey."

The guard tossed the purse in the air and caught it. "And where's your lamb or kid goat for the priests?"

The question took Barac by surprise. "I didn't bring any. We've travelled long—"

"What about your sins?" Glancing back at the other guard, he raised his voice. "No repenting?"

The mocking tone angered Barac, but he couldn't think of a good answer.

"Don't tell me you forgot that tomorrow night is the eve of the Day of Atonement?"

His face flushed, Barac was about to admit it, but Tova spoke up.

"We've been in captivity for some time," she said. "First, the cursed Philistines took us for slavery, and then, the evil men of Dan pounced upon us. We lost count of days."

"Really?" The guard spun the purse, making the coins jingle. "And why did the wicked Philistines and the murderous men of Dan release you? Did you sing for them? Or dance?"

"I did nothing," Tova said. "My husband killed them."

"All of them?" The guard laughed. "Every last one?"

"All who stood in my way," Barac said, drawing his sword, which was red from the fight on the river. "Here's their blood."

The guard's grin faded.

Barac took back the purse and put it in the sack.

The guards looked at each other, and the one in the rear asked, "Who are you?"

"I am Barac, son of Abinoam, chief defender of Beersheba and deputy to Mamreh, son of Judge Ohad."

The barrage of names and titles must have impressed the guards, who stepped aside.

Tova picked up the sack and followed Barac.

The road passed behind the roaring springs in a narrow curve under the cliffs. A short incline took them to an open area where the road split three ways – straight to the north, right to the Samariah Hills, and left through the busy fairgrounds to the open gates of Aphek, where a bigger flag of Manasseh flew from a taller pole.

At the intersection, Tova put down the sack and sat on it. She didn't complain, but he could see in her eyes a plea for rest. They had been walking briskly since the middle of the night and had not slept since the previous day.

"We must continue," Barac said.

Her eyes moistened, but she didn't argue.

"I fear we'll be too late." He felt obliged to explain. "Deborah believes that her True Calling is to speak the word of God to the Hebrews at Palm Homestead, and what day would be more fitting for her first delivery than the Day of Atonement?"

Perhaps because he phrased it as a question, Tova answered. "She'll be safe from an attack on the Day of Atonement."

"From Seesya?" Barac laughed bitterly. "He's not afraid of Yahweh. For him it is Ra, the Canaanite Sun God, who is chief among the Gods."

Tova stood up, her face twisting in pain, and picked up the sack. "Which way?"

Barac took the sack from her hand, pulled out the purse, and put the sack down. "Sit back and rest. I'll buy us a horse."

In the far corner of the fairgrounds, he found a horse trader and negotiated a price of two silver coins for an old horse with a scuffed-up saddle, patchy fur, and no tail, as well as some bread, apples, and figs.

Barac wanted to ask him for directions to Emanuel, but was careful to ask in a way that didn't give away his destination. "Where does the road go from here?"

"The road splits. Haven't you noticed?"

Barac shrugged. "We're tired."

"The main road continues north to Megiddo, which we control now." The horse trader sneered. "Further north, you'll find Issachar, Zebulun, and Naphtali, our wretched brothers who kneel before the Canaanites and kiss the toes of King Javin at Hazor."

"And the road east?"

"To the land of Ephraim." He spat on the ground. "Only until God delivers the rest of Ephraim into our hands."

"Why?" Barac scratched his head in order to seem bewildered. "Aren't you brothers?"

"Indeed," the horse trader said. "And who was the firstborn?"

"Manasseh?"

"Exactly, which means our tribe should have inherited all of Joseph's share of Canaan, not divide it with the usurper Ephraim. Learn your Holy Scriptures, boy, or God will punish you. The Day of Atonement is upon us!"

Barac reclined his head and spoke in a contrite tone. "How far is Shiloh?"

"Follow the road east for about a day, where it joins the road from the south that brings all the pilgrims from Emanuel, Bethel, and Jerusalem. From there, it's about half a day to Shiloh."

Barac and pulled the horse through the fairgrounds. Judging by the position of the sun, he surmised there was still a good part of the day to travel. If they rode fast and made the turnoff south before dark, they could continue through the night and reach the small path to Palm Homestead shortly before the main road reached Emanuel. Meanwhile, there would be pilgrims on the road from Emanuel, heading the opposite way for Shiloh, and they would know if Deborah had arrived yet. Finally, after all the setbacks, Barac felt hopeful as he pulled the horse by the reins out of the crowded fairgrounds and onto the short path back to the intersection. Only then did he notice a group of soldiers surrounding Tova.

One of the guards from the checkpoint saw him and pointed.

Barac let go of the horse's reins, drew his sword and raised his club while rushing forward.

The soldiers shoved Tova to the ground and aimed the tips of their spears at her.

The guard yelled, "Drop your weapons, or she dies."

Slowing down, Barac struggled to control his rage and the overwhelming urge to attack the men and cut them down, but he knew they wouldn't think twice of killing a woman, and Tova would be dead before he reached them. With a shout of anger, he threw his sword and club to the ground.

They tied his wrists behind his back and took his weapons and the horse. Tova's hands were tied up in front of her so that she could carry the sack. They led them through the gates into the city, up several streets, past remnants of charred stone walls, and into the ancient palace that had been visible from across the river.

The entryway was immense, fit for three horses abreast and three more stacked up. A cavernous hall was missing part of its roof, but the stone walls were solid. The floor, though littered with parts of the roof, was lain with huge slabs of white stone that had been sanded down as perfectly as the smooth face of a pond on a windless day. In the corners of the hall stood sculptures of tall creatures, each with a naked female body and the head of a bird with full hair, trimmed straight over the eyes and above the shoulders. Two more stone creatures, also with human bodies, but with male organs and heads of lions, stood beside an empty throne that appeared carved out of the same smooth slab as the floor.

The soldiers made Barac and Tova sit on the floor and left the hall. Their voices could be heard from outside, chatting and laughing.

After a while, Barac called out to the soldiers, but they ignored him. Time passed slowly, the lights and shadows moving gradually across the vast room as the sun went down. When darkness came, the meek moonlight cast enough light on the strange sculptures to make them seem alive. Tova leaned over and buried her face in the nook of his neck. Barac felt her shaking.

53

That morning in Bethel, Ramrod put on a plain robe and rode to his relatives' homestead nearby. He returned with his two elderly uncles mounted on donkeys. They followed behind the caravan of lepers as it slowly advanced on the road north from Bethel to the Samariah Hills.

In the late afternoon, Deborah saw Emanuel in the distance, and her heartbeat quickened. She dropped the sheer veil over her face. Yael did the same. They set up camp by the roadside, just south of the Weeping Tree, where Tamar's bones had dangled for many weeks, where Deborah had spent a night tied to the trunk while blood dripped from her lacerated back, and where Seesya had received a good whipping, though not as good as the stoning he deserved.

Ramrod sent one of the lepers to the gates with a request for the priest to come out, accept their gifts, and give them a blessing. Deborah started a fire, and the lepers borrowed burning branches to start a dozen more fires, where they sat down to eat in groups, talking quietly. She worried that Obadiah might send someone else in his stead, but a while later, the old priest's familiar white-clad figure came up the road from the gates. He reached the large encampment and stopped, leaning on his wooden staff, a lone figure in the bleak twilight.

The lepers got up and gathered before him. Obadiah seemed stunned by their large number, all congregated in one place, but quickly recovered and got on with the task at hand. He raised his hands, fingers parted in pairs, and recited the traditional priestly blessing: "May Yahweh bless you and protect you. May He show you kindness and grace. May He illuminate your path and grant you peace."

The lepers chorused, "Amen."

Deborah approached him, setting aside the sheer veil from her face.

It took Obadiah a moment to recognize her in the twilight. He stumbled back, his hand shooting to his mouth.

"Don't worry," she said. "I'm not afflicted."

"Not worry?" He glanced back at the gates. "Are you trying to get us both killed?"

"No one will recognize me under these leper's rags."

"God's mercy!" He groaned. "Don't you know anything? Seesya's only surviving soldier, whom you foolishly sent back—"

"Mishneh?"

"Yes, that poor boy stood at the gates of Emanuel to praise your courage and compassion until Seesya returned by way of Moab with a broken jaw, a burning fury, and a five-dozen group of Canaanite mercenaries he'd hired along the way with promises of generous pay."

"What happened to Mishneh?"

"He had to go into hiding."

"Where?"

Obadiah leaned forward, lowering his voice further. "At my house, in the back of the temple – the one place that the faithless son of Judge Zifron doesn't frequent."

"You did the right thing."

"But you didn't. Sending him back was a foolish. Now every man and woman of Ephraim talks about what happened in Ein Gedi, fueling Seesya's fury."

"People should know the truth. It's good."

"It's good, yes, if you wish to die."

"I wish to marry," she said. "This is Ramrod, son of Malkishua of Ephraim."

Ramrod set aside his black veil, too.

"I remember you," Obadiah said. "You told Seesya she was heading to Ein Gedi."

Lowering his eyes, Ramrod nodded.

The priest turned to Deborah. "Why would you marry this weakling?"

"Palm Homestead," she said. "I need a man of Ephraim."

"Then find a real man of Ephraim." The old priest waved dismissively at Ramrod. "This one isn't a man, but a chaff of straw, afraid of his own shadow—"

"Enough," Deborah said. "Everyone is afraid of Seesya, even you, a man fortified by faith, wisdom, and a priestly white robe. Now, will you marry me to this good man?"

Obadiah turned to Ramrod. "Are you a good man?"

"Yes," Ramrod said. "I am."

"Then be good and go back to where you came from. Deborah is not for you."

"Why?"

The priest sighed. "When Moses reached Canaan, the Hebrew tribes were afraid to enter it, and he sent spies to explore the land. Do you remember what they told him when they returned?"

Ramrod shook his head.

Deborah answered. "We saw giants in Canaan, and we felt like locusts next to them, and that's how they perceived us."

"Next to her," Obadiah gestured at Deborah, "even I feel like a locust, as you do, I'm sure, and before long, she'll perceive you as a locust, too."

His face burning, Ramrod said, "I'm not a pest."

"You're not a giant, either, and Deborah needs a giant – a mighty, smart, and fierce husband to match her courage, brilliance, and ferocity. Only such a man will be a proper match for Deborah. Without such a husband, she's in great danger."

"I'll protect her."

Obadiah rested a hand on his shoulder. "I'm giving you wise advice, boy. This marriage will end in disappointment, anger, and tears. She's not for you."

"I'm not a boy, I'm a man who has betrothed a woman." Ramrod held up Deborah's hand with the ring on her finger. "She's betrothed to me, and I won't release her."

The priest looked at Deborah. "In the name of God, don't go through with this marriage."

"His uncles are here," she said. "They can verify his ancestry."

The older of the two uncles said, "I swear by Yahweh that this is Ramrod, son of my dead brother Malkishua of Ephraim."

The other one said, "I swear to it, too."

One of the lepers brought over a goat.

Obadiah swayed, steadying himself with his staff. "Seesya will kill me."

"Marry us," Deborah said. "Do it now, before your faith falters under fear."

"Have you dipped three times in a ritual bath?"

"She did," Ramrod said. "I swear to it."

Ramrod's uncles lifted the goat and turned it over, one holding its front legs, the other holding the rear legs. The goat brayed.

Glancing back toward the gate and the fairgrounds, Obadiah said, "Under the laws of Yahweh, this man, Ramrod, son of Malkishua of Ephraim, takes Deborah, daughter of Harutz of Ephraim, as his wife."

Deborah looked away from the goat. She imagined reaching Palm Homestead, a bright sun shining on the lush fields and green orchards.

"With this offering," the priest continued, "we ask God to sanctify this marriage, make the bride's womb fertile, and give her many sons to continue her husband's name."

Over two hundred lepers chorused, "Amen!"

Obadiah drew a knife from under his white robe, held it over the goat's neck, and recited the traditional marriage blessing: "Blessed be Yahweh, our God, king of the world, who created man in His own image and made the woman to lust after her husband and obey him in all matters until death."

The goat bleated and thrashed as he brought down the blade and sliced the neck with a single pass. The goat went silent, its legs kicked hard, and Ramrod's uncles struggled to hold it.

Deborah breathed deeply, determined not to faint. The goat was dying to honor God as He blessed this marriage, which needed every available blessing to succeed. She thought of her palm tree, its canopy of fronds rustling in the wind.

Ramrod took her hand, pressed it lightly, and led her into a small tent a few steps away. Obadiah followed them and stood beside the tent. Yael held up the flap as Deborah crouched and got in. A palm-sized oil lamp softened the darkness inside. The cot was covered with a sheet of white linen. Ramrod squeezed in, too, and Yael dropped the flap.

Deborah sat at the edge, her back to the pitched cloth wall of the tent, forcing her to lean forward. Ramrod sat across from her, his back to the opposite wall, and also leaned forward, which brought their faces close. The oil lamp illuminated his face. He smiled – a nervous smile that made his lips seem even thinner. She wondered how long it would be before the patchy plumes on his gaunt chin grew to a full beard over his ungainly features.

"Well," he said. "Here we are."

She nodded and gripped her hands together. The six-starred ring pressed on her finger, reminding her of Barac, of his smiling face, his sweet lips, and his strong arms. The memory filled her with an urge to push aside the flap and crawl out before Ramrod tried to touch her.

They heard Obadiah chanting words from the Holy Scriptures.

A hissing sounded when the goat's entrails landed in the fire. The odors followed soon enough, and Deborah had a hard time breathing. What had she done? There was no way she could go through with this – with him! She had to get out!

A knife appeared in Ramrod's right hand.

Deborah tensed, but he put the blade to his left palm.

She grabbed his hand. "What are you doing?"

He leaned closer and whispered, "Making sure they think you're a virgin."

Stunned, she watched him nick his palm and hold it over the white linen. His blood trickled, staining the linen, spreading in a dark circle.

Satisfied, he pulled out a strap of cotton, wrapped it around his hand, and held it forward for her to tie a knot.

"That's it," he whispered. "We just have to wait a little longer to make it believable."

Deborah was relieved. "Don't you want to, I mean, be my husband?"

"I do, but not like this." He took a deep breath and kept his voice low. "We need time to get to know one another. I have to earn your trust and prove to you that I can be the husband you want, a husband who shows you the same honesty, loyalty, and respect that he expects you to show him."

Filled with gratitude, Deborah's hands shook as she struggled to tie the strap over his wound, while her eyes filled with tears.

Ramrod smiled. "Don't cry. Please don't. The old priest already thinks poorly of me."

She laughed, put her arms around his bony back, and hugged him. Hesitant, he placed his arms around her, as well.

54

It was dark when a man marched into the hall, followed by two guards with burning torches. He had a short silver beard, wore a long leather coat, and his boots knocked on the stone floor as he walked to the throne and sat down.

"Welcome to Aphek," he said in a booming voice. "How is my old friend, Judge Ohad of Simeon?"

Tova started to get up, but Barac stopped her and remained seated, remembering the lesson he'd learned with the guards at the gorge. The men of Manasseh respected arrogance, not politeness. He grunted but didn't answer.

The man stretched his legs forward, one boot on top of the other. "Have you gone mute, young man?"

Barac glared at him. "The bounds on my wrists tie up my tongue, too."

The man laughed. "Feisty, aren't you?" He clicked his fingers, and one of the guards put down his torch, knelt by Barac and Tova, and untied their hands. They moved their arms around, bending and straightening them.

"Now, can you answer?"

"Judge Ohad could not be a friend of a man whose thugs abuse innocent travelers."

The amusement faded from the man's face. "Watch your tongue when you speak to the judge of Manasseh."

"And you speak to the chief defender of Beersheba and deputy to Mamreh, son of Judge Ohad."

"So I've heard. Let's start again. I am Orran of Manasseh." His tone resumed its friendliness. "We have no quarrel with Simeon and wish to send New Year's greetings to Judge Ohad."

"I saw him a few days ago." Barac chose his words carefully,

"Judge Ohad and Mamreh visited the southern parts of Simeon's land, near the Ramon Crater. I returned to Beersheba in preparations for an attack by the army of Judah."

Orran took a moment to digest this convoluted answer. "My guards had the impression that you just escaped Philistine captivity. Are they wrong?"

Barac inhaled deeply, taking his time to answer. "Once Beersheba was safe again, I travelled west to gather the valuable herds of Simeon from the pasture lands near Gerar, east of Gaza. A Hebrew farmer betrayed me to Philistine relatives of his wife." To change the subject, he asked, "How did you become a friend of Judge Ohad?"

"We have traded through traveling caravans. When you rode Judge Ohad's horses, you were sitting in saddles made by my tannery."

Hearing this, everything fell into place, and Barac knew who this man was and why the guards had held them here to be questioned by him.

"You make good saddles," Barac said. "Surely a rich man like you can afford to feed those he unjustly imprisons."

Tova giggled, probably out of nervousness. Orran sent one of the guards to fetch fresh bread, a chunk of cheese, and a jug of wine, which he placed on the floor in front of them.

Barac broke off two pieces of bread, gave one to Tova, and said, "Blessed be Yahweh, king of the world, for giving us bread from the land."

"Amen," Orran said. "Now, if you tell me how you got out of Philistia, and why you came to Aphek, I'll tell you why my men held you here for me."

While chewing, Barac spoke casually to give credence to his words. "To get out of Gaza, I regretfully had to burn down the temple of Dagon, kill a horde of Philistines, commandeer a ship with its crewmen, sail up the coast past Jaffa, and row into the mouth of the Yarkon River, where I slew a few attackers from Dan, before rowing further upriver, releasing the ship and its crewmen, and enjoying a vigorous walk along the river to Aphek." He took a sip of wine. "By the stench of it, I think we passed by your tannery on the way."

The soldiers laughed, and Orran smiled.

Barac wiped his lips. "If not for this delay, I'd be on the road to Shiloh now. We should all seek redemption for our sins before the Day of Atonement."

Orran gave him a long, searching look, perhaps sensing there was more to the story. "The Philistines deserve what you did to them, as do the men of Dan. Which brings me to the reason my men held you until I arrived."

Barac raised the jug in a faux toast and sipped from it.

"It has to do with a terrible crime," Orran said. "Some time ago, all my Philistine slaves disappeared from the tannery in the middle of the night. No one saw them on the roads in any direction. It was a mystery at first, but we figured out they used the roofs of the pavilions to float downriver. Our foreman, an Edomite slave named Kassite, rode away on horses he stole from the guards, together with a few other Edomite slaves and one Hebrew slave."

"A Hebrew slave?" Barac took another sip of wine. "Was he the brains behind this debacle?"

"Worse than a debacle. We had to start from scratch – hire a free Canaanite tanner as a foreman, overpay conniving traders for new slaves, beat them into obedience, train them to do the work, beat them again when they damaged the hides, brand them on the cheeks to prevent new escapes, and throw away a fortune in damaged hides the new slaves destroyed, intentionally or not. That escape cost me dearly."

"A terrible crime." Barac passed the wine jug to Tova. "A sin against God."

"Have any of the Philistines mentioned the name Borah?"

"Borah?" Barac chuckled. "Is that a name for a man, or a donkey?"

"It's not a laughing matter." Orran got up and walked back and forth in front of the stone throne. "The Hebrew slave, Borah, organized the escape, I'm sure of it."

"Why?"

"Because I never bought a slave named Borah. My foreman, Kassite, acquired that slave without telling me, I'm not sure why, and then, he had the audacity to show up at my house and ask me to release him – some nonsense about getting old and wanting to see his homeland again before he dies. Who ever heard of a slave demanding freedom due to homesickness? I should have chopped off his other foot right there and then!"

The man's cruelty was unsettling, but Barac knew he had to keep his cool. "It's hard to escape without feet, but also difficult to serve a master. Have you found out anything about Borah?"

"There is a rumor that Borah is actually a girl named Deborah, the rebellious wife of Seesya, son of Judge Zifron of Emanuel. Do you know him?"

Barac could feel Tova tense up, and was thankful he had not mentioned Emanuel in his travel plans. "I serve only one judge at a time," he said with a forced smile.

Orran walked over, his boots knocking on the floor, and crouched before them. He smelled of the tannery by the river.

"Try to remember," he said. "Did any of the Philistines mention the escape?"

"We didn't converse much with them. Have you reached out to Seesya, son of Zifron?"

Orran shook his head. "Our tribes aren't on the best of terms these days, but I'm a patient man. One day, I'll catch that wretched creature called Borah and mete out punishment worse than stoning, burning, and hanging combined!"

Barac rose to his feet, struggling to contain his urge to strike the man.

Orran stood up, too, and they faced each other up close.

"Take comfort," Barac said, "in the faith that our God always delivers justice."

"I'll deliver it myself. Justice will be done."

With boldness that surprised even him, Barac opened his arms. "Let us embrace as brothers," he said. "And pray that Yahweh decides to forgive our sins on the Day of Atonement and bless our new year with prosperity and health."

"And justice," Orran said, embracing him. "Justice!"

55

When Deborah came out of the tent, she almost bumped into
Obadiah of Levi, who stood not a step away. She hoped he hadn't
heard them inside the tent.

He picked the sheet off the cot with the tip of his wooden staff,
held it up in the light of the fire, and declared, "I bear witness to the
stain of blood from the virgin maiden Deborah, daughter of Harutz
of Ephraim, as she was possessed by Ramrod, son of Malkishua of
Ephraim, who is now her husband under the laws of our God."

Ramrod straightened his robe and bowed. "Thank you."

With a swing of the staff, the old priest tossed the sheet into the
fire. "You own Palm Homestead now, but I strongly urge you not to
go there. Take your new wife, go back to Ein Gedi, and pray that
Seesya dies in one of his violent raids. If you try to assert your
inheritance rights, he'll kill you and her and all these helpless lepers
you've brought along."

"It's not my decision," Ramrod said. "Deborah will decide."

Obadiah sighed. "I was afraid of that."

"Afraid?" She smiled. "Do you still doubt, after all the dangers
I've survived, that God is my shepherd?"

The old priest smiled. "Faith is a sun that lights up the dark
corners of fear."

"And of false faith, too."

"Of course," he said. "Still, I advise caution. Faith is comforting,
but it's wise to hedge every risk with a practical plan beyond mere
reliance on divine intervention."

"I'm relying on Judge Zifron."

"How?"

"Tomorrow is the ninth of the Days of Awe. At sunrise, I'll go
with my husband and my people to take possession of Palm

Homestead. I'll arrive in the afternoon, too late for anyone to notify Seesya before the start of the Day of Atonement. When he hears about it, I'll already be settled with some defenses in place, and the news will have already spread around the whole area that Palm Homestead has returned to its rightful owners."

"That won't stop him," Obadiah said.

"His father will stop him. Judge Zifron knows that there can be no second pardon for Seesya. He has avoided death by stoning once, getting mere lashing for the murders of my parents and sister. If he kills us, the rightful heirs, the people will accept nothing less than his death by stoning. That's why his father will stop him."

"Things have changed since Seesya came back with the Canaanite mercenaries. There's a rumor that he signed a secret treaty with the Canaanite ruler, King Javin of Hazor."

"What treaty?"

"For the future subjugation of the tribe of Ephraim, its people, and land."

"In exchange for what?"

"What do evil men seek? Power, wealth, and revenge."

"Judge Zifron will never agree to it."

"His father is powerless against him. In fact, everyone is powerless against Seesya."

"Yahweh isn't powerless." She raised a fist. "He will strengthen my hand, and I will strike down His enemies."

Without another word, Obadiah of Levi turned and walked back toward the dark gates of Emanuel.

Ramrod blew the horn to mark the ninth of the Days of Awe. The roasted goat meat was shared among the lepers, and everyone settled down to sleep.

56

Barac was relieved to find the gates of Aphek still open at night. In the fairgrounds, darkness shrouded the merchants' tents, but the grassy slope by the river was alive with bonfires, laughter, and singing, as men enjoyed wine and loose women. The sight of such debauchery near the Day of Atonement was jarring, and Barac was happy to leave it behind. With Tova mounted behind him, he urged the horse on the road east, up into the dark hills.

Orran had invited them to stay overnight as his guests. When Barac declined, expressing his desire to make up for lost time, Orran mentioned that a brazen wolf had recently preyed upon travelers and livestock in the Samariah Hills. Tova's eyes widened in fear, but Barac's mind was set and his heart told him that Orran was exaggerating the risk because he was still suspicious and, therefore, reluctant for them to leave. But now, surrounded by darkness, Barac was beset by doubts, for it wasn't only his own life he was risking, but Tova's life, as well.

Soon, the lights of Aphek were left behind. The road meandered up the slopes of the Samariah Hills, whose outlines were drawn against the starry sky. The horse slowed down, breathing heavily, but as the road flattened out, it recovered. Tova dozed off, but kept waking up every time dogs barked at them from dark homesteads.

On a quiet stretch, it was Barac who was startled when a wolf howled nearby. He hoped Tova wouldn't wake, but a second howl, even closer, made her sit up and cling to his back. The horse quickened its steps to a fast trot. Barac unsheathed his sword and held it ready, though he knew it would be hard to hit an animal in the dark. Behind him, Tova whispered a prayer.

The wolf howled even closer, and Barac imagined it giving chase, nibbling at the horse's hind legs, and causing the panicked beast to throw off the two of them. He recalled the tiger's claws bearing into his chest and its jaws clamping down on his head, but what truly scared him was the thought of Tova becoming prey. He stabbed his heels into the horse's ribs and shook the reins, urging the old beast to go faster while Tova continued to pray.

As if answering her prayers, coming around a curve in the road, a dot of light appeared ahead. It was a fire, which promised human presence and safety. The horse neighed, and Tova said, "Thank you, God!"

Filled with gratitude, Barac leaned forward and praised the horse, whose old legs must have neared their limits. With his eyes focused on the light ahead, Barac didn't notice the gray shadow on his right until it was running even with the horse. Barac looked down, barely able to believe his own eyes at the sight of a large wolf so close that its panting was audible. The animal's legs moved with blurry swiftness, and the predator seemed to be flying, not running.

The wolf turned its head, and its jaws opened in a wide grin, exposing white fangs that stood out in the dark.

Without thinking, Barac hurled his sword downward. It stuck the animal's back, causing it to flip over several times.

A terrible howl sounded behind them. Barac didn't look back, but kept urging the horse forward.

A man stood watch near the fire while the rest of his group slept under the sky. He told Barac that they were on the way back from Shiloh, where they had sacrificed sheep and goats while praying for God's help against Manasseh's violent expansion, which threatened their town of Bet Horon in southern Ephraim. While Barac and Tova stood with the man, their horse stepped away to the edge of a large pond. Much of the pond was in the dark, away from the light of the fire. Tova followed the horse, and when Barac went over to check on her, he saw her robe on the ground by the water's edge, and her head bobbing above the dark water.

"Come in," she said. "It's wonderful."

He glanced back and saw that the man by the fire had turned to look the other way.

When Barac waded in, completely naked, the water was shockingly cold. Rather than enter slowly, he dived in, splashing

Tova. She laughed and splashed him back. Once he adjusted to the cold, the water felt, as she had said, wonderful. The pond was shallow, and they had to lean back and wade to keep their bodies under the surface.

He felt her hand taking his.

"I'm pure again," she said. "Can you tell?"

He laughed, and his breath quickened. Her words were more than a statement of physical cleanliness. On the night of their marriage, when he had possessed her, the resulting blood made her impure and forbidden to him for at least seven days, at which time she had to dip in a ritual bath or a natural body of water, such as a pond, to purify herself and become ready for his bed again. There was no bed waiting for them here, but as she faced him, only her head above the water, it was clear that this pond was better than any bed.

Barac caressed Tova's wet hair and kissed her lips. She kissed him back, took his hands, and lowered them underwater, placing them on her breasts, which were as large as ripe pomegranates, but supple, like fresh dough.

"God have mercy," he said, breathing hard.

Tova giggled and curled her left arm behind his neck for support while locking her legs around his waist. Reaching down with her right hand between their bodies, she guided him into her warm body.

57

The night passed quietly. Deborah shared the tent with Yael while Ramrod and his uncles took turns standing watch. At dawn, the lepers began to pack up. In the nearby fairgrounds, the merchant caravans came to life as women started preparing the morning meals and men set out goods on their stalls. When the gates of Emanuel opened, local vendors emerged with their goods.

Soon after, Obadiah of Levi appeared, riding a donkey. His white robe was covered up with a travel robe. He carried his staff in one hand and a long ram's horn in the other. Prodding the donkey with a wooden stick was a man whose face was shadowed by a low hanging hood. When they reached the Weeping Tree, Obadiah's companion pulled back the hood and revealed his face. It was Mishneh, the soldier whose life Deborah had spared in Ein Gedi after Seesya's ambush.

"Good morning," Deborah said.

Mishneh bowed.

"I'm not a queen," she said. "Thank you for telling the people what had really happened in Ein Gedi."

"I made you a promise."

The priest knocked the ground with his staff. "There's no time for niceties."

"Did you come to join us?"

"No, we came to warn you again. Then, we're going to Shiloh."

"What about the people of Emanuel? Who will lead them in sacrifice and prayer at the commencement of the Day of Atonement tonight?"

"My townspeople kneel in prayers to false Gods these days. Besides, as soon as Seesya hears that I proclaimed your marriage and property rights, he'll sacrifice me at the altar of Ra."

"He wouldn't dare to touch Yahweh's priest."

"Dare?" Obadiah leaned forward, lowering his voice. "Seesya has lost all restraints. What you did to him – getting yourself acquitted at trial while he was convicted of murdering your parent, the humiliation of getting whipped in public, the defeat of his ambush in Ein Gedi – you have deformed his face and transformed his juvenile nastiness into a fiery malevolence that knows no boundaries. Hearing you've returned, he'll ride with his Canaanite mercenaries to Palm Homestead and spill a river of blood. I beg you, Deborah, come with us to the Holy Temple. You'll be safe in Shiloh."

"I wasn't safe there last time."

"No homestead is worth dying for."

"I won't die at Palm Homestead. God won't let it happen."

Obadiah sighed. "I shall atone for my cowardice and pray for you and your poor flock." He nodded at Mishneh. "Let's go. We must reach Shiloh by sunset."

Mishneh nudged the donkey with the stick, directing it back toward Emanuel. They went past the gates and continued north. Obadiah kept looking back over his shoulder for a long time as if trying to etch into his memory a final glimpse of Deborah.

The lepers' ranks had swelled further since the previous day, with more lepers hobbling out of the nearby hills to join the caravan. Deborah sent Ramrod to the fairgrounds with silver coins to buy large quantities of wheat flour, honey, and cheese, as well as live goats for milk and cheese, and animal hides to make more slings.

As soon as Ramrod came back and packed the supplies, Deborah urged Rogez forward. She led the long convoy with Ramrod and Yael, all three of them wrapped in black rags like lepers. Most of the real lepers were on foot, with the weakest riding in the carts, followed by the numerous newcomers. The fairgrounds quieted down, and people looked away. A man yelled, "Pick up the pace, wretched ones!" Another shouted, "You won't make it to Shiloh, invalids!" And a third screamed, "No atonement for you, only curses!" Many of the spectators laughed and hurled pieces of garbage at the lepers.

Leaving Emanuel behind, they proceeded up the road at a pace that Deborah found excruciatingly slow. Her mind filled with memories of life with her parents and sister at Palm Homestead. She wanted to let Rogez run at top speed, but the convoy could only move as fast as its slowest members.

She noticed new fields of wheat and barley along the road. Men and boys toiled in the fields, their backs bent and their faces weary, while foremen on donkeys wielded whips. The workers wore full beards and white caps, as customary for the God-fearing poor among the Hebrew men of Ephraim, but the foremen were beardless as those who had adopted the Canaanites' ways. She also noticed that no houses were built near the fields, which meant that the workers either slept on the ground, or walked every day from Emanuel.

At midday, Deborah turned right off the main road onto a narrower road heading east.

A while later, the sky clouded over, and a drizzle started, soon developing into a heavy downpour. The hills disappeared, as if behind a waterfall. The convoy slowed down to a crawl and stopped. Everyone got soaked down to their undergarments. A creek near the road filled up with raging water, which soon overflowed and burrowed secondary rivulets down the slopes. On both sides of the road Deborah saw ponds forming in low depressions, with whole bushes disappearing underwater. She thought of Noah and the great flood, which the Holy Scriptures described as a punishment for men's unrepentant sins. She shuddered with a sudden chill and wondered if the storm was a divine warning about what awaited her in Palm Homestead.

After a long time, the downpour eased up, turning into rain, then a drizzle, until it stopped, leaving them amidst gray mist under a foreboding dark sky.

Deborah pushed aside her doubts and prodded Rogez. The convoy moved on, sluggish on the muddy road. It was the first rain any of them had experienced in a long time, and it would have been invigorating if not for its ferocious excess. Glancing back at the convoy, whose size she still found hard to believe, Deborah noticed that the dirt road was black from the dye that had run off their rags. At the same time, white patches appeared through the black dye on Rogez's back.

Further up the road, more tilled fields appeared on both sides. Here and there, she noticed irrigation channels, which were overflowing after the downpour.

When the sky finally cleared up, the sun was low over the horizon behind them. As they passed another hillcrest, Palm Homestead appeared on the right.

It was as beautiful as she remembered it, nestled in a wide valley among gentle slopes, its fertile soil rich with crops. The surrounding slopes carried dense orchards of apple, pear, pomegranate, fig, plum, and carob trees. In the rockier patches of the hillside, silver leaves glistened on the gnarled branches of ancient olive trees. A great palm tree towered from the top of a small hill near the one-room house.

No smoke rose from the chimney of her family home, but it seemed in good repair, its thatched roof full and solid. A donkey was tied to a stake by the door. A short distance away from the house was the waist-high round wall above the small opening of the ancient water cistern. A pulley had been installed over it, and a water channel, which was marked with lines of white stones, connected to smaller conduits that branched off to carry water to the fields, where a few men were working.

Deborah stopped before entering her father's land and dismounted. She unwrapped the black rags, revealing a plain robe underneath, strapped on the sword and the sling, and returned the copper spear to the sheath attached to the saddle. Ramrod and Yael also changed out of the black rags. Yael stayed behind with the lepers while Deborah and Ramrod rode together to the house.

A bearded man came out. He carried no weapons, only a whip.

She stopped Rogez. "I am Deborah, daughter of Harutz of Ephraim, who owned this land until he was murdered by Seesya, son of Zifron. And this is my husband, Ramrod, son of Malkishua of Ephraim. We are the rightful owners of this land."

The man grinned. "We've been wondering if you'd ever dare to come back."

"What is your name?"

"I'm Eleazer, debtor for life to Seesya, who's going to come here with his Canaanite mercenaries as soon as he hears you're back."

"Will you be the one to tell him?"

Eleazer gestured at the low sun. "The Day of Atonement is upon us."

"What about your workers?"

He looked down at the whip in his hand, chuckled, and tossed it away. "We're all your guests now."

Deborah gestured at the road. "I have a lot more guests."

Noticing the lepers, Eleazer groaned and turned away, twisting his face in disgust.

"They're not only my guests," she said. "They are my friends."

He glanced at her hands and feet.

"I don't have the curse," she said.

"Not yet. You'll get it soon enough, mingling with them."

"God decides whom to afflict, and it could be you even if you never as much as look at a leper in your life. Sins will get you punished, and being unkind to other people is a sin."

"Lepers are not people."

"Saying such a thing is also a sin."

Eleazer didn't answer.

"Where would be a good spot for them to camp?"

He pointed at a moderate slope abutting the entrance to Palm Homestead.

"We'll tell them," she said. "In the meantime, instruct the workers to collect figs, pomegranates, and any other fresh fruit that's ripe. Everyone needs to eat before sunset."

A roaring noise drew their attention. It came from the ancient water cistern. Approaching it, they looked over the circular wall. Gray mist circulated upward through the opening. The thunderous sound reminded Deborah of the waterfall hitting the bottom of the shaft in Kassite's abandoned copper mine.

Ramrod stepped back. "What's this noise?"

"Underwater tunnels," Eleazer said. "The rainfall was as heavy as I've ever seen it, and now, all the water that filtered into the ground up on the hills is flowing below our feet into the cistern."

"I've heard the tunnels' flow many times," Deborah said. "My sister and I used to press our ears to the ground every time it rained, but in all the years I lived here with my family, the most we could hear was rippling sounds, nothing like this."

They stood for a long moment, listening to the roar from below, their faces moistened by the rising mist. Eleazer was the first to speak.

"God is angry at you for bringing them here." He gestured at the lepers without looking.

"Or at you," she said. "Farming a stolen homestead is a sin."

Ramrod raised his hand to hush her, but didn't say anything.

Eleazer chuckled. "We'll never know who's the worse sinner."

"I'll know," Deborah said. "God will tell me."

Both men looked at her, their expressions a mix of dread and incredulity. In Ramrod's eyes, though, she saw a glint of admiration, as well.

58

Laughter had woken Barack and Tova up that morning. With the sun already up, the men from Bet Horon were taking a plunge in the pond.

Tova rekindled the fire and boiled water in a clay jar, which she spiced up with rosemary leaves from a bush. It won hearty praise from the men after their swim, and they were happy to share a large honey cake and a sack of pomegranates. Barac asked them about the road ahead, which they had travelled in the opposite direction the previous day. They assured him it was easy to follow and fairly safe, with an occasional homestead and other pilgrims. The distance to the turnoff south to Emanuel was about three-quarters of a day away, which delighted Barac, because it meant they could ride east and reach Palm Homestead, before sunset would usher in the beginning of the Day of Atonement.

Barac rode back down the road to collect his sword. It was still embedded in the wolf's backbone, which had been stripped of all flesh by scavengers.

The ride proceeded at a good pace on the well-trodden road, which rose over hills and dropped into valleys. They passed by several homesteads and stopped at midday to drink from a spring. Further to the east, Barac saw a mass of dark clouds resembling a solid wall above the horizon, but the sky above them remained blue and clear.

They resumed the journey at a good pace, but soon the horse became restless and kept trying to veer from the road. Barac leaned forward to rub the horse's neck while urging it to keep going. A slight wind brought with it cold air, and Tova buried herself under a blanket. As they passed over a high ridge, he saw the distant hills ahead shrouded in gray mist.

Descending into a valley, they passed by a homestead. The small house stood on a flat boulder far from the road. A man waved from the door. Barac waved back, but the man kept waving, and Barac realized he was actually beckoning them to come over. The distance was too great to yell back that they had no time to spare. Barac waved one more time and urged the horse down the road.

Near the bottom, the horse stopped before crossing a dry streambed.

Barac shook the reins. "Move on."

The horse whinnied.

"What's wrong with you?" He kicked in with his heels. "We don't have time for this."

Rocking its head, the horse stayed put.

"Go!"

The horse stepped sideways.

"Wait," Tova said. "Horses get spooked for a reason."

"What reason?" Barac pointed at the rocky streambed. "I don't see a snake, do you?"

Tova looked over his shoulder. "No, but it could be something else."

"I'll give him something else." Barac pulled the club from its saddle sleeve, reached behind Tova, and patted the horse's rear. The horse neighed and turned around a full circle in place.

Tova laughed.

"It's not funny," Barac said. "We must reach Palm Homestead before sunset. Deborah might be there already, and Seesya won't be far behind."

"Let me try." Tova reached back and slapped horse's rear with her hand.

The horse leapt forward. Barac grabbed the reins, while Tova rolled backward, saved only by pressing in her knees, which Barac caught in his armpits, preventing her from going over the back of the horse, which stopped again, now standing smack in the middle of the rocky streambed. Tova started laughing, and as always, it was contagious. They laughed while trying to prod the stubborn horse, stabbing their heels and shaking the reins, to no avail.

Stuttering between giggles, Tova said, "A donkey in horse's clothes!"

They laughed harder, but then, Barac noticed another sound. It was deep, almost like a growl, or a rumble, coming from higher up in the gorge, which curved to the left, out of sight. It seemed as if the rocks around the horse's hooves were shaking.

Tova's laughter died down. "What's that noise?"

Finally, Barac understood what had spooked the horse. "Slap him again! Quick!"

She did, twice, without any effect.

A wall of water appeared around the curve from upstream.

Barac turned, grabbed her arm, and yanked her off the saddle. "Run, Tova, Run!"

The raging water was coming fast while Tova fell to the ground and scrambled the rest of the way across the streambed and up the opposite bank. Barac jumped off the saddle and made it almost out of the way when the water yanked him off his feet and carried him downstream.

59

Ramrod and Yael directed the lepers to spread up the hillside and set up their tents. Those who already had slings were tasked with cutting the leather hides brought from Emanuel to make new slings for the lepers who had joined along the journey from Ein Gedi and teach them how to shoot.

Deborah entered the house. She used her father's fire starters to start the stove. Watching the flames, she pressed the fire starters to her cheeks, remembering the warm evenings her family had spent together in front of this stove.

Ramrod came in and sat on the hard-packed dirt floor beside her.

"I grew up in this room," she said. "It's familiar, yet feels so empty without my family. I miss them terribly."

He wiped her tears with his hand. "We'll name the child for your father."

"Or my mother, if it's a girl."

"What was her name?"

"Raquellah."

"It's a beautiful name."

"She was a beautiful woman."

"As you are." Ramrod looked down, embarrassed.

"It feels strange to be back here, after all the obstacles I've faced, the foreign places I've passed through, and the longing I've constantly felt. And in all my dreams about returning to Palm Homestead, I never imagined arriving here with a husband and a baby on the way." She glanced at him. "I know it's not easy for you, either."

"What do you mean?"

"The baby."

He shrugged. "It's not the baby I worry about. It's the father."

"You shouldn't." She sighed. "Barac is out of my life forever. I made my feelings very clear to him, and I'm sure he's doing his best to forgot about me and the brief time we had together."

Ramrod didn't respond.

"Do you think I made a mistake coming here?" She heard the tremor in her own voice. "Is that it? You agree with Obadiah of Levi?"

He tilted his head, neither agreeing, nor disagreeing.

"Don't hold back," she said. "I trust God, but I'm not free of doubts. It's one thing to risk my own life, which I've done many times without hesitating, but it's quite different to put you, Yael, and the lepers at risk, and to place my unborn child in the path of an evil man like Seesya."

Ramrod took a deep breath and clenched his fists as he finally spoke. "God is with you, I believe it. No harm will come to anyone here."

She smiled, knowing he had spoken from the heart. "And the baby? Will you accept this baby as our child?"

"Will you?"

"I don't understand."

"Swear to me that you'll never reveal the baby's true lineage to anyone, especially not to the real father."

Deborah pressed a fist to her heart. "I swear in the name of Yahweh."

"Then it's our baby," Ramrod said. "And we'll have other babies after it, many children, enough to fill this place with happiness." He waved around the room. "We'll name them for your parents and sister, and for my parents, too."

"And for Miriam," Deborah said. "We'll have a girl named Miriam."

Ramrod took her hand and kissed it. "Miriam brought us together."

On her way out of the house, Deborah touched the empty cavity about two-thirds of the way up the doorjamb and remembered she had a mezuzah scroll in her sack. She took it out, showed it to Ramrod, and told him about the old healer in Tamar, who had mistaken her for her mother and given her the mezuzah scroll.

"I remember her words exactly," Deborah said. "Take it with you, Raquellah, and put it on the doorjamb of your home in the land of Ephraim. Yahweh will see it and protect you and the children you'll bear in His honor."

Ramrod fitted the mezuzah scroll in the doorjamb cavity and said, "May her blessing come true in every way."

Outside, the sun touched the horizon while the lepers finished setting up their tents and ate the last meal before the fast. The workers sat near the water cistern and ate, too. Yael arranged a meal of bread, cheese, and fruit for the three of them in the house.

Ramrod recited a blessing. "Thank you, Yahweh, king of the world, for the plentiful blessings of food you shared with us today."

When they finished eating, Deborah put on her armor, brushed the dust off her boots, and picked up the copper spear. Ramrod went ahead of her up the small hill. He rolled a large rock and set it down by the trunk of the palm tree.

Deborah sat on the rock under her palm tree and held the copper spear upright, its bulging butt on the ground. Above her, the canopy of fronds rustled in the soft breeze. The air, infused with the scents of her childhood, was cool from the rain. She looked around at the thriving Palm Homestead and, for the first time since her parents died, felt at home.

60

At least Tova was safe, Barac thought while the water churned him like a roll of tumbleweed in a whirlwind. It was a strange sensation, not painful or scary, but dizzying in a disjointed way that felt almost wondrous. He could tell which side was up by the surface light, which kept going on and off as he rolled over repeatedly. He thought of Deborah, when a boy had pushed her into the rushing river in Aphek after a slingshot competition, and her horse saved her from drowning. Who would save him?

The current tossed him upward, and his head popped above the surface, allowing him to inhale sharply before the mighty force of the water sucked him back under. Rolling again, he held his breath, wondering whether this dreamlike experience would turn out well like Deborah's underwater adventure. The sense of wonder, however, was cut short when his arm hit something hard, then his leg, and his arm again. In the water near his face he saw a wooden log, traveling beside him at the same pace. He grabbed the log and tried to mount it, only to make it spin, pushing him deeper. His knees scraped on rocks, then his stomach, and his face, which he turned sideways in the last moment before his head became lodged between the rocky bottom and the log. It hurt almost as much as the tiger's jaws, and the lack of air made his chest burn. The current was weaker, and the light told him the surface was very close.

The thought of drowning in waist-high water made him angry. He craved air so much that the only thing to do was to open his mouth and take in whatever may come, but Deborah's face appeared before him, and she looked at him, her green eyes sad, her pale cheeks dotted with golden freckles, her lips moving with words he yearned to hear. He gave a mighty shove with his legs and managed to shift the log enough to release his head and burst out of the water.

Panting loudly, Barac looked around. He was in a flooded basin after the force of the rapid current had propelled him outward at a sharp curve in the gorge. He waded through the muddy water to a rocky slope, crawled out of the water, and collapsed on the ground. Rolling onto his back, he looked up at the clear blue sky and tried to understand where all this water had come from. The answer, he realized, was in the mass of dark clouds he had seen further to the east — rain clouds, which must have dumped their contents on the Samariah Hills, filling up all the dry streams and sending flashfloods down the gorges. He thought of Deborah and wondered how she had fared through this powerful demonstration of God's fury.

"Barac!"

He sat up and saw Tova running along the opposite side of the gushing gorge. He waved, groaning as pain shot through his shoulder. Getting up, he wobbled, and almost fell. He found a broken branch, long enough to serve as a walking stick, and motioned for Tova to head back upstream. Feeling something against his thigh, he looked down and saw the empty sheath of his sword.

It was a slow trek, walking along the fast water, whose roar made it impossible to communicate except by hand gestures. The sun descended behind the hills, and he worried that they might remain separated in the dark, leaving Tova across the water without protection from predators.

Coming around a curve, Barac saw the corpse of their horse lying in the mud with its hooves still in the current, which flickered them, creating the illusion of life. Crouching next to the horse's head, he caressed the wet plume of hair between the eyes and felt an overwhelming guilt for causing this needless death.

Their sack was still attached to the saddle. Barac untied the sack and slung it over his shoulder, where it dripped water down his back. Later on, they reached the road where it had all started. On his side of the stream, Barac found the club he had dropped. The water between them wasn't as high or fast as it had been when the flash flood had hit them, but Barac decided not to risk being swept away again, and they continued going upstream on opposite sides of the water.

61

When the sun slipped beneath the horizon, Ramrod put the horn to his lips and blew it in a long, drawn-out blast that echoed from the surrounding slopes. Seated under her palm tree on the small hill by her family home, Deborah felt the echoes in her chest, which swelled with gratitude and hope.

The lepers made their way down the slope near the road and walked over to stand at the foot of the small hill. Eleazer and the workers stood together by the cistern, looking up at her. Yael went into the house.

"The Day of Atonement," Deborah declared. "The Sabbath of all Sabbaths has begun."

Blowing the horn again, Ramrod pointed it up at the twilight sky.

"It's upon us now," Deborah continued. "The holiest day of the year. From this moment until the next sunset, tomorrow night, we will deprive ourselves of all food and pleasure. This deprivation is not because we lack food, of which God has given us plenty, or because we lack joy, which we feel in abundance on this fertile Promised Land of our ancestors Abraham, Isaac, and Jacob. Rather, this deprivation cleanses our mind of earthly things in order to focus on self-reflection, atone for our sins, and seek Yahweh's forgiveness. We do not have a priest here to recite from the Holy Scriptures—"

"I can!"

The voice came from among the lepers. One of them stepped forward. He was missing both hands and limped badly as he came to the front of the group, his voice emerging through the sheer black veil over his face.

"I am Akhlan of Levi. Before this curse afflicted me, I was a priest in the land of Manasseh."

"God bless you, Akhlan of Levi." Deborah raised the copper

spear and pounded the ground the way General Mazabi had used to do. "Let us hear the words of the Holy Scriptures."

"And Yahweh said to Moses," Akhlan recited. "Tell the People of Israel this: On the tenth day of the seventh month you shall observe the Day of Atonement. You shall deprive yourselves and do no labor, you and the stranger living among you. For on that day you shall atone to repent all your sins, before God you shall repent. The Sabbath of all Sabbaths it shall be, and you shall torment yourselves, this is the law. And the person who didn't torment himself shall be cut off from among you, and the person who worked shall be cut off from all the nations. This is the law forever, in all the generations, in all your settlements, from the evening of the ninth of the month, from sunset to sunset, you shall observe this Sabbath of all Sabbaths."

He turned and limped back through the crowd of lepers, blending in until he was indistinguishable from the rest.

"Let us sit down now," Deborah said. "With awe in our hearts, we'll reflect on our deeds, atone for our sins, and ask for His forgiveness."

As twilight gradually turned to darkness, hundreds of lepers sat on the ground at the foot of the small hill and contemplated their sins over the past year. Deborah thought about all she had been through since celebrating the last Day of Atonement as a grieving orphan, taking shelter in Judge Zifron's house. On her path to this moment, she had committed many sins – lying, hitting, even slaying, as well as causing others to lie, hit, and kill – but had she really sinned? Everything she had done since the stoning of Tamar had been instrumental to her True Calling, a long quest to return here and serve God the way her father had dreamt. And wasn't her safe return to Palm Homestead on the eve of the Day of Atonement a divine message, confirming the truth of her quest? Had not God, by providing countless shortcuts along her path, affirmed that His divine voice had issued her True Calling?

For a brief moment, Deborah allowed herself to think of Barac and recall her searing pain and raging fury upon hearing that he had married another girl. Her anger had cooled down, but she couldn't reconcile his passion for her on the battlefield at the Ramon Crater with Leah's description of Barac's eyes shining upon the pretty girl in Beersheba and the bloodstains left from the consummation of their union. Still, Deborah had to admit that Barac had the same right as her to take any action in furtherance of his True Calling – to become a great warrior and lead the northern Hebrew tribes against their Canaanite oppressors. Hadn't she rejected him for the same reason – that his ineligibility to inherit Palm Homestead stood in the way of her True Calling? Should she not grant him the same forgiveness she had granted herself for virtually the same hurtful act of rejection?

The darkness had by now turned into a starry night, softly lit by the rising moon. Deborah sighed, resigning herself to never knowing the correct answers to her doubts. Barac was gone from her life, pursuing his own quest in the north, but she wasn't worse off for it, sitting under her tree at Palm Homestead with a good man of Ephraim by her side and hundreds of faithful Hebrew men and women before her, as her father had dreamt.

Deborah pounded the copper spear on the ground to get the lepers' attention.

"To earn God's forgiveness," she said, "we should forgive those whose acts or failures caused us pain or distress in the past year. Let us bear no grudge, resentment, or anger against any man or woman who has wronged us."

Propping the spear against the trunk of her palm tree, Deborah extended her hands forward, fingers parted in pairs, and recited the priestly blessing over the silent crowd below. "May Yahweh bless you and protect you. May He show you kindness and grace. May He illuminate your path and grant you peace."

The lepers responded with a roaring chorus: "Amen!"

62

It took them until sunset to climb high enough to where the low water level allowed rocks to poke through and serve as steppingstones. As soon as Barac crossed over, Tova hugged him tightly and began crying.

He held her. "No reason to cry. We survived."

She kept sobbing.

He patted her back. "Is it the horse?"

She shook her head while her sobs subsided.

"Then what's wrong?"

She whimpered. "Nothing is wrong."

"Nothing?"

Another headshake.

"I don't understand."

She pulled back, still holding him, and looked up, her eyes tearful.

"Please tell me." He dabbed her cheeks. "Why are you crying?"

"Because of you," she said, her voice trembling.

"But nothing happened to me, I'm fine. Really. Look." He stepped back. "I'm in one piece."

"You're silly." Tova laughed through her tears. "I'm crying because you really love me, that's why. Don't you understand?"

"No." He chuckled. "For the life of me, no, I don't understand."

"You pulled me off the horse, yelled at me to run, and saved me from the flash flood, all before you thought of saving yourself. What man would do such a thing – save a girl before saving himself? The only explanation is that you really love me."

She hugged him again, and he put his arms around her. What could he say? It was true that he had saved her before trying to get himself out of the way, which could be a sign of true love. However, it was also true that, for days now, he had risked both their lives repeatedly in order to reach Palm Homestead in time to save Deborah from Seesya. By the same reasoning, it meant that he loved Deborah more than he loved either Tova, or himself.

"We should start walking," he said. "It will be impossible to find the road now."

Tova held on to his arm as they headed in a north-easterly direction, which he identified based on the fading glow of sunset in the west. It would have been safer to walk back down the gorge all the way to the bottom, where they had first encountered the flood, but he wanted to save time by making progress in the general direction of their destination.

As darkness thickened, it became harder to maintain direction through the hilly landscape. He began to worry they were lost and exposed to danger. How long before a predatory animal picked up their scent and stalked them? On foot, with only a wooden club for defense, they would make easy prey.

As if reading his mind, Tova said, "Don't worry, husband. We are safe. I'm sure of it."

"Why?"

"Because God has tested us enough."

"You think?"

"Judah's attacks in Revivim and Beersheba, Tsruyah's betrayal in Gerar, the Philistines' slavery and near drowning in Gaza, Dan's deadly ambush at the Yarkon River, Judge Orran's harassment in Aphek, the wolf's stalking on the road, and the flash flood to top it all off." She looked up at the night sky. "Anything else you want to throw at us?"

"Hush, wife," Barac said, chuckling. "The Day of Atonement has just begun."

"We've paid for our sins," she said. "And then some."

"I hope you're right."

"You'll see."

And as she said it, they came over a hill and saw a small fire glowing near a house. Dogs began to bark, and a man came out with his three sons. Barac greeted them and, while they held the dogs, told them what had happened to his horse. They were God-fearing men of Ephraim, who delighted at the opportunity for an act of charity on the Day of Atonement.

Other than food and drink, which were forbidden, they offered Barac and Tova warm hospitality, including a cot with clean linen, a warm blanket, and the safety that would make for sound sleep. The temptation was nearly irresistible, but Barac declined and explained their need to keep going as fast as possible in order to save the life of a friend in danger. He took his purse out of the sack and offered to buy a horse. The man refused the coins, citing the prohibition on buying and selling on a Sabbath, especially the Sabbath of Sabbaths. Besides, they owned no horses, only two oxen and three donkeys, the stronger of which he gave to Barac as a gift.

The road to Shiloh, as it turned out, passed near the homestead. With the man and his sons wishing them God's grace, Barac and Tova mounted the donkey, prodded it downhill to the road, and turned right toward the moon, which was rising in the east.

63

In the house at Palm Homestead, the fire in the stove had gone out. It was forbidden to start a new fire until after the next sunset. Deborah shared a cot with Yael, while Ramrod slept at the other end of the room. The workers slept under a tree behind the house, and the lepers on the hillside slope near the road, sharing tents or makeshift lean-to shelters attached to their carts.

Sometime during the night, Deborah heard a donkey braying, but when she went to the door and looked around in the moonlight, she saw nothing. Back on the cot, her head resting on her sack, she closed her eyes, fell asleep, and faced the glowing yellow eyes of the eagle.

"I came to congratulate you," the eagle said.

"Thank you." Deborah smiled. "God chose the holiest day of the year to be my first day back home."

"Sad, too, isn't it?"

She nodded.

"I enjoyed what you said under the palm tree."

"About forgiveness?"

"Yes." The eagle sighed. "Often the worst pain gives us the clearest insight."

"I'm not in pain anymore. I forgave Barac and prayed for the success of his quest."

"Yes, of course. Forgiveness is virtuous and wise, especially as you're carrying his child in your womb. I wonder, though, do you really feel safe without that brave boy standing by your side, ready to die for you, as he'd shown in Emanuel and at the Ramon Crater?"

"He's standing by another girl now." Deborah could hear a hint of resentment in her own voice. "He has his battles to fight, far in the north. My place is here, with those who love me standing by my side, I'll prevail. I'm sure of it."

"It won't be easy." The eagle clicked her tongue. "You're back in the lion's jaws."

"Not a lion. A jackal, maybe. Or a coyote."

"Each has a mouth full of sharp teeth."

"I'm not in anyone's mouth. Under God's law, this land is mine."

"Your husband's land."

"Our land, together. We are the rightful owners of Palm Homestead. No one has the right to take it from us, not even Judge Zifron and his son. No one!"

The eagle chuckled. "Don't yell at me, girl. I'm on your side."

Deborah was embarrassed. "Forgive me."

"I do, but not Seesya. He will never forgive you."

"Forgive me for what? Didn't he force me to act? Didn't I harm him only to survive his attacks?"

"Well, how should I put it?" The eagle sighed. "You know how insecure men are about their manhood, right? Seesya's first night with your sister, and then with you, deepened his insecurity. Your continued existence is a constant reminder of it. Besides, he's already shown his greed for this land and its water cistern by murdering your parents. For a wicked man, every murder deepens his thirst for blood."

"He doesn't even know I'm here," Deborah said. "And it's the Day of Atonement. No Hebrew man would dare commit murder on God's Sabbath of all Sabbaths."

"I recall hearing something about a band of Canaanite mercenaries he now commands." The eagle raised her wings and tilted her head in an almost human gesture of apology. "It's your first night back at home, I know, but we don't want it to be the last one, do we?"

"It won't," Deborah said. "God didn't bring me back to be killed."

"God protects those who protect themselves."

"If Seesya sends his Canaanite mercenaries to attack me, I'll have a little surprise ready for them."

"Good," the eagle said. "That's what I was hoping to hear."

64

In defiance of her species' reputation for obstinacy, the donkey carried on through the rest of the night, bearing Barac and Tova on her back through an endless succession of ascents and descents. A few of the creeks at the lowest points were overflowing, which required leaving the road to climb up high enough to cross safely where the water level ebbed, then ride back down along the opposite side to find the road and continue east. The detours lengthened their trip, but were necessary to avoid another near-death plunge, or worse.

At one point, however, a wider stream blocked the road and, unlike all the creeks that preceded it, did not diminish as they rode up along the side. It meandered between the hills in a general easterly direction, gushing loudly, until the donkey uttered a plaintive bray and stopped abruptly at the edge of a large body of water under a foggy mist.

"I hear no waves," Tova said. "At least we're not back to the Great Sea."

Barac got off and helped her dismount the donkey.

"Where are we?" Tova crouched and put her hand in the water.

"I don't know."

She licked her hand. "The water is fresh. Could it be the Sea of Galilee?"

"We haven't gone that far."

"Then what is this?"

An early dawn infused the fog with pale ruddiness, which brought out the outlines of hills around the water.

"It's a large pond," Barac said. "The flood probably created it."

Voices came from a nearby hillside. Walking toward it, he saw tents and people sleeping under the sky. A few piles of embers glowed where fires had burned during the night. A clutch of coyotes nibbled at a trash heap a short distance away. He picked up rocks and threw them at the animals until they ran away.

Pulling the donkey along, they walked around the edge of the pond until their path was blocked by another gushing stream that poured into the pond. By the glow of dawn through the fog he could tell that this stream was coming from the south. The high volume of water worried him. How far would they have to ride along this flooded stream before finding a safe place to cross?

The blow of a ram's horn came from the hillside. When the blow ended, a murmur rose as more people woke up.

Out of the foggy twilight, a figure advanced toward Barac and Tova. It was a man in a white robe, a white cap, and a long white beard, carrying a ram's horn and leaning on a wooden staff. He walked to the edge of the pond, knelt down with a ponderous groan, put the horn and staff on the ground, and rinsed his hands and face.

Barack walked over to help the old man stand up.

"Thank you." He accepted the horn and staff, which Barac picked up for him. "May Yahweh favor you on this Day of Atonement."

Barac was astonished to recognize him. It was Obadiah of Levi from Emanuel.

The priest peered at his face. "Don't I know you from somewhere?"

"I'm Barac, son of Abinoam."

"The blacksmith's son? Seesya has bragged that he killed you. What are you doing here?"

"I was wondering the same thing about you."

Obadiah sighed. "I suspect we're both on the road for the same reason."

"Deborah?"

"Yes, that inimitable girl of earthly beauty and spiritual fervor, who has devastated both our lives – all because of her father's slumberous dream." Obadiah raised the ram's horn to stop Barac from responding. "Yes, I know, she is true in her faith and devoted to her calling, but if not for her captivating beauty and alluring personality, neither of us would have risked our lives for her."

Barac shook his head.

"Don't deny it, boy. The consequences of Deborah's relentless pursuit are ruinous for all around her. Look at us, standing right here on the Day of Atonement, confined by floodwater and steep hills, stranded in the wilderness without an altar to make a sacrifice, or a scroll to recite the Holy Scriptures."

Words of protest and retort came to the tip of his tongue, but Barac had spent all his childhood and youth watching this man with reverence during Temple ceremonies, and the memories kept him from arguing.

"How is your father?"

"He went back to Naphtali. I pray that he is well."

"Are you trying to reach Palm Homestead to stand with Deborah against Seesya?"

Barac nodded.

"It saddens me to tell you something that might upset you." The priest rested his hand on Barac's shoulder. "The night before last, I blessed her marriage to a young man of Ephraim, who then possessed her, with ample blood evidencing the consummation of their union."

The words dropped like a punch to the gut, and Barac turned away, stumbled to the water's edge, and bent over in pain.

Tova ran to him and held him as he trembled. "What's wrong? Are you ill?"

"His heart is broken," Obadiah said from behind. "The girl he loves is now another man's wife. Not for long, though. In a day or two, Seesya will kill them both."

While the old priest made his way back to the hillside, Tova comforted Barac, who sat down on the wet soil, surrendering to her caresses and soothing words. He felt no shame, only sorrow and confusion. Had he fooled himself to think that his heart had accepted Deborah's rejection? Or had he accepted her rejection only under the assumption that she would forever remain untouched by another man? That was a foolish assumption, because her need for a husband of Ephraim to inherit Palm Homestead had been the very reason for rejecting him.

With that thought, the priest's words rang in his head: "The girl he loves is now another man's wife. Not for long, though. In a day or two, Seesya will kill them both." Through his sorrow, Barac absorbed the implication, because for Seesya to kill her in a day or two, Deborah must be at Palm Homestead already!

He stood up. "We have to go on."

"How?" Tova gestured around. "The priest said we are confined on all sides."

65

At dawn, Deborah stepped outside and breathed in the fresh air of Palm Homestead. In honor of the Day of Atonement, she did not put on her armor or practice with her weapons. Rogez was in the corral behind the house. His water trough was dry. She went to the water cistern to fill up a bucket. The water level was almost to the top. Going back, she almost tripped on the channel the workers had dug to divert water to Judge Zifron's fields.

While giving water to Rogez, she noticed that Eleazer and the other workers were gone. She went inside and woke Yael and Ramrod up to tell them.

His face contorted in fear, and he ran out to see for himself. "On the Day of Atonement? Don't they fear God?"

"They do," Yael said. "But they fear Seesya even more."

"We're doomed." Ramrod's voice trembled. "By now, they've reached Emanuel and told him we're here."

"Maybe not," Deborah said. "They could have gone to join their families."

"No one travels to visit relatives on the Sabbath of all Sabbaths."

"The lepers' presence might have spooked them."

"Seesya spooked them," Yael said. "They did it to save their lives."

Ramrod was on the verge of tears. "Sinners!"

"Not really," Deborah said. "The sanctity of life supersedes all other sanctities."

"Maybe I should go to Seesya, too." Yael combed her long hair with her fingers. "Nothing calms a man better than the company of a pretty girl."

"Yes, go," Ramrod said. "I'll get the horse ready."

"Please," Deborah said. "Don't be ridiculous."

Yael smiled. "Why not? Men like me. They trust me."

"Let her try," Ramrod said. "She can do it."

Deborah shook her head.

"Why not?"

"We're the rightful owners, and we're not alone."

"But we are," Ramrod cried. "The neighboring homestead owners don't even know we're here. If he comes today, we'll be alone. Your plan failed!"

Deborah pointed at the lepers. "We have them."

Ramrod's eyes were wide with fear. He ran inside, reappeared with the horn, and blew it. The sound was squeaky, ending with an odd shrill. He took a deep breath, and blew again, producing a wobbly sound that mimicked his tremulous voice. He paused, bent over, and retched, but only a few drops emerged.

Yael looked at him, shaking her head.

In her mind, Deborah heard Kassite's voice: "When circumstances force a choice between getting killed and becoming a killer, most men fall apart, beg for their lives, or start weeping like children, whereas the truly brave harden up with firm resolve, total focus, and icy determination to kill."

The words took on a fresh meaning – a sad meaning – as she realized that her husband belonged with most men, not with the brave few.

Yael whispered, "Do something."

Deborah took Ramrod's thin arm and helped him stand.

His eyes were wet. "We must run away before it's too late."

"You don't win a fight by fleeing," she said, quoting the eagle.

"You don't stay alive by fighting the impossible."

"I've beaten Seesya before."

"Not alone. You told me how much help you got from all those men – Obadiah, Sallan, Kassite, Barac – even that Moabite boy, Zariz."

"They're still with me, every one of them, all the time." She knuckled her head. "Right here, whenever I face a hardship, their wisdom speaks to me and their courage fortifies me."

"Then listen to their wisdom now, because if they love you as I do, they'll tell you to run. Run, Deborah! Run!"

"I'm not leaving Palm Homestead again," she said. "You can

leave, if you want."

"What's the point of leaving without you? I'm afraid for you." Ramrod was weeping now. "All I wanted was to have a life with you – anywhere, anyplace, even in a cave. And my wish came true when you came back and agreed to become my wife."

"Then stand by me. If Seesya comes, we'll fight him together."

"Oh, Deborah, don't you see? It's a fight we can't win."

Searching her mind for an answer, she recalled what the eagle had said to her in the seemingly inescapable tunnel at the bottom of Kassite's abandoned copper mine. "Defeatism is self-fulfilling, but so is the determination to win."

Ramrod took a deep breath. "Do you really believe we can beat Seesya and his Canaanite mercenaries?"

"I do," Deborah said. "We fight for Yahweh, and He will deliver us to victory."

Wiping his eyes, Ramrod said, "Then I must believe it, too."

They hugged.

Yael cleared her throat. "Better start preparing."

Ramrod filled his lungs with air, put the ram's horn to his lips, and blasted a thunderous blow. Many of the lepers emerged from their tents and gazed in the direction of the house. He blew again.

Yael pulled Deborah inside. "Dress up, girl. Armor, weapons, the whole show."

"I'd rather not carry weapons on the Day of Atonement."

"Pardon me," Yael said. "Maybe because I'm of the Cainite Clan, I misunderstood what you said about how saving lives takes precedent over all your holy laws and prohibitions."

Deborah chuckled. "You understood it correctly, but we're not sure Seesya is coming. If he does, I'll get my weapons."

"It's not for Seesya that you need to suit up. It's for those lepers, who followed the famous Deborah, the daring warrior on her white horse, the fearless slayer with her silver sword, the righteous proclaimer of God's justice - you have to look the part, or they'll lose heart."

When Deborah was dressed and armed, Yael checked her from head to toe, pulling and straightening, until she was satisfied.

"You're ready. Go and pump them up for battle."

"Aren't you coming?"

"Battles aren't for me," Yael said. "I'll stay inside the house, have something nice to eat, and make myself pretty."

They laughed, and Deborah stepped out, carrying the copper spear. Ramrod accompanied her up the small hill to the palm tree and blew the horn again. The lepers gathered, looking up at her, many through sheer veils, others with exposed faces gouged by their affliction.

"It is the Day of Atonement," Deborah said. "God decreed that we torment ourselves and repent our sins. However, it seems that others might be coming here to torment us. We should be ready to make them repent their sins."

The lepers turned to each other, murmuring.

Akhlan of Levi stepped forward and asked. "Who might come here to torment us?"

"Seesya, son of Zifron," she said. "He killed my parents here and tried to steal this land and its water. I was hoping he would not hear of our arrival until word had spread over the Samariah Hills that the rightful owners are back, but his foreman and workers snuck away during the night to inform him." She gestured toward the house. "A murderer such as he might not honor the Day of Atonement. If he comes here with his Canaanite mercenaries, we must defend ourselves and teach him a lesson in true faith. Are you with me?"

"Yes." Akhlan looked around at the other lepers. "We are with you, Deborah."

"And I am with you," she said. "Let us prepare for a battle that we hope will not come."

"Tell us what to do," Akhlan said.

"We'll defend Palm Homestead from the two slopes overlooking the entry from the road." She pointed. "Spread up and down the slopes, collect stones for your slings, and practice shooting without hurting others. Make sure you keep a pile of stones ready to sling at the attackers. When they appear, Ramrod will blast the horn. A continuous sound will signal you to get ready. A stuttering sound will signal you to sling your stones, one after the other, with careful aim and deadly force, until we smite the enemies of God."

Their murmurs had the tone of nervous doubts, but Akhlan

picked up two stones and clicked them against each other repeatedly until the lepers quieted down.

"My friends." He turned his head from side to side as he spoke through the sheer black veil over his face. "We are the wretched, the despised, the miserable pariahs among the tribes of Israel. Everyone looks away from us with revulsion when we pass by, when we come to purchase food, or when we go to the temple. Everyone treats us with fear and hate, everyone except for one person, in all of Canaan." He pointed his wrapped fingerless hand. "Deborah!"

Their murmuring quieted, and many of them nodded.

"Think about it," Akhlan continued. "God cursed us to live shamefully, but today, He blessed us with an opportunity to die honorably. I believe He will reward those who stand with Deborah." He turned up toward the palm tree. "Will you bless us?"

Deborah extended her hands forward, fingers parted in pairs, and recited: "May Yahweh bless you and protect you. May He show you kindness and grace. May He illuminate your path and grant you peace." Then, she added the sentence the priest in Arad had recited over the men of Judah before the attack on Beersheba: "May He fortify your hearts and give you victory."

The lepers chorused, "Amen!"

66

Barac took Tova's hand and followed Obadiah of Levi. The early sun illuminated the stranded men and boys. Their robes and blankets were soaked from yesterday's downpour, and many of them had no belongings, likely lost in the floods.

The priest sat on a rock beside a younger man and pointed at Barac. "Another admirer of Deborah."

He pulled back the hood of his robe. "I am Mishneh of Ephraim."

Barac remembered the name from Deborah's story of the ambush in Ein Gedi. Mishneh was the soldier she had spared. "Will you fight for her against Seesya?"

"I'm ready." Mishneh patted his sword.

Obadiah of Levi grunted, but didn't speak.

"Good," Barac said. "We need to reach Palm Homestead as soon as possible. Do you know the lay of the land?"

"The pond wasn't here before yesterday. It covers the intersection of the road from Emanuel with the road connecting Aphek and Shiloh." Mishneh marked a circle in the wet dirt with his finger, then five lines connecting to it. "The Irzil Creek is usually dry, but the heavy rain filled it, together with the Shiloh Stream right here. They overflowed and filled up this basin, covering the whole area, trapping all these travelers. Some, like us, were on the way from Emanuel to celebrate the Day of Atonement in Shiloh, and others were returning from Shiloh after making sacrifices during the Days of Awe. We are on higher grounds here, blocked off from the roads by the flooded basin and the two overflowing streams."

"Can we walk upriver to cross the Irzil Creek?"

"We might walk for two days without a chance to cross over and find ourselves in the land of Benjamin, or Judah, far away from Palm Homestead."

"Calm down, boys," Obadiah said. "If God wanted us to travel on the Day of Atonement, He would have already drained this flooded basin."

Mishneh turned to him. "If God wanted us to spend the Day of Atonement in Shiloh, He would not have flooded the roads. I think He was upset that we left Deborah at her time of need and wants us to go back to help her."

"I agree," Barac said. "As soon as Seesya hears she's back, he'll rush to Palm Homestead with his Canaanite mercenaries. We have to go now."

The priest shrugged. "We can't go anywhere until the water recedes."

"Yes, we can. Blow the horn."

Obadiah did it, and the sound of the Ram's Horn drew everyone's attention.

Barac mounted a rock. "Faithful men of Yahweh! A terrible wrong is about to take place! A sin greater than all sins combined!"

The men and boys moved closer in, eager to hear.

"The Promised Land of Canaan was divided by Joshua to give each family a homestead to pass down from father to his eldest son, or to the husband of his daughter, for all the generations. Many of you heard about the recent trial in Emanuel of Deborah, Daughter of Harutz, accused of being a rebellious wife by her supposed husband, Seesya, son of Judge Zifron. The trial ended with her acquittal and release from the unconsummated marriage to Seesya, who was found guilty of murdering her parents and sister in order to steal the family homestead. Not surprisingly, Judge Zifron spared his son from stoning."

Some of the men booed.

"I agree with your anger, because a murderer should pay with his life."

Everyone voiced their agreement.

"Deborah finally returned with a new husband of Ephraim to live on the homestead they inherited by God's law from her father. Today, Seesya will be coming to murder the rightful owners again!"

The men shouted angrily and waved fists.

"Think about your own homestead, your own family, and your

own children. Should we allow murder of rightful owners and theft of fertile homesteads in the Promised Land of Israel?"

A chorus responded, "No! No! No!"

"I agree," Barac said. "And I believe that's why God opened the sky and poured all that rain yesterday. He wanted us to gather here and stand up for His laws and for His justice. If we do, He will grant each and every one of us full redemption for all our sins on this Day of Atonement!"

They cheered.

"We start there." Barac pointed to the south end of the flooded basin, which was coming into full view as the sun burned off the fog. "We'll build a dam of rocks to block off the creek where it pours into the basin. We'll cross over the dam, take the road south, and then east to Palm Homestead. Along the way, we'll collect sticks and branches as our weapons of righteousness, for it is in God's name that we will prevent Seesya from committing another murder and theft!"

A swell of enthusiasm carried the men into a frenzy of work, running back and forth with stones and rocks. Even the littlest boys helped, tossing small stones into the water. Barac and Mishneh stood at the edge beside the inflow of the Irzil Creek and directed the work.

Faster than Barac had expected, a dam rose across the stream, gradually blocking its flow into the large pond, diverting the water aside, where it forged a channel to the west.

When the dam was complete, a great cheer came up.

Barac pointed at the hillside. "Collect your belongings and come back here to cross to the other side of the water."

A few moments later a queue formed. Barac estimated there were over one hundred men ready to march to Palm Homestead and defend its rightful owners.

The first to cross was Obadiah of Levi, followed by his donkey, led by Mishneh, who came back over the dam and helped Tova cross with their donkey. A column of men and boys followed. Barac stood by the dam, cautioning each one to watch their steps lest they slip into the pond and drown.

The pressure of the water coming down the stream kept nudging at the dam, and rocks began to tumble. Barac urged the men to cross faster. The growing current over the crumbling dam pushed over more rocks, which disappeared in the dark water. The rest of the men quickly skipped over the gap in the dam. Last was a father carrying his young son of five or six, who was wearing a multi-colored shirt. Barac shouldered his sack and stepped onto the dam behind them.

All went well until a stone gave way. The father slipped and fell across the dam, his legs in the stream and his head in the flooded basin. Two men jumped onto the dam from the other side and grabbed the man's arm, while Barac tried to catch the boy, who slipped into the pond and sank like a stone in the water, his multi-color shirt fading away in the dark depth. As they pulled the father to safety, he screamed, "My son! My son! My son!"

Barac hurled his sack to Tova.

She caught it and yelled, "No! You can't swim!"

Inhaling deeply, Barac jumped into the churning water.

67

With Akhlan issuing directions, the lepers fanned out all over Palm Homestead to collect stones. Some ventured far across the road, where the hills were rough and rocky. There were over three hundred of them – men and women, young and old, strong and frail. With their black rags and bent backs, they reminded Deborah of the morning before Tamar's trial, when the maidens of Emanuel had been sent to collect stones for the execution, spreading out over the Samariah Hills like an army of squirrels gathering nuts for the winter.

During the morning, no travelers passed on the road, which was rarely frequented even on workdays. Deborah and Ramrod helped the lepers make tidy piles of stones on the slopes overlooking the entrance from the road to Palm Homestead.

Back under her palm tree, Deborah sat on the rock, feeling lightheaded from the lack of food and water. Her mind simmered with reflections of the past year and worries that today's confrontation might surpass all previous battles in its scope of viciousness and death toll. Yet, as the sun passed its apex and began to descend in the west, she felt a cautious sense of hope that the Day of Atonement would conclude peacefully.

Her thoughts were interrupted by a shout from one of the lepers, who pointed at the road.

Getting up quickly, Deborah became dizzy and leaned against the trunk of the palm tree as she shielded her eyes to look.

About fifty or sixty men marched up the road. Their hair was pasted down and cut at the shoulders, their faces were clean-shaven, and their bare chests glistened with either sweat or oil. They wore short skirts with horizontal lines in different shades of gray, walked barefooted, and carried machetes, battleaxes, and short spears. They stopped on the road near the entry to Palm Homestead.

Deborah gripped the silver hilt of her sword. Were these Seesya's Canaanite mercenaries? Their arrival by foot explained the length of time it took them to march from Emanuel, but where was Seesya?

A man on horseback rode up from behind the troops. He was dressed the same as the others. Attached to his saddle was a pole with the golden effigy of Ra, the Canaanite Sun God, with its man's body and hawk's head, crowned with a solar disk and a coiled serpent. It was the same effigy Seesya had brandished at her trial in Emanuel and, later, at the ambush in Ein Gedi. The man was too far for her to make out his face. Was this Seesya, dressed as a Canaanite?

Ramrod groaned.

The man rode through the group of Canaanites, which parted to make way, and turned right into Palm Homestead. As his broad face and square jaw came into view, she saw that he wasn't Seesya.

"Blow the horn," she said to Ramrod.

He blew it continuously.

The lepers stood, dotting the slopes on both sides like charred tree stumps after a forest fire. They picked stones and fitted them in their slings' pouches.

The Canaanite leader glanced left and right at the lepers and continued into Palm Homestead. He stopped his horse at the foot of the small hill and gazed up at her.

"I am Evedra," he said. "My master is Seesya, son of Zifron."

"I am Deborah," she answered. "My master is Yahweh, God of Israel."

Evedra smirked.

"Why do you invade my land on our holiest day, brandishing a false idol?"

"False is your insult to my God, and false is your claim to this land." Evedra waved at the fields and orchards. "All this belongs to my master."

"You are mistaken." Deborah untied the sling from her hips. "This land is called Palm Homestead. It's been in my family for generations." She dangled the sling by her side and picked up a stone. "Under our God's laws, my father's ownership of this land passed down to me and my husband, Ramrod of Ephraim."

Evedra glanced at the stone in her hand. "Under Canaan's laws, when a man dies without sons, his land passes to the local ruler. A trespasser must leave, or be killed. Which will it be, girl?"

"You are the trespasser." Deborah fitted the stone in the pouch while clasping the hook and tab. "Go back to Emanuel and tell Judge Zifron that Deborah, daughter of Harutz of Ephraim, thanks him for guarding my father's land. His compensation has been its harvest and water until I returned to live on it with my husband as rightful owners under our God's laws."

Raising his battleax, Evedra tilted it so that the sun reflected on the blade. "Is that your husband, hiding behind you?"

"Go in peace." Deborah began to rotate the sling. "While you still can."

Evedra smirked and focused on Ramrod. "Where is your weapon, little husband?"

Ramrod put the horn to his lips and blasted it continuously.

With a burst of laughter, Evedra turned his horse back toward the road, but as Deborah lowered her arm with the rotating sling, he shifted sharply in the saddle and hurled the battleax at her.

Ramrod's horn blow was cut short with a high pitch as Deborah dodged the spinning battleax, which swished by her head and lodged in the trunk of the palm tree with a loud thwack. While falling down, she saw Evedra turn his horse and gallop up the small hill.

Rather than waste time on getting up, she let go of the sling, drew her sword and, gripping the hilt with both hands, swung the blade up just as Evedra's horse came upon her. The point of the blade jabbed the horse's chest, and the beast neighed, reared up, and lost its balance, falling backward. Evedra jumped sideways before getting crushed by his horse, which struggled back to its feet and sprinted away.

With terrifying howls, the Canaanite mercenaries rushed from the road into Palm Homestead.

"Blow the horn," Deborah yelled. "Stuttering sound!"

Ramrod did it, and the lepers deployed their slings, raining stones down on the bare-chested Canaanites, who charged forward, wielding their weapons. Meanwhile, Evedra managed to stop rolling downhill and sprang to his feet. He drew a short sword and ran back up the small hill.

Deborah got up, her sword in the ready. She glanced at the slopes and saw that the Canaanites had split in two and were moving against the lepers, who kept shooting, scoring hits among the attackers, whose terrifying howls mixed with painful wails. Evedra made it halfway to the palm tree before he registered the change in his subordinates' tone and the staccato sound of the stones hitting their human targets. He paused and looked at the slopes, where the lepers, who numbered five times more than his troops, had blunted the attack, knocking down about a third of the Canaanites, who were either writhing in pain, or motionless.

"Give it up," Deborah said.

Evedra looked at her and back at his men, some of whom had turned to flee.

"I can stop the slings," she said. "Will you call your men back?"

He lowered his sword.

Deborah said to Ramrod, "Blow the horn – continuous sound!"

He did, and the lepers stopped shooting.

Evedra ran down the small hill and back to his men, yelling orders. The Canaanite mercenaries picked up their fallen comrades and hurried down from the slopes and out to the road.

Ramrod stopped blowing. He stepped over and stood by her side, watching the Canaanites' retreat. "We won," he said shakily. "We won!"

"One battle," she said. "Not the war. Not yet."

The lepers stood on the slopes, watching their attackers retreat, and cheered.

Evedra and his men regrouped on the road. One of the mercenaries brought the horse back. The pole was broken, and the effigy of Ra lay on the ground, shattered into pieces.

"Why aren't they leaving?" Ramrod shaded his eyes with his hand. "Will they attack again?"

"Not likely," Deborah said. "It would be futile to repeat the same tactic. They might go around and try to surprise us through the hills."

Many of the Canaanites turned to look toward Deborah.

"Should I blow again?" Ramrod raised the horn. "Show them we're ready to fight once more?"

"Wait."

Evedra stepped to the edge of the road, staring at her while raising a fist, which ignited a primal howl from his men.

The lepers shouted back, but their voices were weak, barely heard over the Canaanites' howls, which continued unabated.

"I don't understand," Deborah said. "What's the meaning of this?"

"It's nothing." Ramrod had to yell to be heard over the howling. "They're angry about losing."

"No," she said. "There's always a reason."

"What reason?"

"To distract us from something."

As she started to turn, Deborah heard Rogez neighing at the corral by the house. Through the glare of the afternoon sun, she saw a figure running uphill toward her. She sheltered her eyes, but with the sun blinded her. A glint came from a raised sword, and she responded instinctively with a motion she had practiced countless times, angling her sword just as he hacked downward. Their blades collided and bounced off one another, her hand barely keeping grip on the hilt.

He laughed – a menacing laughter she remembered well – and swerved his sword, slashing at her sideways, while she brought her left hand to join the grip and tilted her blade just in time to block his.

Behind her, Ramrod screamed.

Deborah skipped aside, avoiding another slash, and Seesya circled her, getting to even ground beside the trunk of the palm tree.

The Canaanites' howling changed tone, and she glanced to see them rushing forward for another attack at the lepers.

"Blow," she yelled. "Stuttering!"

Seesya jumped forward in a feigned assault, startling her, and retreated, laughing again.

"Ramrod," she shouted. "Blow the horn!"

His horn emitted a stuttering sound.

With the sun no longer in her eyes, Deborah was shocked by Seesya's appearance. His jaw was set in a grotesque mold of wooden sticks tied with threads. It cradled the broken jawbones while setting his lips in a permanent crooked smirk.

The staccato of raining stones resumed, mixed with the Canaanites' howls.

The ugly laughter reemerged from Seesya's gaping mouth.

"Day of Atonement," Deborah said. "It's for self-reflection, not bloodshed."

"Yahweh's little witch," he said, barely coherent. "Back in my grasp."

The horn died out.

From the corner of her eye, Deborah could tell Ramrod was backing away.

"Husband," she said. "Get the battleax!"

Seesya glanced at the battleax, lodged in the tree trunk.

Ramrod continued stepping backward, down the slope of the small hill. Deborah glanced at him and knew, by the look of sheer terror on his face, that he wouldn't fight by her side. Behind him she caught a glimpse of the battle raging between the Canaanites and the lepers, stones flying down and battleaxes flying up, while machetes and spears took down the lepers at the bottom of the slopes.

"Little husband's gone." Seesya jiggled his blade like a slithering snake. "Gone like your old priest, off to Shiloh with his tail between his crooked legs." He jabbed his sword, which she parried. "Gone like your showoff boy, the blacksmith's son, off to Simeon or who knows where. Gone like your conniving basket maker, off to Edom with his fake elixirs." Another jab, easy to deflect. "Who's left by your side, stupid girl? Only lepers, whose fingers, ears, and noses will fertilize my land, may Ra bless them."

"You talk too much," she said.

With another jittery laugh, he swung his sword and hit the handle of the battleax, causing it to dislodge and fall to the ground, taking with it her copper spear, which was leaning against the tree.

Deborah attacked, aiming her blade straight as a spear at his chest. He parried, blocked, and repositioned himself to face her, but now she had the sun behind her.

"Nice," he said. "Little witch has been training."

"To defend my land from murderers and thieves."

"Says she who rides my stolen horse and wields my stolen sword. Thieving little witch."

Deborah willed herself not to answer and imagined him to be one of her pretend opponents at dawn near one of the campsites. With the hilt gripped at level with her belt, she tilted the blade toward his face, ready for his next move. Had he practiced every morning for weeks, as she had done? Had he worked his muscles daily to exhaustion, as she had done? If not, perhaps his superior skills and strength would fade more quickly than hers, as his arms grew tired.

He lunged forward, and Deborah parried, blocking his thrust. He came at her again, and again, his blade swinging in from the left, from the right, from above, and from below. Deborah shifted and jammed, dodged and circled, ceded ground and recovered it, descended to a lower elevation and stepped up the other way, but she didn't counter-attack him, only deflected his efforts while keeping a smirk on her lips to irritate him into more futile attacks. The sword grew heavy in her hands, but she knew from all those early mornings that real exhaustion was still far off. She used the trunk of her palm tree as a center point for their deadly dance, and with her lithe figure, she was quicker than Seesya, whose panting became heavier while his blade grew slower. At one point, her boot banged against a stone, and she tripped, barely escaping a swift jab of his sword. Keeping the location of the rock in her mind, the next time around, she positioned herself at the right distance to step back out of his range momentarily, shove the tip of her boot under the stone, and kicked it upward, hitting his nose, which began to bleed.

"Witch!" Seesya dived forward, chopping down with his sword.

It was close, and though her blade nudged his out of the way, Seesya got close enough for her to catch a whiff of his foul odor of male sweat and garlic breath. He faced her again, his sword down for a moment, his dark eyes burning with hate, the wooden cradle under his broken jaw reminiscent of a menacing dog. She wanted to look away, but couldn't, and recited silently the last part of the priestly blessing, "May He fortify your heart and give you victory."

The knocking sounds of stones continued to mix with the Canaanites' howls and the lepers' screams.

"Praying to your Yahweh?" Seesya sneered. "He's gone like your other friends, off to Shiloh to help the priests get fat on the burnt offerings."

His mockery of God sickened her. "I feel for your mother."

"My mother?" His eyes narrowed. "Be careful what you say,

witch."

"Poor Vardit – she had such high hopes for you, her firstborn son." Deborah quoted from memory. "The moment he was born, when I heard his first scream, I felt a divine presence in the room. That's why I named him Seesya, because I saw Yahweh right there."

He didn't speak, but his blade slowly descended, pointing at the ground.

"Sees-Ya," Deborah said. "He who rejoices in Yahweh's presence."

He raised his blade, pointing at her. "I spit on your Yahweh!"

"And I spit on your undeserving name."

With an enraged cry, Seesya attacked her again, slashing and hacking while Deborah jammed and blocked, skipped aside and swerved, her agility shielding her from his powerful fury until they found themselves on opposite sides of the trunk of her palm tree.

"Go on, pray," he said, panting hard. "Your invisible God isn't coming."

"Who do you see when you pray?" Deborah kept shifting on her feet, ready to move. "Ra?"

"Yes!"

"He who rejoices in Ra should be called Sees-Ra."

"You're right," he yelled. "From now on, my name will be Seesra! Do you hear, everyone? I am Seesra!"

"Finally," Deborah said. "A moment of honesty in the life of a sinner."

"Finally, I'm going to kill today."

"Between the two of us, you're the one bleeding out."

He wiped his nose on his forearm, still breathing heavily.

"All this killing," she said. "Just because you couldn't do it on our wedding night."

A growl escaped his gaping mouth, and he sprung to the right, his sword rising as he came at her around the tree. She jumped back and would have avoided him altogether, but he tripped, lost his balance, and swiveled, his shoulder banging into her. They fell together, and in a blind, frenzied tangle of arms and legs, turned on each other, their swords crossed, the blades at each other's throat. Deborah felt the cold, sharp iron against her skin and knew he was feeling her blade against his neck.

They froze.

The sounds of battle quieted down, both the Canaanites' howling and the staccato of stones. There were no victory cheers, only moans of pain. From where the two of them were locked in a stalemate, slightly below the top of the small hill, her line of view was blocked. What did the silence mean? Was everyone dead or mortally injured on both sides? How could it happen again, so soon after the battle in the Negev Desert? And where was Ramrod? And Yael?

The sharp iron against her throat drew her mind back to the fact that her life was hanging in the balance. Up close, his odor was nauseating and the contraption around his jaw was even more grotesque, especially with the blood from his nose trickling through the wooden sticks. His eyes burned with rage yet blinked in indecision. He wanted to kill her, but not at the cost of his own life.

"Let it go," she said. "Killing me won't restore your manhood."

"Yes, it will."

"How?"

"Your mother, your sister, and you cursed me. When I kill you, all three witches will be dead, and the curse will be lifted."

His words reflected not only the depth of his hatred, but also the rawness of his motivation, delusional as it was.

"Remember what the High Priest said in Shiloh?"

He tried to shift away from her blade, but she pressed on while quoting Shatz Ha'Cohen.

"If women's curses had any power, all men would turn into lepers."

He scoffed, pushing harder on the crossed swords.

Deborah felt the burning of a fresh cut as his blade nicked her neck. "There's no curse. It's the sin of killing our mother that has haunted you, making you unable to—"

"Shut up!" He spat a glob of blood, which dangled from the wooden sticks over his jaw. "It's your curse!"

"If you kill me, God's wrath will descend on you, worse than any woman's curse."

"Really?" He glanced up. "Where are you, Yahweh? Come and get me!"

A horn blasted a long, continuous blow. It wasn't the thin sound of Ramrod's horn, but the sonorous sound of a fully-grown Ram's horn.

When the sound ended, a man's voice boomed. "Hear, O Israel!"

Deborah recognized the voice: Obadiah of Levi.

"Yahweh is our God," he bellowed. "Yahweh is one!"

A roaring chorus of many men repeated after him. "Yahweh is our God! Yahweh is one!"

Seesya craned his head to see what was happening, and Deborah saw her chance. She shoved him while untangling their swords and jumped back, away from him.

He recovered quickly, rising with his sword, facing her.

She picked up a stone in her left hand. "Don't get closer, or I'll smash the wooden monstrosity holding your jaw."

His eyes narrowed, measuring her, gauging his chances.

Moving higher, closer to her palm tree, Deborah had a better view of the whole area.

The surviving lepers at the upper slopes and the remaining Canaanite mercenaries lower down had stopped fighting and turned to watch the road, where two donkeys led a long column of Hebrew men. Obadiah of Levi rode one of the donkeys, and the other was ridden by a man holding a small boy in a multicolored shirt.

As they turned into Palm Homestead, the priest lifted his ram's horn and blew again. The man riding beside him raised a club, whereas the little boy in multicolored shirt waved a stick, smiling happily. She gazed at the man's face and could not believe her eyes.

Barac!

The column of men behind Obadiah and Barac was armed with wooden planks and thick branches.

Seesya cursed.

Advancing into Palm Homestead at the head of the column, Obadiah and Barac passed between the slopes, glancing at the suspended battle between the lepers and Canaanites, and stopped at the foot of the small hill. The column stretched all the way back to the road, and the men turned to either side to face the remaining Canaanites, who were now caught between the lepers above and the newcomers below.

Through the silence, the priest's voice came loud and clear. "I, Obadiah of Levi, priest of Emanuel, come here to bear witness that this land, known as Palm Homestead, belonged to Harutz of Ephraim, who was murdered by Seesya, son of Zifron, leaving no sons, but two daughters, Tamar and Deborah. I bear witness that Tamar died unjustly and that Deborah was married under God's laws to Ramrod of Ephraim, who possessed her as his wife and, by such marriage, inherited from her father. I bear witness that Ramrod of Ephraim and his wife Deborah are now the rightful owners of Palm Homestead. I swear to all this in the name of Yahweh on this sacred Day of Atonement."

Deborah dropped the stone. "It's over, Seesra."

He stepped forward, aiming his sword. "It'll be over when one of us is dead."

"I've slain too many men." She held up her sword in the ready. "If you want to see another sunrise, leave my land."

"Your land? Ha! I own the Samariah Hills!"

"You're only the son of the judge in these hills, not their owner."

"Forget my father. Ra will make me ruler over all of Ephraim."

"There's your Ra." She pointed at the broken pieces of Evedra's banner on the ground below. "Not so powerful, is he?"

"My Ra is whole." He waved his sword. "And my patron, King Javin of Hazor, has an army of steel chariots as numerous as your lepers."

Seeing in his eyes the fervor of one who believed he was in the right, Deborah remembered what Umm-Sallan had said: "Good and evil always compete for man's heart, which is why even the worst man must convince himself that his evil actions are in actuality good, just, and necessary."

"Your Gods are false," she said. "My God is true. He sent all these good men to stand with me against you and your foreign mercenaries."

On the slopes, Evedra yelled a quick order. A dozen or so Canaanites ran to the foot of the small hill and formed a protective half-circle. Barac got off the donkey, which a pretty girl with wide hips and ample breasts pulled away with the boy riding alone. A line of men stepped forward with Barac to confront the Canaanites. A second and third line formed behind them, ready to fill in for those who would be stricken down. They held up their sticks against the mercenaries' machetes, battleaxes, and spears.

"Hear O Israel!" Obadiah's voice was stronger than ever. "The rightful owners!"

Barac stepped forward, facing Evedra up close.

"Hear O Israel," the Hebrew men chanted. "The rightful owners!"

"Leave, Seesra," Deborah said, taking strange pleasure in pronouncing his mutilated name. "And take your mercenaries with you."

He kept his sword aimed at her, but his eyes were on the standoff down below. She wondered, was he starting to doubt the powers of his false Gods?

"Hear O Israel," Obadiah bellowed. "The rightful owners!"

"The rightful owners!" The Hebrew men repeated after him while the rest of the column spread out, encircling the whole area. "Hear O Israel! The rightful owners!"

Evedra raised his sword at Barac, who raised his club. The other Canaanites held up their weapons, and the Hebrews wielded their planks and branches, chanting repeatedly.

"Hear O Israel! The rightful owners!"

Watching this, Deborah's chest swelled with pride. At the same time, she knew that the Canaanite mercenaries, with their superior weapons and training, would flood Palm Homestead with Hebrew blood, before their ultimate defeat by the overwhelming number of the men who had come with Obadiah and Barac. Did God want her to win back Palm Homestead at such a horrible price?

Weak from fasting and fighting, Deborah closed her eyes to pray for an answer. She felt his arm grabbing her shoulder, swiveling her, while his sword rose to her neck, and her sword tilted as if by its own will, the blade pointed downward beside her hip, the tip at his crotch.

"Drop your sword, witch, or I'll cut your throat!"

"I'll cut your manhood." She held the hilt with both hands, ready to heave downward.

"You'll be dead!"

"And you'll be a woman."

The Hebrews stopped chanting.

"And then," she said, "they'll kill you, and you'll be a dead woman."

He laughed. "They're armed with sticks. Tell them to leave, or they'll all die here."

"They won't listen to me." From behind her, his breath stunk. "You should slosh mint water in your mouth before approaching a girl again."

"I'll slosh with your blood, witch."

"Deborah," Obadiah called from the foot of the small hill. "God is with you!"

Hundreds of men held their breath. She did, too, to avoid Seesya's odor.

"I'll let you go." He tightened his grip, "if you tell them this land is mine."

"It's not yours," Deborah said.

"Tell them, or we'll both die here, together with many men."

"I've survived worse odds."

"I mean it!"

"I don't tell lies, and neither should you on this Day of Atonement."

He inhaled deeply and shouted, "Ra gave me these hills!"

No one responded as hundreds of tense eyes stared up at the the small hill.

"All the Gods stand with me," he yelled. "Do you hear? All the Gods love me!"

"Look at the sky," Deborah said. "I think the one true God is getting angry."

The sun disappeared behind a solid bulk of clouds, advancing from the west, rapidly covering the sky. At the same time, the mild breeze built up to a mighty wind, lashing them with prickling sand and the salty scent of a distant sea. The last patch of blue sky disappeared as the clouds formed a low, dark, solid mass, similar to the pervious afternoon.

The bright day turned to bleak twilight.

Over the howl of the wind, they heard knocking, like the staccato of stones hitting targets from multiple slings in rapid salvos, though no one was slinging stones. Deborah felt his hold loosen. She used one of her hands to grab the hilt of his sword and turn it a quarter of the way so that the edge of his blade was no longer at her neck, but the flat side of the blade, which was cold, but harmless. At the same time, raising her leg forward, she kicked back, slamming the heel of her boot into his shin. He shouted, let her go, and reached down to grab his shin, while she turned and struck him on the head with the butt of her sword, where the silver hilt was fixed with a large black gemstone. He dropped to his knees, holding his head, and she stepped backward, aiming the tip of the blade at his chest.

From the west, a pale mist advanced.

The noise grew louder, the mist denser. She saw white pebbles bounce off the rocky ground nearby and realized that the source of the knocking was hail.

As chunky pieces of ice pelted him, Seesya bent over with his arms over his head. The Canaanite mercenaries, shouting in fear, did the same.

Stepping up to her palm tree, Deborah pressed her back to the trunk and beckoned Barac. He ran uphill to join her. They stood shoulder-to-shoulder under the canopy of fronds, which protected them from the falling hail. It surrounded them like a pale curtain, and the drumming noise was punctuated by men's cries of pain.

Deborah smiled at him. "You came to stand with me against God's enemies."

"It's nothing." Barac gestured dismissively. "I happened to be in the area."

She laughed.

The noise gradually subsided, and the storm moved on.

Deborah looked around in wonder. A white carpet covered Palm Homestead. On the opposing slopes, the lepers seemed like gray mounds, slowly emerging as they brushed the hail off their black rags. The Hebrew men and the Canaanite mercenaries stayed crouched, except for Obadiah of Levi, who had remained upright through the storm, which piled hail on his white cap and on his shoulders.

Seesya rose to his feet. His sword lay on the ground, but he didn't reach for it. He looked around, his face pale above the bloody contraption over his jaw.

Through the silence, Deborah heard a horse whinny. She turned to look.

Ramrod was leading a golden-brown stallion with a banner of Ra on a pole attached to the saddle. Yael walked alongside it, wearing bejewel sandals and a long gown of red-and-blue stripes. Her black hair rippled in thick locks around her shoulders, down to her waist. Her face was made up with white powder, blushed cheeks, and red lips.

The Hebrews and Canaanites stepped aside to let her pass. She made her way up the small hill and stopped in front of Seesya.

"I am Yael," she said. "A woman of the Cainite Clan."

He stared at her. "I am Seesra."

"Seesra?" Yael smiled and tossed her hair. "I like it. A strong name."

Deborah was about to protest, but Ramrod gave her a look that made her understand. If Yael succeeded, a great deal of bloodshed would be averted. Deborah held her tongue and watched.

"Come, handsome." Yael took his hand. "I know how to lift bothersome curses."

He followed her to his horse. She rested her hands on his shoulders, and he helped her onto the saddle. She glanced at Deborah and winked.

Mounting behind Yael, he took the reins from Ramrod and trotted toward the road. Evedra hurried after him while barking orders. The Canaanite mercenaries collected their weapons and ran, leaving their dead behind.

The surviving lepers supported each other as they came down from the slopes and gathered closer. Deborah remained by her palm tree while Barac rejoined his motley Hebrew army at the foot of the small hill. He looked up at her, and she smiled at him, knowing that neither his departure from the ravine at the Ramon Crater, nor his marriage to another, had in any way diminished their bond.

Sheathing her sword, Deborah picked up the copper spear and pounded it on the hail-covered ground three times. "Hear, O Israel!" Her voice was clear and sonorous. "Yahweh is our God! Yahweh is one!"

"Yahweh is our God!" The lepers and the Hebrew men repeated

after her, their voices reverberating like thunder from the hills around Palm Homestead. "Yahweh is one!"

"The king of the world has spoken." Deborah sat on the rock and quoted from memory. "If you follow my laws and keep my commands, I shall bring you rain in season. The land shall give you its full harvest, the orchards their ample fruit, and the vines their copious grapes. Your threshing shall extend to your vintage, which shall overlap with your seeding, and you shall eat bread to satiation and live safely on your land."

"Amen," the crowd cried. "Amen!"

Behind her, the sun was setting on the Day of Atonement. The wind picked up, and the palm fronds rustled above. Deborah tilted her head back to look at the sky and smiled, remembering her father's words: "You're a true Hebrew, the seed of glorious ancestors. One day, you will sit under your palm tree and deliver His message to the people, to us, the ancient Hebrews. I believe it with all my heart."

Epilogue

(Seven Years later, as told in the Book of Judges, Chapters 4-6)

The People of Israel continued to sin against God, and He delivered many of them into the hands of King Javin of Canaan, who ruled from the city of Hazor in the Galilee. Seesra lived near the gentiles' iron mills and commanded King Javin's mighty army, including a force of nine-hundred iron chariots, which he used to oppress the Hebrew tribes in northern Canaan.

At that time, the prophet Deborah, a fiery woman, was the judge of Israel. She sat under Deborah's Palm in the Samariah Hills of Ephraim. The oppressed people came to her and pleaded for justice.

Deborah sent for Barac, son of Abinoam, from Kadesh Naphtali in the Galilee, and said to him, "God has finally called upon you to act. Go back north and recruit ten-thousand men from the tribes of Naphtali and Zebulun. While you assemble your army on Mount Tabor, I will draw Seesra with his Canaanite soldiers and iron chariots to the muddy Kishon River at the foot of the mountain, delivering them into your hands."

"If you go with me, I'll go," Barac said. "But if you don't go with me, I won't go."

"Fine, I will go with you," she said. "However, you should know that there will be no fame for you this way, because God will deliver Seesra into the hands of a woman."

Her argument did not sway him.

Rising from the rock under her palm tree, Deborah joined Barak on the journey north. There, they issued a call to arms, and ten-thousand men from the tribes of Zebulun and Naphtali answered it, ready to fight the Canaanites. With Deborah by his side, Barac assembled the Hebrew army on Mount Tabor.

As it happened, at that time, the Cainite Clan camped nearby at a modest forest by Kadesh. When they informed Seesra that his Hebrew enemies had gathered fighters on Mount Tabor, Seesra summoned the whole Canaanite army, including all of the nine-hundred iron chariots, and marched to the Kishon River.

"It's time," Deborah said to Barac. "Today, God will deliver Seesra into our hands."

Rushing downhill from Mount Tabor, ten-thousand Hebrew fighters swarmed Seesra and his army, whose iron chariots were sluggish in the muddy valley. Seesra jumped off his stranded chariot and ran away on foot. Meanwhile, the Hebrew fighters chased the remaining Canaanite chariots and soldiers all the way to the gentiles' iron mills, killing all of Seesra's men. Seesra alone escaped and made it on foot to the tent of Yael, a woman of the Cainite Clan, which enjoyed the patronage of King Javin.

Yael came out of her tent and said, "Get inside, quick. You'll be safe with me."

Seesra entered her tent and collapsed. Yael covered him with a blanket.

"I'm thirsty," he said. "Give me some water."

Instead, Yael gave him warm milk.

"Stand outside the tent," he said. "If anyone asks you, tell them you saw no man here."

Yael stepped out of the tent, but after some time, snuck back inside while Seesra was dozing off. She took a copper tent peg and a mallet, approached him quietly, and hammered the tent peg into the side of his head. Seesra shouted and sat up. She collapsed to the ground, but he dropped back and died.

At that moment in Hazor, Seesra's mother, Vardit, ran to the window, looked out, and cried, "Where is he? Why can't I hear the sound of his chariots?" Comforted by her servants, she said, "You're right. He is busy after the victory, collecting all the plunder – fair Hebrew maidens for his bed and colorful embroidery for me, to wear around my neck."

While Yael was waiting outside her tent, she saw Barac riding fast down the road and stopped him. "Come into my tent," she said. "I want to show you something."

Barac entered and saw the dead Seesra on the ground with a tent peg in his head.

Later that day, the Hebrew fighters captured King Javin and beat him until he died, bringing an end to the House of Javin in Canaan.

When the triumphant army reassembled in celebration, Deborah stood with Barac and declared: "So shall all your enemies perish, God!"

Following the victory over Seesra and the Canaanite army at Mount Tabor, the liberated tribes of Israel enjoyed peace on their land for forty years.

The End

A NOTE TO THE READER

While the *Book of Judges* describes Deborah's stunning success as a prophet, a judge and a military leader, who liberated her people from Canaanite oppression, it says nothing about her youth and upbringing. How could a girl, growing up in a world controlled by men, rise to rule over them? What hardships fueled her tenacity? What setbacks steeled her resilience? What battles transformed her into a formidable leader? These are the fascinating mysteries we aspire to unravel in this novel series, which began with *Deborah Rising* (HarperCollins, 2016).

To ensure accuracy in describing how people lived in the ancient Mideast, I consulted countless books and articles. They are too many to list here, but I am particularly indebted to the scholarly works of William F. Albright, Yigael Yadin, Avraham Biran, Israel Finkelstein, Benjamin Mazar, Amihai Mazar, William G. Dever, Joyce Salisbury, Carol Meyers, Thomas E. Levi, George Hart, Bruce Routledge, Richard Elliot Friedman, Geraldine Harris, Richard Wilkinson, Boyd Seevers, Gale A. Yee, Brian Schmidt, Alan Dickin, Monroe Rosenthal, Isaac Mozenson, Diana Vikander Edelman, Hershel Shanks and Claudia Valentino.

We are blessed with wonderful friends and family members, who read my manuscripts at various stages, provide insightful observations, and offer enthusiastic support. They include (in alphabetical order) Margie and Arie Adler, Sarai Azrieli, Talya, Ben, and Elan Azrieli, Hagit and Michael David, Rabbi Dr. Israel Dreisin, Don Eddins, Monica and Prof. Michael Finkelthal, Risa and Dr. Opher Ganel, Rachel and Joel Glazer, Prof. Sharon Glazer and Tamas Karpati, Julie and Hanan Gur, Dr. Jennifer and Nir Margalit, Linda and Dr. Bernard Rosenbaum, Glenna Salisbury, Wendy and Avner Skolnik, Stephen J. Wall, Stephanie and Ernie Wechsler, and Carol Wilner.

As always, this novel would not have come to life without the tireless support of my wife, Fiona, a dedicated physician who finds time to read the first draft of every new novel and provides astute critique, perceptive comments, and inspiring encouragement. Fiona and our children fill my life with love and laughter, which sustain me daily.

Last but not least, I owe a debt of gratitude to you, my readers, for choosing to spend your precious time with my books, for recommending the books to your friends, and for posting thoughtful insights and reviews on social media. There is no greater joy for a writer than a supportive community of readers. Thank you!

ABOUT THE AUTHOR

Avraham Azrieli is the author of books and screenplays. His first novel was *The Masada Complex* (a political thriller), followed by Israeli spy novels *The Jerusalem Inception* and *The Jerusalem Assassin*, as well as *Christmas for Joshua* (an interfaith family drama), *The Mormon Candidate* (a political thriller), *Thump* (a courtroom drama featuring sexual harassment and racism), and *The Bootstrap Ultimatum* (a mystery involving the commercialization of Memorial Day). Most recently, he has written a series of novels inspired by the true story of the first woman to lead a nation in human history, starting with *Deborah Rising* (HarperCollins, 2016), and continuing with *Deborah Calling, Deborah Slaying,* and *Deborah Striking.*

Beside fiction, he has also authored *Your Lawyer on a Short Leash - a guide to dealing with lawyers* and *One Step Ahead – A Mother of Seven Escaping Hitler's Claws* (an acclaimed WWII true story, which inspired the musical By Wheel and by Wing).

While growing up in Israel, Avraham received extensive Talmudic education, before attending law school and serving as a law clerk at the Israeli Supreme Court in Jerusalem. He later earned an advanced law degree from Columbia University in New York City, served as a law clerk for the Federal District Court, and started his legal career with Davis Polk & Wardwell. He has represented clients in numerous complex court cases before trial and appellate courts, including the United States Supreme Court. He currently lives near Washington DC with his wife and children. Like Ben Teller, the protagonist in *The Mormon Candidate* and *The Bootstrap Ultimatum,* Avraham often rides his motorcycle in the mountainous forests of western Maryland.

To learn more, please visit www.AzrieliBooks.com

ALSO BY AVRAHAM AZRIELI

Fiction:

The Masada Complex
The Jerusalem Inception
The Jerusalem Assassin
Christmas for Joshua
The Mormon Candidate
The Bootstrap Ultimatum
Thump
The Elixirist
Deborah Rising
Deborah Calling
Deborah Slaying
Deborah Striking

Nonfiction:

Your Lawyer on a Short Leash – A Guide to Dealing with Lawyers
One Step Ahead – A Mother of Seven Escaping Hitler's Claws

Author Website:

www.AzrieliBooks.com